SEMUS BRACELET

TESSA LAROCK

PublishAmerica
Baltimore

ISBN: 1-60474-901-6 (softcover)
ISBN: 978-1-4489-0490-7 (hardcover)
PUBLISHED BY PUBLISHAMERICA, LLLP
www.publishamerica.com
Baltimore

Printed in the United States of America

This story is dedicated to my brother Joey who passed tragically at the age of 20. You will always be remembered.

With special thanks to my family, especially my mother and children, who have always believed in me.

Egypt's billowing waves of heated sand readily consume its victims like vicious waves of the tossing sea. Men and beast have lost their sanity and their lives to its cruel sadistic nature, though *some* have arduously ventured to battle its supremacy in an attempt to remain alive. What lies beneath that blanket of brutal grit? Is it sandstone and granite? Or is it the fury of an incensed deity?

CHAPTER 1

The scorching sun blazed relentlessly down upon the small box truck as it raced along the sandy road spraying a fountain of dry sand behind it. Three Middle Eastern men dressed in long flowing robes frantically ran behind the truck. And realizing they were unable to seize the vehicle, they slowed to a stop and raised their angered fists while blasting out threats in an Arabic dialect. Turning, they then headed back inside the regime gates and wondered how they would explain their incompetence.

"*Whoa! Yeah!*" Laddor yelled triumphantly, his adrenaline pumping furiously as he banged his fist against the steering wheel. "*Whoa!*" He swiped the back of a clammy arm across his sweat beaded forehead. "*Man, those camel-kissin' amateurs!*" he stated excitedly to the plastic bobble-head as he removed it from the pocket of his vest and placed it on the dash. Shooting her a glance, he briefly watched as her grass skirt jolted briskly to and fro with the rough motion of the jarring truck. Then he smiled.

"Man, they never knew what hit em! One minute the jewels are there—the next minute," he threw his arms up in the air, "*SHAZZAM! They're gone! Damn, am I good or what?* And wait until Cherry sees *this haul!* Maybe she'll be a little nicer when she sees what I got her. *Eww, Baby!*" He licked his lips lavishly. "Come to Papa sweet Cherry and let me pick of your tasty fruit!"

Shifting the truck into high gear, he motored toward the docks which were located one hundred and fifty miles to the east. Taking a big swig of cool water from the metal canteen hanging loosely from around his sweaty neck, he thought of his girl….and air conditioning.

KEY WEST, FLORIDA AUGUST

"Reynolds?" Cherinne, the striking, chestnut-eyed blonde, called to her butler. "Has there been any sign of Laddor yet?" She sighed heavily as she seated herself in a chair nearest the vestibule door. "He said he would be here when I finished with my studies and returned from school; that was weeks ago," she mildly pouted.

Rising to her feet, she glanced out one of the enormous bay windows of the northern sitting room. "By the way, I've checked in his room and he may need an exterminator. What a mess."

"No, miss—in answering your first question, I have not seen him." Reynolds appeared before her in a crisp tux, a middle-aged man with slightly graying hair and pleasing eyes to match. "Would you like for me to phone them for you?"

"Phone whom?" She lowly grumbled, while her concentration was elsewhere and she was becoming slightly irate.

"The exterminator, miss. You mentioned something of needing an exterminator."

She waved the remark away. "Oh—no, I was just talking out loud. Besides, the only bug we *really* need to get rid of is *him*."

The butler studied her briefly, aware that her feathers were becoming quite ruffled. "I assume you mean Sir Laddor," the name brought a sour taste to his mouth as he thought of the nuisance.

"Yes, *him!*" She threw her hands in the air. "He's always running off, getting into God knows what; then, comes running back to me to fix whatever damn mess he's gotten himself into!" She briefly observed the quiet just beyond the double-paned glass, the dryness of the earth and sweltering heat of the day. Succumbing to a short choppy pace upon the carpet, hands clasped behind her back and eyes to the floor, she cursed every red-hair upon Laddor's head.

"Miss…" Reynolds paused, "you know your father had made it quite clear, when he left you this estate, that there were to be no young gentlemen staying here; that is, of course, until you are rightfully married. I don't believe your father would approve much of the young Sir Laddor, or of him occupying one of the guest rooms."

Her pacing abruptly halted and she looked squarely at the man in irritation; while the tension building between her shoulders and crawling to the back of her neck, was shocking the nerves into the start of a headache. The tension more from Laddor's disappearance than from the man who was always there for her—Reynolds—whose kindness and generosity were more than she could ever ask for.

Knowing her butler was right she unclenched her tight fists and took a deep breath. Her father had specifically told her 'no males in the house'. That meant boys, men, males, Peter Pan, Batman, gentlemen, hotties, chaps or even male dogs. "Reynolds, since when do I listen to what my father says? And, besides—*you're a man* and he's let *you* here with me."

"Yes, but, miss…" he paused, knowing that to start an argument, first off, was not his place; and secondly, she would not listen anyway. "I have been in the service of your father since you were born, and even assisted the Missus, your mother, with the changing of your diapers. So, technically, that makes me not a ruttish old man, but a piece of the furniture." He smiled with a soft twinkle in his tired eyes. "You are like a daughter to me, my dear, so I do feel the need to watch out for your best interest, that's all."

"Thank you, Reynolds." The tension slowly dissipated and her shoulders sagged in compliance like a cushion. "It's just that there have been so many things between my father and me—negative things—which I don't know how to correct right now." She glanced back out the window while her thoughts were focused in the distance and the aged gentlemen patiently awaited his dismissal.

"You may leave me now, for I have some things to think about. Just please let me know if you hear from Laddor."

"Yes, Miss." Leaving the room, he softly closed the door behind him.

Changing his mind, he peeked his head back inside and mildly scolded, "Oh, by the way, you cursed. So you need to put a dollar in the cookie jar."

"Oh, shoot!" she snapped her fingers. She had been trying to clean up her language a little—not that she walked around cursing like a longshoreman, by all means. It just seemed that here of late she had been slightly freer with her words and because of that she had come up with the dollar in the cookie jar rule. "I'll put it in when I go to the kitchen."

Reynolds gave her a wink and quietly left.

Cherinne thought about Reynolds for a moment, while he was, without question, the only rational person she respected. And, although her father, Joseph Havenstrit, had held her respect for years, Cherinne had found she couldn't even put him in the same category with Reynolds. No longer did she see him as that hero from her childhood days, a gallant nobleman who would protect all those within his world, a knight in shining armor. She snorted; that only existed in fairy tales.

Her thoughts turned to the times she had spent with her father as a little girl. How she had sat upon his large lap as he, reading one book after another, had chatted about his many mind-boggling inventions, inventions which would one day make the family super wealthy. He was a scientist—a "mad scientist" to be exact—who worked on several projects at one time, nearly driving him insane.

Finally, one of his inventions sold—something to do with spying equipment for the government. And, though he had made boatloads of money from the contraption, he wanted more. Not that they needed more, because truthfully they didn't. Mother had had money when father married her—not billionaire money, but enough to have their butler Reynolds, a caretaker and two maids, a nice comfortable house, private schools, and pleasurable vacations. However, her father saw only dollar signs before his eyes and continued with projects that seemed to bring in oodles more than was even needed.

Unknown though to anyone, Cherinne's mother had been plagued with an incurable illness, and to their dismay, she died suddenly at a young age. Cherinne was six years of age to be exact. Her distraught father, taking her mother's passing extremely hard, had seemed to lose any *real sense* he *may* have possessed. And, attempting to muddle through the madness and loss, he left his only child with Reynolds for weeks at a time, traveling extensively and digging deeper into his work.

Years went by as Joseph spent very little time at home and Reynolds became more of a guardian and father to Cherinne as she grew. Much of her time was spent at school and on their large estate which consisted of over one hundred acres and comprising stables, tennis courts, an Olympic size pool, and the house that encompassed seventeen bedrooms and eleven bathrooms. Cherinne loved their home, though sometimes it became very big and very lonely.

Joseph, after being gone on one of his many extended trips, arrived home a few days before Cherinne's eighteenth birthday with the sudden announcement he had just taken a new bride. That's when—as Reynolds would put it—"all Cain broke loose."

The young new mistress—half her father's age and extremely garish—fashioned bright red, slippery lips, stuck in a sneering grin, which frequently produced a bubble from some sort of gum. Sporting bursting boobs, which popped from clothes that seemed to be two sizes too small, she spent a great deal of time lining her closets with the most expensive in the latest fashions of clothing and shoes, claiming she never had enough. Cherinne's dislike of her new step-mother amplified to the point she despised the young floozy who had made it known to her that she was now the head mistress of the estate: her name being Scarlett.

Cherinne's eighteenth birthday had included an elegant dinner prepared by the servants and her father attempting to appease her with a brand-new black Porsche. Hugging her, he had wished her happy birthday, then, warily snuck in *another* of his heart-wrenching announcements, "Cherinne, I'm moving to France with Scarlett." Laying a guilt-ridden hand upon her shoulder, he stared into her melting chocolate eyes. "Now, you're welcome to come, or you may stay at the estate with Reynolds—it's your decision, honey."

Numbly, she peered through the slightly bent glasses to her father's graying stare, with the years of madness taking their toll—his khakis inches above his ankles, a five o'clock shadow that had grown well past midnight and the aging process being wretchedly unkind. This just wasn't the man she had known as a child—the one who had read to her and treated her like a princess. He had become old, chasing after a young skirt, living vicariously; and as a result, he was being consumed by his meaningless desires—the desire for aggrandized wealth and the desire for a tight ass, nothing of which included her.

Serves him right, Cherinne deliberated as her thoughts briefly drew to the present and she searched the landscape again for Laddor. Sighing cantankerously, her thoughts quickly returned to her father and the bubblegum chewing female.

Cherinne had glanced at the shiny new car then back at her father, who had just used her birthday present like that of an infant's pacifier. Being plagued with guilt, he quickly grabbed her hands and placed the jingling keys within them. 'Happy birthday, sweetheart.'

Cherinne rubbed her thumb over the gold then looked at Scarlett who stood watching with a dim-witted, triumphant grin pasted to her excessively-blushed face. "Whatever, Dad," was all Cherinne could think to say as she quickly turned and raced the sting of tears back into the house.

Reynolds had achingly watched and listened from the front room window as Cherinne had entered the house and hurriedly closed the large door behind her. Leaning against the thick oak frame, she stared blindly into the heavy stillness while puddle-sized tears formed behind her enormous brown eyes; then quietly, she slid to the floor. Watching her from a distance, he wanted more than anything to comfort her in her time of need, give the young lady the love and attention that her father was not. Abruptly, Cherinne broke down and cried.

Hearing the footfalls and chatter of the master and new mistress of the house, Reynolds coughed into a fisted hand—a simple warning to the young miss that her father and new stepmother were approaching. And, wishing to save her the mortification of having the obnoxious new stepmother, who had won the first *and* the second round, discover her *new* step-daughter in tears upon the floor, he rushed to intercede at the door. Shocked by his presence and ashamed he had seen her weeping, Cherinne leaped to her feet and bolted upstairs to her room.

"Where are you, Laddor?" Cherinne sighed deeply and gazed out the enormous picture window overlooking the front lawn. She watched the spray of water as it cascaded gently downward, spouting from the ornamental water fountain, which sat on the opposite side of the drive. Several sprigs of green grass, sprouting close to the fountain, reached desperately for the cool nourishment of the few drops that had bounded from the concrete and scattered upon the lawn; while the noonday sun blasted hot rays from a cloudless sky, withering everything in its path to a crispy brown. Cherinne's mother had watched the mesmerizing scatter of the water's droplets much in the same way when she was alive; but, that was many years ago.

I'm gonna' strangle him when he gets back, Cherinne thought. With that in mind, she decided to go for a swim.

Doing the perfect swan dive, her slender body cut through the cool of the aqua water, while her long golden tresses trailed along gracefully behind her. Her swimming lessons as a child had paid off and she had even joined the swim team when she had gotten to high school. Cherinne was an avid swimmer and loved the water; but Laddor, when they had first met, had avoided it like the plague. Their fun with Mr. Dolphin in the estate's adjoining pool and trips out on the boat had somewhat cured that, though he still disliked being completely submerged; while she assumed it had something to do with his hair.

Giggling slightly to herself, she recalled his first venture out on the cabin cruiser as he had stood trembling uneasily on the edge of her father's boat, the *Chastity*. Yawling and shivering, he had debated on whether or not to take the plunge into the depths of the Atlantic Ocean. While the orange of his vest, clashing abruptly with the wine color of his wafting locks and cranberry trunks, had made him appear more as a target for the enemies' missiles than a weekend vacationer.

Cherinne, just settling herself into the comfort of a lounger, was abruptly startled into a panic when a dreadful shriek rose from alongside the boat, as Laddor mustering the courage, had disappeared beneath the cool blue waters. And, as she peered over the side to see him thrashing about wildly, she removed her sunglasses, smiled and dove in.

15 MONTHS EARLIER

School had been out for a few weeks and Cherinne had received her diploma with honors while graduating top of her class. She had planned on taking a well deserved vacation far away to rest, needing to decide on what she was going to do with the rest of her empty life—besides going to college. Her father was gone, off gallivanting somewhere in France with *Licorice Lips*. That being the kindest thing she could think to call her new step-mother, since Scarlett's mouth reminded her of two engorged pieces of blinding red licorice which snaked across her pasty face. Besides, she couldn't break her own cursing rule; and what she really wanted to label her wasn't anything she'd be proud of thinking, yet alone saying.

Each month Cherinne received a nice allowance scribbled with a quick note and an "I miss you, Love Dad." Soon, Scarlett was sending the checks which included no "I miss you" at the bottom, or "Love Dad"—nothing; and, while they slowly dwindled in amount and regularity, they eventually, didn't arrive at all.

Regretfully, Cherinne ended up having to release the hired help, which had left just her and Reynolds. She couldn't bear to see him go, for he was the nearest thing she had to a father or family. Cherinne believed that to be the period during which her choice of words became a slight bit more unsavory and her mood more sullen. But, she had figured on this, so each month she had budgeted and tucked away most of what had been sent, which provided for the two. She hadn't graduated at the top of her class by being an idiot; but the nest egg she had saved wouldn't last long, *especially* after Laddor arrived.

When Cherinne had decided to take her new Porsche 911 Turbo out for a spin, she had no idea how that day would add to the insanity already steering her life. She cranked over the fine tuned engine and ran a hand over the crisp Italian leather, drew in a breath of the new car smell, threw in a CD, then headed out of the estate. A long drive down by the shoreline would brighten her spirits, she thought, and maybe clear her muddled head.

She drove through the little town of Clearwater sporting a mint green jumpsuit, plastic-framed white sunglasses and a new white hair tie to match. Smiling to herself, as bystanders stopped and stared, she cruised smoothly along looking better than a million bucks, but truthfully, bored out of her skull. Most of her friends were away for the summer break and she certainly hadn't wanted to hang out at the estate with Reynolds for the next three months.

Sighing, she threw the shifter into sixth gear. Then reaching a long stretch of straight road, she slowed and pulled to a stop. A Cheshire cat grin grazed her glossy pink lips as she glanced into the rearview mirror— all clear. Suddenly, she mashed the gas pedal to the floor. The car quickly lurched forward, jolting her heart into a thrumming bash, and she smiled manically while gripping the leather wheel with firm closed fists. Not bad—zero to sixty in 3.9 seconds and 6 cylinders with 480 horses under the hood. Nice! Her adrenaline flowed as her golden hair whipped wildly in the warm wind and the music filled her ears. She focused on the approaching road.

Pushing the sprite little sports car, which hugged the asphalt tightly and seemed to have a temperament of its own, she rounded each and every curve that ran along the jagged cliffs and away from town. *Beautiful*, just *beautiful*. Daddy—you surely didn't go wrong here; thoughts of her father entered her mind.

Cherinne pulled along the road to a secluded spot that overlooked the water, where the waves crashed forcefully along the jagged shore and climbed upon the rocks. She needed some work, she thought, as she slipped from behind the wheel and stood in the warm breeze leaning against the car. Her college courses, which would be starting in the fall, were already paid for by her father and she had planned on going into law. But for now, she needed cash—cold hard cash.

Taking one last look at the alluring blue, she hopped back into the driver's seat, started the car and carefully backed around. The sun setting in hues of reds and yellows brought to mind a book she was reading and she intended on burying herself in it before turning in for the night; so she headed for home.

Cherinne slowly cruised through town, making her way past the education center and several shopping malls. She slowed to a red light, pushed back her sunglasses and watched as a young couple—hand in hand—lazily made their way to the far curb. Chatting excitedly amongst themselves, they strolled indifferently past those along the busy street, oblivious to all around them. Nice—she thought; but, *not for me.* After seeing her father's mess, she wanted no parts of a relationship.

Suddenly, the car jolted forward, as she felt a thump from the rear and the passenger door flew open. A sweaty young male immediately scrambled into the adjoining seat.

"Drive! Drive!" he shrieked hysterically at her as he slammed the door closed and locked it.

"No!" she screeched while tearing through her purse for her pepper spray and swearing beneath her breath for not locking her doors. "Get out! Get out of my car you sweaty barbarian!" Beads of perspiration flew from his long, flaming auburn locks, which thrashed about as his gaze darted nervously from her to the rear of the car. "You're getting sweat all over the leather...and me! Look at my jumpsuit!" She held the spray canister near to his face; her slender finger trembled on the mechanism's trigger.

"Are you crazy, lady? That shit burns!" He grabbed her hand rougher than meant. The canister quickly came alive and heedlessly discharged its contents as a foggy layer over the inside of the entire car and windshield.

"*Nooo!* Look what you did, you stupid animal!" Her eyes flared from the stinging chemical and she gulped back the tears that suddenly burst to her eyes. Infuriated, she blindly began to swing her petite fists, striking out in a maddened frenzy as he raised a sweaty arm attempting to ward off the pelting of hardened blows. "Get out! Get out!" She screamed frantically through a deadly sanguine-colored glare.

Her small fists thrashed about wildly, till he caught her wrists and secured them tightly—the red of his eyes matching that of his hair. "I'm sorry!" he shouted in a rushed apology. "But *drive!*"

Three offhanded male characters, sweating profusely and out of breath, rapidly converged upon the car. "Laddor..." One said condescendingly, drawing a breath; his voice was a muffled vibration through the window. "Get outta' the car." He jerked the door handle with one hand and brandished a gun, from within his jacket, with the other, while the other two men made their way around to Cherinne's door.

"Crap!" The shriek escaped her lips as she began to swoon and bile choked at her throat. The fog of spray, thickly plastering the windshield, had made it near impossible to see clearly what was happening outside the car. Groaning, she shook her head in an attempt to free her thoughts, as her mind raced in several directions at once while her world had tumbled into a well of confusion.

The two men stood boldly next to the car; arms crossed they glared in at Cherinne, like a hawk eyeing its prey. "Open the door, sweetheart." One rapped with the butt of his gun upon the door; his grin reeked of antagonism.

"No," she replied wearily, hearing the quiver in her own voice. The small hairs tingled on the back of her neck.

The nose of his bootlegged berretta appeared against her window just inches from her terrified face. "Now, open the door," his patience had receded now to complete annoyance and the counterfeit grin had disappeared.

"No!" she yelled anxiously, uncertain as to what she was doing when she slammed her foot to the floor. One second, two seconds, the car blasted forward, as if it had snapped to life, while its tires screamed and it veered wildly into a fishtail. Clutching the steering wheel with shaking hands, she realized, too late, she was unable to see.

"You crazy broad!" the male they referred to as Laddor squawked, while using his sleeve to clear some of the gunk blocking her view. "Clean off your windshield!"

The annoying blare of car horns sounded and a muffled curse, from whom Cherinne was unsure, as she raced blindly through the intersection away from the men. Her heart banged against her chest, threatening to tear through the skin. But, determination was set in Cherinne's mind, and she would have been able to see through mud.

The Porsche wailed through town, slowing for no-one, while time swallowed them in a dimensional pause as the ticking of the clock was just a leisurely blur. Clearing the town's limits, and no longer feeling threatened, she pulled to the rim of the road. Cherinne inhaled deep; and attempting to slow her pounding heart, she focused on the situation at hand. Rubbing the sting of her eyes with the back of her hand, she then wearily turned the golden key and shut the engine off. Sighing deeply, she laid her forehead against the gunk spattered steering wheel and closed her burning eyes. The smell of chemicals and muskiness of a boy's locker room clung heavily to the air and Cherinne suddenly remembered she was not alone.

The blood began to boil beneath the surface of her skin. It flared in crimson streaks along her neck and cheeks; and when she opened her eyes to the barrage of staining splotches covering the front of her jumpsuit, which just hours before had been crisp and clean—in fact, only worn this once—she shook violently. The realization of being almost killed; and now both her car *and* her clothes were ruined, she no longer had control.

Cherinne slowly turned her head and glared at her passenger. Invisible claws tore at every red hair from the stranger's head—the person responsible for bringing more chaos to her already troubled life, *and*, he may have even dented her car. Unseen smoke rose from her ears and nose while her face twisted in a leering grimace, giving her the appearance of a mad bull. Opening her door, she angrily climbed from the automobile, her white sandals clicking heavily upon their heels as they charged toward the rear of the car. No dents. Sighing with relief, she then marched to the passenger's side of the car and rapped sharply on the chemical covered window with readied knuckles. Her passenger, like an undisciplined child investigating every knob and gadget, was paying no heed to the fact that he was liable to lose a lock or two from the crown of his measly head.

Cherinne immediately burst into a seething rage. How dare he touch her things, especially, after he had just defiled her car and her clothes!

"Get outta' the car! You freaking lunatic!" she screeched with raised fists, her blonde-gold tresses sparking on end, as she stomped white heels into the stony earth, while resembling an escapee from the mental facility. She brusquely banged on the window. "Get out!"

"No!" Terror riddled his enormous azure eyes, near as when the three men sporting guns, had him surrounded. "You might hurt me," he mewled, leaning into the driver's seat.

"I'm gonna' hurt you!" She stammered, "You...you...red-haired baboon!"

"Hey," he stated through the layer of mace. "There's no reason for name calling! Besides, I always thought I was quite good looking." He thought about it for a moment. "At least, that's what my mother always said."

"Shut up!" Cherinne snapped. "I'll get you out!" she grumbled stomping back around to the driver's side. Climbing in the car on her knees, she reached across the console and angrily grabbed a fistful of sweated red locks.

"Ow, ow, owww!" he screamed. "Let go of my hair! That hurts!"

"Not until you get outta' my car!"

Laddor's hands shot in the air, as if surrendering. "*Okay, okay.*" Slowly, he opened his door and climbed out. "*Jeesh,*" he mumbled to himself, "and here I thought—nice car, nice looking chick, *maybe* nice attitude. *Man*, was I ever wrong." He shook his head.

Cherinne stormed again around the car, "What are you mumbling about?" Pausing briefly, she now took in full view his handsome features and striking shaded hair which added ambiance to his height.

Staring down at her musingly, he smiled to himself. "Man, you're shorter than what I thought."

"Oh, shut up!" She stomped her feet, fuming in anger. "And, what was the snide remark about *attitude*? You come out of nowhere, invade my space—*my* space. Then, you sweat all over my brand new car and jumpsuit, get pepper spray all over my windshield—*and* almost get me killed! And, I'm not supposed to have an *attitude*! What kind of lunatic are you?" Cherinne's thinned eyebrows met in a crooked scowl.

"Hey," he said in a silky tone as he, with his forefinger, smoothly wiped away a bead of sweat appearing upon her forehead.

"Don't touch me!" She slapped his hand away.

Again his hands shot up in protest. "Look—whatever your name is. What is your name?"

"Cherinne," she snapped.

"Look—Cherry."

"*Cherinne!* It's *Cherinne!*"

"Well, *Cherry*," he said, while giving her the once over, "My name's Laddor. Laddor—with an 'O'—Zeandre. And..." he stated matter-of-factly. "I'm sorry."

"It's not *Cherry!*"

He glanced at the car then back at her. "Well, it all looks *cherry to me*," he snickered; his eyes sparkling matched his expression.

"*Ugggh!*" she groaned stomping back toward the driver's side. "You're hopeless!"

"Hey," he called to her, as he smiled with big white teeth and an ornery grin. "I'm just callin' it as I see it—*Cheerrrry!*"

Climbing in the driver's seat and starting the engine, she shoved it into first and began to pull away.

"Hey! You're not gonna' just leave—are ya'!" he yelled to her, his sparkle suddenly turning to alarm as he hurried toward the Porsche. "Don't leave me out here! I don't have a ride!"

Cherinne slowed to a stop and rolled down the window. "I don't care!" An ominous laugh drifted from inside as the tires slowly crept into motion.

"Awe, come on, doll!" Breaking into a full run, he yelled in desperation, "I'll clean your car!"

The words glided through the clearing heat of the upcoming evening, and Cherinne grimaced at the thought of the appalling chore; the thought of spending hours scrubbing out the car—enough to make her cringe, or, possibly even cry. And Reynolds would definitely find the job repulsive, doing it reluctantly, but with a darkened mood that would probably last, if she was fortunate, only a week.

Regretfully, she pulled the car to the shoulder and stopped. Glancing through the splatters of gunky spray decorating her rearview mirror, she watched as Laddor—with an 'O'—ran toward the car. He is kinda' cute, Cherinne thought as she smiled to herself. And, as the young man with the long flaming multi-colored locks, climbed into her car with a broad canary-eating grin on his face, she had somehow felt she would be breaking her father's rule.

PRESENT

"*Cheerrryyy! Oh, Cheerrryyy!*" Cherinne could hear Laddor holler out as his boots crunched along the thirsty grass just outside the fence. Diving below the surface of the ten-foot section, she popped up under a large vinyl dolphin that floated lazily about in the crystalline ripples of water. It was Laddor's favorite; and he rode it through the water like a bucking bronco—waving his arms and kicking his legs wildly—while she laughed and tried to get away from him as he chased her around the pool.

Holding onto the raft, she hid herself from view, while she could hear him unlocking the latch and approaching through the gates. She was angry with him—angry he had run off, and just angry that she liked him and still had him staying in her house.

"*Cheerryy! Oh Cheeerryy!*" he sang out, "*I know you're out here.* Reynolds told me you were, and you're hiding from me." He pushed several of the floats away from the edge of the pool with the tip of his boot and taunted her. "Are you mad at me, Cherry? Is that why you won't come out and give ol' Laddor a big wet kiss?"

Cherinne clenched her fist and fumed, whispering angrily beneath her breath, "I should bust him one."

"I have something for you, Cherry baby—something *really nice.* Now, come on out and I'll give it to ya'. Then, maybe you can share some of your sweet fruit with poor ol' Laddor here."

"*No!* I'm not coming out! I'm mad at you, Laddor."

"Aw, come on *baby.* Don't be like *that.*"

She doesn't answer.

"Hey, what if I come in and play with Mr. Dolphin with ya'—will ya' forgive me then?"

"No! And, you leave Mr. Dolphin out of this!"

She could hear the plunk of removed boots hitting the concrete and the unzipping of pants as Laddor slipped them from his body. "Laddor, what are you doing?" Peeking around the dolphin float, she saw only shoes and clothes heaped in a pile by the pool. "Laddor?"

"*Yee ha!*" he hollered out, as he suddenly sailed recklessly through the air and landed with a thud atop the unsuspecting rubber raft, sending water spewing across the pool in a cuffing wave. Spying Cherinne ducking below the surface, he raced in her direction.

"*Whoa, yeah! I'm comin' for ya' Cherry baby!*" Whooping and hollering he kicked the dolphin, as he, wanting her to laugh, waved his arms around wildly. The plastic float immediately came alive while thrashing him in an attempt to buck him off.

Cherinne surfaced with determination to hold her scowl. But, as she watched his carrying on, sporting only a small pair of black skivvies and jerking about on the poor elastic mammal, her heart softened and she covered her mouth to giggle. Laughing aloud, Laddor urged the trouncing float onward, chasing her from one end of the Olympic-sized pool to the other. Diving beneath the blue waves, she'd then pop her head up ever so often and eagerly splash him.

Catching her in the corner of the pool, he bragged, "I got you now, Cherry baby!" He dove from the dolphin and cornered her. And clutching his large hands about her tiny waist, he playfully pulled her beneath the surface. Their eyes met amidst the flourish of bubbles and his fingers regretfully slipped away, while his dislike of being completely submerged, forced him speedily up for air. Cherinne quickly took the opportunity to escape.

"Oh, no, you don't." Laddor reached a strong arm out and grasped her slippery ankle. Her heart pounded angrily within her chest, either from the hold he had on her—not physically—but emotionally; or, from the idea that he could just waltz in and out of her life whenever it suited his needs or desires. And, foolishly, she had laughed and carried on, as a young schoolgirl, giving in to the hidden feelings she possessed.

Her anger escalated with the mixture of emotions that mounted upon her chest. "Let me go, Laddor! I'm still mad at you." She thrashed about in the tumult of evolving waves in the attempts to get away.

"No," he pulled her firmly within his arms, while her tanning oil had made her quite slick. Her body easily slid along the auburn hairs of his rippling chest and she gasped as he effortlessly spun her to face him. The seething anger in her pounding heart rapidly changed to a forbidden excitement and she caught her breath.

He stared down at her suspiciously, through large ocean blue eyes. Water dripped from his thick lashes and his fiery wet locks clung to his chiseled face. Snaking along his perfectly shaped physique to the middle of his back, the hues of red—a wine connoisseur's varied selection—were richly dark, yet warm as honey. She could feel his heart beating steadily, humming against her goosebumped flesh, as he had her secured tightly against the cooled heat of his wet skin.

"Come here, Cherinne." His moist lips, searching hers out, pressed with a gentle urgency against hers and his tongue slipped lightly over her teeth. "I've missed you," he breathed in a pressing force of warm air.

Cherinne gasped as a surge of current rushed through her body, causing her knees to buckle and her legs to grow weak. Opening her eyes, she blinked back the drops of water sitting lazily along her feathery lashes. Every nerve in her body tingled to his touch as he slid his hands over the small of her back and firmly drew her in. She heatedly quivered within the cool of the water; and catching her breath, she replied in a low rasping voice, "Well, you wouldn't miss me so much if you weren't running off all the time."

He studied her face momentarily, as the sun reflected the rivulets of water which ran along the gleam of her long metallic strands; he thought she looked beautiful. They stylishly glided along her neck and collarbone where they slipped ever-so quietly into the top of her bathing suit; and, continuing to just below her breast, added curvature to her already perfect form.

Waiting for a response that never comes, her brimming rose-colored lips parted slightly with another mention of her disappointment at his disappearances. But, being consumed by the energy soaring within his loins, he bent and kissed her again. "So, you do miss me," the words seeped from his mouth to hers.

"Nooo…I would just like to know where you're at—that's all." She slowly tore herself away, along with his hands which had quickly begun to search out areas forbidden to anyone's touch. Near to a pant, he pressed her once more against him then nestled his face within the curve of her neck, while his gentle kisses along her damp skin brought a rush of added bumps to her flesh.

A trying whisper escaped her lips, "Laddor, you have to stop." Pushing him gently away she gathered his open palms in hers and examined him with large questioning eyes, "Where have you been? You up and disappear for days—sometimes even weeks." Releasing her hold, she pouted, "You're probably with someone else."

"Awe, *Cherry.*" He wiped away a droplet of water as it slipped down her cheek. "You're the only fruit for me." Grinning broadly, he attempted to embrace her again and then suddenly remembered the jewels. "Hey!" His eyes gleamed with excitement; the raging heat now calm as the pool water surrounding them. "You've gotta' see what I got ya'!" Hurriedly wading to his clothes, he grabbed his jeans. Rummaging around in the pocket, with a grin the width of Texas, he quickly spun while concealing something behind his back. "Now, close your eyes—and no peeking."

Cherinne closed her eyes, liking surprises—good ones anyway; especially since her father was gone—they were few and far between. She hesitated then reopened them. With Laddor's surprises not always being the best, they most times cost her time *and* money. "Laddor, this isn't gonna' set me back any; is it?"

"Ah, Cherry…*sweet Cherry.*" The ring in his tone made her weary. "When have I ever cost you?" He rethought the remark. "Never mind…" he mumbled, "…don't answer that. Now, close those lovely brown eyes of yours."

Stopping before her and pausing momentarily, his eyes swept the entirety of her body to the height of the water which began at the full of her slender hips. The heat of his groin rapidly rekindled again into an agonizing flame; and, reaching a trembling hand toward her, he remorsefully willed it to her face. Holding her chin within his long fingers, he only touched her lips. She'll surely want to thank me after I give her this; the thought crossed his over-eager mind as he pulled the bracelet from behind his back.

It was of the finest of gold—an Egyptian heirloom—broad and beautifully carved, while the etchings upon it were of a beautiful Egyptian woman, possibly a goddess or princess. Holding one hand out to a feline and the other to a mighty spear, the female tilted her head back as if chanting a summons to the gods. A beautiful array of earth colored jewels surrounded the enchantress and lined the edges, with several proudly adorning the center and shimmering brilliantly in the rays of the afternoon sun.

"Laddor—what are you doing?" Cherinne asked impatiently. "You'd better not be tryin' somethin' funny!"

"No," he sighed regrettably. "I'm being good."

Taking her right arm, he opened the bracelet and latched it on.

"*Laddor*...that had best not be handcuffs. You know how I feel about relations before marriage."

"*No*, I promise; it's not." He stepped back. "Now, open your eyes."

In a state of warranted doubt, she opened her eyes; and seeing the magnificent gift, she beamed from ear to ear. The golden metal of the band shined magnificently, crowned with a layer of brilliant multi-colored jewels—every possible gem forged from the verve of the earth which reflected a rainbow of remarkable hued rays bursting into a gemologist's delight.

"Oh, it's beautiful! Thank you, Laddor!" Cherinne, leaping into his arms, repaid him generously with an affectionate kiss, beings she had just discredited him so, and extremely happy it wasn't a sexual toy.

"Does this mean I get to make wine with Cherry today?" the warm words slipped slyly into her ear as he placed a hand on her bare thigh, which she had absentmindedly wrapped around his waist at the excitement of her new gift.

An angered rush of blood quickly welled to her head and she stiffened at his words. "That's grapes, you stupid moron." She wiggled away. "Is that all you ever think about, Laddor? You're such a perv…

Suddenly, she disappeared beneath the water.

"*Cherry?*" Laddor reached for her hand. "Cherry—quit jokin' around—I'm sorry. It's just I…"

Her eyes were wide and raked with fear as she struggled just beneath him. Thrashing the water wildly, she tore desperately at his legs with her hands and nails while she attempted to fight her way free of the invisible anchor that was threatening to drag her to the bottom.

Laddor yelped in a sting of pain as blood trickled to the puckered slits upon his legs and streamed within the surrounding water. Frantically, he thrust his arms beneath the surface and tried to pull her up for air, as his heart pounded within his chest and he feared she may drown before his feet. Cherinne's mouth, opening to a throng of quickening bubbles, attempted to scream; when suddenly she burst from the water and her body shot skyward, like a rocket launching from its pad.

Coiling herself into a fetal position, she then slowly began to open like a fruit being peeled, while unknown forces, controlling the whole of her limbs, laid her spread-eagle before the watching sun. Its rays glistened off the dripping strands of her dangling hair, like falling stars, radiating a sparkly crystallized glow which gleamed in harmony with the amethyst of her bathing suit. A deep-throated, low moan escaped Cherinne's lips as she hovered, bound, beneath the azure-blue of the cloudless sky and vulnerable to the environment's every element. While the bracelet, seeming to feed off the energy of the daystar, or the universal bonds beyond, came alive, casting a multitude of radiant prism rays into the heated sky—a blazing star.

"*Cherinne!*" Laddor shrieked in panic as he watched, through shielded eyes, her body slowly revolving above him while she called out words of a foreign tongue. "*Arabic?*" he stated confusedly. "Is she speaking *Arabic?* What *was* she studying while I was gone? I thought it was DNA identification." Laddor scratched his head. "Cherinne?"

Dark ominous clouds rumbled and twisted, rolling along the perplexed sky and bringing with them a blanket of pitch black, which shrouded the hot afternoon sun. While the bracelet, shooting forth the fine multicolored beams of brilliant rays in every direction, possibly reached as far as thirty or forty feet—like that of laboratory laser beams.

"Wow!" Laddor exclaimed in uncertainty while gazing through the thick of darkness at the incredible array of dazzling lights. His astonished stupor quickly screeched to a halt as he suddenly realized the beams had become deadly, intending to rid him of his existence.

"*Holy Shit!*" He cried out while dodging this way and that as several rays drilled effortlessly into the concrete slab surrounding the pool. Searing pinholes shot through the fence, and continued on, to pierce near-by trees and bushes that smoked and sizzled then quickly burst into flames.

"*Shit, shit, shit!*" he shrieked nearly being blasted within an inch of his life. His heart pounded loudly in the abrupt darkness and he ran for the gate. Slamming it behind him, he groaned, "What'll I do?" He could still hear Cherinne as she called out steadfastly in the controlled Arabic language, while unknowingly adorning the bracelet which was now on a rampage. "*Oh, man,* is she gonna' be pissed at me now," he mumbled beneath his breath. He peered back inside, then hurriedly closed the gate as Reynolds came jogging hastily around the fence.

"What in blazes is going on?" the butler shouted as he took a deep breath. "Is Miss Cherinne alright?" His peppered brows furrowed in suspicion as he glared at the red-haired nuisance through narrowed slits.

Laddor rolled his blue eyes futility, trying desperately to avoid the poisonous glower, which he—more often than not—received from the austere butler. "*Well,* Reynolds…I'm not sure how to answer that."

"*Get outta' the way, you foolish boy!*" Reynolds roughly shoved him to the side and flung open the metal gate. A violet ray of light suddenly shot past his ear nearly piercing it with precise accuracy. "Holy Mother of God!" He slammed the gate closed then eyed Laddor with unbridled contempt. "*Boy,* what have you done," he seethed from behind clenched teeth.

"*Me?*" Laddor retorted defensively. "I was just being nice to Cherry!"

Disgust with the young man hung heavy between the two, as Reynolds balled his fists, knowing he could easily get off a descent shot there in the dark. "I can just imagine. You're here for no more than thirty minutes and already things are in a shambles. And, where in God's name, are your clothes?"

Laddor glanced down at his clingy wet underwear. "Uh….I was swimming."

"Yes, I can see that," Reynolds stated sarcastically as he glanced at the blood puckered slits upon the young man's legs wondering of their origin.

A loud splash sounded from beyond the walled enclosure. And, peering inside, they could see that the bracelet's tirade had finally come to an end; while the dark clouds, which had suddenly appeared from nowhere, vanished.

Cherinne lay face up at the bottom of the cement pool with her eyes wide in a frozen stare. While her body remained motionless, except for the long strands of her hair, which floated idly upward, away from her face.

"Is she dead?" Laddor whispered, as icy chills burned hot across his damp skin.

Throwing the young man an irate stare, Reynolds snapped, "For your sake, she'd better not be!" Hastening toward the pool, Reynolds immediately removed his shoes and dove in, followed quickly by Laddor. Reaching her water-logged body first, Reynolds drew Cherinne tightly into his arms then made his way upward toward the pool's edge. With a grunting heave and Laddor's help, he hoisted her onto the warmth of the concrete block and climbed out.

Laddor also made his way out as Reynolds, soaked to the bone, laid Cherinne before him. Kneeling, the butler checked her vitals signs.

"*Don't touch her!*" The command was sharp and painful as Reynolds took Cherinne's hand and called to her. "Miss!" He patted her hand. "Come on miss!"

"*Come on!*" Laddor pressed in a whisper. Desperation mounted in his voice, while the aching increasing in his chest brought tears which pressed against the back of his eyes. He refused their coming.

Suddenly, her body lurched forward. And, with a strangling gurgle, water was spewed forth from her blue lips. Gasping for a breath and groaning, Cherinne blinked her eyes which had never closed.

"*Oh…thank the heavens!*" Reynolds exclaimed as Laddor, unaware of the tears streaming his cheeks, had quickly snatched her up in his shaking arms.

CHAPTER 2

"*Laddor!*" Cherinne yelled as she tugged at the bracelet while Reynolds searched diligently for a pair of pliers. "*Where* did you get the bracelet?"

Laddor fearfully cowered in a chair just beyond her reach. "You won't hurt me if I tell ya'—will you?"

"I just might."

He hesitated then said, "Well then…I can't."

Quick as lightening, Cherinne was bounding from her chair and snatching a fistful of drying hair. Her damp bikini clung ever so tightly to her tense body; and, if it hadn't been for the hair pulling, Laddor thought he may have rather enjoyed it.

"Tell me, you red haired rooster! You have two seconds to start crowin'…or I'm gonna' turn you into a freakin' hen!"

"*Miss Cherinne!*" The shock reverberated in Reynolds's voice as he entered the room. "A young lady should learn to *always* restrain herself when angered, even if she is dealing with a….," he raised his brows, "…troublesome cock."

"*Hey! Who you callin' troublesome?*" Laddor howled in defense.

"I shall make you into a hen myself—you red-haired buffoon—if you don't straighten this mess out," Reynolds stated coldly as he glared down at the young male. Handing Cherinne her robe, he assisted her to her feet.

Plopping down wearily on the brocaded cream and lavender loveseat,

Cherinne examined the bracelet closely, while Reynolds attempted to pry it loose with the pliers. "Laddor...*please* tell me about the bracelet. I promise I won't maim you, or do anything to quash your manhood. *Now please.*"

"Well, in that case," he stated, "get some hiking boots on and I'll just show ya'."

A portion of the hundred-acre grounds ran rocky, due to its being on a coral island and it colliding with the Gulf of Mexico; so the boat landing for the estate sat nearest to Mexico. Fortunately, their patch of woodland sat on a downward slope, nearer to the main house, making the hike in the extreme heat possible for Reynolds—with his state of mind more the concern than his health.

The white box truck, being well obscured within a clump of several trees, was just inside the eastern property limits of the estate: the hike there giving the three ample time to discuss what had happened at the pool.

"I just wanted to do something nice. That's all." Laddor whined defensively. "I thought the bracelet was gorgeous, just like my *sweet Cherry.*" He ran a quivering finger along her arm to see if he was able to touch her yet. Without even passing him a glance, she abruptly gave him 'the hand'. It was a gesture, where Cherinne jerked her hand open firmly, palm side out toward him, somewhat like a crossing guard. And, if he didn't stop *immediately*, what he was doing, she was liable to inflict lots of pain upon him. Well, he got the hand—so that meant she was still really pissed.

"Miss Cherinne, are you aware that you were speaking Arabic while you were in that trance?" Reynolds asked.

"I'm not sure," Cherinne tried to recall. "I know I was speaking something other than the English language; but it was all like a dream. Flashes of images raced through my head—many of great wars. I think it was during King Tutankhamon's reign, or around that period; and I—or someone—was fighting using the bracelet. There was something to do with a god named Seth, but I'm not sure. It all happened so fast."

Laddor hurried into the patch of trees ahead of them and busied himself removing the camouflage tarp that covered the beastly looking truck. "Well, this is it," he grinned proudly.

"Now, wait a minute," Cherinne stated coolly, "I'm no idiot, but, I know this truck wasn't here before. I've hiked this part of the estate just recently, and *nothing* was here."

Laddor climbed up on the back bumper and unlatched the rear doors. "No, Cherry Baby, I just brought it today. I have to show you inside. Now, close your eyes."

"*No, Laddor,*" the reply was sharp. "The last time I did that, I ended up a floating zombie and tried to kill you *and* Reynolds."

"Okay, then—look." He threw the truck doors open.

The blinding sparkle of gold, diamonds, amethysts, pearls, rubies, and many stones Cherinne had never seen before—including precious metals—rushed in a massive heap upon the canopy floor. Earrings, necklaces, bracelets, toe rings, belly button rings, anklets, and jewelry she didn't even know where someone would wear, spilled before her feet.

"*Oh, my God!*" The words escaped Cherinne's lips before they were even a thought.

"*Mother, Mary and Joseph!*" Reynolds clutched his chest and hastily made the sign of the crucifix.

A roaring laugh preceded Laddor's intensified grin. "Whaddaya' think of this, Cherry Baby! *Did I hit the jack-pot—or what?*"

Cherinne was speechless. Surrounded by a collection of dazzling splendor, she stooped and picked up a ring that lay atop the massive pile of wealth. The ring was absolutely stunning; a pewter band intricately carved and lined with a multitude of diamonds. Holding it up to her other hand, she imagined what it would look like embellishing her finger; while the setting sun shone upon the stones, as they twinkled softly in flecks of multi-colored light.

"Miss Cherinne," Reynolds gently took her hand. "You know what they say, 'curiosity killed the cat.' Please do not be tempted to put any of this jewelry on."

Replacing the ring to the pile, she sighed.

Laddor jumped from the back of the tailgate, beaming with accomplished delight. "So, Cherry baby, whaddaya' think?"

"Laddor, where'd you get all this stuff?" Cherinne breathed the words in a hushed whisper.

"*Man…*" He waved his hands enthusiastically, as he did quite often. "It was a piece of cake! I got a tip from this guy who had just gotten back from the Sinai Peninsula. He had information on a stake of over a billion dollars! A *billion dollars* of jewels that was located in Luxor!"

Laddor suddenly got 'the hand' again. "Now wait," Cherinne retorted. "Are we talking about Luxor, Egypt?"

He shook his head 'yes'.

Her reaction was sudden, quicker than Laddor could calculate, as she suddenly sailed through the air and slammed him to the grassy earth. "What the Hell were you doing in Luxor, Egypt, *Laddor?*" She shouted the words within an inch of his terrified face.

"Cherry, baby, I was just thinking of *you!*" he cried from beneath her.

"My ass!" she hollered aloud.

He raised a brow. "*Yes! I was thinking of your ass,*" he stated coyly in his defense.

Glaring down at the frightened male, her tone was condescending, as if she was speaking to a two year old. "Whose jewels are these? And, you had better tell me the truth."

"Sir Laddor, I believe you have just ruffled the wrong feathers, and, I would answer truthfully, if I were you," Reynolds remarked snidely while barely obscuring a grin. And, though he knew Cherinne's reaction was inappropriate, he wished he would have done it himself.

"Uh…he stammered. Well…" Cherinne roughly grabbed a handful of hair. "They belonged to some prince—Prince Racid—Richard—Rasheed! That's it! Prince Rasheed! The jewels belonged to Prince Rasheed Tarun," he stated proudly. "Now, I told the truth—are you gonna' let me up?"

"Are you *crazy?* You stole jewels from the Arabs!" His head pounded in a game of paddleball against the hard ground. "Are you *trying* to get us killed?"

"Ow, Ow, Owww! Cherry, I…was…just….think…ing…of…you," he cried out as she angrily banged his head to the earth. His red locks, entangled tightly within her fist, flopped about as an uncontrollable scarlet mop.

"Ugh! I'll be prosecuting guys like you!" Shoving him one last time, she then, exhausted, rolled to the ground on her back beside him and gazed skyward.

"Now *that's* what I'm talkin' about," he hoisted himself to an elbow. "You're layin' there just waitin' to kiss and make up." His smile was ornery as he winked. "But, shouldn't we get rid of Reynolds first?"

"You moron," Cherinne cracked him forcibly with a closed fist, sending him dazed, into a milky-way of stars.

"Miss Cherinne," Reynolds pointed out, "Not only has your Mr. Laddor stolen from the Arabs; *but* he has also acquired jewels that possess some kind of mystical power. Do you think it's possible that there may be others who are looking for them—especially since the information was obtained from some *unknown* who had just returned from Egypt?"

Cherinne pondered his words for a moment, then glanced again at the bracelet locked to her wrist. Quickly hopping to her feet and shouldering the small pack she had been carrying, she announced, "I think it's time to call Joseph. Laddor, get that truck covered and let's get back to the house."

The phone rang several times before Cherinne heard Scarlett pick up the line.

"*Hello?*" Scarlett sing songed the greeting. Cherinne cringed.

"Hey, Scarlett…it's Cherinne."

"Hey, what's up?" Scarlett replied cracking gum loudly in Cherinne's ear.

"I was wondering if my father was around. I need to speak with him."

"Well, if it's about the checks…"

Cherinne rolled her eyes, "No. I just need to speak with him."

"Well, in that case, hold on." She laid the phone down and Cherinne could hear her step-mother's obnoxious holler. "*Joseph!* It's your daughter."

"Oh, I could just puke," Cherinne whispered beneath her breath as a minute or so went by. "She makes me sick!"

"Hello, Cherinne?"

"Hey, Dad."

"Hey, honey! How are you?"

Turning her wrist, she looked at the bracelet. "Well, it's been interesting." She added, "…to say the least."

"You getting your checks?"

"No, Dad. I haven't gotten a check for months."

"Oh…I wonder what happened there."

She could imagine him scratching his head while she just wanted to blurt out, *Gee—I wonder!* "Anyway, Dad, I need a favor. I need to make a trip to Luxor and I was wondering if you could arrange for Deverell to fly us in the Amphibian."

"Luxor? Is that Luxor, Egypt?"

"Yes, Dad, Luxor, Egypt. I need to…" she paused knowing she couldn't tell him anything about the jewels. If Scarlett found out Cherinne had all these diamonds—that woman would appear quicker than Cherinne could say, Licorice Lips. "A friend from school is sick," she lied. "I need to go see her."

"Well, that's fine, sweetheart, but who is the 'us'? I distinctly heard you say, 'us'."

Oh shit, she thought, while she had forgotten about the stupid rule and Laddor living in the house. She lied again—not wanting to. "Reynolds. Reynolds is coming with me."

"Oh, okay. I'll make the arrangements. When would you like to leave?"

"Tomorrow."

"*Tomorrow?*" he stated surprised. "Let me see what I can do. I'll call you back in a few hours."

"Thanks, Dad."

"I'll call you soon." He hung up.

Cherinne slowly set the receiver down, realizing she had never lied to her father before. But, also, realizing there were a lot of things she could never tell him the truth about either.

Reynolds waited just outside the study listening to the conversation. "Reynolds, I know you're out there. I can hear your breathing," Cherinne announced. "You can come in. I'm restraining myself."

"Miss…" Reynolds eyed her curiously, "how is it you were able to hear my breathing? I was practically holding my breath the entire time."

"Um…I'm not sure," she stated preoccupied with thoughts of taking the trip. "Joseph will be phoning shortly, so please inform me when he does. I shall be resting in my room. Oh, and what is Laddor up to now? If you see him, please tell him to stay off my balcony."

"Yes, ma'am."

Laddor laboriously made his way up the trestle. Then, hoisting himself up onto Cherinne's balcony, he watched as she entered the room, glanced around, then wearily sat on the edge of her bed. Fidgeting with the bracelet, she tried to remove it. Then, getting frustrated, she flopped back on the bed and closed her eyes.

Laddor stood absolutely still and peered around the corner, knowing that if she found him there he was toast.

"Laddor," she suddenly called through the closed paned doors. "I can hear you out there."

He didn't answer.

"I'm not going to pulverize you—yet. I'm too exhausted. So, wait there and I'll come out."

Dragging herself from the comfort of the soft, king-sized mattress, she then made her way out onto the balcony. It overlooked the swimming pool and showcased a view of the rolling hills, all the way to the rim of the roaring ocean. Sighing heavily, she thought of the damage that had been done to both the fence and the pool *and* the cost of repairs. "That'll be a nice little sum of money I really didn't need to part with," she grumbled beneath her breath.

Silently emerging from behind the door, Laddor slipped behind her. Wrapping his arms around her waist, he whispered into the back of her hair, "Cherry…does this mean you're not mad at me anymore?" He slightly turned her and his enormous puppy-dog eyes, begging for forgiveness, met hers. "I'm *really* sorry. I never meant for any of this to happen. I just wanted to surprise you, give you something nice, for all the nice things you've done for me."

The sun was passing through a hue of red and orange horizon. Finally settling into submission, it was disappearing behind a roving cloud. Cherinne turned to face the dusk and stated wearily, "No, I'm not mad; I'm too tired to be mad." A few strands of hair, wafting in the gentle evening breeze, brushed her paled cheek. Fingering them briefly, she then tucked them behind her ear. "I just wanna' get this mess straightened out." She touched the cool of the bracelet's gold edging then remarked, "It *is* a beautiful bracelet."

"I'm sorry, Cherinne." Turning her toward him, he bent and brushed a soft kiss against her lips.

"*A hem*," Reynolds cleared his throat. Disapproval was apparent in his tone and fixed stare. "Madam, your father is on the telephone."

Cherinne blushed. "Thank you, Reynolds—I'll take it in the study."

Making her way to the study—by way of the kitchen—she passed 'the cookie jar.' Stopping, she dug the few bills out of her robe pocket and dropped them in. "I have a feeling, after this week, I'll owe a lot more than *that*," she groaned sourly.

The conversation with her father was brief. Thanking him again, she hung up.

"Laddor, Reynolds, you two can come out from behind the door," she stated as she opened the safe which was tucked securely behind a wall-sized portrait of her and her mother. "All the arrangements have been made. It's time to pack, so travel light."

Reynolds approached Cherinne, "Miss Cherinne, is there a possibility that maybe I should stay at the estate and tend to things while you are gone? And, do you think it wise to leave the jewels in the truck unprotected? I know we have security alarms and all, but wouldn't it be an unnecessary risk to leave them where they are?"

Pondering that briefly, she replied. "Yes, I guess you're right. Maybe you should stay here and see about getting the pool fixed. Also, bring the truck into the garage—at least until we figure out what we're gonna' do with the jewels." Removing all her cash from the safe, she then turned to Laddor. "Well, I guess, Mr. Zeandre, you and I are off to Egypt."

CHAPTER 3

Deverall appeared agitated. The seaplanes engines were running, while he stood thrumming his fingers methodically against the Amphibian's fuselage. He was still as scruffy as Cherinne could remember, with baggy khaki shorts, an aged muscle shirt, battered straw sandals and a hat to match that brimmed a pair of dark sunglasses. And, to top it off, he had twice the amount of beastly hair sprouting from every crack and crevice.

Reynolds, fretting over a soiled car, drove the Rolls Royce slowly across the runway and parked. He assisted Cherinne from the car and retrieved the luggage from the trunk.

"What's the hold-up?" Deverall yelled over the roar of the engines as he pointed to his watch. "We were supposed to leave more than twenty minutes ago."

Cherinne had thought him to be nearing fifty while he had served her father as a pilot for years. And, from what she knew, he had been through three wives, and only the Lord knew, how many children. His tactics were a slight bit rusty, but he got the job done and was a helluva pilot.

"Mind your manners, Mr. Deverall," Reynolds commented, "especially around Miss Cherinne. I won't be attending this trip to keep order. But…" He looked at Laddor distastefully, briefly thinking he could leave the responsibility to him, but then, thought better of it. "Miss

Cherinne will be reporting daily to me and to her father. So, you had best mind your p's and q's."

Deverall guffawed shrewdly, *"Yeah, right.* Well…my question is: who the hell's this red-haired roach, she has taggin' along? Mr. Havenstrit said absolutely nothin' about some 'flame boy' hitchin' a ride."

"Hey! I resent that! I'm no *flame boy!"* Laddor squalled as his face, burning three shades of red, nearly matched the color of his hair.

Deverall pulled out a pack of cigarettes, tapped them, then removed one with his yellowing teeth. Giving Laddor the once over, he circled him like a steer you are about to purchase. Releasing a gruff, he slyly stated, "Ya' know, I had myself a red-haired woman a few years back. She was wilder an alley-cat and beastly in the sack." Continuing to circle Laddor, he grinned then chuckled maniacally, "a red-head…..Ya' know they say, that any man who has had a red-headed woman automatically receives magical powers. This trip may prove to be quite fun."

Laddor quickly hid behind Cherinne as she glared angrily at the obnoxious pilot. "Mr. Deverall, may I remind you, you are in the employ of my father *and* me. And while so, you shall act in a respectful manner."

"Oh, don't get your panties in a wad, sweetheart. I'm just partial to red-heads that's all. So, I won't tell Daddy that he's along—if you won't." He snickered with a cough. "Now, fuel isn't free, so let's get this party started."

"Miss Cherinne," Reynolds whispered as she shouldered her pack and they loaded the rest of their belongings. "If this barbarian gives you any nonsense, you let me know. I shall contact your father immediately."

Cherinne gave Reynolds a peck on the cheek. "Don't worry—if I can handle those college frat boys, I can handle Mr. Deverall. I'll be in touch soon. Now, take care, Reynolds."

"You, also, miss." He gave her a squeeze and looked to Laddor. "Now, you take good care of her, boy, or I'll come hunting you."

"Yes, sir," Laddor grinned skeptically. Then suddenly tripping over Cherinne's bag, he spilled to the ground. "Oww!"

Deverall belted out a loud cackle. "What an idiot!"

"Oh, Laddor, come on." Taking his hand, Cherinne led him inside the plane to find a seat amongst the dozen or so to choose from. Settling herself, she watched as he fidgeted nervously with the strap of his belt.

"You know I hate flying Cherry," he whispered lowly in her ear, "especially with that creep behind the controls."

"Yeah, I know. That's why I put you in the aisle seat. Oh, and I've been meaning to ask you, Laddor—how did you manage to get the jewels to the United States?"

"A barge of course, Cherry," he announced with pride. "It was—"

Suddenly grabbing her hand, he was interrupted from his thoughts as the plane began to jerk and jolt, as it traveled along the runway and was positioning itself to take off. Closing his eyes, he placed his head back against the leather seat. "Come on, baby, come on," he whispered, while the engines roared and they could feel the pressure of gravity burning within their ears as they gradually climbed toward the sky.

Letting out a puff of heavy air, Laddor began to snore. Drool ran from the corner of his mouth and slipped from his cheek onto Cherinne's shoulder where he was resting his head.

"*Laddor!* Wake up—you're drooling on me." She shoved him with an elbow.

"Huh?" Smacking his lips, he wiped his cheek with the back of a hand. "Where are we?" He looked around the plane at the other empty seats and a few slatted crates sitting behind the cabin area, then out the window at the ground below. "Oh. We're still on the plane. *Maannn,* and I was having this awesome dream, too, Cherry." He leaned toward her ear and sighed, "ya' wanna' hear about it?"

She looked at him questionably, knowing that his dreams were usually very risqué and somehow always involved her.

He told her anyway.

"See, you were wearin' this little pink nighty." A broad smile brightened the whole of his face as he recalled the image. Laying his head back against the seat, he closed his eyes and brought her into focus. "*Oh, baby*, did you look *hot.*"

Cherinne rolled her eyes.

Deverall scooted to the edge of his seat. Removing his earpiece, he strained to listen.

"Anyway, I was lying out at the pool, and it was hot—and I mean *hot*—

just minding my own business," he added nodding his head in a sanctimonious manner. "When suddenly," his eyes flew open, "Cherry, you come sauntering out in this little pink, see-through nighty." He waved his arms around. "*Geez!*" He then wiped a bead of sweat from his forehead, "I'm gettin' all worked up just thinkin' 'bout it!"

Cherinne shook her head with disgust.

"Anyway, you come moseying on out, in this little pink see-through—"

"Uh, Laddor, I already heard this part. I get the picture."

"Well, anyway, you know what you're wearin', and you come sauntering on over to me—smellin' *sooo good*, like coconut oil or somethin'. And, I'm just minding my own business, just trying to relax a little on a hot afternoon; when you have it in your pretty little head to try and corrupt me by seducing me—right there by the pool and with Reynolds inside, no doubt!

Anyway, you come over, stand beside my lounge chair, then slowly slide your long silky leg across me—mounting my lap—then gaze, face to face, into my eyes." Shifting in his seat, he wiped away another bead of sweat. "Then, you—" he looked around, as if telling a most important secret, and whispered into her ear.

Cherinne's face contorted into an angry, fierce-looking scowl, "*Laddor! You're disgusting!*" She elbowed him hard. "Get away from me!"

"What! What did she do?" Deverall, nearly falling from his seat, yelled, a look of perverted desperation shadowing his anxious face.

Cherinne gave Deverall a nasty glower, appalled to find he had been listening.

"She—" Laddor began.

"Shut up, Laddor!" Cherinne suddenly swung her backpack, making contact upside his head.

"Oowww, Cherry!! Whaddaya have in there? Books? It was just a dream!" he stated in his defense while rubbing his head.

"I don't care if it was written on stone tablets! Your dreams are perverted!" she said as she glared at him.

"Yeah. But, you're always so hot in them and you always make me *so happy.*"

"Laddor, a ten dollar bill and that bear you sleep with makes *you happy.*

I doubt very seriously anything I could do would make you any happier than that."

"Oh, but that's where you're wrong, Cherry." He rubbed a finger along her smooth thigh and gave her a large grin.

"Stop it!" She pushed his hand away.

Deverall cackled obnoxiously. "Woof! Now, that's somethin' to think about!"

Glowering at the two perverted men, Cherinne wondered as to how she had gotten herself mixed up with them. "You two are disgusting! And, Mr. Deverall, you had best just navigate this plane and not think about me, or pink lingerie, or anything like that. And, Laddor—"

"Oh, pull the panties outta' your ass, sweetheart," Deverall remarked. "I wasn't thinkin' about you. I was thinkin' about Red and that teddy bear."

Laddor shrieked and cowered behind Cherinne as she stood with a dumbfounded expression upon her face and pointed a commandeering finger at Deverall. "Well, that includes any lecherous thoughts about Laddor, here, also."

"Aw, you're no fun at all," he grumbled while replacing his ear piece. Thinking twice, he turned and added, "Hey, Red, you have any more dreams about Miss Havenstrit—you see me first. The same goes for you too, sweetheart, you have any about 'Flame Boy'—I wanna' hear em."

Deverall cackled maniacally as Cherinne and Laddor exchanged a look and cringed.

Laddor then whispered to Cherinne nervously, "Cherry, honey, you wouldn't tell that ol' pot-bellied fuzz-ball about any dreams you had regarding *me*, now would ya'? I seriously think something's wrong with that guy. And, to top it off—he keeps lookin' at my ass."

She glanced at Laddor, as he sat and fidgeted nervously within his seat. Grinning wide, she mewed in mock pleasure. Her tone was patronizing, "Well, Laddor *baby*, now you know how I feel."

"Oh, but, Cherry baby, your ass is worth looking at." He leaned against her and gave her that canary-eating grin while trying to place a roving hand high upon her leg. Quickly getting the hand, he pulled away as if he had touched a hot skillet.

Hours had passed while Laddor lay with his head on Cherinne's lap and slept like a new-born baby. Shifting slightly in her seat and feeling as if she had been riding a wooden plank, she sighed and thought about how she'd be lucky if she didn't end up with an enormous patch of blisters on her rear by the time they arrived in Egypt. A picture of herself in a bikini with big red blisters protruding from her hind cheeks entered her mind. She giggled—nice, *real* nice.

Closing her eyes, Cherinne listened to the planes motors as they purred along and cut through the cloud covered sky; and drifting into an agitated slumber, she began to dream. It began with Laddor picking grotesque scabs from her rear and repeating over and over, "But, Cherry baby, your ass is worth looking at…but, Cherry baby, your ass is worth looking at."

Cherinne groaned and flinched restlessly, as the dream slowly began to turn into a sweat-ridden nightmare, centered in the midst of a battlefield, where thousands of warriors fought valiantly in the rage of a blood-thirsty war. She could see herself amongst those who fought, as she rode upon a magnificent winged chariot, whose forged metal blazed in ravaging red and orange flames, as it cut along the blackened sky.

She was an all powerful universal goddess, dressed in garments made of long pearly-white silk, which flowed gently in the breeze as they pressed firmly against her skin. The haltered top, which was wrapped delicately around her neck, meshed together across her breast in an intricately detailed array of scintillating jewels; while the bodice formed snuggly to her slender waist, revealed an exceptionally shaped figure. The sheer material of the broad leggings, near to the length of her legs, hugged her thighs tightly as their delicate cloth whipped wildly in the midnight sky. Several necklaces adorned her neck, while her arms were lined with a vast variety of bracelets, one of which she was now wearing. Holding her arm firmly before her, she swept it broad, like that of a swinging pendulum, as she sent the beams of multi-colored light, shooting from the one main armband. Aiming, with precise accuracy, she fired into a legion of mystically formed creatures which possessed the head of a boar and the body of an ass.

Cherinne suddenly bolted forward and her eyes flung open to the quiet of the aircraft's engine. Her heart banged with the blood in her ears, and a cold sweat had drenched her neck and back. Clutching an armrest in the death-grip of one hand and Laddor's jacket in the other, her knuckles had shaded from pink to white and her fingers ached along with her hammering chest. She strived to measure that of her sporadic breaths and slowly settled back against her seat. Laddor slightly twitched, as his head was still in her lap along with, she noticed, a puddle of drool.

"*Ewww,*" she remarked, vigorously pattering her legs to wake him. "Laddor," she whispered, "you're drooling on me again."

"What?" He raised his head, attempting to clear the cobwebs of sleep. Smacking his lips, he pushed back his mop of disheveled hair.

"Look." She pointed at her white shorts. "You made a mess on my shorts. It looks like I wet myself."

"Hey, Red," Deverall yelled back as he angrily chewed on the stub of an unlit cigar and leaned forward in his seat. Rubber-necking exceedingly to nearly touching the aircraft's windshield, he noticed something just beyond the plane's nose. "Any more wet and juicy dreams?"

Laddor stood and stretched tall, while rubbing his stomach with one hand inside his uplifted shirt, and the other disappearing into the back of his blue jeans, which scratched his hind quarters generously. "Nope, not this time," he yawned. He ran his hand through his mussed hair and lazily sunk back into his seat. "Sorry, man."

"*Humph!*" Cherinne huffed in annoyance then noticed as Deverall was gazing fixedly at something out the windshield of the plane.

"Deverall, what's goin' on?" She quickly climbed over Laddor and smacked his hands, as he, nabbing the opportunity, had used them to support, or rather grope, her hind end. Ignoring his whiney protest, she moved through the seats toward the cabin.

"Deverall, what…?" Her voice was lost in a gaping open-mouthed pause while terror raced along her puckering skin and ran throughout her bones. Frozen moments fled till she was able to find her voice in a croaked whisper, "*Oh, my God! What is that?*"

"I'm not sure, sweetheart, but you'd better buckle in and hold on tight."

Cherinne, hurrying back to her seat, obliviously gazed through a wide blank stare at Laddor, who was rummaging in her pack. Her heart banged ruthlessly against her rib cage in the attempts to escape from her chest and burst through her black camisole. And, fumbling to her seat and with her buckle, she anxiously squawked, "Put your belt on. Oh, and by the way, Laddor, I *do* love you."

"Aww, Cheerryy, did you just say you love me? Aww, I love…" he leaned in for a kiss.

"Laddor, just put your belt on!" The command was frantic and panic plagued her face as she grabbed his hand and stared mindlessly toward the front of the plane.

Realizing something was seriously awry, he squeezed her trembling hand. "What's wrong?" her fear echoed within his own voice.

"There's something out there." The nervous quiver in her tone sounded above the roar of the engines, as she pointed a shaking finger in the direction of the window.

A heavy dark cloud, thick as pea soup, gradually ascended about the small plane and enveloped them within its massive black shadow. The ominous form, seeming to possess some sort of diabolic aura, which permeated from within its inner core, was like that of an unholy inferno that raised the hairs upon the skin and caused the human body to involuntarily shutter. Appearing to be something of a decomposing substance, the huge mass commenced to freely run down the windows, while slowly beginning to form into broad outstretched clawing fingers.

"*Oh, my God! What is that smell?*" they crowed in unison, as a vile stench filled their nostrils and drew the taste thick upon their pallets.

"*Oh, shit!*" Deverall exclaimed. "Hang on you two!" Aiming to toss the mutation from his aircraft, he veered left then right. "They don't call me 'Bushwacker Deverall' for nothin'!" he bellowed, chewing ferociously on the remains of his cigar butt. Manning the control wheel with his left hand and beckoning to the ominous form with his right, he shouted, "Come on you *sonsbitches! Bring it on!*"

Snaking themselves, as liquid serpents, around the small plane, the black forming fingers, or boggies, clutched the Amphibian in a tightfisted unrelenting grip. While an oily dark slime covered the windows, leaving behind an inky film that made it impossible to see out.

Darkness filled the inside of the compartment while the rancid odor drew nauseous bile to Cherinne's throat and her head began to reel. Immediately, she covered her nose and mouth with her shaking hands.

"Cherinne! What the hell is it?" Laddor muffled a cry from behind a hand, while the whites of his eyes, bulging in fear, gleamed in the flickering shadows.

"I don't know," was barely a whisper from her choking throat and chest.

The liquefied mutation bore down upon the small craft as the Amphibian fought its way through the dense mass, while its motor roared in determination to break loose. The dark form squeezed the plane within its grip, sending an ear-piercing moan of bending metal reverberating loudly within their ears. It yanked them haphazardly about the open sky. Drinks, their luggage, tools, medical supplies, a Chobits book—anything that wasn't bolted down, crashed against the seats, while seeming to make Cherinne a target as she ducked in fear of being pelted. Emergency lights flickered on in a maddening frenzy and air masks sprung from upper compartments to dangle in their terrified faces.

Thoughts of a child, she had once seen, shaking a plastic tube filled with gel, raced through Cherinne's mind. The child had gripped its small hand around the tube, and, as he had squeezed, gel filled one end or the other, stretching the lining to a transparent nothingness. The child had shook the tube fervently and laughed. Then, finally, the lining, from too much pressure, burst; and the child ran to his mother crying and covered in the sticky goo. The plane was now that tube, being squeezed and shook, it urged the bile to abruptly rise in Cherinne's throat, soon to be sprayed everywhere as sticky puke. Screaming out in terror, she drew at heaving breaths while again she white-knuckled the arm rest.

"Have to focus! Have to focus," she whispered as she, looking at the spot on her shorts through unclear eyes, thought she had probably, out of sheer fright, wet herself. While Laddor, slumped forward and passed out, was fortunately oblivious to the chaos surrounding them. Using every ounce of effort she could muster, she aspired not to spew her tuna sandwich, from lunch, over him or herself. And, dimly hearing the many curses of Deverall, as he fought the yoke, determined not to allow the so-

called 'sonsbitches' to make a monkey of him, she closed her eyes and attempted to remain conscious.

"I'll show you!" Deverall shouted out, appearing to have gone stark raving mad as he pounded a fist upon a large button just above the control panel. More metal creaked eerily as if the plane were being torn in half; then a low droning noise slowly began to rise from beneath the cargo area.

Seconds passed, seeming to consist of hours, when suddenly, an ear-piercing scream was heard as a half dozen razor sharp blades rapidly burst through the Amphibian's hull. The steel blades, thick as plywood and the length of a grown man, plunged deep within the mutated claw that had ensnared them in its massive slimy grip. Recoiling, the creature immediately drew its immense fingers back in a painful fit of defeat while its ear-splitting screeching filled the whole of the atmospheric layer. And, as suddenly as the shadowy horror had appeared, it disappeared.

Deverall cackled aloud, as triumph ruptured through his veins. "Take that! You menace from Hell! You don't mess with Busher Deverall, especially when he hasn't had a drink all day!"

Deverall launched into the control panel, sending it flickering wildly, like that of a lighted carnival at night; while it flashed various signs of distress in radiated colors of light. The demented pilot, in the efforts to keep the Amphibian airborne, broke into a full blown sweat and cursed the dark demon that had attacked his flying ship, also the mother that had delivered it.

The sound of his bellowing voice gradually awoke Cherinne from her hazy stupor and her breathing slowly returned to normal, while her heart raced like that of her Porsche, wanting to rip through her sweated skin. Reaching a shaky hand for Laddor, she nudged him, basically just wanting to feel something other than the cold pitiless vinyl of her seat. "*Laddor*," her voice shook as she touched his shoulder.

"Huh?" He stirred. "Are we still alive?" Raising his slightly disoriented head, he ran his gaze around the plane, which looked to have already crashed.

Cherinne cracked a thin smile. "We're not out of the woods yet. Deverall's earning his keep."

Laddor glanced at the man who was busier than two squirrels gatherin' nuts before a hail storm. He then turned to Cherinne and grabbed her trembling body into his arms. "Oh, Cherry, I thought we were dead for sure."

"Hold me, Laddor," she whispered, burying her face in the lapel of his jacket. While the possibility of death was still evident and she briefly thought of how she may never hear the words she so desired—words of love, which she had so hastily spewed in their dire moment, that may never be returned.

"*May Day! May Day!*" Deverall shouted into the radio.

Through a haze of static, a voice coldly replied something in Arabic.

"Yeah, *whatever,*" Deverall slammed down his headset and grumbled, "Who the hell speaks Arabic? Hang on Red…sweetheart. We're goin' in for a landing."

While Cherinne had flown about the world with her father for many years and had encountered many uneasy, bad-weather flights, she now had a completely different definition of turbulence. Deverall, managing to keep the Amphibian from plummeting nose first, like a huge stone into the heated sand of the desert, worked in a maddened frenzy to maintain an upright position. Piloting the seaplane with pitching jolts and jars, he diligently strived to maintain control. And feeling as if their heads would be knocked loose, the aircraft finally succumbed to his demands and collided with the sea in a mountainous spray of water.

"*Water!*" Laddor cried petrified. His closed eyes sprung open while he had been clutching to Cherinne for dear life. Waving his hands frantically in the air, he squalled, "We're gonna' *drown?* We survive: the hand from hell, a plane crash and a lecherous old hairy pilot—to *drown!*"

Growling, Deverall trudged from the cockpit toward Laddor and shoved him to his seat with a thick hand. "Oh, shut up, you flaming sissy….," he stated irritably, "…no-one's dyin' on my watch." Making his way toward the back of the plane, he grabbed a lifeboat and threw open the emergency door.

"Come on. Let's get the hell outta' here and get ta' dry land." He kicked the lifeboat out the exit and it instantly sprung open. Grumbling, he tossed them both a life vest, "Here, put these on—especially you, Red. I have a feeling a 'flamer' like you can't swim."

Grudgingly consenting, Laddor put the vest on; while he was surprised the mangy pilot had emergency equipment on board at all, as the aircraft had seemed no more than a flying bucket of bolts. He wiped a bead of cold sweat from his forehead, while observing the ocean of water around them; then he turned to the obnoxious pilot as if the comment had just sunk in.

"*Geez!* What's up with the flame-boy shit, anyway? I keep tellin' you— *I'm no flame-boy!*"

"Can you swim?" Deverall's shaggy brows curled together as he jeered with big yellowing teeth.

Laddor stared at the aged man through slated eyes, endeavoring to meet the man's gaze which was hidden in the shadows of the aircraft. Then, slumping his shoulders in defeat, he regretfully answered, "No."

Stepping into the light, Deverall's eyes glinted in satisfaction along with a dirt-colored grin which reeked of triumph. "There! That's proof— case closed."

Stepping forward, Laddor clenched his fists and readied himself to advance on Deverall. Cherinne quickly grabbed his arm. "Come on. He's just screwin' with your head."

Deverall chuckled. "Yeah, I'm just screwin' with ya'," he affirmed, cracking Laddor smartly on the ass as he was carefully climbing into the boat after Cherinne.

"Hey! Watch with the touchin'!" Laddor yelped in annoyance.

Deverall released a full-fledged laugh and Cherinne hid a giggle behind her hand.

"*Aww*, not *you too*—Cherry," he whined.

"You're just too cute, Laddor. And, that red hair—well, it just makes you more...uh...*irresistible*." She giggled again.

"So, now that sissy boy is in the boat and we're all alive—where we headed? According to my calculations, flying so called 'dead reckoning', with all that slimy shit on my windshield—we should be smack dab between Egypt and Saudi Arabia, near Quseir. And, *this*....my young companions...." He spread his arms wide, "...is the Red Sea."

CHAPTER 4

The Red Sea is a great arm of the Indian Ocean. It separates the Arabian Peninsula from northeastern Africa. The waters are tinted a rusty red color from the algae that resides there, and even the seaweed, surrounding hills and reefs are red. Not quite the red of Laddor's hair, but red. Hot desert sands blow, settling across the waters in a cloud that produces reddish streaks. It is the Great Red Sea; the sea that Moses parted during the exodus of the Children of Israel and the water is thick with salt.

"Cherry! Why'd I hav'ta do all the rowin'?" Laddor rubbed his forearms and shoulders.

"That'll build up those scrawny little muscles of yours, Red," Deverall remarked. "And, make you into a *real man*—if you catch my drift." The scruffy pilot sat up and stretched while he had drifted off to sleep and had been snoring at a dull roar. Cherinne was relieved that it had finally ceased.

Shifting everything into place, he then cleared his throat, which sounded as if he was drawing secretion from the depths of hell and spat across his shoulder into the water.

Laddor poked a finger at the ballooning bulge hanging over Deverall's belt. "Looks like you're the one who needed the work out, old man."

Deverall, lifting his t-shirt to expose his well rounded stomach, encrusted with an oversized navel, stated, "You talkin' bout my 'goody basket'?" Grabbing it with both hands, he shook the excess roll of fat proudly. "I'll have you know—this is bought *and* paid for, and contains lots of skunky-ass beer," he flashed yellowed teeth while his grin crossed a scrub of five o'clock shadow. Then, leaning toward Laddor who grimaced at the sight, he stated in a hushed undertone, "The ladies love this." He rubbed it lavishly with both hands. "When we're in the sack, they wrap their loving arms around this and…"

'The hand' quickly shot up in front of Deverall's face. "I think I'm gonna' be sick," Cherinne quipped wearily.

Disappointment quickly appeared upon his face. "Aww, but you haven't heard the best part, sweetheart…the part where they smear peanut butter on it and…"

Deverall's lips continued to move; but fortunately for Cherinne, Laddor had cupped his hands tightly over her ears. But, as she watched the twisted facial expressions on Laddor's face, she knew the peanut butter story couldn't be good.

Water, splashing gently along the sides of the yellow raft, added to the calm of the moment, while a mild breeze was wafting along the downy swells of the shifting sea. The odor of salt was thick upon Cherinne's nostrils, sending a tingling sense along her sinus cavities, occasionally causing her to sneeze. And, gazing up at the cotton-candy clouds hovering overhead, she wondered about the dark creature or cloud that had nearly swallowed the Amphibian.

Deverall suddenly stood to his feet and shouted, "Laannd hhooo."

Cherinne shrugged her shoulders theatrically while she and Laddor exchanged a doubtful glance. Together, they stared out across the vast rippling of water to blue nothingness, while neither could see hide nor hair of land.

"Uh…Deverall…we don't see any land. Are you sure you're not suffering from heat stroke or something?" Cherinne asked.

"Yeah, old man, you sure you didn't get hit in the head with somethin' back on the plane." Laddor gripped the sides of the raft as Deverall's weight shifted and the raft teetered.

"Sit down!" Laddor suddenly squalled. "...Before you tip the damn boat over!"

Deverall gave his red-haired companion an eye narrowing look. A devilish grin glinted within his eyes and he shifted his weight purposely. Water proudly sloshed alongside the see-sawing raft and splashed carelessly into the small boat; and Deverall, watching Laddor squirm nervously, laughed. Double-stepping, he continued with his little game and increased the raft's rocking.

"Deverall, if you tip this boat over I'm gonna' make sure you don't get a red cent for this trip!" Cherinne snapped without a smile. She gripped at the thick black handles affixed to the raft. "You did a helluva good job piloting the Amphibian. But, if you put us in the water, I'm gonna' make sure the only piloting you ever do is for a school of fish!"

"Aww, you're no fun, sweetheart. I was just screwin' around. Besides, our journey together is just about over. We'll be docking *very* shortly."

Laddor stretched his long body out in the raft, while endeavoring to make himself comfortable. "Well, I'll believe it, when I see it," he quipped in a low mumble. "Anybody who does that shit with peanut butter has definitely got somethin' growin' on their ass and brain besides hair. And, if you say you see land, then you definitely aren't right—peanut butter, or not."

"You'll see, Sissy-boy. I can smell those camel-jockeys a mile away." He drew in a long breath of air through nostrils which produced near as much hair as his ears. "Yup, that there's camels I smell. Land is just ahead."

Deverall rowed while Laddor lay peacefully with his head back and his sunglasses pulled down over his eyes. Twitching ever-so-often, he moaned lowly and garbled something slightly beneath his breath. And, slipping into an exotic dream-state, filled with no one but him and Cherinne, he began to mumble, "No, not again, Cherry. You have ta' let me rest."

Cherinne watched and listened closely, as thunderclouds of anger shadowed her face. It was true; she did love Laddor, but all he ever thought about twenty-four-seven was how to get her in the sack. And that, in her book, was forbidden for now—until marriage anyway. The 'Forbidden Fruit' as Laddor would always say.

"*Oh, Cherry,* stop," he mumbled. "That might hurt." He stretched his lips in a desperate reach toward the dreamy figure of her, while she thought he resembled that of either a blow fish or a feeding infant.

Deverall elbowed Cherinne with a large sweaty arm. "Hey, look—Sissy-Boy's havin' himself another full-blown tits and ass dream." Deverall chewed his cigar stub excitedly as he observed the red-haired young male with a look of envy.

Laddor, mewing like an alley cat, begged, 'Tie me up, you lynx'.

"*Whoa! Yeah!*" Deverall leaned forward and eagerly glanced between Cherinne and Laddor. "*Man,* Sissy-Boy has it *goin' on.* No wonder he sleeps so much."

The toe of Cherinne's hiking boot quickly made contact with the delusional young male who seemed to find erotic sexual favors most every time he closed his eyes.

"*Owww!*" Laddor bolted upright, still hazy from sleep, as pleasure was suddenly replaced with confusion and a jolt of pain. "*Hey,*" he looked groggily at Cherinne and Deverall. "I was in the middle of somethin'." Which one of you kicked me?"

Deverall quickly threw a thumb in Cherinne's direction and declared, "*She* did it. I was rather enjoying the show—why would I turn off the set?"

"Cherry, whaddya' do that for?"

"*Humph!*" She turned her back to him, "You make me mad, Laddor—that's all."

"Aw, Cherry." Placing a warm hand upon her shoulder, he gently pulled her toward him, while wrapping his arms around her waist and cooing into the back of her hair. The tension between them slowly began to diffuse and Cherinne started to giggle.

Deverall suddenly slammed his hat to the floor of the raft. "*What the hell is that?* You coo like a baby in the back of that gorgeous girl's neck! Be a man! Bite her! Make her bleed!" He stood to his feet. "Do *something,* other than blubber like a baby with a wet nurse! Stick your tongue down her throat till she almost chokes! Lick her eyeballs—*something,* besides that damn cooing!"

Laddor stood tall to his feet—inches above Deverall—as he clenched his fists in knots. "I'll have you know, my Cherry does not like biting." He stared down at the scruffy pilot in an all out challenge as he handed Cherinne his sunglasses.

Scratching the shadowy growth on his thick chin, Deverall briefly pondered a reply. Then, suddenly, bellowing out a long gutteral laugh, he slapped Laddor on the back. "Boy, Red—that's the most courage you've displayed since I first laid eyes on that flaming mop of yours. Keep it up." A devilish twinkle appeared in his eyes, as he chuckled and slapped him again.

Laddor returned the back-slapping with a wary, unsure grin, and Deverall responded with more of the same. The slapping became more vigorous and energetic, as their eyes met and they suddenly became aware they were both teetering on nervous, wobbly legs, and that the boat had broken into a hair-raising hap-hazardous swing.

Deverall, reaching for Laddor, managed barely to grasp only fistfuls of flailing crimson hair; while Laddor, terrified of falling in, clutched at the shifting pilot's t-shirt, as his arms worked frantically along with his legs to keep afoot.

"Oh shit!" Deverall exclaimed as his weighty stomach suddenly threw him off-balance. Double-stepping and reaching for anything but hair, he finally made contact with Laddor's life jacket. The pilot's weight, throwing Laddor off balance, immediately sent them both airborne and sailing into the cool steady-moving current of water.

"*Cherry!*" Laddor screeched as his arms waved desperately amidst the mêlée of auburn hair and he splashed head first into the colored sea, disappearing beneath the dark red surface along with Deverall. A spray of wetness spattered Cherinne's front and awoke her from a state of bewilderment, while she was unaware she had been holding her breath. She scrambled to the edge of the raft.

A few tense moments passed till Deverall, popping his head up above the water's edge, spit the saline liquid from behind a grimace. "Salty shit." He glanced around for Laddor. "Hey, where's Red?"

Cherinne scanned the whole of the surrounding ripples of water— water that stretched for miles. "Laddor?" His name drifted softly across the tips of the gentle waves to be swallowed by the vast crimson sea.

"Red!" Deverall shouted. His eyes rapidly darted to and fro as he stuck his head below the surface and searched for the young man. He lifted his head from the water. "Damn! The blasted water's the same color as his hair! Dipping below again, he then resurfaced—this time—holding an orange life vest. "Cherinne, here's his vest." He pitched it in the boat. "It was caught on a reef below. It's unhooked so he must have gotten free of it." Deverall dipped below again, while Cherinne quickly removed her vest, held her breath, and dove in.

A sting of tears formed in Cherinne's eyes as she attempted to see through the haze of red; and her mind, galloping in several directions at once, frantically searched the depths of the water. Laddor, she prayed, please don't die on me. *Please!* Holding her breath, as long as humanly possible, she thanked God she had always been such a good swimmer. Minutes passed as she scanned the murky darkness, while her lungs, burning within her chest, felt as if they would explode. She forced her body upward toward the surface.

The sun shone brightly upon her face, as she broke through the surface, and gasped for fresh air. Wiping the tears from her stinging eyes, tears which no longer stung from the salt, but for someone she loved, she looked around for Deverall.

"Cherinne," She could hear Deverall call to her through a panting breath, "…I have him here!" Quickly, he hoisted Laddor over the edge of the raft.

Hurriedly swimming toward the small boat, with her heart pounding loudly within her head, Cherinne began to tremble.

Deverall pressed sharply on Laddor's chest. "He's swallowed a lot of water," he stated gravely while Cherinne made her way back into the raft. "*One…two…three,*" he pushed with two hands pressed against Laddor's motionless chest, "*one…two…three.*"

Deverall placed his fingers to Laddor's unresponsive pulse just below his jaw. Then, cocking the young man's head back, he opened his mouth. Inhaling deep, Deverall then placed his mouth over Laddor's and released a lengthy, stale wind of stinky cigar breath which blasted into Laddor's water-filled lungs.

Eww, Cherinne thought as she observed the pilot with his large hair scrubbed lips to Laddor's. A foul taste suddenly formed in her mouth.

Deverall licked his lips lavishly. *"Mmm, peppermint candy,"* he muttered to himself, as he bent again to exhale his lot of dragon breath into Laddor's unmoving body.

"Stop! I'll do it." Cherinne pushed the sopping pilot to the side. Brushing away the dampness clouding her eyes, she placed her trembling lips to Laddor's. *"Oh, please, Laddor, please…"* she whispered as she drew another breath of air and exhaled into his lungs.

Suddenly, he coughed and his long body wrenched forward in a spasmodic jerk. Red sea water spewed from deep within his chest and he gasped for air. His dripping red locks, cascading loosely about his lowered face, made it impossible for Cherinne to see his expression. And, without warning, he grasped her hand in a conjoining grip as her tears broke free and flowed easily down her heated cheeks. Endeavoring to sniffle back the aching within her heart, she was unexpectedly bombarded with an inexorable flood of emotions. And, throwing her trembling arms around him, she burst into a fountain of hiccoughing sobs.

"Oh geez," Deverall remarked while removing his sopping wet T-shirt and quickly ringing it out. He laid it over the edge of the raft, then began to unzip his clinging wet shorts. "Twice I save this boy's ass and *he's* the one gettin' all the reward."

"And what reward is that, Deverall?" Laddor's weary tone was raspy.

"Well, *geez,*" he stated while pointing a finger at Cherinne. "I don't have hooters like that pressing up against me—now, *that's* a rack of lamb. How'd the hell *you* get all the luck?"

Cherinne quickly glanced down at her top and shrieked at the sight of her breast pressing firmly against the clingy, wet material where there was little left for the imagination. Laddor also looked, as both men gawked open-mouthed in a fixed stare. Cherinne's face rapidly welled into a raging flurry of anger and humiliation. And, clenching her teeth, she balled her small fists into tightened knots, driving one into Laddor's chest and the other into Deverall's bulge of excess fat. A wail of complaints was all she heard as she made swift, direct, contact.

"Humphh!" She rummaged angrily through her overnight bag; and

quickly selecting a hunting vest which she had picked up in Africa, a few years back, when visiting with her father, she hurriedly slipped it on. Securing all the snaps and latches it adorned, she made sure to cover anything that might even resemble a breast.

"*Cherrrryy!* Now, what'd you do that for? I didn't do anything." Laddor whined while rubbing his chest.

"Yeah, we can't help it you have that beautiful set of knockers that only begs to be looked at or—"

Cherinne planted another blow to Deverall's lower abdomen.

"*Ughh!*" Deverall lurched forward while holding his stomach. "*Man,* can you haul a punch!"

"Serves you right, *you old pervert,*" Cherinne declared as she zipped her bag.

Laddor nudged her. "Hey—look." She followed his finger across the water to the shoreline in the far-off distance. "It's land."

CHAPTER 5

The bright yellow raft drifted lazily just beyond the small port of Quseir, which to Cherinne's surprise was amazingly beautiful. Lovely palm trees lined the shores where several sea-bound vessels were docked either loading or unloading cargo and the water was pristine. The soil-rich red mountain ranges, breathtakingly gorgeous, surrounded the white beaches which lay before them, just beckoning for a sunbather's oily body to lie upon their sands. It was a tourist's dream come true.

Deverall grabbed his dried shorts and slipped them on. Cherinne was thankful; for the sight of him sitting in his boxers had been more than discomforting, forcing her focus elsewhere. He secured the raft. "Well, kiddos—I guess this is where we part." He scratched in unmentionable places. "Your father—Mr. Havenstrit—said that you could take a bus from here to Luxor. It's about a three hour ride. There he'll have a car awaiting your arrival." He handed Cherinne her bag. "How much time will ya' need?"

Cherinne glanced around at the port just below them and the beautiful beach just inviting her to lie upon its golden sands. "Give us seventy-two hours. That should also give you time to make any repairs to the Amphibian, if there was any damage done when that thing attacked us. What do you think that was anyway?"

Deverall removed his sunglasses and suddenly grabbed her wrist which adorned the bracelet. "I suspect it has something to do with this." He closely examined the exquisite piece of jewelry. "I've noticed that every time you were in distress the bracelet produced a mystifying aura, like it was glowing or something. It happened when that cloud or *thing* attacked; then also when the Flamer here…" he pointed to Laddor "…fell in the water."

Cherinne looked closer at the artwork engraved on it; unaware it had done anything.

"You probably just didn't notice it, cause you were scared or thinkin' of somethin' else." He released her wrist. "Your father never mentioned the details of this trip; but I have a feeling that a lot of shits about to go down and you and Red here are snap dab in the middle of it." He turned to Laddor. "I know you're a sissy-boy an' all, but here…" He pulled a flare gun from within his knapsack and handed it to Laddor. "If anything happens and you need my assistance, don't be afraid to fire this baby off. I'll be close. I wanna' do some repairs and check the status of the Amphibian's blades; I think one of em' got bent when it punctured that thing. Sure was a helluva modification job your old man did on that little plane. It's like a flying beast," he smiled. "Also, I wanna' check me out one of them there harems. They may not have peanut butter here," he patted his potbelly with a maniacal grin pasted on his face. "But, I bet they have some kinda mystical oil that may even make things grow a little—if you catch my drift." He elbowed Laddor and chuckled deep.

"Good bye, Mr. Deverall," Cherinne firmly stated as she grabbed her bag and shouldered her pack.

"Now remember…"he yelled after them, "shoot the flare if anything goes wrong."

Laddor turned and flicked him a military salute.

Deverall muttered quietly to himself as he glanced around at his surroundings. "Egypt—let's see…" He rummaged around in his sack till he found a small book mapping out the area. Paging through to "Quseir," he studied the lay out. "I think I'll start here and try ta' get a few parts." Shoving the book back into his bag, he then brandished his trusty bootlegged Mauser, which he jammed into a holster, concealed beneath the vest he was now wearing. Grabbing an extra cartridge, he made his way toward the docks.

Vendors lined the lively streets of the village's marketplace in an attempt to sell their wares, as they, clamoring in their native dialect, busied themselves in the hopes of a thriving, prosperous day. A small white bus made its way toward Cherinne and Laddor as they stood on the street corner beneath a sign picturing an automobile with, what they assumed, was the word 'Bus' written in Arabic. Cherinne unzipped the side pouch of her backpack and pulled out an Arabic-English translation pamphlet. "Basic Arabic," she read aloud while shuffling through the pages. "Laddor, are you sure I spoke Arabic when I was out at the pool?" She recalled the fact that she had been speaking a language which was foreign to her ears; but yet, she was able to understand most everything she had been saying. She had heard the name of Seth and had called out to those who she assumed were her comrades; all in a language she had thought to be Arabic or possibly ancient Egyptian. She scanned the pages of the book—"please, please?" She ran her finger down the page. "Oh—it's minfadlak—Luxor, minfadlak. I think I've got it," she stated happily.

"Reynolds was sure that's what it was," Laddor replied. "He had done a little research on it in the study; and, *I* also think it was. You have to remember, I was just here, and it sounded very near the native tongue." He took her hand as the bus's brakes screeched loudly and it pulled to the corner. "Now, stay close; I don't want anything happening to you over here and I don't want us getting separated."

Laddor grabbed their bags with one hand and lead her with the other; and, as they stepped onto the small bus, all eyes shifted to him and Cherinne. Laddor's flaming red hair and eyes the color of sapphires, plus, his height, drew attentive stares, while Cherinne, trailing along behind caught near as many with her long, blonde waves and large, chocolate colored eyes—eyes which made Laddor melt each time he looked into them.

Feeling like an insect under a microscope, Cherinne grasped Laddor's hand tighter. "Luxor, minfadlak," she said joyfully to the bus driver, while adding 'shukran'—thank you. Nodding impassively, he closed the doors.

Several women scattered throughout the bus wore traditional head coverings or veils to conceal their faces. Cherinne thought that they were possibly from a nearby village and may have been on their weekly visit to town—perhaps where they had visited the local bazaar or market for supplies. Their eyes shifted uneasily across her and Laddor and she could see the furrowed lines of disapproval just above their gaze. Two young village girls, perhaps high school age, giggled amongst themselves and pointed a finger at Laddor. Sparkling with delight, they watched him as he passed their seats.

Without warning, the bus, shifting into first gear, lurched forward and merged onto the road. Someone coughed and the gears grinded into action. Loosing her balance, Cherinne bumped into Laddor nearly sending him stumbling, while he was aiming to keep himself, their luggage and her afoot. Cherinne staggered into a gentleman who, in grabbing her waist, was able to catch her, just before she plummeted onto his lap. Flustered by his touch and somewhat embarrassed, she quickly apologized and grabbed Laddor's arm to pull herself away from his grip. Producing a thin smile, he put his hands up slightly in a gesture of innocence as Cherinne gave him a faint, but weary grin, and moved on.

A young boy and his father curiously watched as Cherinne and Laddor found their seats toward the back of the bus, shuffled their luggage about noisily, then finally got settled.

Suddenly feeling exhausted, Cherinne laid her head against Laddor's shoulder. She sighed heavily; while, the trip had, in no time, become a burden.

"Cherry, are you feeling okay?" Laddor brushed several strands of hair from her face which was slowly taking on the color of milk.

"I don't know. All of a sudden, I feel so tired and weak. Maybe we could find a motel as soon as we get to Luxor where I can grab a nap. Then, later we'll go see that prince of yours." Closing her eyes, she listened to the hum of the bus's engines and the stir of people around them. "Laddor," she whispered softly. "Can you stay awake till we get there? I—" She nodded off mid-sentence while breathing lightly and holding his arm securely.

The ride was quiet except for the working of the bus's motor as it hummed along its directed course, with an occasional grinding of the gears, as the road would rise or fall. Laddor watched the small boy, who he had guessed to be maybe seven or eight, as he busily occupied himself with a hand-made wooden toy. The young boy's father smiled and relayed something to his son in Arabic, then patted the boy's hands. Bored with themselves, the two young Egyptian girls began a game of their own. Peeking up over the back of their seat they would giggle then quickly duck back down before Laddor, playing along, would spy them with a smile and a wink.

Cherinne suddenly began to twitch and lowly moan; and, slipping into that surreal world, suspended between a dream and reality, she started to stir. Laddor held her close, while, fortunately, the low utterances which began to gradually slip from her moving lips, where drown out by the noise of the bus.

Laddor watched despairingly as the bracelet steadily began to glow, seeming to awaken and come alive. While the jewels upon the armband flickered brighter and more intense the further into the dream Cherinne withdrew. Her body quivered periodically and he momentarily wondered what she was experiencing, whether in the throes of battle, fighting for her life, or possibly fighting for someone else's. Ancient Arabic began to spew forth from her lips and Laddor glanced around nervously as several people, hearing their native tongue, began to turn and stare. Holding her securely within the vice-like grip of his arms, he wondered what would happen if the bracelet went on a tyrade. A bead of sweat ran down his face.

Suddenly, Cherinne reeled forward and her eyes sprung open as she called out loudly to some unknown, mystical force.

"*Oh shit*," Laddor muttered beneath his breath, while the bracelet, quickly ascending to the air, seemed determined to pull her along with it. Grabbing Cherinne's arm, he tried to lower it to her lap. But, as the jewels blazed intensely upon the bracelet, which was firmly affixed before her, he knew the armband was now in control.

"*Cherinne!*" he whispered in alarm as the bus suddenly detonated into a blast of colorful rays. The deadly laser beams shot uncontrollably throughout the enclosed area, cutting through vinyl seats, the gray ceiling of the bus and through the aged wooden floor. Chaos filled the screeching air as a throng of people screamed in terror and pushed and shoved toward the front, while others threw themselves to their knees and fervently prayed to Allah.

"*Cherinne!*" Laddor struggled to keep hold of the arm as it swayed methodically before her in a full pendulum swing, aiming to deliver its curse of death upon those in close proximity. "*Cherinne!*"

The bus veered sharply left and rapidly abandoned its lane which ran parallel to the rock encrusted wall. Spanning the width of the road and shoulder, it smashed through the guardrail and banged violently along the rock-strewn crag. It sailed into the ravine and sent the occupants, along with luggage, perishables, books and other items tossing about inside as they uncontrollably plowed along the narrow gorge. Tearing metal screeched in a raging scream with every fleeting moment, as Laddor was suddenly thrown into Cherinne with the force sending both their heads smashing against the bus window. A lightning bolt of pain struck within Laddor's forehead; and seeing white then black before his eyes, he groaned. His head thrummed with the sound of breaking glass and screaming, as the bus suddenly screeched to a halt and tipped over on its side.

An Egyptian woman, near to the front of the bus, rose wearily to her feet. Releasing a blood-curdling wail, she tugged at her torn garment and ran a hand along the spatters of blood covering her front, seeming confused as to whether it was her blood or anothers. Breaking into a rash hysteria and crying out words in that of her native tongue, she searched out the two Americans. Her dark eyes, wide with delirium, darted frantically between Cherinne, the bus-driver and the small boy, while she pointed a shaking accusing finger at Cherinne.

"*Mish kuwayyis! Mish kuwayyis!*" Tears spilled from her eyes and a fist sized bruise welted her cheek. "*Antee radi!*"

Shaking his head, as if something was loose, Laddor gently ran a hand over the knot forming quickly on his forehead and the trickle of blood stinging his eye. Confusion clouded his thoughts as he attempted to clear the haze from his mind and focus on what was before him. Gazing through the beams of yellow sunshine, which shone through the windows of the bus, he briefly watched in bewilderment the particles of dust which floated lazily about the air. Like flecks of powder upon a fairy's wings, they danced before his blinking eyes, appearing to be crystallized snow. A gutted moan rushed from his aching body as he, slowly rising, pushed himself off Cherinne, who was trapped against the window beneath him. He briefly observed her injuries to determine their severity.

Cherinne's head, rammed partly through the broken pane, oozed dark, sanguine blood which ran from an open gash into her quickly caking hair. "*Cherinne?*" Laddor choked out her name, bearly hearing his own voice above the delirium of those on the bus. Brushing the loose strands of his own hair away from his sweat-beaded face, he drew a deep breath and looked around—his main goal, to get them out and find Cherinne help.

The father lay close with his son cradled in his arms. Blood ran from a quarter inch sized smoldering hole just below the boy's collar-bone where the father had his hand attempting to slow the bleeding. Their eyes met and the father's face, twisting in uncertainty, betrayed agony; it compelled Laddor to speak, to silently console the man who dazedly turned his blood covered hand, wondering whether his son would live or die.

The boy achingly placed a shaking hand to his chest; and opening his teary eyes, he moaned, then whispered in a low voice, words only his father could hear. With a quaking hand, the father pulled a patched cloth from within his pocket and placed it to the wound.

Laddor glanced through the mirage of occupants for others who may have been injured. The young girls who had, just moments earlier, teased gleefully, were now terrified, clawing at the bus's doors, along with others who aimed to escape. Blood splattered the nape of the driver's neck as he lay slumped against the steering wheel of the bus with two dime-sized holes seared into his back which readily leaked blood. "Oh shit," Laddor breathed dolefully, feeling as if he had suddenly been sucked into the throes of a bad dream. "He's dead."

Cherinne opened her groggy eyes and winced. Groaning in pain, she was awakened to an exploding ache within her head which brought her semi-alert. "*Laddor?*" She reached a trembling hand toward the swell of blood matting quickly in her hair and whispered his name again,

"*Laddor?*" Closing her heavily lashed lids, she succumbed to the tears which peeked their way from the corners of each eye and raced along her heated cheeks.

"Cherinne." Laddor gently moved her head away from the shards of broken glass. "You'll be okay, honey." His voice quivered slightly as he found his bag and quickly rummaged through it for something to apply pressure to her wound. Using a bandana he had within his things, he lightly fashioned it around her head endeavoring to slow the bleeding.

Slowly, she re-opened her tear-swollen eyes. "Is this my fault?"

"No. No, it's not, Sweetie." He brushed a fore-finger along her cheek. "Just be still till I can get us outta' here."

The bus, resting recklessly on its side, leaned against a small palm. Possessions along with people lay against the frames of the windows and scattered along the bus's inner walls. Those who weren't injured climbed over the seats one by one till they reached the exit doors at the front. They banged and pushed upon the exit—mostly panicked women and the man that Cherinne had happened to stumble into.

"Gas," Laddor muttered. The odor of fumes was pungent, bringing terror to his slowly clearing senses and turning them cold. Vaguely remembering seeing an emergency door when they had boarded the bus and made their way to their seats, Laddor glanced over his shoulder to see he was correct. He briefly recalled the days he had practiced jumping from the back of his schoolbus, his many rides to and from the orphanage, then to middleschool, then highschool, while his elementary years had been spent at the Catholic monastery. He rolled his eyes at the length of time that has passed. Then wearily edging his way in that direction, he tried the handle—jammed. He glimpsed at the young Egyptian boy and his father making sure they were clear; then bracing himself he positioned his feet to face the door handle. Drawing his knees back and summoning all his might, he forcibly kicked his legs. His heavy boots slammed the bar and it creaked. Kicking the handle again, it broke free of its restraint, allowing the door to now be opened. The smell of gas was now over-whelming, creating a burning sensation within Laddor's scratchy nose and throat. And, forcing the exit door open, he shoved their luggage out to the ground to clear the way for Cherinne, the boy and his father.

The Egyptian wedged his way around the top of two seats with one arm, while supporting his son with the other. Pausing momentarily, he grabbed the wooden toy and shoved it into the pocket of his galabiyah— a long shirt-like garment which was cumbersome for his ensuing plight. His face was crossed with fear and determination, intertwined as one; while his son whimpered soft words to him as if encouraging him to proceed forward.

Smoldering gray smoke filled the whole of the bus and a frizzled hissing of open flames prompted both men to move. The Egyptian's dark, near black eyes, grabbed Laddor's gaze in all-knowing horror; and glancing at Cherinne, he quickly scurried toward the exit. Impervious to the sudden lamenting of the boy, he hurriedly closed the gap between life and death for him and his son.

Laddor could see the two young girls—the last of the fleeing lot— climbing through the hydraulic doors. Relieved, he gathered Cherinne gently within his arms and balanced on all fours upon the windows' casing, careful not to place weight on the glass in fear of breaking through.

Cherinne moaned with each thud of Laddor's knees to the inch wide metal framing. "Hold on, honey." He breathed laboriously as he made his way in the direction of the open door. A low droning hiss quickly raced along the gas submerged verdure, just beneath his knees, separated merely by a pane of glass. Laddor glimpsed in frozen horror at the flames wildly snaking along the ground in a determination to mesh with the fuel of the bus's tank.

"*Holy Shit!*" He lunged forward, tossing Cherinne roughly through the exit while his heart leaped within his chest and he scrambled into an awkward dive. Thudding to the ground, he rolled to his feet.

The Egyptian man, gathering his wits and his son, glanced his shoulder with an urgent shout and waved for Laddor to move. "*Ifajar! Ifajar!*"

Scooping up Cherinne and their bags, Laddor high stepped it into a dense area of palms and tall grasses while speeding along behind the fleeting man. A cold, fearful sweat mingled with that of pumping adrenaline as Laddor ran blindly through the patch of trees. An eerie moan of warping metal, followed by a loud screeching whistle, raced through the quiet of their surroundings, while Laddor, unsure as to what he was hearing, just knew it couldn't be good. Immediately throwing himself and his son to the ground, the Egyptian continued to shout in an alarmed panic, motioning for him to get down.

Laddor took a giant leap as a fizzled whistle blasted through the foliage and struck his back like a vibrating iron fist. Slamming forward, he lost his grip on the bags and Cherinne, as they abruptly crashed in a thunderous collision with the rumbling ground.

Cherinne released a stifled cry as she, banging roughly to the ground, ended up face down near the Egyptian. The gash in her head throbbed with insurmountable pain and fresh blood oozed over what had begun to clot.

Painfully, she turned her head as time froze and consumed her within its grip, while her body rested in a cluster of tall pasture grass and her face lay in the dirt. Gazing face to face with the Egyptian father, and wanting to speak, or possibly even scream, she could only blink her lashes. The sound of the explosion, resonating as a large clanging bell within her ringing ears, accompanied by excruciating pain, brought nausea to boil in the pit of her stomach. Afraid to move or even speak, with the possibility that Laddor may be severely injured, or worse dead, a tear traced Cherinne's cheek.

"Laddor?" Her voice cracked in a whisper and she was surprised at its sound. A vision of his riding Mr. Dolphin fluttered through her mind, and her laughing, as she could see his red hair dancing along before her eyes. "Laddor?" she whispered again as her heavy lids closed and her thoughts faded into darkness.

CHAPTER 6

A brusque hand brushed over Cherinne's forehead and someone rolled her gently to her back; she moaned. Pain raced in seering streaks throughout her head, as waves of exhaustion ebbed over her, and she attempted to open her eyes which felt as lead weights. Croaking something indiscernible from a parched throat, she could hear someone calling her name. A hazed vision of Deverall's roughly cracked face appeared close to hers as he seemed to be beckoning to her through dreaded eyes. She strained to listen; but the ringing of the blast still filled her ears and her head felt somewhat *puffy*. "Laddor?" her mind stated, though her voice conveyed something that seemed to come from a frog.

'Sweetheart', Deverall's lips formed in a slow motion set. He turned his head and yelled to someone behind him while Cherinne could barely make out the words "she's awake." Cherinne thought it odd—Deverall being there, in the middle of nowhere, lending a helping hand. He seemed to be more than just a dirty old pilot and she was kind of glad to see him. Placing his hand at the base of her neck to support her head, he then held a metal canteen to her lips for her to drink. The coolness of the water ran down her throat like a smooth sweet honey, like rainwater nourishing a dry flower.

Cherinne suddenly saw Laddor's face. An alarmed anxiety glazed his eyes as he dropped to his weakened knees beside her and pulled her close

69

to his body. His face was quickly in her hair; and she could hear him lightly inhaling, breathing in her scent. Feeling his body trembling, she raised a fragile hand and touched the back of his head; her hand ran the length of his hair. As her ears slowly began to open, like the blossoming of rose petals, she could hear his sobs as he called out her name. Tears welled in her eyes and she cried along with him. "*Laddor*," she whispered close to his ear.

"Hey, Red—let's get her outta' here." Deverall laid a hand to his shoulder.

Carefully cradling Cherinne in his arms, Laddor rose to his feet; and though he was taking extra precautions to be gentle, she cringed in pain. Raising a weakened hand, she touched the flowing locks of red that cascaded along his breast, while a thin smile, half grimace, wavered upon her lips as she saw the determination set within his eyes. And, feeling the straining of his working muscles, as he ascended the steep embankment, she wished they were going home. Cherinne touched Laddor's sweat beaded face, which arduously attempted to demonstrate courage, but, failing miserably, ended up portraying that of rueful sympathy. She briefly thought of her mother's funeral, where she had observed that same look upon the many in attendance; and, while her tears had momentarily ceased, they appeared again, but this time stronger.

Deverall followed along behind Laddor, as they crested the hill and made their way toward an awaiting vehicle. Opening the rear passenger door, Deverall waited till they were in then closed it. Climbing into the driver's seat of the running vehicle, he pulled onto the road and steered the car in the direction of Luxor.

The backseat of the vehicle was small and cramped; and Laddor shifted awkwardly, while his long lanky legs were folded near to knots, as Cherinne lay across his lap drifting in and out of consciousness. The engine of the small car purred along quietly while she could barely hear the crackling of voices sounding out in Arabic over the automobile's radio. And though the temperatures outside remained unbearably hot, the air conditioning, which was primal, blasted just enough air to keep the three from suffocating.

Suddenly, Cherinne felt a cold chill rush along the back of her spine and send a shiver racing throughout her body—not from any Freon, but from something else. She knew it was the bracelet.

"Shouldn't we get her to a hospital?" Laddor suggested to the pilot.

"Probably," Deverall replied, "but, do they even *have* a hospital, let alone one way out here?"

"Sorry Cherry," she heard Laddor whisper as the car came to a stop. Opening the door, Laddor unfolded his body as he carefully worked to steady her weight without causing her any more pain. Fortunately, she had always been petite—five foot, a hundred and four pounds; whereas, Laddor on the other hand was just above six foot, barely hitting two hundred pounds. He made her feel like a midget at times; but she didn't mind, she kind of liked it that way.

Regretfully, Cherinne opened her heavy eyes, wishing the ride would have been longer, possibly even a week; and as she peered through squinting lids at the desolate area and the leering block building, she wondered where they were. Quickly, they made their way into a side entrance of a dimly lit corridor. The air was skin chilling cool, dark and dank and she wondered as to why they weren't at one of the lovely resorts she had seen in the brochure—ones she had requested through the web.

The stench of cheap aftershave, along with the smell of a marijuana cigarette, or bad-choice of incense, seeped from beneath a closed door they passed on their trek into what seemed like a dungeon. Cherinne buried her face in Laddor's lapel, preferring the scent of sweat and cologne his jacket emanated. And, while her head throbbed madly and her body felt as if it had been broken, she breathed deep, feeling somewhat at peace.

Producing a key from within his short's pocket, Deverall shoved it quickly into the knob of a door; and, using a solid hip, he jostled it. The door creaked upon its hinges and opened. Then, she could hear the sound of luggage being tossed, which she hoped was hers, onto the floor inside the room. Laddor shuffled in and gently laid her upon the bed, then left her momentarily to rummage around in what, she assumed, was the bathroom. Cherinne grimaced, while her view took in that of the stained ceiling which peeled readily large remnants of plaster and bore bad tidings of a leaky roof. *Where in God's name am I?* In the attempts to keep from being defiled by the squalor of the morbid room and the itchy blanket, she drew herself up on her left side and clutched her knees to her chest. The mere thought of what kinds of activities had gone on previously in the single bed before their occupancy made her shudder.

Returning with a damp cloth, Laddor knelt beside the bed and rubbed it gently across her face. "I'm sorry, Cherry." Empathy was large in his eyes. "You should be staying at the Ritz, with a king-size bed, a bottle of wine and maids bearing snow white towels with little bottles of shampoo and conditioner." He laid the cloth across her head then searched his bag for medical supplies. Surprisingly, her injury had healed greatly from the time the accident had occurred, so applying a small amount of antiseptic to the hair line cut, he retrieved a bandage and secured it.

He turned to Deverall, "Damn, old man—couldn't you've at least gotten us a room with the paint sticking *to* the walls. Why the hell'd you get this dump anyway?"

"Oh relax, Red—it was cheap and came with the car; a package deal. It's not so bad; at least the toilet flushes. Besides, the shurTa bolis, or whatever the hell they're called, is looking for you two. What the hell happened on that bus anyway?"

Laddor dabbed Cherinne's cheeks with the damp cloth, then headed back into the bathroom to retrieve fresh water. "It's a long story," he called from within the dilapidated cubicle—a room someone threw a toilet and sprinkler in, and decided to call a bathroom. "And, I'd be able to explain it a lot better if there was some damn air conditioning in here." Returning, Laddor wiped a bead of sweat from his forehead and removed his blazer. His muscles gleamed with sudation and his t-shirt clung desperately to his heated body as he bent over Cherinne and replaced the cloth. "And, can *you* explain what the hell *you* were doing down in that ravine? How'd you know where we were?"

"Are you kiddin' me?" he stated, fiddling with the knobs on the air conditioner vent. "Piece of shit!" He slammed his fist cantankerously against the controls. "Fortunately, I had decided to just trail along with you guys instead of wandering off on my own; I'll search for ladies later. Anyway, I wasn't far behind you in my rental, just a few miles back or so. I was tuned in to a local channel; and, of course, not understanding one blasted thing that camel-jockey was spewing—I'd get more from the braying that screams from a camel's ass—"

Laddor raised a thin dark brow; only the left, used often to show doubt or orneriness.

Deverall continued. "….Anyway, when I saw the fire, I pulled over and ran to the edge of the bank, where the guard rail had been ripped apart. I saw the bus lying near on its side and the few towel-heads standing not too far off. That's when I noticed you," he threw a thumb in Laddor's direction, "high-tailin' it with sweetheart toward them there palm trees. You looked as if the Devil himself was hard on your heels. And, if it wouldn't have been for the severity of the situation I may have chuckled—you lumbering all those bags and that girl in your arms. It was somewhat amusing." He sniggered, then his eyes widen with excitement. "But, *holy nuts! Did that Mother blow!* When that bus exploded those camel-jockeys probably thought it was some sort of bombing. Shit was flyin' everywhere! That group, standing by, hit the deck; and to tell you the truth—I about shit my pants!"

Laddor's brows met in a full scowl, "so that's what I've been smellin'."

Deverall brushed him off with a wave of his hand. "Anyway, on the way here, I kept hearing mention of 'shurTa bolis' and 'otobis' on the radio. I know shurTa bolis is police, because when I was filling out the papers for the rental car, the chick behind the counter kept pointing to the word on the form and in broken English saying *police police*. Some dark faced fat chick with lots of jewelry wrapped around her stupid neck. I wanted to choke the little…."

"Man Deverall, you sure are *spicy*," Laddor inferred. "Enough about the chick; how would you reckon they're lookin' for us? We didn't do anything wrong."

Deverall's face grimaced as he raised an arm to remove his dank shirt and proceeded to inhale the sweaty bouquet wafting from beneath his armpits. "Damn, it's hot! I sure could use a shower. Well, think about this Red: A little boy was shot with *something* through the shoulder; and, from what you told me, some poor slob has holes blasted all in his back, deader-n-dead. What the hell do ya' think they're gonna' tell his wife? Besides, you never told me exactly what had happened." Walking over to

Cherinne, who had dosed off, he grabbed her wrist and held it up. He eyed the bracelet suspiciously, turned it to and fro, then stated, "I think it has something to do with sweetheart's jewel-piece here." He continued to examine it questioningly. "Tell me if I'm wrong. Plus—can you explain ta' me how her head injury is about near healed."

Silence momentarily filled the room with Laddor unsure as to how to answer. He wondered himself about Cherinne's injury, certain he hadn't imagined it.

Turning to face Deverall and elaborate on the situation, Laddor was abruptly met by the roll of excess that protruded from the pilot's front. It distracted him briefly from his thoughts as the over-sized navel, crawling with straggles of graying hair, seemed to stare him in the eye. They snaked over the bulge to a larger bushy patch of hair that covered a chest that looked to have been…deflated? "*Eww*," slipped from Laddor's lips. "Ya' know, Deverall, if you're gonna' be traveling with us, you could at least do something about keeping *that* covered." He pointed a finger at the mass while removing his own shirt to be relieved of the heat.

"What? This?" He patted his stomach like a bongo player taps his instrument to produce practiced music. "*Ol' Mirella.*"

"That's original."

"It sure is," Deverall stated proudly. He pulled up a chair, ready for firewood ages ago, plopped into it and stared off, lost in a memory; then he spoke. "The name is Spanish; it means *wonderful.*" It all started with this little Spanish gal I met on one of my flights for Mr. Havenstrit. She was darn-sight the prettiest lil' thing I had ever seen; and her name was Mirella. She loved this goody basket o' mine and told me so each and every day. She used to love to lay her dark mane right here," he pointed to a spot just above the crater size navel. "She would sing so softly her senorita song of love, while she would look up at me with those warm dark eyes and that angelic face." He wrung his hands, removed his hat, then ran a hand through his hair. "Oh, how I miss her."

"Well, what happened to Mirella? And, I thought you liked red-headed women?"

"Oh sure, I love red-heads. They are beastly women; none to be trifled with. They can rock a man's world, then send him cryin' back to Mommy in a blink of an eye. Yes, they are mystical creatures; part tomato, I think."

"*Tomato? Man, you* are *insane, Deverall.* I'm a natural-born red-head; and no-one in my family ever said anything about an Uncle or Aunt tomato. I think you seriously have a screw loose. Anyway, finish the story, it's gettin' late and I wanna' shower and get some rest."

"Well, there's not much to tell. We spent a lovely couple of weeks together; and when the job was finished, I got in my plane and left. I haven't seen her since."

Laddor glanced at Deverall; and as the pilot began to remove his shorts, he quickly looked away. "Well, *you idiot....* why don't you go back and see her if you miss her so much?" Laddor rummaged in his leather bag to retrieve shampoo, conditioner, clean clothes and a razor; while the thought of a refreshing shower was most appealing and his body was pasted with sweat.

"Oh, maybe someday...after I get this playfulness outta' me. A stud like myself certainly can't tie himself to one woman at too young an age; too many lassies wantin a little of this first," he chuckled, as he rubbed his bulging stomach.

Laddor's exasperated eye rolling was a signal he'd heard enough. "You're hopeless." He made his way toward the bathroom door, which, with the punitive dimensions of the room, was only a few steps away.

"*Hey Red!* Don't think you're showerin' first." Jumping to his feet, Deverall had forgotten the shorts dropped about his ankles. "*Oh shit!*" The weight of his 'goody basket' and entangled feet, throwing him off balance, sent him crashing upon Laddor, who slammed face-first to the floor. Deverall, wiggling about in an attempt to free himself, sweated profusely atop Laddor who had quickly pictured a sumo wrestling match within his stunned mind.

The ruckus of the two men colliding to the floor, abruptly awoke Cherinne. And, attempting to shake the cobwebs of sleep from her achy head, despite the screaming of her body, she sat up. "*Laddor?*" She shuddered, as the dingy room hadn't been a dream, but was actually a nightmare. "*Laddor?*" Glancing over the edge of the bed, she caught her breath and her eyes flew open. "*Oh my God, Mr. Deverall...what are you doing? Please refrain yourself, sir?*"

Turning toward her, he produced a slaphappy grin which opened to a dental-hygienists sweating toil. "Hey, sweetheart, you're awake. We were just about to get in the shower. Wanna' join us?" A gutted laugh escaped from behind his yellow fangs.

"*Get off me, you smelly windbag!*" Laddor hollered, attempting to wriggle himself free from beneath Deverall's overpowering weight. "Cherry, would you tell him to let me up."

"*No.* I'm not letting you up till you say you love me." Deverall's jesting plea for nuptial unison was nauseating, almost near as nauseating as that of the overpowering odor of rotten cheese, which drifted throughout the air. Deverall smiled sheepishly. "*Sorry.*"

"*No Way!* You didn't just release toxic gases on me from that overgrown hump you call an ass, *did you?*"

"*Hey,* I said I was sorry. That's what happens when I get excited."

"*Geez man! Get the hell off me!* You smell like somethin' that's been festering in my grandma's shoe!" Laddor shoved the obtrusive pilot away; and as Deverall collided with the bathroom door, he rolled to his back and smiled.

"See sweetheart, that's how you keep your man in control—brute force," Deverall chuckled. Then getting up, he quickly raced into the bathroom, slamming and locking the door behind him. Creaking pipes protested, with the clanging and moaning of many years use, while they could hear the water shoot forth from the showerhead and Deverall releasing a taxed groan, as the warm water washed over his large body.

Laddor's sigh and discouraged look as he glanced around the room at the dingy linens, stained repulsive rugs and lopsided pictures, portraying scenes from some snow capped mountain, were just a few indications that conveyed shame and remorsefulness as to having caused this mess. The low monotone of an Arabic song drifted lazily through the swell of humid air as he strained to see, through the crack of the sooty curtains, darkness arriving as one by one the shadows fell. All this was his fault: the accident, Cherinne's injury, his almost drowning, and this shit-hole. He looked at Cherinne—a delicate flower whose root had been trampled, a broken china doll in need of mending. While he hadn't meant for any of this to occur; he had just wanted to give her a small portion back of what she had given him—love.

A speechless union had formed between him and Cherinne the moment he had first laid eyes on her, though she hadn't been aware, he was. He remembered that day in the city, as if it were yesterday. He had been job hopping from one worthless employer to the next, never the brightest candle on the mantle, when a simple task had quickly turned into a nightmare, with her smack dab in the middle. His entire life seemed to run that course, as vague images, like smoke, breezed through his mind of a past meaningless life; starting with his childhood.

He had been orphaned at the age of three, after his father had raved, insisting that red hair was not of his lineage and the sight of the boy repulsed him so. A dark stony pair of eyes would scrutinize every inch of him; while the hand that extended from those fear-inspiring eyes would hold his boyish cheeks firmly, turning his head from left to right, then scowl angrily. An irritated snort usually followed then a heavy hand that thwarted his chest knocking him to the floor, or whatever else was near. Laddor's mother begged for Laddor's father to just *leave the boy—pretend he wasn't there* or even *that he existed,* while her pleas continued to fall upon deaf, unwavering ears.

As Laddor grew, his locks seemed to intensify in variegated colors of crimson and fiery scarlet to an indescribable mane of beauty; every beauticians unsuccessful aspiration. His mother cut, shaved and even covered with knitted caps, the gorgeous strands; even shaved his tiny eyebrows to hide the unexplained pigment. But, no matter her efforts, Laddor's father refused to accept him and wanted him gone.

Laddor's mother, teary eyed and delirious with grief, finally gave over to her husband's demands. A chilled morning came when she awoke Laddor from his sleep, dressed him warmly, then led him by his tiny hand to the front doors of the nearby monastery. Puddle sized tears filled her eyes as she hugged her son and choked out an '*I love you.*' Then quickly grabbing his hand, she shoved a small gift into it and clutched him to her chest again. Then hastening to her feet and without turning, she fled toward home. Tears spilled down Laddor's cheeks, as he watched her go; not quite realizing the ramifications of her actions. He yelled for her. "*Mommy, come back.... please don't leave me!*" Then, he remembered how she had firmly told him on the way there that he could not follow her, that this was to be his new home.

"Mommy," he had asked in the smallest of voices, "Will you come to live with me? I'm scared, and I don't want to be there without you." Unable to look him in his big blue eyes, her voice had cracked as she answered, "I can't, honey; but, I will see you someday."

While his tiny heart ached miserably and he choked back the small lump forming in his throat, he had continued to watch her till she disappeared from sight.

Snow had begun to fall in crystallized cotton candy flakes and he stood alone in the quiet of the white storm slowly brewing. Droplets of water, careening from sludge encrusted gutters, quickly turned to elongated icicles as the temperature dropped and the wind suddenly turned blustery. Blinking back the feather light flakes from his long lashes and swiping a small hand along his stinging eyes and sniffling nose, Laddor shuffled his snow boots about on the snow covered stoop. Then, looking at the gift in his hand, which was wrapped in lovely golden paper and secured with a small red bow, he gently placed it into his pocket. Glancing again at the path in which his mother had taken, with emptiness brimming within his small heart, he sat upon the edge of the cold stone step. Then, covering his face with trembling mittened hands, he began to cry.

As a young boy in the monastery, the sisters had often spoke of the impending evil spirit—the so-called Devil. Laddor would think back to that Christmas morning, nearly nineteen years ago, as he had sat shivering and cold in the loneliness of the wet snow, seeing his mother for the last time; and knowing he had already met him. And, the day they stood before him announcing that she had taken her life; Laddor knew that the devil had won.

Cherinne lay quietly on her side upon the bed; everything his heart had ever desired and more. Sure, he had teased about tumbling around in the back of the Rolls and had spied her often through the doors on her balcony. But, all of it was just a ruse, a way of showing her he cared and cared deeply. If she decided to never sleep with him, that would be okay, disappointing, but okay. She was there for him and had accepted him the way he was. And, when Laddor had shown Cherinne the gift, the final gift from his mother which he had carried all those years, she had taken it gently in her hands while lowering her head, and wept. The gift was miniscule to most; a small silver flute, an ocarina, enclosed in a little wooden box. But, to Laddor, it meant both the beginning and the end to his life; the final gift of Christmas past. After that day at the monastery, where he had stared up at the gargantuan sized cathedral with the doors broad and wide and the handles too high for him to reach, he grew to hate the snow and the holiday of Christ. And though, Cherinne would stow him away to her father's winter cabin, which was much more than just a snowy retreat—out sledding and pelting him with a snowball or two and surprise him with something under the tree—the memory of that morning never faded, only surfaced those times of the year. So, hot cocoa along with her in front of the warm fireplace were the only things that ever took him from the south, plus his meeting with an old friend who was setting him up for a job, a *real* job, which had nothing to do with running.

"*Laddor?*" Cherinne reached a hand toward him; while the arm entrapped by the mystical bracelet, laid firmly beneath her cheek. Opening her large chestnut eyes, she recognized the 'look'; the look of the past that glazed his eyes frequently and made her want to embrace him, reassure him she was always going to be there. Taking his hand, she studied the etchings and lines that brought character to his chiseled features; then she soothingly spoke through a voice as warm as honey. "Laddor, it's okay."

"Cherry…" Seating himself upon the edge of the bed, he took her hand. "I'm truly sorry." His fingers ran along the cool of the thick gold then brushed a long lock of hair away from her face. Their eyes interlocked; and, as she looked into those fathomless pools of blue, which seemed to be able to see beyond the very depths of her soul, she yearned to pour herself into them and drown. And, while they now held her captive—captive to a feeling she had sworn to never allow to empower her, she knew she was unable to escape. Placing a hand upon the muscle of his heated back, she ran it along his well-proportioned physique.

"Kiss me, Laddor." Her head swam as she pulled him toward her and was submerged within those mesmerizing pools. The soft of his lips were against hers and momentarily she forgot the horrific circumstances of the past few days, while her sense of control was being tested and she knew she had to stop.

Suddenly, the bathroom door banged open and Deverall emerged; his eyes flipped open wide. *"What the hell! This isn't the Love Boat!* Now, I'm finished in there; but, I have to warn ya'; there's no hot water."

Laddor, tearing his lips from Cherinne's, lept to his feet, leaving Cherinne with her lips braced in a partial pucker. *"Damn you, Deverall!* You expect us to take a cold shower?"

"Aww, quit your whinin', you bawl-baby. It looks like you two could use a cold one anyway"

Laddor clenched his fists in knots, while an angry stare seethed from behind eyes that had just been silken as blue velvet. Tensed muscles formed along his glistening back, chest and arms as he placed his fists in front of his face readying himself for a fight. *"Alright, Goody Basket, let's go."* Dancing left to right, his bare feet shuffled along the stain encrusted carpet.

A maniacal grin of pleasure scanned Deverall's face. *"Oh, you've gotta' be jokin'."* Tossing his damp towel to the bed, he raised his heavy fists and thick arms, twice the density of Laddor's; and licking his sweat beaded curled lips, he began to weave and bob. "This is gonna' be fun."

With his jaw clenched and his eyes intense, Laddor moved quickly, as he was slightly more agile than that of the heftier pilot. Jabbing, he threw a right fist which, in catching the pilot by surprise, planted itself directly along Deverall's unyielding cheekbone.

Deverall grinned as he wiped away a trickle of blood that slithered from the corner of his mouth. His tone was silty, *"Nice move.* I didn't know you had it in ya', Red."

Laddor's look was one of firm resolution while he was intent on a victory. Continuing to weave and bob, he made another attempt with a left cross. Quickly throwing a broad hand up, Deverall caught the strike mid-air. "Oh, no you don't, Sissy-Boy. You won't get off that easy." A twisted blow, sent into Laddor's abdominal area, doubled the young man over as he clutched at the blast of pain within his stomach and gasped for a breath of air.

Cherinne's reaction was one of shock and dismay. Shrieking in protest, she glared angrily at the pilot. "Stop it! Someone's gonna' get hurt!"

Deverall turned his attention to Cherinne and Laddor attacked. Thrusting forward at a ramming angle he charged, sinking his right shoulder deep within the pilot's excess. Realizing too late his offhanded blunder—never get distracted during a brawl, especially by a woman— Deverall groaned. His lumpish potbellied body, naked to the waist, slammed in reverse knocking the low-grade, model television off its stand and sending it crashing noisily to the floor.

Red hair swirled in an array of wild unrestrained madness, as Laddor dove atop the disorientied male, bombarding him with a fury of sweaty fists.

A war cry, equally savage and triumphant, escaped the overthrown pilot as he suddenly shoved with bare feet, off the box spring. And to Cherinne and Laddor's amazement, he abruptly curled up and smashed his forehead into Laddor's. The cracking fury of fists swiftly came to a halt, when Laddor in mid-swing began to teeter, as if he had suddenly become intoxicated. His hair, swaying methodically, clung desperately to his dampened skin; and unexpectedly toppling forward, he landed upon Deverall's sweaty heaving chest with a thud.

"Not tonight, Red, I have a headache," Deverall grumbled as he rolled Laddor onto the floor. Sitting up, he wiped the droplets of sudation away from his beaded forehead; then he reached around to rub his back. "Shit, I'da never thought that lil' bugger'd have it in 'im." He glanced at Laddor while touching fingers to his own battered face and catching a drop of blood as it raced from the corner of his mouth. Wincing, he chuckled, "Well, I've always said red-heads weren't to be trifled with." And, slapping Laddor on the back in a gesture of comradery, he stated "Good show, young fella'…now for the prize." Slanted malevolent eyes darted toward Cherinne, who immediately cringed. *"How's 'bout a lil' ol' kiss for the champion?"*

Cherinne's mouth dropped open in appalling shock as the room suddenly began to spin and her head began to swoon. *"What?"* She croaked out.

Cracking a painful smirk, he coughed out a chuckle, while the look of horror which was plaguing her face, was priceless. "Just kiddin', sweetheart. I'd be too much man fer ya." He cackled slightly at the idea while jerking a thumb in Laddor's direction, "though, you'd throw stones at Red here afterward." Then sniffing the nose-hair curling aroma wafting from his underarms, he announced, "Man, I'm gonna' need another shower."

CHAPTER 7

The sound of clanging pipes and a raging grizzly bear woke Laddor as he attempted to clear the tangled mesh of cobwebs from his mind. Painful flares, like charged electrical currents, raced throughout his head and body, sending his skull thumping in a screaming protest. He opened his eyes. Then, succumbing to the pain and thinking better of it, he closed them. He listened to the sounds within his surroundings, recognizing the bear as Deverall and the screeching of the pipes as the nightmarish bathroom from hell. Reopening his eyes, more slowly this time, he glanced around the darkened room. Slivers of moonlight slipped through the slightly parted curtains, casting eerie gray shadows upon the walls; daylight would be arriving shortly. Placing a hand to the blast of pain raging within his forehead, he thought, *Yes, Deverall,* I am *now* part tomato since I have this humongous growth on my face. *Great,* not only am I a fool; but, now I look like one—Cherry is probably really pissed.

He closed his eyes again, grateful for the pillow beneath his head and the blanket covering his body, which was stretched out across the poorly carpeted floor. Though, life would be much better if Deverall weren't breathing noisily in his ear and shifting about so much. He shoved him with an elbow. "*Damn you, Deverall—you can be such an ass!* Laddor cursed beneath his breath as the pilot moaned. Thinking about the fight and what had led to it, Laddor elbowed him a second time—just for good measure—especially since the big oaf had ruined the passionate kiss that he and Cherinne had been so rudely interrupted from. Then, recalling Deverall's impressive head-butt, he attempted a slightly, painful grin, deciding he'd have to master that move sometime, just not anytime soon. He gingerly touched his blossomed tomato.

Laddor turned his attention to the screaming of the bathroom plumbing, as he could hear the water begin to rush from the spigot and Cherinne open the door to the shower stall and step inside. Tuning in to the sounds of her in the shower, he listened as she hummed softly, like she always did when she bathed. Something he knew from spending quite a bit of time on her balcony, either at the estate or the cabin—sometimes freezing his ass off. Listening intently to the cascade of the water, he allowed his imagination to slip through the walls and gravitate inside the small cubicle, as he hopelessly watched.

Cherinne stood in all her beauty, while her rosy-golden skin glistened beneath the droplets of water as they molded to her beautifully carved shape, then tore themselves away and fell graciously to the tiled floor. He watched as she palmed shampoo into her lovely flaxen hair, and messaged it through, while her fingers ran the length of the long wet strands, which clung tightly to her body and added definition to her perfect form. Laddor groaned and scolded himself for subjecting his mind to the torturous thoughts, knowing it would only lead to unrelenting, dissatisfying agony. Throwing caution to the wind, he succumbed to the perilous pleasures and turned his attention back to what was going on behind the bathroom door.

He watched as she applied the sudsy coarseness of a loofah to her moistened skin and ran it tenderly over the smoothness of her curved neck; the spot where he loved to bury his face and gently cover with kisses. Traveling easily over the tenderness of her breasts, the sponge then ran along the tautness of her abdomen, to trace the inner silk of her thigh and explore the firmness of her calf while reaching to her ankles…

"*Laddor?*" The bathroom door suddenly creaked open, spilling light into the early morning gloom of the room, and tearing him from the illicit fantasy. Cherinne peered into the darkness while wrapped only in a small white towel; he knew she was watching.

Freezing in motion, Laddor held his breath while feeling as if he had been caught in the act of something heinous. Though, it was more like being caught with his hand in the cookie jar, and the proof wasn't in chocolate on his face, but something surging in his loins.

She whispered to him again. "Laddor—I know you're awake. I could hear you groaning and you were gasping for breath. Are you okay? What were you doing?"

What? He thought. *How is that possible, with the grizzly bear making that entire racket?* His mind raced for an answer. "No, Cherry," he finally answered in a muffled tone from within the dark. "That wasn't me."

"*Laddor,*" she scolded mildly. "*I know you're lying.* I can hear your heart pounding louder than thunderclouds movin' along the gulf. If you don't tell the truth, something's liable to explode."

Yeah, I'd say. He rolled his eyes. Why don't you tell that to your witnesses when you have 'em up on the stand. "*Uumm,* I was dreaming." There—it was half truth. She should be happy with that. *Besides*—he had been in a fight; wasn't there any reward for the gallant hero, even if he did lose.

Satisfied with his answer, she closed the door and returned to doing all those things that Laddor wished he could help her with. His awe-inspiring illusion now shattered, while the agony was still alive. Sighing heavily and holding his breath, he poked his tomato. That would cure it.

A few minutes later, the bathroom door re-opened and Cherinne stepped out smelling fresh as a spring flower; her aroma was tantalizing to the senses. Recalling the images of the soap bubbles, Laddor breathed deep.

Light had begun to filter slowly into the dreary room and life outside the ratty hotel had begun to come alive. A low murmur of prayer resonated throughout the air—not in unison—but spanning in various tones, pitches and tongues throughout Egypt and the entirety of the mid-east. The heat of the day crept in from the desert, bringing with it unwanted sweltering temperatures which drifted throughout the stillness, while only prayer and the braying of several camels was heard.

Laddor forced himself to an elbow, while his abdominal area, tight with pain, felt as if it had been shoved to meet that of his spinal cord. A miserable day of soreness and humiliation were best faced head-on; so, brushing his hair away from his face—his teeth grimy with nighttime film—he prepared mentally for a cold shower.

Cherinne painstakingly watched him, the knot on his head the size of her fist. "Laddor," she carefully stepped over Deverall's feet and knelt beside her hero. "I left you some hot water. You might wanna' get in and get cleaned up." She fingered a strand of long red hair then placed a delicate kiss next to his bruise. "You fought valiantly," she whispered close to his ear.

"Hey, Red," Deverall called to Laddor as he made his way toward the car. "Make sure you lock up before we go. I wouldn't want a TV or somethin' disappearin' and endin' up on my Mastercard. Damn derelicts around here are liable to steal anything." Starting the car, he tapped the stirring wheel and tuned in the radio, while Cherinne was waiting impatiently in the backseat.

She gazed in the direction of the room's door; and, while she was unable to see Laddor through the shadowy hall, she was able to hear him. "What's he doin' in there?" She strained her neck to see. "I can hear him; he's in the bathroom and he sounds like he's in pain."

Deverall turned from the front seat to face her; his face displaying the evidence of a losing battle from the night before. A thick, hair encrusted arm appeared across the leather and he raised a heavy brow in question. "Uh, sweetheart, I hate to break this to ya': But, you can't hear lover-boy from here. You probably hear some kid bawling somewhere or somethin'. But there's no way you could hear him from here."

Her face took on a confused state and she smiled in uncertainty. "Sure I can. I can hear him saying, 'Ow that damn Deverall', then he's fiddling with something in a plastic case. Now he's dropped whatever he's messing with and cursing because it's broke."

"No. I'm sorry, sweetheart, you must be hearin' things. Look," he pointed to the building. "See, that's cement block—and *you* have your window up." Pointing to the wall of solid block, then to his head, he stated in a slow condescending tone, "We are *hu-man be-ings. We don't hear things through eight inch stone. You are not Lind-say Wag-ner.*" She looked at him strangely. "Oh forget it." He waved it away. "She was before your time; *way* before your time." Cherinne continued to listen to something intently. Taking a breath, he decided to play along. "Alright, I'll humor ya'."

Opening his door, he climbed out and made his way toward the hall. Standing just inside the shadows, within sight, he called to her through cuffed hands, making sure her window was down. "Okay—you can hear me, right?"

She replied, "of course."

Deverall called again. "Okay, now roll your window up."

Quickly cranking the window to the top, Cherinne watched as he put his hands over his mouth. The muscles on his face twitched as his lips moved. He then waved to her to lower the window. "Okay, now what did I say?"

Smirking, she nonchalantly replied, "You said, 'this is stupid'."

Deverall's mouth dropped to his chin in disbelief and his eyes shifted over her face; he wondered as to how she could have possibly heard him. "Well, you just got lucky that time. Let's try again. Roll your window back up." He made his way deeper into the shadows, certain she couldn't hear from that point. Then covering his face tightly with his hat, he whispered into it. Quickly, he ran out to have her lower the window; and with a broad grin, he asked, "Now what, smarty-pants?"

"You said, 'this hat stinks.' There!" She stuck her tongue out at him. "I told you I could hear Laddor; he's comin' out the door now."

Deverall spun around as Laddor emerged from the darkened hallway with something in his hand. Worry raised the young man's wine colored brows near to his hair as he approached the car. Slipping by the pilot, who was frozen in stupidity, he opened the door. "Cherry," he placed her mascara case in her hand which was broken in two. "I'm sorry; I borrowed it to try and cover the bruise." He pointed to the lump upon his forehead thickly coated in rose shaded make-up. "I'm sorry—it dropped."

Snorting, she threw a triumphant gaze in the dumbfounded pilot's direction. "I know Laddor—I heard it."

The Tarun Regime

Fahimah lay as a cat upon the over-sized bed, laden with silken sheets and the scent of musky oils, while basking in the morning sun which blanketed her in its warmth. Stretching her achy muscles, taut from her intense workout the day before, she stuck her toes toward the ceiling and ran a small hand along her smooth thigh. With a yawn, she combed long nailed fingers through her mussed hair; the golden locks cascaded lazily upon the smoothness of her silky white skin and camisole while she knew the prince couldn't help but watch.

Rasheed, a tall overly-handsome Egyptian with large dark midnight eyes and wavy charcoal hair, dressed only in sandy trousers, took his place by the wall of glass. He regarded Fahimah's every move, as she rehearsed the same routine each morning, drawing more attention to herself than he could find energy to give. Sighing, she playfully rolled onto her taut belly; then she laid a fine chiseled cheek upon her folded arms.

"Rasheed," she pleaded in a silky voice, "please, come and play with me. I'm bored."

His gaze narrowed as she closed her large kaleidoscopic eyes which possessed the ability to persuade him into most anything her heart desired. "Not now, my pet; fore you are like the cheetah—possessing nine lives—and *I*, on the other hand, have only *one*. You shall be the death of me—you and all your beauty, added to your craftiness. Besides, we know the bracelet of Semus is near. You have been unbearably rambunctious; to the point the instructors have had to turn you out on your own, while they are unable to match your energy without coming near to death." Rolling, she swung her feet to the floor and sunk her toes deep within the lush carpet. Her head was down and he could not see her face. "Does the bracelet still beckon to you?" Fahimah tossed her head, giving no reply. The sunlight glimmered like gold upon the crest of her hair, creating a magnificent glow; she appeared as an angel—however, the prince knew better.

Retrieving a small piece of taupe yarn from the adjacent nightstand, which had been confiscated from the innards of a jeweled hair-bob, damaged during her sparring practice with one of her trainers, Fahimah ran it methodically between her fingers. "Well, if you won't play with me, Sire; then I shall play myself." She rubbed the fibrous wool with three fingers gently to and fro, along her smooth bare thigh. Twisting and turning in a methodical rhythm, it rapidly began to change colors and grow in length.

"RABBA!" she abruptly shouted the command, as the string suddenly came to life, and quickly began to grow. It wound its way up her thighs and progressively coiled its way along her calves and feet, rapidly consuming her legs. Fahimah mildly groaned as it snaked its way along her panties. She stood to her feet. Her heart raced within her chest and she lifted her arms high above her head, while the twine continued to cover every inch of her arching body. A blustery howling wind surrounded her in the wild throes of an untamed vortex, whipping the locks of her flaxen hair about in a wild frenzy and casting golden light about the room. Rasheed marveled at the motions and moaning of her body, questioning as to whether they to be from pain, or possibly that of sadistic pleasure.

Fahimah disappeared, completely consumed within the immense amount of woolen string, while the thrashing wind ceased to nothing more than a whisper. The prince watched with a quickened pulse, wondering in amazement, as to what trickery she had up her sleeve this time, while he could still hear the muffled sounds of her mystical chant. She was the majesty of her craft, calling out to the great spirits—subduer of both eminence and power—changing both mind and matter with a touch of her hand and a breath from her lips. Her chant increased in strength and clarity, becoming a bewitching shriek which sent cold shivers racing along the prince's skin. Briefly, he pondered, as to how he managed each night, to slip into those lovely arms, as she would amorously take him in.

A low forced wail echoed from within the yarn cocoon and Rasheed briefly glanced at the enormous window beside him, realizing it may need replacing after she was finished. He would discuss that with her later.

Suddenly, a hail storm of string exploded in every direction. Thousands of pieces of thread shot wildly from the mass, sending woolen strands, sharper than needles, hastily discharging like porcupine quills throughout the room—piercing the floor, ceiling, bedpost, wood framing and furniture. They crashed through the large picture window sending glass exploding in sharpened shards along the floor and toward Rasheed who rapidly dodged the strands as they raced within a hair's breath away, nearly maiming him in the process. Scowling, he observed a trouser leg, which had taken four, and the glass surrounding his sandaled feet.

The whirlwind of needles, lasting for a matter of moments, finally came to an abrupt halt; while the illumination surrounding her arched form, diminished to a slight flicker. Her body suddenly became limp; and, immediately, grabbing the bed, she sank to the carpeted floor. Her chest rose and fell while she gasped for a solid breath not yet mastering the immeasurable power contained within the thread. Rasheed clapped his hands; and, avoiding shards of glass, carefully made his way toward her. "*Bravo…bravo…*my *lovely Fahimah*—you *never* cease to amaze me."

The palace guards banged brusquely upon the broad chamber doors and Rasool, the military's commander, shouted in a muffled voice through the thick of the wood, "Your Highness…are you okay? We heard the sound of breaking glass."

The prince quickly replied. "Yes—now leave me." The mere sound of footfalls retreating reached his ears and he returned his attention to the princess who lay in a heap upon the floor. Bending, he brushed a lock of dampened hair away from her sweat-laden face and briefly studied her rosy features.

"Yes, my pet, you have answered my question." He placed a kiss upon her moist brow. Then, gently cupping her within his arms, he laid her upon the bed.

"Now, I shall play."

Cherinne studied the land as they left the city limits of Luxor; where the meager destitute were forced to look upon the mega rich. Beautiful widespread motels and resorts beckoned to tourists who came from all over the world to observe the Valley of the Kings and the wondrous pyramids. They tossed money in the direction of those who already possessed millions; while the hordes of poverty-stricken searched the bottoms of their coin purses for change, enough to buy bread. The history and geography all astounded her as they traveled along the sandy road and headed away from civilization, toward the unknown vastness of the desert and Prince Rasheed's royal residence.

"Laddor, how much farther?" she asked meekly while the car motored steadily along and a sickened feeling rose from the pit of her stomach to her throat. Mile upon mile of dry, antique-white sand lay before them like waves of the open sea; and Cherinne began to feel as if they were being swallowed by its billowing vastness. The spiritual energy of the bracelet, seeming to slowly come alive with each passing mile, appeared to be drawing them closer to its owner. Laying her head back, she closed her eyes; while the motion of the car was making her nausea worse, as Deverall watched the road with his foot slammed to the floor.

"Cherry, are you sure you don't wanna' get the car that your father has for ya'? It'd be a lot nicer than *this thing*," Laddor asked as he turned in the front passenger seat which supplied a slight bit more room for his long legs.

"No. Let's stay together," she whispered while fighting back the urge to vomit. Briefly opening her glazing eyes, she glanced at the bracelet then quickly slipped it behind her back; while the jewels upon it had subtly begun to glow and she didn't want Laddor to see.

Reaching a hand toward her, Laddor gently grasped her shoulder. "*Hey, are you okay?*" He elbowed Deverall. "Pull over, man."

Deverall pulled the car to a stop and Laddor hopped out. He opened Cherinne's door. "*Cherry?*"

Sweat streamed the length of her heated cheeks and her eyes suddenly flung open. "*Let me out!*" Clamoring from the backseat, she pushed past him. And, taking three steps from the car, she crashed face first upon the sandy shoulder.

"*Cherry!*" Laddor, bending to help her to her feet, noticed the shimmering of the many jewels as the bracelet was rapidly beginning to come alive. "*Oh shit*," he anxiously whispered, "Whaddaya want me to do?"

"*Get back!*" She cried out as her body suddenly plowed through the sand as if she was being drug by the wristlet.

Deverall lumbered from the car and grabbed Laddor by the shoulder. "*What the hell's goin' on?*"

A ring of terror reverberated in Cherinne's shrieking voice as she was lifted high into the air. Sand ran from her clothing and hair and her body slowly began to unfold before the heated sun.

"Run."

Deverall glanced at Laddor, then at Cherinne in confusion. "*What?*"

"*Run!*" Laddor yelled this time, as the jewels building to an apex, suddenly exploded in a prism of colored rays, blasting the sand about them.

"*Holy shit!*" Deverall shouted high-tailing it toward the car with Laddor close in tow. "*What the hell?*" They dove behind the rental, which, in taking the brunt of the blasts, was drilled full of holes.

"*A wwwwwww—ccoommee oonn!*" Deverall wailed. "I didn't take out the *insurance!*" He glared angrily at Laddor. "*Alright, Sissy-Boy*—you mind tellin' me what the hell's goin' on."

Quickly catching his breath, Laddor replied, "*Well…*"

"*Ah*, forget it." Deverall cautiously glanced over the hood. "I think I get the picture."

Cherinne's chanting voice drifted with clarity across the desert dunes; while the ancient Egyptian words, calling out to the drifting sand, disappeared into nothingness.

Fahimah's eyes flew open as she sat up and drew the silky blanket around her suddenly perspiring body. She glanced at the broken window which now allowed the late afternoon breeze to easily filter in, then at the prince who lay peacefully at her side. She listened intently to the voice which drifted across the open wind and called out her name. The bracelet.

Gravity grasped Cherinne within its fingers and yanked her back toward the sand engulfed earth; while the bracelet had become no more than a flickering hue.

Rushing from behind the car, Laddor raced across the heated sand; and dropping to his knees, he clutched her still body within his arms. He brushed away the sand caked to her sweat-laden skin and tousled hair, then removed the strands of sandy locks from her face. "*Cherry?*" It was a repeat of her condition as when she was possessed at the pool and on the bus. *"Damn it!"* Laddor cursed through gritting teeth. "Deverall, get my canteen of water from the car."

"I'm already on it, Red." He quickly handed Laddor the metal flask.

With a shaking hand, Laddor placed the canteen to her lips. *"Cherry?* Come on, honey—wake up." A few drops careened along her pale lips.

Looking spitefully upon the bangle encasing her wrist—now an enemy in need of destroying—he balled his fists in anger. And, gazing over the slopes of sandy hills rising and falling in the distance, Laddor made a vow—a vow to the profound skeleton hidden behind this enigma. Fury masked his eyes that gazed off into the distance while the terse words burned from his lips. "I swear, as God as my witness—I will rid Cherinne of you, you demon—*you* and *your damn bracelet!"*

Deverall grasped his shoulder and whispered, "Hey, Red—I think she's awake."

"Laddor…" Cherinne choked from deep within her chest, as she blinked away the few grains of sand which lay upon her lashes. "…I gotta' get this thing off."

Gathering her into his arms, Laddor headed toward the car. "Come on; let's get this done." A determination was in his voice that neither had ever heard before.

CHAPTER 8

"*Hiyahh!*" Fahimah spun in the perfect pirouette, slashing vehemently at one of her instructors, just grazing his chest with her outstretched sword. He pinched his eyes in disgust which seeped with a bitter resentment of the young female, who had the agility and cunning to overcome his gifted skill as a warrior. Striking again, the tip of her blade reached his stiffened jaw and drew a slight trickle of blood.

"*Ugghh!*" Why you little…" The ill-tempered commander hissed through clenched teeth. He lunged forward, forgetting his reserve while thirsting for the taste of blood.

"Rasool—" The prince suddenly appeared from within the shadows.

Surprise and annoyance caught the leader of the militia and he abruptly halted; though his adrenaline continued to rapidly pump in the attempts to push him forward, while his need to destroy this new Egyptian Princess was obsessive, as his hatred for her was intense. How could *she* be revered as anything but a troublesome whore? She was not of this country, with her fair skin and golden hair; yet, the prince worshiped her and gave in to her every whim, something that disgusted him. Control by beauty, and what only a woman possesses, was a sure sign of weakness. He despised this blonde haired creature and intended to rid the palace of her presence; even if that meant a secretive act of insubordination.

"So, I take it my lovely angel has gotten the best of you?" Prince Rasheed chuckled mildly.

The warrior quickly bowed in reverence. "Yes, my Lord," he stated sourly, shifting his eyes from one to the other. "She is surely a godsend." He feigned a smile as his eyes roamed along the thick stone wall that stretched skyward—a colossal sized arena—perfect to conceal the screams of a dying wench. He swiped away the blood on his cheek with a closed fist. "I look forward to sparring with her again; she is most exceptional." He caught the prince's gaze, knowing better than to challenge the man in a fixed stare—death came quickly to those who would defy the prince.

"Good." The prince smiled broadly at Fahimah as she tossed her hair and her eyes glinted in triumph. Ambling over to Rasheed, she cast a challenging glance in her opponent's direction—daring him to make the move she knew was stirring within his blood; and sliding her arm within the prince's, she pulled him snuggly against her while shifting her bare feet. The shimmery material of her skirting, easily slipping open, revealed a long slender leg—bare to the upper thigh; and attempting to draw his eyes away from the silk of her skin, the warrior lost the battle. With great effort, he quickly tore his gaze away; then, he glanced at the prince who observed him in amusement. The prince smiled; familiar with the weakness that comes from being in the presence of such a beautiful woman. Rasool quavered in anger, as his flushing cheeks revealed more than exertion from the heat.

"You may take your leave, Rasool. My lovely is finished for today." Prince Rasheed regarded the princess; sweat moistened her face and glistened upon her chest that slowly rose and fell. He ran a hand along her hair. "Now, I would like to see your true ability. What surprises do you have instore for me today, my love?"

Fahimah watched as Rasool left the arena, making sure he was well out of sight. Running a finger along the prince's cheek, her eyes met the sharp, dark, celestial spheres from which he observed her, while she would perform perfectly. "Watch, my sweet prince." She removed the choker from around her neck and held it up for Rasheed to see. It was a simple black velvet ribbon—slender—with a beautiful emerald jewel secured in the center and two golden clasps at each end.

Snapping the choker, she raised it toward the sky and called out in the language of their land, "dauwar 'ala, dauwar 'ala, seek and destroy!" She tossed the neckband, which rapidly came to life and dove beneath the surface of the sandy floor. They watched as it raced along, trowelling underground and left the arena. Seconds later a bloodcurdling scream, of a strangling guard just outside the gate, ascended the palace walls. The incensed choker shooting from the earth, had wrapped itself quickly around the unsuspecting guard's neck and had tightened its grip, choking him as he struggled for a breath. His limp body slammed to the ground in a resounding thud, and the necklace, slipping from his throat, immediately searched out another victim.

Rasheed raised a furrowed brow, rather displeased at the unnecessary loss of the soldier's life, while Fahimah nonchalantly shrugged. Then, they turned to observe the choker's path as it tunneled its way back inside the arena and rapidly snaked its way along the sandy floor. A look of marked betrayal glanced Rasheed's face as he observed the choker racing in his direction. But, as the necklace exploded from beneath the ground's surface and screamed toward the prince's exposed throat, Fahimah, dove through the air and caught it within her grasp. Landing easily on her feet, she paused as if to speak, then decided better of it. And without a word to the prince, she carefully replaced the choker around her neck and left the arena.

Unaware he had been holding his breath, Rasheed exhaled and watched as she went.

Cherinne laid her head upon Laddor's shoulder; grains of gritty sand still remained within her clothing and hair. Wearily, she brushed it to the floor. Laddor rode with his face to the warm wind, gazing out his window which had been shattered during the bracelet's tirade. Binding his swirling hair, he laid his head back and closed his eyes.

"Hey, Red—we could try and cut that thing off; maybe use a blow torch or somethin'," Deverall suggested.

"No." Laddor replied with his eyes still closed. "We tried pliers, tin cutters, just about any tool you could think of; and a blow torch would probably burn her." He glanced out over the sandy dunes that gently rolled along, meeting with the setting sun which was lazy upon the horizon. "We're close now. I'm sure the owner of that thing will know what to do."

Deverall, glancing in the rearview mirror, spoke to Laddor's reflection. "And, who did you say this bracelet belonged to...some prince or somethin'?"

"Yeah, it's a Prince Rasheed." Laddor sighed. "I did some research before we left. Apparently, he's some big wig sheik who lives out here in the middle of the blasted desert in his big palace. There wasn't much mentioned about him or what he does or doesn't do. It's kinda' like the Arab world just doesn't recognize his existence."

"Well, explain to me again, how you got the bracelet?" Deverall pressed. "Sweetheart here looks like she's been through the mill and back, and I have a feeling there's a little more to the story than what you're lettin' on."

The air of the car rapidly gathered thick with tension as Laddor stiffened in defense. "Look, I screwed up...okay? Are you satisfied? I screwed up big. My whole life has been one big foul up after another. Cherry here, is the only good thing I have ever had; and all I wanted to do, was give a little back to her. But, I blundered again, and hurt the only person that means anything to me. Is that good enough for you, Deverall? Just because you don't give a rat's ass about anything or anybody doesn't mean I don't."

Laddor closed his eyes again with regret eating away at his inner core—like the way he had just treated his new friend.

They rode in silence, Deverall no longer pressing for answers and Laddor no longer wanting to talk about it. The battered car motored along the dust covered road, cresting one dune after another, till the pilot leaned forward in his seat. "Hey, somethin's ahead."

The palace sat in its splendor along the splash of red tint, painting the horizon; while the setting sun cast enormous shadows over the sand, adding to the mammoth sized structure. Fire lanterns lined the entrance within the gates, flickering against the gentle breeze, which had suddenly begun to stir.

Deverall let out a low whistle. "Boy, Red, when you pick em', you pick em'." He gently patted the Mauser lying in the passenger seat.

Cherinne watched out her window, awe struck at the beauty and grandeur of the realm before her. It spanned a vast area of sand, covering near that of five city blocks. The main palace structure was a great round building with numerous pillars, highlighted by a dome of shimmery marble, which glistened with a luxurious hue. Thick granite covered the whole of the royal residence, carved intricately with various details, while the rest of the regime was more akin to that of the finer sections of Luxor with some structures with high raised roofs, and some with shorter, not quite as elegant, towers. Monumental gates attached to a giant-sized wall surrounded the fortress of high reaching structures and stone towers, while a flag, bearing the symbol of an Egyptian goddess, waved majestically in the warmth and peace of the passing day. Cherinne's heart beat anxiously, while the bracelet hummed in a low, yet eager, vibration upon her wrist, as if happy to be going home.

Laddor grabbed her hand and without looking in her direction said, "Well, here we go."

Fahimah raced wildly through the palace halls. Her bare feet skimmed the cool of the beautiful mosaic tile as her heart pounded excitedly within her chest. "My lord, my lord!" she called out rapidly opening and closing one door after another in search of the prince. Then hastily bursting into his private study, which was normally forbidden, she drew a breath.

Rasheed sat amongst a stack of documents, submerged in his work. Raising a questioning brow to her, somewhat annoyed at the outburst, he wondered as to what had her so troubled.

"*Fahimah?*"

"My lord, Rasheed!" she announced out of breath while unable to contain her enthusiasm. "The bracelet of Semus is here! *It is here, My lord!*"

Laying his pen down, he stood and observed her with amusement; while her vibrancy, without fail, had always brought him a deeply gratifying pleasure—yet he was apprehensive. "Are you sure?"

She nodded her head fervently. "Yes! Three travelers have arrived and are waiting at the gates. One carries the bracelet in their possession."

Rasheed glanced out the window, then back at the beautiful enchantress, who he allowed to hasten him from his office, away from critical material which required immediate attention. The jingling echo of her many golden bracelets was heard as she led him eagerly through the many corridors toward the front entrance of the palace. And, while her flood of excitement was contagious, he feared for her being reunited with the jewels—a bond that no man *or prince* could ever come close to breaching.

"Fahimah—slow down. You shall drag me before our guests in a disheveled state. I am a prince; and must present myself to them in such a manner that is respectable and worthy of honor. And..." he grabbed her by the shoulder and looked at her sternly, "...you are not to be greeting *anyone* without a veil—especially those who are unknown to my regime." Sighing loudly, she gave him a disappointed look along with a pouting lip.

Brushing away a waft of hair cascading over her eyes, he spoke to the wide, kaleidoscopic pools with kindness; yet, his tone was firm, "Now, go, and make yourself presentable for our guests; show them how lovely a princess lives in this palace." He tapped her gently on a hind cheek, as if he was conferring with a child, "Now be off."

The jingle jangle of her bracelets was music to his ears as she heeded his words and hastened eagerly toward her quarters.

Deverall lumbered from the car and stretched, showing all angles of his goody basket. *Nice,* Laddor thought, as he helped Cherinne from the car—a beat up old jalopy, Cherinne looking like she's been sleeping on the beach, me with a tomato on my forehead, along with Deverall's busted lip, and the fat pilot giving them a glance at his huge navel which resembled that of a large eye laced with lint. Great—maybe they'll think we're from the circus.

Reaching back into the car and shoving his pistol into his shorts, Deverall gave Laddor a wink. "Well, ya' never know with these camel-jockeys. Didya' ever see Lawrence of Arabia?"

Laddor shook his head in bewilderment as to how he had ever gotten mixed up with this blockhead. Then, he thought, maybe it was possible Cherinne was thinking the same thing about him. "Are you up for this, Cherry?" He took her arm and brushed some of the sand from her hair.

She glanced up at him while a look of dismay and uncertainty hid behind a wane smile. "I guess I'm as ready as I'll ever be."

"It'll be okay." He kissed her gently upon the forehead. "I'll grovel for forgiveness, then tell em to get that damn thing off." He also smiled in uncertainty; fore maybe they were really pissed and would just execute him on the spot.

The gates to the palace slowly parted as four heavily armed guards, each sporting weaponry from automatic weapons to long blades of sharpened steel, stepped forward dividing with two at each gate. They stood to attention, then bowed in reverence as two people appeared. The man, seemly stately, with jet black curls and piercing eyes wore the long robes worn by most Egyptian men; and the female was clothed in a lovely, white garment wrap, which covered from her neck to her ankles—exposing nothing. She peered through a small slit of the veil that covered her hair and face, as she and the prince stepped forward. The prince eyed the strangers skeptically and his gaze darted toward the piece concealed within Deverall's waistband. Snapping his fingers and speaking in Arabic, he signaled to one of the guards, who slowly removed a semi-automatic from within its holster.

Rasheed ran a glance over Laddor; and, viewing the large bruise upon his forehead, he rolled his eyes. Aware there was someone cowering behind the red-haired American, who he was unable to see clearly, the prince waved a hand and in broken English stated, "Please—come out into view, where I may see you. I cannot introduce myself properly to someone who is hiding. Unless, of course, you have something to hide; then maybe my guards should remove you from my presence." He smiled showing the brightest of teeth then winked at Fahimah.

Feeling self conscious of her appearance, after being dredged through the sand like a child's toy, Cherinne now stood before royalty, looking as if she could be the house servant or possibly even a beggar. Taking a deep breath, she stepped out slowly from behind Laddor.

The prince's smile quickly disappeared, as his mouth dropped to his chin in marked shock and betrayal. "Fahimah! Rish'sh! This is deceit." The guards rapidly pulled their weapons as Rasheed pointed an accusing finger at Cherinne. Abruptly, he then turned toward the woman standing beside him, anger glaring upon his face.

Backing away, Fahimah placed her hands on her heart; she pleaded, "Amir, ana bala zamb! Bala Zamb!" Quickly, she tore the veil from her face; while bewilderment filled her eyes. "It is *I*." She spoke fluently in English coated heavily with an accent.

His eyes darted venomously from the princess to Cherinne. They were mirror images of the same person, just clothed in different garments.

Deverall whooped, "*Whoa yeah! Dou-ble trou-ble!* Well, I'll be dipped—there's two of 'em!" He nudged Laddor, "Hey, Red, ya' have any gum?"

"Shu Aish hada sharr?" Prince Rasheed demanded.

"Yeah, that's what I'd like to know!" Laddor shouted out, awkwardly catching Cherry, who had suddenly fainted. "Who the hell are you people? And, who is she?" He pointed in the princess's direction.

"My lord, Semus Suwari!" Fahimah pointed an enthused finger at the bracelet which had suddenly begun to glow. Her face relating happiness rapidly darkened with facial thunderclouds, as she, realizing the implications, suddenly exploded in anger.

Racing from the prince's side she skimmed across the sand, as her feet sprayed small fountains of grains behind her swift determined movements. "Thief!" she shouted heatedly as her eyes flashed in multi-colored rage and she quickly bound through the air making her target Cherinne. Releasing a war-cry, equal to that of an aggressive animal, she was determined to fight for that which was rightfully hers.

Angrily hurtling in a downward swoop, she made solid contact, sending Laddor, who was too stunned to move, crashing to the gritty ground and spilling Cherinne, who was unconscious, to the earth.

"Holy shit!" Deverall hastily drew his pistol; but only to drop the weapon as he heard the sickening sound of several cartridges being expertly slammed into their chambers. Peering shakily into the cold barrels aimed directly at his head, he placed his quavering hands in the air. "Okay, chief…I give up."

Grabbing Cherinne's wrist with a venomous resolve, Fahimah tugged at the unyielding bracelet, while wrath burned as flames within her eyes.

"Give me my bracelet! *Give it to me now!*"

Startled into alertness, Cherinne's heart pounded roughly against her chest, as the princess had her pinned in the sand, aiming to rip her hand from its paining socket.

Fahimah slammed Cherinne's bewildered face to the desert surface and ground it into the hot white granules. Attempting a scream, Cherinne swallowed a mouthful of gritty sand and her throat closed quickly. The rough granules, filling her lungs, had lodged within her esophagus as she laboriously struggled for air. Peering through a muddled consciousness and terrified eyes at the image of herself fighting in desperation to attain the immovable armband, she wondered if she was dreaming.

Laddor shook his head, aiming to clear the haze of stupor from his jumbled mind. "Cherry?" His senses were awakened to the harrowing situation at hand and he hurriedly crawled on all four toward the two scuffling females, as Fahimah clawing wildly in a frenetic passion, strived to retrieve her possession.

"Hey, you, get off her!" Laddor yelled as he reached for the princess. Swinging, she viciously cocked him in the tender spot just above his brow, sending stars before his eyes. He grabbed his forehead. "Owwww! You crazy…"

The guards quickly shifted their aim at Laddor, seeing that he had reached for one of the royalty.

"Istanna! Wait." The prince raised a hand to the four over-eager men whose fingers were itchy on their triggers; and then he turned to the princess, "Fahimah! Salak!"

Whipping around in irritation, her eyes fumed with fury, as she studied the Lord Rasheed.

"Fahimah, *please*, behave," he implored in a more soothing tone.

Her fiery gaze lashed back at Cherinne while she felt she has been dishonored in front of strangers—strangers who had disrupted the course of things and had stolen what was rightfully hers and the regime's.

In stormy annoyance, Fahimah swiftly shoved a palmed fist into Cherinne's chest, lodging the grains of sand deeper within her throat, making it near impossible for her to breathe. Achingly gagging, for a raspy breath, Cherinne choked for much needed air.

Fahimah then rose to her feet; and glaring angrily at Laddor and brushing herself off, she abruptly turned and marched back in through the palace gates.

Laddor quickly knelt beside Cherinne, as she painstakingly gasped for a breath. "Hold on honey!"

She raked at her polluted throat as her eyes glazed with fear and confusion and her body heaved in an attempt to draw air. Laddor turned to Deverall and then to the prince. "She can't breathe! I need some water!"

Rushing to her aide, Prince Rasheed pulled a leather waterskin from within his tunic; and lifting her convulsing body gently into his arms, he placed the rim to her purpling lips. The cool water lightly trickled along her lips and traced her harrowed cheek, as she observed him through a grateful stare. Then coughing, she laid her head back and closed her eyes.

"She has swallowed quite a bit of sand. Let us take her inside." Gently cupping her in his arms, he signaled to his guards and carried her in through the gate. "Follow me."

Laddor and Deverall had both visited numerous places throughout their time; but nothing had prepared them for the splendor of the palace's architectural design and décor as they entered the two oversized brass doors. Each was inlayed with black and gold and inset with a black and silver eight-pointed star. An imperial guard opened each door permitting them entry to the main hall where they arrived in a colossal-sized atrium. It was immaculately decorated, with sculptured statuettes and an array of floral tapestries. An extravagantly detailed vaulted ceiling contained four large glistening chandeliers—each casting a lovely light upon the rich grey and blue veined marble flooring where several full green trees grew lavishly to the ceiling. The vestibule to the palace was enthralling, while they hadn't yet entered the main residence.

Laddor grudgingly followed along behind, while the mere thought of the prince carrying Cherrine was repulsive, yet the act of him actually doing it was appalling. Laddor bit his venomous tongue which desired nothing more than to give the prince a severe lashing, especially when the female—of his—was too hot-headed to be controlled. Making their way past several beautifully carved sculptures and pillars adorned with the finest of gold, Deverall oohed and aahhed. And, with wide-eyes and an open-mouth, he fingered several pieces.

"Please, do not touch anything," the prince stated kindly. "These are ancient artifacts passed down through generations of my family and the oil from your fingers is like that of acid.

I shall take your friend to the guest's quarters, where we shall tend to her needs. And, what did you say her name was—*Cher-ry*—like the fruit, yes? How unusual."

"It's her nickname, *Amir*," Laddor remarked irritably. "Her name's *Cherinne*—Cherinne Havenstrit; and the princess really did a number on her. Maybe your pet should be kept on a leash, if you can't control her."

"Ahh, so, you believe that Princess Fahimah is my pet and I should restrain her on a leash. That is also very interesting. I didn't think that you Americans made it a practice to put your women on leashes. Gee, and, our belief to have them just wear a veil to cover their beauty from the leer of lecherous men has been deemed as—how should I say it, *cruelty*." He chuckled lightly. "How very confusing." Stopping in front of a set of double doors, he announced, "Here we are." Patiently, he waited as the guards opened them.

The guest quarters were immaculate, twice the size of Cherinne's bedroom back home where Laddor wished they could be now, fighting over who would get the last plate of chili spaghetti, Cherinne's favorite dish. A multitude of lovely vases sat throughout the enormous room stuffed with gorgeous flowers in every color of the rainbow imaginable. While baskets of mouthwatering fruits invited the hungry to taste of their sweetness; and a wet bar, stocked with spring water and bottles of exquisite wines, invited those who wished to celebrate, or just needed a well-deserved drink. The over-sized, canopy bed was large enough for two people to perhaps get lost on or possibly invite all their friends, and several heavily cushioned wicker chairs and couches sat about, looking to never have been sat upon.

Deverall let out a low whistle. "Man, Saheeb, you sure are packin' some dough-rai-me here in Disney Land. The only thing missin' is that big stupid-ass mouse. Mind if I grab a drink?"

The prince laid Cherinne upon the bed. "By all means—help yourself." Going into the bathroom, which was twice the size of the dilapidated room Deverall had taken them to, he returned with a folded, damp cloth. Laddor quickly took it from him, not wanting the prince to take care of Cherinne, then gently laying it upon her forehead, he observed as she lay peacefully with her arms at her side.

Rasheed quietly studied her seemingly calm features also, thinking how much she was identical to the princess, but somehow softer, like while Fahimah slept. "Your princess is lovely, just like my Fahimah." Careful, as not to disturb her, he quietly took her hand and closely examined the bracelet of Semus. Then sighing, he gently laid her arm on the bed.

"We should get her changed into something slightly cleaner till she feels like bathing." The prince's warranted suggestion was received in a frightful panic as Laddor's eyes suddenly bulged from his head in astonished repulsion. Deverall cackled in amusement, knowing that first off: Cherinne would kill him if he ever attempted such a feat; secondly, Laddor would bust a nut after the first two buttons were opened; and thirdly, *another man helping*—Deverall was shocked that Laddor hadn't passed out at the proposal.

"What?" Laddor barely croaked as a cold shiver ran to his boots.

"You do not agree?" The prince raised a dark brow and pointed out, "she is covered in sand." Watching Laddor squirm uneasily, Rasheed quickly became aware of the situation. Adding fuel to the fire, he then remarked, "I undress Princess Fahimah all the time—and she does not seem to mind."

Laddor grabbed the thick bedpost to steady himself as his head spun, while just the thought caused his loins to twist in knots.

Rasheed chuckled mildly, "For a man who has big enough backbone to steal my jewels, you sure do seem spineless when it comes to your woman. Maybe, *your Cherry*, has *you* on a leash—eh?" The prince eyed Laddor debatably.

Laddor shook with anger. "You don't know anything, Amir. Cherry has no leash on me. *I* am the king of my castle." He reached a quavering hand toward Cherinne's shorts button as a cold sweat suddenly broke on the back of his neck and his face reddened. The room began to spin and he held his breath, as his heart beat loudly, and drowned out the quiet of the room while the other two men watched in an amused attentiveness. "Shit!" Laddor finally cried out. His legs turned to over-cooked pasta and he dropped to his knees beside the bed. "I can't. She'd kill me."

Deverall, sitting at the bar guzzling down a beer, burst into obnoxious laughter and slapped a hand to his thigh. "Damn, Red, you *really are* a sissy-boy."

Prince Rasheed laughed along with him, as Laddor shrunk into a chair in shame. "Will you feel better if I have one of my wives take care of this matter—is it, *Red?*" the prince asked.

"Did you say, '*wives*'!" Deverall piped up practically spitting his beer upon the lush carpet. "Damn, Saheeb—you have that luscious blonde, that looks just like sweetheart over there; *and* you have wives on top of that? Man, Princey—another Hugh Hefner!"

"You say Hugh Hefner?" Rasheed tapped a finger to his upper lip. "Hmm—this name does not ring a bell with me; but yes, I have seven wives—all beautiful as the lovely flowers, which bloom within the palace gardens. They occupy the entire east wing." He chuckled. "And not one wears a collar."

"We are very well established here with: a doctor on call, a smithy, our very own wine cellar, and all other varies needs and necessities. And, the best part is, our water flows from the dry arid desert like that of milk and honey—a sure gift from the gods. We lack for nothing."

The excited pilot rose from his seat, "may I shake your hand? My name is Deverall—Busher Deverall; but my friends just call me Deverall. I would be honored to be at your service."

Rasheed smiled and extended a hand to the pilot, "Prince Rasheed Daivyan Khalil Tarun. It is my pleasure to meet your acquaintance. And…" he raised a brow glancing at Laddor "…I assume you are *Red?*"

"*No!*" Laddor shot an irate look in Deverall's direction. "It's Laddor, with an 'O'. Laddor Zeandre." He rose and grabbed the amir's hand, briefly shook, then nodded his head. "Yes, I would prefer that a female do it."

"Ahh, yes." The prince snapped his fingers again and the bedroom door quickly opened as the two guards stood to attention.

"Aiwa, Amir Rasheed?" They both bowed reverently.

"Haneefah, ana taz."

One of the guards replied, "Na'am, mitl ma bitrid." He turned and left while the other remained behind.

"He has gone to retrieve Haneefah, my number one wife. She will be along any minute."

The silence was deafening as the three men stood looking to one another then at Cherinne who slept peacefully upon the bed. "Cherinne just hasn't been herself since we got here. She seems to be either sick or sleeping a lot," Laddor remarked. "I know a lot has happened, but, that's just not like her."

"It is the bracelet—the Semus Bracelet," the prince pointed out. "She is bound to it…"

A gentle rapping upon the door interrupted the prince's explanation as an Egyptian female entered the room. Laddor guessed her age to be maybe the same as his, twenty or so. It was hard to tell with the covering of the veil and her head was lowered, plus, she never took her eyes from the floor. Bending to a knee, she took the prince's hand and placed it to her lips, adorning it with a kiss. "Haneefah, faDlik naDif fauq minfadlik Miss Cherinne." Nodding her head in compliance, she glanced briefly at Cherinne, then rose and quickly headed into the bathroom.

"Please come with me, Gentlemen," he notioned toward the door. "I believe we have much to talk about."

CHAPTER 9

The Prince led them through several long corridors; each was lined with exquisite pieces of ancient artwork mounted upon walls reaching nearly forty feet. Large portraits of a long lineage told the tale of the prince's past history and how the regime was established. Beautiful velveteen tapestries adorned herculean sized windows portraying the first signs of nightfall which was spreading across the desert. The echoing of their footfalls bounded from one wall to another, as they followed the prince, trusting that it wasn't a trap and that he wasn't taking them to the guillotine. Laddor thought that his jesting about the jewels being stolen had seemed rather odd.

Rasheed paused in front of a double set of doors. "This is my study, so please make yourselves comfortable, for I shall need to attend to my Princess Fahimah, while she is a delicate creature, and is in need of my attention."

"Sounds more like Princey's on a leash too," Deverall whispered to Laddor with a chuckle as they exchanged a glance.

The study was large enough to be a public library while thousands of various books lined every shelf which ran from the floor to the high ceiling. A solid, well-built desk of mahogany sat dead center neatly stacked with papers, a few textbooks, a laptop and the usual pens and pencils. To the right of the desk sat tables with fax machines, several computers, maps laid out marking various points of destination, a satellite phone and several other electronic pieces neither Deverall nor Laddor were familiar with.

Deverall made his way over to the many maps and charts lying upon a table. "Damn, Red…ya' think that maybe Saheeb's a terrorist? Look at all this shit." He ran a thick finger over the charts checking the coordinates on the map. "Look at this—it's New York."

"Fahimah—unlock the door…*please*. You know I do not make it a practice of groveling and I shall have to call the guards to open the door; and neither of us really wants *that*."

The door suddenly flung open and Fahimah appeared along with a clenched fist, which caught the prince in the eye.

"*Ugghh!*" Rasheed back stepped as she threw another punch. Quickly, regaining his composure, he grabbed the left with a fleeting hand as the tiny fist sailed through the air toward his face. "Fahimah! Stop it, this instant!"

Running from the door, she jumped on the bed, and slipped beneath the covers. "Leave me alone!"

"Fahimah, what has come over you? You know it is punishment by death for striking me. If someone of the royal household would have seen you, I'm not sure what I would have done. Surely one of the guards would have terminated you immediately; and, besides—*that hurt*."

"*I don't care! Imshee, Rasheed. Get away!*" She cried from beneath the blanket in gasping breathes perilously close to sobs. "They might as well kill me; my life is over now anyway!"

"Ahh, Fahimah, my dear." Making his way toward the bed and sitting upon the edge, the prince then placed a hand on her trembling shoulder, while she hid beneath the coverlet. "What do you mean?"

Throwing back the silken blanket, she revealed red, tearstained eyes. "*She* has my bracelet—*my* jewels—and I am *nothing* without the bracelet. She will take my place! *Plus, she even looks like me!*"

Suddenly bounding from the bed, she cried from behind trembling lips, "*I won't allow it! I shall kill her!*" Rushing from the bedroom and into the corridor, Fahimah rapidly made her way toward the guest area and Cherinne.

"Fahimah!" Rasheed raced from her quarters and into the hall. Listening for the jingling sound of her many anklets, whose sound had suddenly become a ringing march of death, he turned the corner and rushed in their direction.

"Hey…" Deverall, retrieving his cigarettes from his breast pocket observed as he was glancing out the study door. "Wasn't that the princess who just ran past? I wonder what the hell's goin' on."

Curiously, Laddor peeked his head out alongside the pilot's to see the prince, with a swelling eye, rushing around the corner.

Rasheed shouted, "Catch her! She has lost her senses and is going after your American female!"

"*What?*" Tension erupted within Laddor's shoulders, running the length of his arms to his fists. "Oh no, she's not!" Wasting no time, he joined in the pursuit.

"Hey, wait up! Deverall called to the two men; while his heavy footfalls thundered along the walls and ceiling, as he moved like a freighted train down the hall.

Reaching the guest room and throwing open the double-doors, Fahimah startled both females who sat quietly upon the bed. "*Imshee, Haneefah! Imshee!*" Fahimah pointed a demanding, shaking finger at the princess then toward the hallway.

A marked sign of confusion drew upon Haneefah's face, as Fahimah demanded she leave. Yet these were not the direct orders from Prince Rasheed and she still needed to assist their guest with preparing for her bath.

"La, Fahimah. No," she retorted with uncertainty, "Amir Rasheed…"

"*Get out!*" Fahimah angrily grabbed her and shoved her toward the door then locked it.

Sitting wearily upon the canopy bed, Cherinne looked at the princess in a confused shock, as Fahimah glared at her in blistering fury. "*You!*" She pointed a finger at Cherinne who trembled in fear. "You had better give me that bracelet—or I'm taking it along with a hand!"

"*What?*" Cherinne choked out unable to believe her ears.

"*Give it to me!*" Fahimah sailed through the air, near lightning on her feet. Landing atop Cherinne, she slammed the unsuspecting American's head to the wooden headboard of the bed with a ringing crack.

A bolt of pain shot throughout Cherinne's skull while she wondered as to how she had gotten into this mess and if she would die at the hand of a girl who looked to be her twin. Shaking her head, she tried to think as the rush of pain consumed her thoughts and the bracelet began to emanate a strange glow, seeming unsure who to deem master.

"*Oh, God,*" Cherinne moaned as she struggled to get the princess off, while her body refused to cooperate. Fighting the haze of oncoming darkness, she labored ardently to keep from having her face smashed in.

"*I'll kill you!*" Fahimah shouted, thrashing about as a wild animal and landing several blows to her look alike.

Suddenly, the bracelet exploded to life, ripping Cherinne out from beneath the incensed princess and dragging her across the room. "Not this again," she groaned as her impelling body knocked over a marble, pedestal stand, which supported a large hand-carved, vase. Crashing to the floor, it spewed water and flowers in a stream of sodden color across the white carpet; while her body, speedily winding along the carpeted floor, tipped potted wicker baskets and sent greens to spill in a heap of soil. Then, promptly, she shot toward the ceiling and rapidly spun in a violent tumult.

"*Ahh,* so you want to play, *eh?*" The princess remarked silkily. "Then, *we shall play.*" Pulling the small piece of yarn from within her wrap and baring an arm, she rubbed it swiftly against her skin. "*RABBA!*" A gusty swirl of wind whirled about the air, as the yarn began to grow, and snake its way along her body. Quickly, Fahimah was enclosed within its cocoon as the first colored rays of the bracelet blast throughout the room.

Cherinne's body twisted and turned wildly, in an irrepressible uncertainty. "*Whoa!*" she howled in the attempts to control her body which was tossed about like a rag doll. Glass exploded in a sea of ruins and pin-size holes blasted through walls and anything in the burning rays' path.

Fahimah's cocoon suddenly burst open in an explosion of needles, as a torrent of jagged quills madly raced in every direction.

"*OOhhh GGoddd!*" Cherinne cried out as sharp quills pierced several parts of her body, while it was like receiving acupuncture from a madman. "*Hheeellpp mmmeee!!*" Tears streamed her heated cheeks as she began to weep from the unbearable pain.

Rasheed banged upon the locked guest room doors. "*Fahimah! Open this door!*" He hurried down the hall and shouted into another corridor, "Ana azi musa ada" Two guards immediately rushed to his aide. "Kasar hada la-taHt! Break the door down!"

The guards quickly shouldered the heavy doors. A loud crack and the sound of splintering wood filled the corridor, as the doors suddenly broke free of their hinges and opened. A prism of heated beams and razor sharp needles saturated the hazardous chamber, expelling a threat in every direction.

"*Great Allah!*" Prince Rasheed whispered despairingly. The guards, unsure as to what action to take to secure the situation, watched and listened as Cherinne cried out for help, while Fahimah, in her blaze of fury, desperately attempted to slay her.

"What the hell's goin' on in there?" Laddor anxiously shoved by the prince to be nearly pelted by a throng of needles. "*Holy shit!* What was *that?*" He glared at Rasheed.

"Fahimah," the prince stated flatly. "She has spun her cocoon; which, in a matter of seconds, transforms into a million prickly quills that race at the speed of light toward their victim. It is a devastating series of needles that would fell a mule in an eye's blink; and by the looks of it, she has made contact with Miss Havenstrit. But, fortunately, your female has the power of the bracelet and has not been destroyed; though for some time, she will be in severe pain."

"*Severe pain*! You say it like she broke a nail! Can't you control that lunatic of yours?" Laddor grabbed the amir by his robes. The guards, swiftly pulling their weapons, aimed directly for Laddor's contorted face as the two men had locked angry stares. Rasheed quickly signaled to them to lower their weapons and spoke. "No, she cannot be stopped at this point. But, the attack shall not last for more than a few seconds. Fortunately, for your Cherinne, Fahimah has not mastered the technique to its fullest."

"*Damn it!* That's not good enough, *Amir!*" Laddor, gripping Rasheed's robe tighter, clenched his fists in knots.

Deverall immediately stepped between the two. "Hey! Now none of this will help get sweetheart outta' there." He peeked inside the door, only to jerk abruptly away, as several quills were impelled suddenly within an inch of his head. "*Holy Shit!*" he chirped as he patted both men on the shoulder, "Ya' know, these are your two broads—I think I'll stay outta' this one" He smiled wearily.

"Thanks, Buddy," Laddor stated as he frowned.

"Come." The prince nudged Laddor as he hastened into the guest area. "It has stopped." Rushing into the room, Rasheed hastily grabbed Cherinne as she was suddenly crashing toward the floor and broken glass.

Quicker than Rasheed could react, Laddor grabbed Cherinne from within his arms. "Hey, your woman's over there. *I'll* help *mine*."

The prince put his hands up as a sign of innocence, "I was just trying to assist; I beg your pardon." He then quickly turned and hurried toward Fahimah who lay in a quiet heap upon the floor. Her breathing was shallow and blood was slowly soaking her garment. "*Fahimah?*" Crimson red stained his robe and was sticky to his touch. He quickly tore the cloth of her wrap away to examine her injuries. Blood ran from two nail sized holes—one to the abdomen—the other to the chest. "*Fahimah?*"

"*Yunaadi doctoorra! Yunaadi doctoorra!*" He shouted the frantic command as fear glazed his dark anxious eyes. Attempting to slow the bleeding, he held his flattened palms to her wounds while burying his face in her hair. "*La Fahimah, la.*"

"Cherry?" Laddor laid her gently upon the bed as tears flowed in rivulets from her eyes and she gave him a wane smile.

"Laddor," she barely whispered. "It hurts so badly. I can't move."

"Hold on, honey." Over a dozen quills were lodged in various places, deep within her skin. The slits, swelled and puckered were bleeding. "Now, I'm gonna' try and pull em' out; so, it may hurt a little." His hands trembled and his heart ached terribly. Gazing through misted eyes, he grabbed the first needle which was taut, almost to the bone. "Okay—are you ready?"

Cherinne dug her fingers into the loose fiber of the mutilated mattress, which had been destroyed during the fight. Squeezing her eyes shut, she nodded.

Laddor's hands moistened with sweat as he took a deep breath and yanked the first quill. Cherinne bolted upright. "*Stop!*" The blood curdling cry rushed from her gasping lips. "*Ohhh Goddd—it hurts!*"

"*Deverall!* Help me out, man!" Wiping the sweat from his forehead, Laddor then grabbed Cherinne's hand. "I'll get help. Just hang on!"

"Hey, Red—the doc's here; he's with the princess. Apparently, she's pretty bad off." He patted Cherinne's hand. "Hang on, sweetheart; help's comin."

An aged Egyptian man—his skin the color of darkened leather—hastened into the room. Dressed fairly modern and carrying a large leather bag, he quickly retrieved bandages, several vials of medicine and natural herbs, which smelled like something a camel may have dropped somewhere out along the desert. Quickly, he called out directions in Arabic to the prince, who willingly assisted in the attempts to slow Fahimah's bleeding. Working fervently on the princess, he then directed the prince to remove her to another room more suitable for treating her wounds. Rasheed, gently cupping her in his arms, made his way toward the doors.

"*Hey, Amir!* What about *Cherinne?*" Laddor stated in annoyance. "She needs a doctor too!"

Prince Rasheed nodded in assent, "Al-Sa'ad al bint, Doctoorra Raghib." He gestured toward Cherinne. The Egyptian doctor looked upon her contentiously; then quickly rummaging in his bag, he retrieved a syringe. With an aged narrow finger, he gave it a flick and the golden droplets slivered smoothly down the needle. Then, shoving Cherinne's underwear up, he swabbed the area with alcohol, and, without delay, rammed the needle deep within her skin.

"*Ugghh!*" she cried, grabbing at the painful injection in her leg. Then, laying her head back against the pillow and reaching for Laddor's hand, she closed her eyes. Her harsh breathing slowed and as the golden liquid seeped throughout her body; her breaths became measured and she slowly went to sleep.

Laddor glared angrily—the doctor's inconsideration to her condition appalling. "*Hey!* That was a little rough; wouldn't you agree—*Doctoorra?*"

"Yeah, like, what are you, some kinda' camel doctor or somethin'?" Deverall asked in annoyance. "I don't see any shit on them there Ferragamos, *Saheeb,* so maybe you're into weird experiments and shit; maybe like Mangela?"

The Egyptian grabbed one of the several needles and yanked it free of Cherinne's side. Tossing the bloody quill onto the bed beside her, he then proceeded to remove the rest. Finishing his task, he wiped any traces of blood staining his hands onto a towel within his bag, then threw the towel to the trash. Returning to his bag and retrieving a box of bandages, he tossed them to Deverall. He then turned to leave.

"Why you arrogant…" Laddor called to his back while banging his left arm over his right with his fist high in the air, the insinuation, 'screw you'.

Grabbing the door handle, the Egyptian paused briefly; then in broken English replied over his shoulder, "same to you."

As he spread out on a couch, blasted through with dozens of holes, Deverall's grisly bear came alive.

Laddor momentary looked around the room at the devastation while a full-blown battle had occurred here and Cherinne had ended up a casualty. Furniture—once beautiful pieces—was all now destroyed; while fresh fruit lay split open upon the floor covered with water, broken flowers, glass and drying blood. Glass laid everywhere from liquor bottles, which had housed the finest of wines, mirrors, and the large windows which had once held wall size views of the sunrise and sunset. Laddor busied himself with removing the bloody quills from the bed and finding a clean blanket for Cherinne. Then, closing the tattered drapes, he laid down beside her.

With a slightly trembling finger, he gently removed the hair from her distraught face. She moaned lowly and lightly shifted her body, still seeming to be in pain. Careful not to wake her, he scooted closer, till his body laid snuggly against her soft skin. Wanting to consume her entire being—to take away the pain and all the catastrophes that had been inflicted upon her since the day at the pool, Laddor slipped an arm around her waist. Tears filled his tired eyes with a picture of his mother's face entering his mind; while the thought of being without the only other person he had ever truly loved, tore at his heart.

Laying his head upon Cherinne's pillow, he buried his face in the locks of her hair and breathed deep. Then, pulling the blanket around them, to ward off the night air that was wafting in through the aimlessly drifting tattered draperies, Laddor closed his stinging eyes and allowed exhaustion to take him over.

"*Laddor?* What are you doing?" Cherinne whispered, gently pushing his hand away as it lavishly stroked her bare thigh. Being rushed from the room, Haneefah had not been able to finish tending to Cherinne, so she remained in her underwear covered by a light smock. "Get up—*please.*" She politely pushed him from the bed, sending him sliding to the floor in a thud.

Yawning, Deverall rubbed his belly and smacked his lips together which released the devils of morning breath. "Would you two keep it down over there?" He rolled over scratching everything surrounding the large crack peeping over the back of his shorts.

"*Crap! What are* you *doing in here?*" Cherinne grabbed the chenille blanket and pulled it tightly to her chin.

"Oh, relax, sweetheart. I saw all I needed and you aren't packin' enough for my taste. I likes my women with a *big* rack of lamb." He held his hands arms-length out from his chest. "And a nice butt I can set my beer on while I'm watchin' the game; not some little bunch that you skinny chicks cover. Humph—little asses—who needs em'. I want a *real* woman with a butt the size of Texas. Now, that's good lovin'."

Laddor hefted himself from the floor, yawned and scratched beneath his shirt. "Ya' know, Deverall, man—you *are* twisted."

Feeling quite better, Cherinne watched the two. Wondering as to whether or not all this scratching was due to some kind of skin condition; or, did it possibly have to do with their manly hair? And, when did it start—at two or three—or maybe even ten or twenty? *She* never scratched, and she couldn't remember any of her friends ever doing it. Strange—men—the species deemed to rule the world. If a world-wide crisis ever did occur, would they be too busy digging and scratching to notice that civilization had up and disappeared around them—totally vanished, while they still had their fingernails scraping along their dried-up old tough skin as they made ready for their day? Who needs global warming when the ones with itchy and scratchy fingers are the ones with their hands on the atomic button? God must've been jokin' when he put man in charge—just another way to get back at Eve for having a better body. How do they say it, 'practice makes perfect?' The first species was a trial, or rather maybe an error; but, the second attempt was success.

A soft rap upon the door awakened Cherinne from her musing. Haneefah stepped forward cautiously and quickly glanced around at the destruction about the room. Then lowering her eyes again to the floor, she waited patiently by the door.

"Hey, Deverall, I think she's waitin' for us to leave," Laddor stated. "Come on, Cherry needs to get cleaned up and dressed anyway. Let's go see if we can find the amir and find out what the hell's goin' on."

CHAPTER 10

"Good morning, Gentlemen." The sound of bare feet lightly covered the marbled floor, as the prince appeared behind Laddor and Deverall, startling them into alertness. His two guards stood at a distance while he appeared to have just awakened, as his eyes were crinkled with loss of sleep and his attire consisted of plain western trousers, no shirt and bare feet. "You must excuse me for not being a better host. The princess required all of my attention last night, for your Miss Havenstrit did much damage—almost costing my Fahimah her life. My apologies," he bowed his head.

"Oh, that's okay, Saheeb; though it sure is a damn shame to have wasted all that booze," Deverall noted.

Rasheed chuckled lightly. "You are a funny man, Busher Deverall—a little crass for my taste—but funny. So…" he turned to Laddor, "…how is Miss Havenstrit this morning? Did the doctor give her something to help with her injuries?"

Laddor regarded the prince through narrow leering eyes, unsure if he was corrupt or just too damn nice and good-looking for his own good; kinda' like an old buddy of his back home—Chris, from Panama City. "Yes he did; but that, so-called *doctor*, was about as congenial and caring as Hitler's henchmen. Look," Laddor stated, "I just wanna' get Cherry the hell outta' this joint, and get her home. So, how's about we get that stupid bracelet—the Bracelet of Semus, or whatever it's called, off her wrist and return it to the princess. That should cool her jets. Then we can leave and pretend this whole thing never happened."

The darkness of the prince's tired eyes shaded to an inky black. "You Americans are all alike…" he stated distastefully. "Want, want, want. You think it is just a matter of returning the bracelet? Appeasing my princess, who *you* stole from? And, I assume *you* are the one who took them—*you* and Mr. Deverall?"

"*Oh no! Not me, Saheeb,*" Deverall raised his hands in innocense. "I had nothing to do with it; I'm just a pilot for hire. I work for sweetheart's father, Mr. Havenstrit. I had nothing to do with stealing from you."

Rasheed scoffed and pointed a finger at Laddor as he glared with black eyes into his. "*You—you alone* stole from *me?*" He shook his head in disbelief. "You are a buffoon; a meddlesome idiot." He poked Laddor's chest in anger. "You have no idea what you have done, do you? You come into *my* home, insult *my* Fahimah, who is almost killed, defame the name of the Semus Bracelet, which is a precious heirloom dating back centuries before the birth of Jesus Christ, *and* stare the prince hatefully in the eye. I should have you beheaded. I despise your kind." He turned away. "Leave my sight, before I change my mind." Then, gesturing a wave of dismissal, he continued. "I shall meet with your female and discuss the situation with her." Rasheed then mumbled, "Why a beautiful woman like that would want an ill-bred lout like you is beyond me; especially when she could be living in the palace with me and be treated as a princess, as she should be."

Laddor's flushed face contorted into angry knots, while his blood boiled and his neck stiffened. "Come again, Amir? I don't think I heard you correctly."

"*Oh,* I believe you heard me correctly. You just do not want to face the fact that you are worthless; an incorrigible donkey's rear-end that brings nothing but trouble to those around you. Face it, *Red…Miss Havenstrit* would not be in this predicament were it not for you…. *and, maybe* your mother would still be alive, also."

"Why you arrogant bastard! What do you know of *my mother?*" Laddor drew a fist and planted it squarely in the amir's face, sending him sailing backward to land in a mound upon the floor. The guards rushed toward the three men while drawing a series of deadly weapons and charging upon Laddor.

"*La!* No." The prince commanded with a raised hand as he touched the blood upon his lip while his heart pounded against his panting chest. Blood raged to Rasheed's head as he bounded to his feet and bolted at Laddor, slamming him into the nearby golden tapestries. Tearing from their brass hooks, the massive wall-hangings toppled to the floor and obscured the wrestling men from sight.

"*Hey, guys,*" Deverall appealed into the heap of fabric thrashing about wildly. "This isn't gonna' help anything." He glanced up at the guards who glared angrily. Their look was one of appalling disapproval while his gaze raced past them to see one of the girls advancing steadily toward them down the corridor. "Hey," he whispered, "one of the girls is comin'!"

Their tussling quickly came to a halt, as they fought their way out of the large-scale tapestry and scurried to their feet. Promptly composing themselves, they looked on the young female, wondering whether it to be Fahimah or Cherinne.

"Princess Fahimah?" Rasheed whispered in uncertainty, knowing that with her injuries being near to fatal, she couldn't possibly be up and about so soon. The braids which normally adorned her hair, one's that she fidgeted with so frequently, had been replaced with long gentle curls which Fahimah very seldom ever wore, especially during the governing hours of the regime. Her attire was lovely—that of the royal regime, not western—and she carried herself proudly; a delightful charm to behold.

"Good morning." Deverall bowed.

Laddor studied her closely—Cherry? He inhaled deep, recognizing the sweet scent of her perfume—yes, it was her. "Hey, honey, how are you feeling?" Rising to his feet, he ignored the deadly stare from the prince, and embraced her with a gentle kiss to the forehead. "You look lovely," he whispered into her clean hair.

She smiled warmly, "I'm feeling much better—a little sore in spots—but thank you. Whatever that doctor gave me really helped." She glanced at the torn tapestry bunched upon the floor and frowned. Then turning to the prince, she bowed reverently and stated, "I am most disheartened by the injuries that the princess has sustained. Please convey my apologies to her."

A snow of stupor flurried along Laddor's face in disbelief that she was apologizing to Fahimah; especially since *she* had been the one who had initiated the attack. "*Cherry?*"

She placed a firm finger to Laddor's moving lips.

"Apology accepted," Rasheed gestured with a nod, "while I shall speak on behalf of my Fahimah." Then, snapping an angery look at Laddor, the prince abruptly turned to leave. Pausing, he glanced over his shoulder and directed his request at Cherinne. "I shall meet with you, Miss Havenstrit, concerning this dilemma after you have been served your morning meal. You may return to the guest area, for another room is ready; then, please meet me in my study...*alone.*"

Rasheed parried with the blade of his sword, a magnificent piece of weaponry, which seemed a mere extension of his body. "*Ahh, nice move, Haneefah*; you are an excellent warrior. Your moves are like that of the lioness; a reserved coolness that strikes only when the cub is in danger."

"Thank you, Your Highness." She sailed through the air. "Though I do apologize for not being as skilled as Princess Fahimah; she is far more gifted than I."

Charging her attack and swiftly knocking the blade from within her petite hand, he landed to the sandy terrain with a soft thud atop her. Haneefah breathed heavily and watched him with warm dark eyes as her chest ascended then fell. Pinning her securely, within the nape of his thighs, he smiled affectionately, then bent down and gave her a gentle kiss. He then promptly hopped to his feet. "You have no need to apologize. You are a valiant fighter, Princess Haneefah." Sheathing his saber, he offered her his hand. "Allow me to assist you to your feet."

Taking his hand, she rose quickly and brushed the sand from her clothing. "Amir Rasheed, if I may have permission to speak freely."

"Why, of course. You have always been permitted to speak openly with me in private." He took her arm in his. "You may be one of my wives; but you are also my best friend. Come—let us spend a few moments together before I must address the issue of the quandary this American has put us in."

121

They exited the arena, from the eyes of an on-looker, seeming to be a young couple in love, as they strolled along arm in arm. Quietly, they sat upon the cushioned chairs beneath the awning of the flagstone terrace. Haneefah was beautiful, with ebony eyes and raven hair; her olive-skin was the texture of silken robes. She was night, while Fahimah was day. She held the prince's hand, but knowingly not his heart; for that privilege alone belonged to Fahimah.

"Rasheed," her gaze remained to the ground, "I desperately fear for your safety, Sire. Princess Fahimah has been badly injured and the bracelet is now in the hands of another woman. I surely am not as capable, as is Fahimah, to protect you. If an uprising were to occur against your regime, you would not have the protection that is needed; and your kingdom, especially Your Highness, would be in peril. Please, Rasheed," she mildly begged as she raised her gaze to his, her eyes pleading, "please, be careful."

"Ahhh, my sweet Haneefah, your warm, beseeching eyes, they seep into the very depths of my soul. Do not fear, my princess; for you shall add worry lines to those lovely sculptured features of yours." Smiling lovingly, he caressed her long dark hair. "Look, I have a score of militia who have sworn loyalty to me and to the capitol and they shall bear the burden, if it be deemed necessary.

Now—run along, for I must prepare to meet with the young lady." He waved her away.

She stood in protest, "but, Sire…"

"No buts, Haneefah…I shall be fine. Now, go—for I shall come to visit you in your chambers later and we will talk then."

She bowed, "yes, Your Grace."

Rasool, a lofty Egyptian warrior—swift with a blade and easily provoked—never ceased to deliver a quick death to his opponent. His eyes, narrowed dark saucers, observed all in their view and beyond; while his dark hair, neatly trimmed and secured back, outlined the features of intense animosity. He paced impatiently while dressed in his battle gear, occasionally glancing through the one window in his office quarters, toward the arena entrance. He watched as the prince and princess, conversing, made their way from the training ground, after a brief exercise, to the terrace; then she was dismissed—leaving the prince alone.

Fool! Rasool scowled angrily from within his smoldering inner self, speaking to the ire fulminating in his mind. Prince Rasheed, you are an incorrigible misguiding *idiot,* the lead commander noted with a strong tinge of disgust. You allow yourself to be unattended—open for attack; *and* even greet those idiotic Americans *outside* the gates of the regime! What an utter fool! Your misconceived delusion of optimism endangers the entire kingdom; and, I don't even want to *think* of that little whore who controls this kingdom on her back!

A hasty rap upon the door prompted him from his brooding. "Enter," he commanded; his voice carried the ring of authority that has commanded multitudes of armies. His captain entered. "What news do you have of Princess Fahimah and her injuries, Salman?" Rasool inquired as he kept an eye to the prince as he made his way toward the southeast entrance.

The young man fidgeted nervously, like most who were in the presence of the commander, his flushed cheeks becoming near the color of a clay pot. "Commander, Sir," his voice quivered slightly. "Princess Fahimah's injuries were near fatal; but, the doctor informs me that she is quickly recovering and shall be back on her feet in a day or two."

Rasool weighed this news with much consideration then turned to the captain as the prince disappeared from sight. "Prepare the men, Captain Salman, and inform me of every move the prince makes. He is your insect and *you* are the microscope. Do I make myself clear?"

"Yes, Sir."

"Also, keep me informed of the princess's condition and these meddlesome Americans. I want an update every few hours." He signaled. "You are dismissed."

Rasool thought back to his earliest childhood memories as an apprentice sword-smith when he was in service to Prince Rasheed's father, Amir Nuri. He had worked diligently as a young lad, while the prince being groomed—deemed to be the future Amir—preferred the frolicking of childhood and undisciplined affairs. He could remember the young prince, his disappearing acts, as he, behaving immaturely, hid from his tutors, making complete fools of them as they would search diligently for him throughout the palace grounds and the whole of the regime. Being preoccupied with the desire to learn of life and mythology, the prince preferred the company of beasts and nature to the ways of sword-play, riding and grooming; and though Rasool saw the prince most every day, Rasheed was usually too busy running and hiding to notice the older boy.

Through time, the sword-smith came to revere the young Rasool and his master craftsmanship; and, as a well-deserved reward, would allow the astute youngster a few days of leisure for his many good works. During those times of well-deserved rest and relaxation, Rasool would curiously sneak along behind the inattentive, unmindful Rasheed, and observe as to how an adolescent prince would occupy himself when he wasn't being tutored or primped.

Irately, Rasool recalled one hot and blistering day, where he had pursued the prince, throughout the inner city of the regime. Rasheed, being slight of build, had speedily made his way through one hidden aperture after another, through underground tunnels and back alleys, along the cobblestone path, far from the main palace and the security of the guards. Rasool had trailed him, worn, but persistently, when, unexpectedly, the prince had suddenly dug himself down into a rocky crevice and disappeared. Patiently, Rasool had waited, knowing that his venture into the craggy hole would reveal his, possibly undesired, presence. But, to his dismay, a fierce sandstorm—a khamsin—was rapidly scouring across the desert sands, heading in their direction. Rasool anxiously shouted down into the hole to the prince, fearing the storm would quickly overtake him, and, also perhaps, seal the only exit from within the earth, making it impossible for the young amir to escape. Relentlessly, the winds began to stir, bringing with them massive amounts of dust and sand that easily cut and tore at the flesh; and Rasool, being pelted unmercifully, dug his way down into the tight fitting fissure away from the blast of desert.

The drumming of wind howled just above the deafening quiet of the hole, while the cool temperatures beneath the earth were received gratefully, and he could hear the storm raging forcefully across the defenseless land. Scrambling to his feet, his head scraped the layer of shale and stone above him. And, peering into the oncoming blackness, he attempted to adjust his wide dark eyes. Rasool shouted to the prince and Rasheed unexpectedly appeared, while the glow of an oil lantern's light displayed the austerity affixed to his normally cheery features. The flickering lamp swayed gently with each and every movement the younger boy made; and Rasool was mildly taken aback, when Rasheed suddenly grabbed his hand and drew him further into the darkened bowels of the earth.

"Come and look," Rasheed coaxed, his voice steady, as if he had anticipated this moment. "You are Rasool, the apprentice sword-smith; you work for my father, the Amir. Your work is very good; for I use the sword that you made for me—very impressive." Pausing within his tracks, he abruptly spun on his heels. And, holding the lantern before Rasool, he gazed into his eyes. "Why have you been following me?"

Back-stepping slightly, Rasool hurriedly searched his racing mind for an answer, an answer that would not have him put to the Rod or worse before a sword's blade. "I...uh..." he stuttered. The coolness of the underground grotto was unable to diminish the beads of sweat forming on his wrinkled forehead; while he was unaware the prince had even realized he existed. "...I was curious as to what you were doing," he blurted out. "I am sorry if I have disturbed or dishonored you in any way..." Dropping to a quivering knee, he bowed. "...Your Highness."

Indifferently, the prince turned, "Oh, it is okay; I don't mind," he stated as he continued walking. He spun on his heels again and eyed Rasool; the air in the grotto rapidly grew thick, "...as long as you can keep a secret."

While a secret was every young boy's delight, fear and excitement interweaved within the young apprentice. Cautiously nodding his head in accordance, his gaze followed Rasheed's pointing finger, as the young prince held the lantern out before them.

Rasool strained his eyes and his pupils enlarged to roving black saucers. A thrilling coldness raced along his swarthy skin as he peered into the cool of the vast darkness. "I beg to sound unwise," he stated apologetically, "but, I can not see anything, only the layers of dirt upon Egypt's underground."

Rasheed grinned impishly and he urged Rasool forward. "Now...*look closer.*"

Bewildered, Rasool heeded his words and took a hesitant step forward; then he dropped to his knees.

Deep gouges had been dug along the earth's facade and the dirt was organized neatly in small piles. He rubbed his hand along the surface with pebbles and grit scurrying just beneath his anxious fingertips. His heart thrummed in excitement as he came to something protruding just above the layer of soil. Carefully grabbing the small article with his fingers and thumb, he pulled it loose from its hold.

It was an earring—a woman's dangling golden earring—with three tear-dropped shaped pearls of different dimensions, the largest at the top progressing to a lesser measure at the bottom. Rasool rubbed it between his fingers, breaking the caked mud and dirt away from the delicate cracks and crevices. And, pulling a cloth from within the pocket of his galabiyah, he worked diligently to clean the piece as if it were one of his many handcrafted swords. He held it up to the fire's light; and though remnants of dirt still remained, it shone beautifully.

Eagerly he turned to the prince, "Please, Your Highness...may I keep it?"

The prince considered this carefully then answered, "Yes—yes you may. As long as you swear upon Allah's head not to tell a soul..." Shouting interrupted their pact as they shook, with Rasool brimming in pleasure at his newfound treasure.

Nodding his head and tossing a thick banded bracelet, too large to conceal in his pocket, to the side, the prince headed toward the entrance. Wearily responding to his father, he climbed to the surface followed by the young apprentice sword-smith.

Several palace guards, a disconcerted tutor and Rasool observed reticently, the irate Amir Nuri as he angrily scolded the young prince. Furious at his son's childish antics and disappearance during such a violent storm, the amir had wanted no part of excuses. Aspiring to appease his father, Rasheed apologized repeatedly, promising to never again be tardy or absent during his appointed lessons. Unbearably annoyed at his son's incompetence, the amir suddenly sent a sharp backhand abruptly skirting across Rasheed's remorseful face, sending him plummeting backward to the sandy ground.

Rasool watched in shocked horror the scene before him. Then, swiftly, a brusque hand grabbed the young apprentice by the collar of his garment and forced him back to the sword-smith's shop, where he received a series of lashes—being blamed for leading the prince astray.

As time went by, Rasool's mastery of the sword became known throughout all of the arid Egyptian land; not only his craft, but his mastery as a skilled swordsman. And, though he had been forbidden to consort with the prince, he was promoted, at a very young age, to lead commander of the palace militia.

The enormity of the prince's discovery never rose upon Rasool's mind; till the day the *Amir* Rasheed ordered an excavation of the hidden treasure, which the young amir oversaw himself. Jewel after jewel was spit forth from the soil: Diamonds, Rubies, Sapphires, Amethysts, all precious gems of the earth including gold, silver, and platinum, and stones that none had ever seen—all excavated from the small rabbit hole dug beneath Egypt's terrain.

The Amir Rasheed had allowed no rest, as men worked in methodic shifts, sifting through dirt and clay and leaving no stone unturned. Every earring, bracelet, necklace, and anklet was searched out as he clutched the Semus Bracelet tightly. The thick of the metal was cool to the touch and the jewels shone brilliantly in the hot afternoon sun, while Rasheed knew this was more than just buried treasure.

Rasool sank into his large leather office chair; it sagged as a cushion beneath his immense size. Removing a key from within his inner breast pocket, he slid it into the lock fashioned within the mahogany desk's drawer. There, he removed a small velvet satchel secured with a drawstring cord at the top. And, untying the cord and opening the delicate fabric, he reached inside to remove the earring. The earring he had dug from the earth so many ages ago. It dangled lightly as he held it between a thick finger and thumb, sparkling the same as thirteen years passed.

CHAPTER 11

Laddor quietly made his way along the corridor wall followed by Deverall. "Come on, Deverall," he pressed crouching down as Cherinne knocked upon the Amir's office door.

"Man—hold up, Red. It's not like he'll jump her bones the minute she walks in there. Besides, while she's keeping Saheeb busy, I can go check out his lovely harem. I imagine he has some real hot mamas in there."

"Is that *all* you ever think about, Deverall?" Laddor wrinkled his face in disgust.

Deverall's eyes twinkled with amusement, as Cherinne entered the door and disappeared inside. "Well...*yeah*; but you're a good one to talk. Isn't that all *you* ever think about?"

Flustered, Laddor waved his arms around. "That's not the point! Cherry is *my* girl! And, now that his is damaged..."

"And, doesn't listen..." The pilot interjected.

"Exactly!" Laddor enunciated agreeably. "She doesn't listen. So, he's gonna' go after *my* Cherry." Sighing, he slumped his shoulders, then quietly spoke. "How can I try and compete with such a rich, powerful—"

Deverall interrupted again. "Don't forget extremely handsome. I guess if I was a woman...he tapped his finger against his stubble ridden chin, "...I would definitely have to pick the Amir; even though I dig redheads..."

Laddor angrily spun around, "Oh, shut up! You're not helping." Then, he put his ear to the door and listened closely.

"Miss Havenstrit." Prince Rasheed stood with his hands clasped behind his back. He watched out the large window at Fahimah moving awkwardly along the garden path on crutches, which had been speedily assembled by a local craftsman. Haneefah guided her along by the arm, while Fahimah's injuries still greatly affected her movements, and she tried desperately to conceal the pain. The prince pointed to a large leather chair across from his desk. "Please, have a seat."

"Yes, Your Highness," Cherinne stated softly as she bowed, then complied by slipping into the cool leather. Glancing around the room, she marveled at the rows of shelves burdened with an over-abundance of books. Her eyes, pausing for a brief moment, ran over the tables lined with computers and stacks of papers while she wondered of their contents. She quickly averted her gaze as the prince turned in her direction. Cherinne glanced at Rasheed, then toward the princess, who Cherinne was also able to see from where she was seated. Princess Fahimah was surrounded by the richness of a vast variety of flowers that bloomed for a short stretch of time after the rains. The gardens stretched wide and long, lined with a large hedgerow which extended beyond the palace walls. It was a labyrinth of beauty, guarded by the stone statues of both men and women, who safeguarded the delicate buds as they made their appearance for only a brief period

The Amir watched Cherinne intently, enthralled at her beauty and likeness to his Princess Fahimah. He searched his mind as to where to begin, while she fidgeted nervously under the stare of his dark gaze.

"Your Highness…" she broke the awkward silence, "…I am truly sorry for what has happened to the princess. I did not mean to injure her and I am glad to see she is up and about. But, I do not understand how it is possible that she still lives, let alone is able to make her way outside; *and* how *I* am near myself today after such a painful ordeal." Cherinne busied herself with the button upon her tunic, feeling slightly uneasy and wishing Laddor was there. Though, she knew he was just outside the door listening; for she could hear him and Deverall rustling around.

The Amir smiled wearily. "Miss Havenstrit…or may I call you by your first name, Cherinne?"

"Please, Your Highness, call me Cherinne."

"Okay, *Cherinne.* I believe that to have you understand the implications of Mr. Zeandre's actions, I had best retrieve my journal. There are many things I will need to explain and it may be kind of difficult for you to follow. Before I begin, may I interest you in a cup of tea, or perhaps a glass of water? I would offer you something a bit stronger—perhaps wine— but it would not be wise to intermingle that of stronger drink with the medication the doctor had given you last night. It is still circulating within your system."

"A glass of water will be fine, thank you."

Removing a crystal goblet from a shelf behind his desk, he poured water into it from an iced crystal carafe and handed it to her. She nodded in appreciation. The prince then pulled a large, leather-bound ledger from within the top drawer of his desk, and placed it before him. Leather strapping entwined itself within four holes holding the journal together, which looked to be twice the age of Reynolds. Running his smooth manicured fingers over the coarse etchings in the leather cover and along the binding, he seemed somewhat enthralled for a moment. Rasheed looked upon the book as a long lost lover; as if deciding whether or not to share of its contents with anyone. Glancing at Cherinne and the bracelet upon her wrist; he then quickly opened the journal to the first page, fearing he would change his mind.

"*Man*, whaddaya thinks goin' on in there?" Laddor pressed his ear tighter to the door. "It's awfully quiet."

Deverall stood idly against the wall eating an aged pack of peanuts which advertised United Airlines. "Hell, Red—how should I know." Maybe he's makin' out with her on his *big* mahogany desk." He jested with a snort. "If you weren't such a sissy-boy, you'd be in there too—not letting them alone."

Laddor shot him an irate scowl and whispered angrily, "Man, now I know why I hate you so much!"

"Hey, don't blame me if you can't hold onto your girl. I think you'd have trouble holdin' onta' black tar—you'd find some way to let it slip through your fingers." He crumpled the paper to the peanuts and dropped it into a nearby vase. "I'm outta' here. I know there's some lovely maiden around here, just callin' out my name." He tipped his hat. "See ya'."

"*Deverall!*" Laddor scrambled to his feet and grabbed the pilot's full arm while fighting to keep his voice down. "Don't leave me here *alone*! I might need your help!"

Deverall's voice sounded comically hopeful, "hey, maybe this'll teach ya to be a *real* man. Just knock on that door and demand to know what your woman's up to." Laddor's chin drooped to his chest as the jeering pilot shook his arm free. "Good luck."

Taking a sip of the cool water, which glided easily down her itchy throat, Cherinne couldn't imagine ever being lost in the desert without a drink. Just thinking about it added to the parched feeling she had since they had arrived. She took another sip.

The amir turned and quickly glanced back out the window at Fahimah, a look of concern creasing his dark brow. They watched together as a maidservant hurriedly retrieved a heavily cushioned chaise lounge for the princess, while Haneefah assisted Fahimah to her seat, positioned within the shade. Then she took her crutches. Fahimah slumped down painfully into the chair and lay back, as the maidservant brought her a glass filled with a rose-colored drink, and worked fervently to make her comfortable. Nodding in gratitude, Fahimah delicately sipped at the liquid, then closed her eyes.

Keeping his eyes to the scene below the prince remarked, "My Fahimah—she is distressed as to my meeting with you alone." He turned to Cherinne and raised a brow. "That is why she lies where she can see me through the glass. Do you feel she has any need for worry?"

Cherinne smiled while reserving a giggle, "Then she and my Laddor are the same; for he listens just outside the door."

"Ahh, so you can hear him through the thick of the solid wood?"

Cherinne nodded. "Yes—yes I can. I can also just barely hear the princess speaking of you right now."

The amir quickly turned back to the window. Fahimah was in the midst of a conversation with Haneefah, as he could see her lips moving. "*Ahh*, this is very interesting. Can you tell me what she is saying?"

Cherinne sat forward and closed her eyes tight, while blocking the sounds within the room around her out, like the sound of the amir's heart beating steadily, slightly quickening with anxiety as she raised a quieting finger to her lips. She could hear Laddor shuffling about just outside the door—cursing beneath his breath at Deverall who had finished his peanuts and gone. Cherinne's face scrunched with lines of concentration, cutting through life outside the palace—camel's braying, a buzzard's cry in thirst for food, the clinking of cubes within Fahimah's glass. Though in Arabic, the voices materialized in an audible dialect and she was somehow able to understand them clearly. Cherinne could hear Haneefah, in her soft gentle voice, saying soothingly, 'Fahimah, you need not worry…Prince Rasheed is not like that. He does love you so. Just because this American wears the Bracelet of Semus, does not mean that he will abandon you for her.' 'Yes', Fahimah replied; her voice faltered. 'But, if he loves me so, then why, while I am injured, does he come to lay with you?' Fahimah paused, and Cherinne wished not to hear anymore; but yet, curiosity urged her to continue to listen. 'Fahimah, I am Prince Rasheed's wife also,' Haneefah replied, 'and dearly love the amir…Yet, he has chosen *you* to bear heir to his regime and that is the greatest privilege of all; for I shall never have the liberty of occupying his quarters with his child.'

The princesses' conversation abruptly came to a halt, swallowed by a sudden, thunderous pounding of horses' hooves and a deep resonating tone which shouted, "Kill them all!"

Cherinne's eyes flew open in panicked awareness, while alarm kindled upon her fearful face. "*Princess Fahimah! Princess Haneefah!*"

"What is it? What do you hear?" Prince Rasheed searched the garden below and ran his eyes along the courtyard, all the way to the front palace gates while seeing nothing out of the ordinary.

With a trembling hand, she placed the glass upon his desk; the tinging of the ice rang in her ears. "They are in grave danger. An army ascends upon horseback, commanded to kill everyone." She hastened to her feet.

Narrowing the space between them, Rasheed grabbed her arm and turned her to meet his gaze; he searched her terror stricken face. "Are you sure? You are able to understand the Arabic language *and* you can hear this?" Her large chocolate eyes swallowed him in their sweet flowing warmth—not the warmth of Egypt, but, instead, the warmth between a man and a woman—while, they, instead of melting before him had the reverse effect, causing him to soften before her, with any resentment or doubts he may have had for her as the administrator of the bracelet gone.

Her look was serious, "Yes, yes I can. I would not lie about such a thing."

He glanced back at the women in the courtyard then hastened to the door, where he quickly opened it to find Laddor stumbling forward with his ear still pasted to the wood listening.

"Uhh," Laddor mumbled in stupidity.

Cherinne sighed and shook her head in frustration. "Laddor—*come on.*" She slipped by the prince and took his arm. "The princesses are in danger."

Looking at Cherinne, the amir viewed her briefly then set a decision into motion. Heeding her warning, he shouted to one of his guards. "Al-hayya al jaish hajam Amiri Fahimah wa Amiri Haneefah!"

He then turned to Cherinne and lightly touched her shoulder. "Remain here—where you will be safe." Then exiting the room, he sprinted through the hall. His snow white tunic flapped behind him as his sandals slapped along the shine of the marble floor and he disappeared from sight.

"Princess Fahimah! Princess Haneefah!" The maidservant ran hastily along the garden path, "the bell—it tolls—we *must* get inside!"

Haneefah quickly rose to her feet and glanced up at the towering minarets, where the colossal bells clanged boisterously in a sanctioned warning to the regime's people. She extended a hand to Fahimah. "Hurry, Fahimah! We will make for the servant's entrance."

Reaching for her crutches, Fahimah achingly climbed to her feet to begin the trek toward the palace, which normally would have taken only a few effortless steps, but now was a painstaking endeavor. It dimmed her already solemn mood. Her heart quickened with each afforded step, while the sickening sound of echoing cries and warranted shouts of the residents within the regime, settled upon her skin. They came from inside the palace gates, which meant an intruder had breached their lands and was heading for the palace. She flinched at the sound of cracking wood, undoubtedly the heavy gates being torn from their hinges, as the enemy charged upon horseback, making their way inside. Limping painfully, she attempted to work the awkward crutches while Haneefah slipped an arm around her slender waist and hurriedly assisted her along.

Haneefah yelled to the maidservant, *"shaf musa 'adi! shaf musa 'adi!"*

Hearing Haneefah's call for help, Cherinne ran to the window to see. In the distance, a battle commenced between the amir's men who were uniformed in royal blue attire, embroidered with the crested flag which soared majestically, high and proud above the palace. Their regal Arab steeds charged mercilessly toward the stalwart gates, each bringing forth *their captain* who was ready to defend the honor and nobility within the palace's walls.

Bandits dressed in robes of black, their faces covered to the eyes, rode hard upon mighty horses, bearing brightly colored ruby harnesses adorned with the flashiest of gold trim and fringes. Each man's gird possessed sharpened steel within an elaborately handcrafted scabbard, while they shouldered sheathes lined with deadly machetes and dirks which were ready to spill innocent blood.

A large number of riders, brandishing broad slaughterous blades, broke through the assembly of palace guards. Their heated outcry was one of a bloodletting call which brought forth a hair-raising chill to Cherinne's skin. Raising their massive swords and drawing evil from some unknown force, a force which worshiped that of death over life, they thirst for the taste of blood. Time was swallowed in a swirling vortex in which she suddenly found herself drowning. It was a world of brutal killing and fear of your enemy, death and destruction—unlike the one she was accustomed to: purchasing a new dress; deciding on which for supper—haddock or filet mignon—sleeping with Laddor. With the realization they were storming in the direction of Fahimah and Haneefah, Cherinne's legs grew weak and her heart banged within her chest.

Laddor also watched through the thick, double glass in a soundless immobile fright; the hairs on his neck bristled on their ends. It was like viewing a silent film, a film in which you were certain the main characters died—in fact, you were sure—while the dreaded feeling intermingled with the buttered popcorn within your stomach, causing you to feel slightly nauseous. Beads of nervous perspiration cased his raised brow and he wiped them away with the back of a hand. Then suddenly, seeing the prince emerging from the far reaches of the palace's exterior, Laddor pointed an excited finger and exclaimed, *"Look! The amir!"*

The prince was garmented, except for the black of his riding boots, in the purest of white uniforms, edged in the finest of gold brocade. Decorated medals lined the whole of his ennoble chest, while the current of air stirred by his horse's intense movement, whipped up the full of his white cloak which flapped madly behind him in the pressing wind. An array of weapons, forged by the greatest of craftsmen and ready to prove their worth, lined his sides.

He rode as a skilled master horseman upon a beautiful white Arabian mare, whose coat was the color of winter's driven snow. She was pristine beauty without spot or flaw; and, her lustrous flowing mane glistened in the afternoon sun. The mare snorted proudly through flaring salmon-colored nostrils, as she took in the heat of the warring air, and ran a race with time.

The amir charged toward the women as they hurried to find cover. A glint of deadly rampant steel flashed from his emerging scimitar and he held the weapon before him: anger and rage extinguished the gentleness of his demeanor, as he spurred the horse forward. Its legs reached in lengthy strides for the shifting ground as they shortened the gap between them and the threat of the merciless bloodthirsty bandits.

"Amir!!!" Haneefah cried out while she struggled to keep Fahimah afoot.

Rasheed stationed himself between the intruders and the fleeing women while his roaring horse pawed the air, as he, with resolved determination, made a stand.

Cherinne shivered—the scene below, a haunting apparition—as the dark riders converged upon the one lone warrior.

"They're not gonna' make it," she whispered beneath her breath. "He needs the aide of the bracelet; I have to go and help." She turned to leave.

"*What?* Are you outta' your *panty wearin' mind?*" Laddor squawked "*You'll be killed!*"

"I have to help!" Her adrenaline pumped and she broke into a run; Laddor trailed at her sandaled feet.

"*Cherinne!*"

Cherinne's heart pounded furiously, as she darted through the many halls while searching for an exit toward the gardens. And, glancing from the empty corridor to the bracelet, she breathed, "Okay now—you've put me through this much—now, make some use of yourself!" With an incited fling, she snapped her wrist, aiming to awaken the sleeping armband.

The bracelet lay cold and numb against her skin; its dormancy was a mockery of its fine golden brilliance. "*Come on you stupid thing!*" Repeatedly thrashing it about, she accidentally made contact with the corridor's wall and the metal cracked. Seeming to scream in a protest of refusal, it rang loudly within her ears, as if it was aware her auditory sense had been heightened. She flinched.

Spotting a set of exiting double-doors, Cherinne altered her direction, turned a corner and blasted through the passage out into the bright warmth of the mid-morning sun. The savagery of the battle's cry echoed off the palace walls and drifted aimlessly out across the sun-warmed sands. Effortlessly, she cleared the marble steps and ran along the brick pathway which led to the gardens where the prince and princesses were located. Glancing at the bracelet again, she afforded it one final shake. A thrumming pain raced up her arm and ran throughout her entire body. "Ow!" She banged upon the bracelet with a closed fist. "I'll make you work."

Laddor emerged from the palace's hulking shadow. "*Cherinne! Get outta' there!* What are you doing? You can't even control the bracelet. You'll end up being killed!" Laddor's imploring words were buried by the resonating sound of rampant warfare: the thunderous beating of hoofs, the earsplitting crack of discharging weapons and the many howling cries of those consumed in battle. Unknowing however to him, he had stumbled into the path of an encroaching assailant and was being eyed like that of hunted prey.

The assailant, noticing Laddor's crimson hair, followed the path of wine colored mane and brandished his ready blade. He spurred his horse forward, driving his steed along the garden path toward the unsuspecting foreigner and relishing in the lurid passion for a hunt. Blazing along the hedgerow, he cleared the cobblestone path and emerged upon Laddor as a massive storming cloud.

Rasheed, seeing the danger the American was in, peeled back his horse. But, realizing it was too late for him to come between the foolish American and the steel of the rider's blade, he reserved his attention for the women.

Turning, Cherinne suddenly saw the threat rushing headlong toward Laddor. Seconds flashed by and Terror was now the administrator of her stolen voice. Glancing again at the bracelet, she struggled to return to her senses, as she trembled in panic and struck the armband one last time. "*Work!!*" the word abruptly screamed forth from her constricted throat.

The colored gems, unexpectedly complying, rapidly burst to life, as if they had been awakened in an irate mood. Cherinne held her arm steady before her, aiming in the direction of Laddor's attacker. But, suddenly, the force of the armband ripped Cherinne from her feet and slammed her to the bricks of the garden walkway. Angrily, it dragged her protesting body along the stone and through the defenseless flower buds, tearing the buds from root, like a gardener with a cleaving hoe.

"*Heeyah!*" Rasheed shouted as he sheathed his sword and raced toward Cherinne. Hastily, he galloped alongside her, praying to Allah that the bracelet wouldn't shoot beneath his horse's feet and drag Cherinne to her death by trampling hooves. Swooping down, he reached an outstretched, gloved hand for the back of her tunic; the tips of his fingers barely touched the cloth. Struggling for a better hold, he grasped the material firmly and pulled her to his horse. The bracelet, with resolved determination, refused to adhere to the amir's wishes of controlling its tirade; and breaking free of Rasheed's grip it grasped at Cherinne in the attempts to yank her from his horse.

"Cherinne—control the bracelet!" Rasheed yelled. The tantalizing odor of sweat mixed with the scent of the prince's aftershave drew thick within her flustered senses while the danger and being so close to another man was unnerving.

Her arm jerked about violently. *"I can't!"*

The prince grabbed her arm and forced it away from his mare. "Don't kill my horse!" Suddenly, the bracelet, seeming to draw an enraged breath, exploded in a rainbow of color. Rasheed held tightly to Cherinne's arm, aiming to control the armband which labored ardently to tear free of his grip.

"Oh dear Allah," Haneefah drew a sharp breath as she observed the amir struggling with the infamous bracelet and the American running to escape his attacker, who had him cornered in the courtyard.

Dropping her crutch, Fahimah, reached for the choker, as the crested jewel upon the velvet mildly thrummed against her edgy throat. Immediately, she shouted out to its supremacy in a commanding voice, "Oh, great Goddess, give me strength!" And, ripping the choker free and snapping it sharply, she tossed it in the direction of Laddor's assailant. *"Dauwar 'ala, dauwar 'ala! Seek!"*

The black velvet raced swiftly through the thick variegated maze of flowers and the emerald blazed like the eye of a lizard. Quickly, it disappeared beneath the dirt and out of sight. Seconds passed and the choker suddenly reappeared and blast its way from within the ground. It climbed the horse's girth and rapidly snaked its way within the surprised assailant's garments and again reappeared around his throat. It immediately proceeded to squeeze. The jewel upon the choker screamed out in a frenzied passion as it emitted an ominous glow, as if it were excelling in strength and triumph. The chords within its grip swelled and contracted, and quickly turning a deep shade of reddish-purple, then appeared as blue.

The assailant's eyes were fixed in a state of panic and fear. Ripping at the black sackcloth concealing his features, he glanced at Laddor in disbelief. Blood and skin infested his fingernails as he raked his throat in the attempts to tear the choker from his swelling neck. His horse danced uncontrollably in a nervous fervor as it sensed the shadowy presence of an unforeseen force; and, jarring its choking captain, the black steed eventually tossed him to the ground. Frantically, the assassin reached for his dagger attempting to cut the phantom weapon free. Unsuccessful, he gave one final sporadic kick and lay completely still.

Unable to watch the horrific display before her, Cherinne turned her head within the amir's chest and drew a tight breath. Closing her tear-filled eyes, she was unaware the bracelet's tirade had even come to an end.

The choker ripped free of the assailant's lifeless body, then speedily raced along the ground, fixing its sights on the amir and Cherinne. Rasheed angrily glanced at Fahimah, who, in avoiding his gaze, had turned her head, while from the corner of an eye, she watched the jewel as it rapidly raced along the terrain, then dipped beneath the surface.

Cherinne wheezed forth a groan, as the weapon, aimed for her, suddenly burst from a crack in the earth.

Rasheed heatedly drew his blade. And swinging, with insurmountable strength and speed, he smashed the blazing emerald. Irately, he then turned to Fahimah, while being disheartened by the actions of his lovely, covetous princess.

Two riders suddenly appeared from the southeast.

"*Amir, look out!*" The bloodcurdling cry escaped Haneefah's lips, and her adrenaline soared. Kicking the straw sandals from her feet, she scaled the delicate garden flowers, and made her way toward the fallen rider's sword. Her robes fluttered vicariously behind her and the white of her tunic hugged the darkness of her olive skin, highlighting her dark tresses as she smoothly ran along the stone. She was beauty in its own right, a dazzling warrior—picturesque. Grabbing the assailant's sword, Haneefah engaged in battle.

The two bandits, charging relentlessly upon driven horses, bore down upon the prince and Cherinne. Swiftly, they drew their crimson dripping blades which thirst for more blood. Rasheed swung his saber in broad slashing strokes, toiling diligently to keep the men at bay. Sweat streamed from his face and his energy level sky rocketed, as he, with unremitting determination, fought to protect those around him. Making indirect contact with one of the aggressors, Rasheed then veered right to avoid the other rider's blow.

Suddenly Cherinne screamed as she found herself careening through the air, as the other attacker, vaulting from his horse, ripped her from the amir's grip. Releasing a startled grunt, she crashed to the earth. Shaking her head in an attempt to clear her muddled intellect, she fought desperately to get him off.

Grabbing her roughly, he stood to his feet and pulled her along with him. "Amir," he shouted to Rasheed, "I have your princess. And, if you do not cooperate, I shall slay her before your eyes!" The intensity of his comprehended words rushed within Cherinne's ears and reverberated upon her tender throbbing drums; she thought she would cry.

The cold tip of his dagger played at the flesh just beneath her jaw. Cherinne gasped in pain as a drop of blood ran the length of her neck and reached within the fold of her tunic. Trembling, she watched from a dirt-ridden face, the enraged amir who swung his scimitar in a high screaming arc, burying it deep within the abdomen of the other assailant. Then, removing his bloody blade from the collapsing corpse, Rasheed slowly turned to coldly stare into the eyes of the enemy. "Let her go," he demanded; his tone was of one who earned the title king.

Tears spilled heavily along Cherinne's heated cheeks, while she was unaware she had even been crying.

Laddor's eyes darted hastily from the amir to Cherinne and the twelve inch blade pressed against her throat. Time ceased to exist and he hesitated, unsure as to what he could do—maybe pray. The heat of the mid-day sun pressed down upon those in the garden and he could vaguely hear the clanging of biting steel as warriors near the eastern wall fought ferociously to keep the intruders at bay. Screams were heard from those who had been beaten, or for those who had been bludgeoned beyond life itself. Wanting to scream or shout, or do any such thing that would release the frustration, anger and fear that was imploding inside him, Laddor refused the notion, knowing it wouldn't help the situation.

With a vicious twist of the wrist, the tip of the blade was shoved a little deeper. Fahimah kept watch of the prince, wondering as to what move he would make—truly preferring for the American to die and angered by the amir's endowing ability to deflect the choker from performing that task. Snorting, Fahimah grabbed her crutch wondering why she had even saved the American male—maybe because he wasn't the one wearing her bracelet *or* the one who had been secured on the amir's horse. Just the thought made her irate.

Suddenly, Haneefah bound through the air; her sword and whitest of robes were stained with the freshest of blood. Releasing a war scream and moving with the swiftest of motion, she rushed upon Cherinne's abductor. And, swinging her blade in rampant passion, she rapidly struck downward removing the unsuspecting rider's sweat-laden head.

The earth spun the color of crimson and splashed its contents onto Cherinne, spraying her white garments in human blood. A grisly spectacle thudded sickeningly just beyond her feet as a startled pair of spiritless eyes glowered up to rebuke her and sent her into an overwrought frenzy. Reeling in a spray of red, she was instantly consumed by the nightmare before her, and, slipping to her knees, she placed her hands to her head and screamed.

Rasheed nodded his head in gratitude and approval at Haneefah, while pride at his lovely bride's ability, was mounted high upon his chest. Several more trained assailants rushed from the front gates, continuing to increase in numbers and make their way toward the gardens and courtyard. Rasheed immediately snatched a dagger from within his gird and tossed it to Laddor. He then readied his battle stance, regretfully, unable to console the distraught American girl.

Quickly, making his way toward Cherinne, Laddor grabbed the dagger and hurriedly shoved the eight inch blade into his boot. "I'm here, honey." Stooping, he ran a consoling hand along her hair, then immediately bent to unsheathe the Scimitar from the lower half of the lifeless assailant, who lay before his and Cherinne's feet. The curved blade measured over thirty inches of brilliant carbon steel, secured with a brass hilt that was gripped by a smooth hardwood handle. Laddor momentarily held the weapon before him, as it glimmered white beneath the warming Egyptian sun: his face betrayed a hint of pleasure.

Rasheed shook his head in a brief moment of amusement while observing the American who probably had never beheld such a weapon before. And, turning to Fahimah who fumbled irritably with her crutches, he inhaled deep. Considering her frustrations, he promised to pay special attention to her needs later, after he hopefully, had rid his regime of this unrelenting foe.

Fahimah seethed with anger and a mild curse slipped from her lips. Her wrestling with the wooden framed sticks added to her annoyance and she fought arduously with the idea of hurling them at someone. The American girl—she was to blame for this—all of this. Good, let her scream, scream her fool head off—something I would have removed myself, had not it been for the amir foiling the previous attempt, Fahimah fumed, finding absolutely nothing funny about the entire situation. Yet— the amir, he seemed to have patience with these people—these *Americans*. He housed them, filled their boorish appetites and even came to their aide when he should have had them beheaded—not only the girl, but the entire lot.

Rasheed's attention was suddenly diverted by a horse and rider who was charging full speed toward Fahimah. The rider bore down in determination to catch her off guard; like a huntsman fixed in the steadfast resolution to dominate the fox as it lay sleeping. The tails of the enemies sable robes snapped aggressively, kicking up in the stale wind, like sheets on a line caught in a blustery gale. His roan gelding tore through a thicket of meticulously trimmed hedges, uprooting clumped masses of loose soil and flowers, sending them spraying about the air as a fountain of variegated petals and brown dirt. Drawing a feathered shaft from within his leather quiver, the dark rider set his sights on Fahimah.

"*Intabih!*" the prince shouted the warning through a horrific stare.

As the bowstring was drawn tight and the arrow loosed free of the Egyptian's fingers, Fahimah turned. Singing proudly, it tore through the thick desert air, and raced for the princess's pounding chest. "*Fahimah!*"

A flash of scarlet, white and bronze streaked along the hedgerow. Haneefah, covered in the swells of besieged onslaught, suddenly scaled gravity and positioned herself between Fahimah and the advance of the speedy shaft. The warrior princess hurled the scimitar. It rapidly spun, like the hand on a 'wheel of chance' at a carnival stand, on a warm summer's afternoon, while spectators cast their biddings on which number to select. The scimitar's blade, reflecting the heated rays of the tireless sun, radiated a burst of flickering light throughout the garden, and time seemed to cease.

The feathered shaft tore through Haneefah's chest and sent her petite body sailing backward, as she slammed against the stone walkway.

"*Haneefah!*" A dreadful panic swelled upon the prince's torn expression as he watched in disbelief.

Deverall's voice suddenly sounded through the collage of wails and battle cries and all eyes turned to him. "*Hey! What the hell's goin' on? I got lost!*" He grumbled loudly. "*Man, Red,* I'm missin' all the action." He drew his Mauser; and eyeing three riders emerging upon the prince, Deverall cocked back the hammer and shot. The echo of gunfire exploded along the palace walls as the three riders and their horses went down.

Hastily jumping from his horse, Rasheed ran toward Haneefah. His hands shook as he dropped to his knees. Gently cradling her head within his arms, he attempted to access the severity of her injury.

"Rasheed—it's bad, isn't it?" Haneefah's voice quivered. "I'm sorry…we're not alone…Your Highness." A trickle of blood slipped from the corner of her trembling lips.

"Don't be silly," his voice broke as he wiped away a strand of matted hair from her sweat-laden face. She was splashed in crimson—an artist engrossed in the throws of a masterpiece—Haneefah's masterpiece being the victory of battle. "You can call me whatever you want." His eyes filled, making it difficult to examine the wound, though he already knew the diagnosis was not good. He grabbed her quaking hand. "I'm going to try and pull the arrow out." His voice cracked and tears now leaked effortlessly along his cheeks.

"No." She choked out in a raspy breath as she looked at him through weary, wet eyes. "It is…too late." Placing a finger to a moistened tear which mingled with the sweat upon his face, she whispered, "Rasheed…I am…" Her lips attempted a smile, but the pain was apparent in her aching eyes and the bronze color leaving her cheeks. Her firm, yet frail body pitched forward in a guttural cough and she grasped at the prince's chest, "I'm frightened." Her eyes slowly closed and her trembling hand suddenly slipped and smacked the cool pavement. Rasheed flinched.

"Haneefah?" He touched her cheek. "Haneefah, *Llaaaaaa!*"

Through a well of tears, he stared into her lifeless face; and grabbing the arrow, with shaking hands, he yanked it from her chest and angrily flung it to the ground. Blood seeped from the wound and spilled upon the walk, snaking its way into the cracks and crags of the stone and disappearing within the earth. Grasping her to his chest, he sobbed.

"*Haneefah?*" Denial surfaced upon Fahimah's face as she awkwardly pushed forward with her crutches to reach the princess. Tossing the wooden menaces to the side, she limped with great difficulty to where Haneefah lay. And, dropping to the ground beside the weeping amir, she reached a trembling hand toward her friend—the only person, who, besides the prince, had ever shown her kindness. The one who had comforted Fahimah in her fits of jealousy—jealousy over the close bond the prince and olive-skinned princess shared, and jealousy over his visits to her chambers. Yet, she surmised—Haneefah knew all this—knew how angered Fahimah was the mornings the amir exited the dark-haired maiden's chambers, for that matter, any of his wive's quarters. And, as he would lightly step along the wooden parquet floor, passing the young princess's chambers, he would be unaware as to the brooding which took place just on the other side of her doors.

"Why, Haneefah?" Fahimah uttered while touching the female's face. "Why did you give your life for me?" She laid her head upon the young maiden's stomach and listened to the silence that filled her ears. Her blonde hair tumbled into an instant dye of red as she slipped her arms beneath Rasheed's and embraced her friend. Tears slipped from Fahimah's eyes as she hid her face in Haneefah's robe.

Their earlier conversation breezed through Fahimah's mind—the last few words her friend had spoken to her—'He loves you so', Haneefah had said. Yes, Fahimah thought, that's why you did it—for the prince—because *you* loved *him* so. Through tears of loss and oblivious to those watching and listening, the princess found her voice and softly hummed a soothing melody—a tune for those with passing spirits. Rasheed buried his face within the nape of Fahimah's neck. The warmth of his painful tears, spilling along her skin and hair, ran moist within her tunic; she cried sorrowfully at their touch.

"Damn shame," Deverall breathed as he made his way toward Cherinne.

Cherinne placed her hands over her face; while the loss for these two people and the death looming around her was quickly becoming an over-whelming weight. Suddenly, she spewed everything from within her stomach, while her head reeled in a pounding ache. She retched again.

"Cherry…" Laddor placed a hand on her shoulder. "Honey, let me help you—"

Suddenly, Laddor's head exploded with excruciating pain as he plowed face first into a patch of the few remaining flowers. Mounted atop a moving black mass of gelding, a goliath sized swordsman brandished his swaheel—a massive weapon in size and weight, which would normally require the strength of two men. It was a monstrous beast in itself, while the handle stood over seven feet tall and the blade added another three. A gleam of sunlight reflected from the enormous tree-splitting blade that curved with broad, blood soaked, razor teeth, which had been forged from the fiery elements of hell. Careening through the thick sultry heat, the weapon created a stir of blinding electricity and produced its own storm.

Releasing a howl, Laddor frantically dodged the gelding's hooves and the dangerous brutality of the cutting blade. Angrily, it swiped past his head and cleaved deep within the earth, while gouging out mounds of dirt, stone and flowers. Laddor was showered in the debris; while the rain of a horticulturist's nightmare covered his body and clothes; and he was also, without consent, trimmed recklessly of a patch of auburn hair. *"Holy shit!!"* he croaked.

"I got ya', Red," Deverall shouted as he aimed and shot. Spinning about, the swordsman swung the massive swaheel, as if it were a mere extension of his body. The bullet struck the white light of the heated blade; and without a quiver, split the rushing shell in half. Deverall cocked his head in bewilderment at the low tone of victory listlessly drifting admidst the wind and emanating from the elements of the weapon.

"Man, that's impressive, Chief," The pilot chuckled. "Let's try that again." He sent off another shot which the dark goliath again deflected easily. A look of anger shadowed the giant's shroud of sackcloth and he glared at the pilot through slitted yellow eyes. Tiring of this game, he then whipped about to see Cherinne, who sat defenselessly upon her heels, frozen in terror.

"Run!!" She could hear the voices frantically shout, but terror held her captive and she was unable to move.

Jumping to his feet and grabbing his newly claimed sword, Laddor held it before him and Cherinne, while he trembled to his boots in dreaded fear.

Sneering, the giant cackled in amusement, while his horse reared and pawed at the air in a venomous attack. The clang of metal bit and teeth ground in Laddor's ears as the black gelding chugged out rank breaths in smoky vaporous gusts, snorting out a vicious threat through flared flesh-colored nostrils and two almond shaped eyes. It emanated an aura of underlying evil.

Trying to avoid a bludgeoning by two thrashing, outstretched hooves, Laddor stumbled backward and dropped the blade. An eerie, throated scoff—a pure mockery of Laddor's efforts—rose from the dark shroud; a sound which seemed to materialize from the fiery abyss of hell. The dark enemy then suddenly turned and reached for Cherinne. Clutching a fistful of tunic and blonde hair tightly, he yanked her roughly onto the monstrous beast, while his strength was that of twenty oxen and he easily plucked her from the ground. Kicking her legs and screaming, she struggled in a panicked fright to break free of his grasp. Effortlessly, he held her in his vice-like grip with long broad fingers and arms the thickness of barrels.

Rasheed quickly wiped away his tears with the back of a blood smeared hand. His mourning heart, in need of grieving, impatiently nudged at his very being—an ache that would only mend by the hands of time. He touched Fahimah's trembling shoulder, then quickly rose to his feet. Watching Cherinne's terror stricken face, he swore to Allah, that he would not allow her the same fate as his Haneefah. Shaking off the numbness, he drew his blade. And, standing battle-ready, he eyed his opponent with the determination to protect Fahimah and retrieve Cherinne from the clutches of this barbarian.

Time ceased to exist, as though the hands of a large clock had tolled its final hour, causing all to come to a standstill, while the noonday sun blazed fiery red from high in the cloudless sky. It reached its heated rays down upon those who lived and those who had died; swallowing any relief that may have existed on the sandy dunes of the continent. Inky shadows—buzzards—rose and fell; their circling, a ritual for searching out fresh blood. The stale air reeked with the festering odor of death, as the carnage of battle lay open prey for those thirsting for slaughter.

"*Put her down!*" Rasheed yelled. His voice seethed with anger.

"And, by whose authority am I being commanded?" The abominable giant exhaled in a multi-toned grouse.

Cherinne's skin crawled from the rancid stench seeping from beneath the sackcloth and she choked back the urge to spew again. She would have if it hadn't been for the fact that her stomach was already empty. Her abductor's breath was a series of rasping hisses which rang close to her ear. With a large muscular arm, he secured her close to his body—a powerfully built form, none to be tangled with—which was hidden beneath the flowing dark garbs. He exhumed the scent of burnt ashes, a smoke laden stench which choked at her nostrils and caused her to gag. She sagged in a weakened state, held within his stony grip, while her world spun in an agonizing nightmare.

"I am Prince Rasheed—Prince Rasheed Daivyan Khalil Tarun…and *you,* may I ask, *are?*…And, why have you invaded my palace, broached my lands, lands which stand beneath a flag of peace?" the amir questioned, never taking his gaze from the giant.

"Princey," Deverall whispered,"Ya want me to take another shot at 'im?"

The amir raised a hand to Deverall—a sign to hold.

"I am a descendant of Seth, the desert god, who represents both chaos and violence." The giant drew a breath. "I have been ordained to recover the jewels of Semus. He grabbed Cherinne's wrist; and turning it roughly, he examined the armband, as the many jewels caught the rays of the sun. "And, I see I have found the bracelet."

Fahimah suddenly cried out, as she was yanked upon another horse, not quite the size and mass of Cherinne's assailant's, but large just the same. She fought venomously, swinging closed fists and kicking in a mad frenzy as fury blinded her to her opening injuries. Blonde hair tossed about wildly, as she fought like a wild animal caught in a trap, against the grasp of a rider who endeavored to restrain her. Bearing her teeth, she spun around and bit down hard within the fleshy nape of her assailant's neck.

"*Bitch!*" He suddenly, with a fisted backhand, struck her temple. A fiery blast of pain quickly sent her pitching forward and her face landed in a coarse tuft of black mane. Fahimah lay motionless, staring in a blind stupor, while the horseman secured her tiny waist to steady her upon his chestnut Arab.

"*Fahimah!*" Rasheed hollered in fuming desperation.

"And now, I see I have the anklets. Very good, Hafiz," the giant snorted. "We ride!"

Rasheed glanced from Cherinne to Fahimah, uncertain, of whose assailant to attack. He knew that to throw his sword—the same attack Haneefah had used—might mean the possibly of hitting the American girl; yet he had to try. The horse, he thought; if he could bring down the horse that would put them afoot. He hurled his blade; then without waiting for the end result, he turned and bolted toward Fahimah's abductor.

A deep throated cackle slipped from behind the black cloth of Cherinne's assailant, as the sword landed just inches from his black gelding. "Stupid fool…" the giant sneered, "…trying to kill my horse. I would never allow such an act of stupidity. Hafiz! We go!"

Cherinne fixed her teary eyes to Laddor's in a frightened stare, as the massive horse, prodded, reared in triumph and released an unearthly bray. "Laddor?"

"Cherinne?" He whispered, shocked at the situation. His body quivering, he raised the sword, as the horse lunged forward to make for the clear. "*Stop!*" Laddor screamed the word with a cracked throat. The swaheel swiftly lashed out—brisk as the wind—it was followed by a gutted scoff, seeming almost to be laughter.

Deverall took another shot. The bullet, just nicking the long handle of the giant's weapon, ricocheted within the stone walls and resounded with a sharp ping. He aimed again and pulled the trigger, but was sad to hear the empty click of the chamber. "*Damn!*" He tapped his vest pockets. "They're in the room."

Irate, the giant turned his face toward the sky and roared aloud in a winded bellowing cry. The blare of baritone reverberated, with a violent stirring up of the white hot sands, and blasted loudly in Cherinne's skull. She cupped her palms tightly over her ears, in the attempts to block out the lurid burning within her head, while her acute sense of hearing threw her into a deafening tizzy. She screamed.

Shouting in an ancient Aramic language, he called out to the desert god Seth—the God of violence and chaos; and holding the swaheel upright before him, he then pounded it harshly upon the ground. A rippling vibration instantly surged along the earth, sending forth a vicious snaking crack that split the ground in two.

"*Run!!*" Rasheed shouted. Wearily, he changed his course, knowing he was unable to catch the fleeing horseman and Fahimah, and headed toward Haneefah who lay lifeless upon the splitting earth. His heart pounded laboriously, as the adrenaline pumped within his veins, and he scooped up the deceased princess's body. "*Run for the stables!*" he yelled to the others while dodging the many branching crags racing like snakes in every direction. The splitting of rock and stone creaked loudly with a skin chilling scream, then groaned as it buckled in a mass of shattering crust.

Laddor, hurdling a large crag and silently thanking his mother for his lengthy legs, jumped another snaking fissure. "*Holy crap!*" he cried teetering backward as the ground collapsed just behind him with a thunderous rumble. Large chunks of stone broke free of the earth, falling headlong into the darkness of the heated vaporous abyss and disappearing within the immense black hole. "I won't let him have you, Cherinne!" he shouted. "I swear on my mother's grave, I'll get you home!"

Laddor leaped a wider crag that was headed directly for the palace and dug itself beneath the foundation. He watched the stone of the palace walls quaver and slightly tremble. Then, releasing a gut-rending groan, the massive structure shifted as a huge section, suddenly, crashed to the ground. "*Oh my God!*" Laddor stumbled on the expression as the west walls rapidly disappeared into a thundering pile of rubble.

"*Holy shit Red! Did you see that?*" Deverall clamored, astounded at the severity of the situation. "*Man*, we gotta' get outta' here!"

Laddor looked to be practicing ballad as he sprang from one solid chunk of rock to another. "I can't. I gotta' get Cherinne!"

"Are you crazy? You're gonna' die out here!" The pilot shouted over the explosion of bedrock as the desert twisted, opened its immense mouth and swallowed a rushing river of flowing sand. "They're long gone; and the amir said to head toward the stables. We'll work on getting sweetheart later." He stopped briefly and they exchanged a look; Laddor then glanced toward the west.

"Don't worry, Red. If they wanted to kill her they would have done it right then and there—someone has other plans for the girls. So, come on! Let's get outta' here!"

CHAPTER 12

The sun lay in a lazy haze of red and gray along the western horizon, resting from another day of scorching heat and awaiting the cool of evening's relief.

Cherinne licked her parched lips, barely able to muster the spittle to moisten them at all. She had watched in horror the destruction that had ravaged the palace and its people; the crumbling of the western walls, as the giant had called upon the supernatural powers of his god, which had brought about mass chaos.

Fahimah was still unconscious; secured within the other riders grip as they rode a few paces ahead. Her head bobbed in rhythm with the horse's pounding hooves and her blonde hair cascaded along the chestnut's neck, intermingling with the grainy black mane. A purplish hue marked her right temple, where the rider's fist had quickly connected during their struggle which had knocked her senseless and unable to fight.

Uneasily shifting her weight, Cherinne tried desperately to keep from making contact with the gargantuan chest of the giant seated behind her. The task was becoming near impossible while being bounced around on the black gelding, whose gate was none of a Tennessee walker. The giant's lurid breath settled in a pasty fog along the back of her neck, and she cringed with each inhale, swearing he had drawn into his inner senses an extra deep breath, smelling the scent of her hair. A nauseous feeling rose within her stomach—the thoughts of what might happen to her and Fahimah once they had arrived at their appointed destination. And, closing her eyes to the nightmares that entered her mind, she slightly trembled with the many images that appeared before her.

Opening her eyes and resting her chin against her chest, she watched the large goat-skinned gloves which controlled the reins just above the saddle horn—neither western nor English, more like a camel-saddle, somewhat primitive. The hard leathered horn rose in a high arc and melded into a small curved section—ample for her—then was separated by a thick rise of stitched rawhide which spread into a much broader, wider seat, which the giant fully occupied.

She whispered a quick thank you to God, for not having to be seated directly between her abductor's thighs. While she was unable to remember ever being *this close* to a man before; except for, of course, her father, her doctor, and Laddor.

Laddor, she thought. Are you okay? He had taken quite a beating while trying to protect her, and when the giant had called upon the god of Seth and the earth was being torn into, her captor had made haste—withdrawing from the fight. That was the last she had seen of the others. And with her captor being clearly such a formidable foe, surely Laddor and Prince Rasheed would have been brought to their deaths? Aren't you coming to save us, she thought; and lowering her achy head and closing her eyes, her body began to awaken to the throbbing pangs of her many injuries.

Dozing, out of pure exhaustion, Cherinne was suddenly startled into alertness. Uncertain as to how long she had been asleep or where they were, she groaned. The only clue now was the sun, which no longer set along the horizon, but had disappeared from the dark earth, while the full of the moon had taken its place. Groaning lowly, she tried to figure out as to how long she had slept, intending to keep track of their location. Yeah, right, she scolded herself—we're in the middle of the desert—she hoped somewhere still in Egypt. And, with no land markings to keep track, like: a tree, house, bush, *frog, anything*—with just sand and more sand—how was she to know? *Ohhhh*...she silently whined beneath her breath...*Where are we?*

Slowly exhaling, a puff of warm air escaped Cherinne's lips as the hot sultry lands which had been blistery, had suddenly turned chilled. She shivered. Closing her eyes to think, and drawing her arms tightly around her body, she became acutely aware of the danger she and the princess were now in. Glancing at the bracelet, a thought entered her mind of getting the bracelet to work and then, perhaps, she and Fahimah could get away. Thinking she would hold tight to the horn, so as not to be drug off like a fool, Cherinne thought she would then turn and blast her assailant.

Devising a plan, she decided to try.

Cherinne coughed; and, shaking her wrist, she placed a hand to her mouth. The giant shifted his massive body within the saddle. His horse never broke stride. No reaction or lights—she coughed again and flicked the bracelet with a quickened snap. *Come on*, she breathed beneath her breath. Reaching for a lock of her hair and fluffing the strands slightly, she snapped her wrist more quickly.

Suddenly, a broad hand reached from the reins and grabbed her arm in a tight grip, as his long fingers wrapped the entirety of the bracelet and more. "Stop that," the giant growled the warning, shoving her hand in her lap.

Cherinne flinched in surprise. Did he know what she was doing, she wondered. Or, did he just not want her moving about because it irritated him so? She decided to try another approach.

Reaching toward her ankle, she jiggled her arm. "*Ow*," she mewled, just a tad late. Great, she thought, I knew I could never be an actress; but that was ridiculous. She tried again. "*Ouch!* Something just bit me." That's better she reckoned, as she snapped her wrist and scratched falsely. With still no reaction from the giant or the bracelet, she tried again.

With a sharp command, the gloved hands suddenly pulled the mammoth-sized horse to a halt. Fear suddenly slapped Cherinne like an angry hand. Her captor rose in his saddle, then dismounted with unrestrained agility; the mass of his body, surprisingly, moved fluidly, even with the gargantuan weapon strapped to his back. The bubble of hope also burst. Great, she sulked—not only was he humungous, but he's also in shape.

His feet dug deep within the sand, high upon his black riding boots which ascended into the hem of his robes. Trudging heavily through the white terrain, he held fast to the reins while making his way around the front of the horse. The gelding snorted and stepped in place, as if urging his master on.

"Hadi," the giant breathed through his shroud, which Cherinne understood as 'quiet'. Running a gloved hand over the soft pink of the horse's nose, he continued around.

The full moon cast a cool glow down upon the desert, making it possible for Cherinne to see beyond the many dunes. She watched her captor as he sifted through the sand and arrived at the right side of the saddle. His eyes roved the horse's flank; then he checked the girth with a quick yank of a strap.

His companion stopped and turned. "What is it?" he inquired eyeing Cherinne.

The giant replied matter-of-factly, "sand fleas." He suddenly grabbed Cherinne's ankle and yanked her leg toward him. She gasped in surprise, wondering as to what madness had come over him as she recoiled in an attempt to pull away; but his hold was firm.

Removing a glove, with the aide of his teeth, he pulled her tunic clear of her calf, up to the thigh, then ran long fingers along her skin. Cherinne cringed and turned her head while bile boiled within her chest. She closed her wide eyes tight and her heart pounded loudly in her ears, as he slowly ran his fingers along her leg.

A round moment passed and he released his grip. Her leg dropped as a lead weight against the saddle as he turned to make his way back around the horse. Cherinne hastily grabbed the wrap to cover the bare of her skin and quickly tucked it securely behind her calf, never feeling so violated in her entire life.

He effortlessly mounted his horse and settled in behind her. His breath came hot upon her neck. "Nice try," he stated in a silty tone. "Keep it up, and I'll do much more than that."

Cherinne swallowed hard and choked back tears of protest as he spurred his horse forward to ride in silence.

With Haneefah lying loosely in his arms, Rasheed made for the stables. Passing through heavy metal gates, he pushed through to an empty corral.

After the clamoring of battle, the smell of straw and hay were refreshing to the senses and the quiet was comforting. His clicking boot heels sounded off the dust laden wooden floors, as he quickly made his way inside one of the expansive barns. It was meticulously cared for with burlap sacks full of rich oats and grains stacked neatly along each partition. Rows of empty iron hooks lined the whole of the east wall, where riding tack had hung previous to the battle which was ensuing at that very moment.

"*Ib!*" The prince shouted out to the empty stalls—an echo was his only reply. "Ib! Are you here, boy?"

A door burst open somewhere and he could hear the sound of footsteps quickly approaching from the rear section of the barn. Unsure as to whether it was friend or foe, Rasheed slipped into the shadow of an open stall.

"Your Highness—I am here!" A young strapping lad, raven haired and bronzed skinned, with animation in his wide eyes answered. He wore a galabiyah; the long garment hung just to his ankles and revealed bare feet. He glanced about questioning, "*Your Highness?*"

Rasheed quickly emerged from the shadows with Haneefah still clutched to his rising and falling chest. Ib gasped aloud as his dark eyes, large with apprehension and concern, realized it was the princess. He bowed quickly, then quietly whispered, "Your Highness—is Princess Haneefah dead?"

"Yes," the reply was somewhat terser than the amir meant. "I need a place to rest her body. I would like to use your quarters."

Ib's brows furrowed in confusion. "My quarters?" he stammered. "But, Your Highness—I mean no disrespect; but I have no quarters."

Rasheed regarded the boy for a brief moment then stated, "well then—where you sleep."

Nodding, the lad hurriedly led the amir along a straw strewn isle toward a cubicle at the far end of the barn; quickly swinging the cubicle door open, he motioned him inside.

Rasheed's narrowed gaze scanned the full of the dusty, dimly-lit twelve by fifteen foot compartment—a meager stall, probably once used to house birthing mares or the fouls themselves. Sighing heavily, he took

Haneefah inside. A small bed lay along the far wall, fashioned of bundled straw and twine. It was covered carefully with a gray woolen cover which lay atop the rough, prickly matting to protect the skin from being scraped raw—followed by another gauntly chestnut throw to block the chill. A plate of partially eaten food sat upon the gritty floor, along with an open book—one of the few items the boy possessed.

Ib brushed by the prince. "Excuse me, Your Highness." Gathering up the plate and quickly closing the book, he placed them carefully in a far corner.

Wearily, Rasheed laid Haneefah's still body on the bristly straw mat while Ib readily hastened to gather one of the horse blankets for her head. Returning with it rolled, he handed it to the prince, who quietly positioned it beneath the princess's dark hair. Gently removing a blood spattered lock from her sallow features, he fought back the tears that raged to return.

"Your Highness…" Rasheed's glazed eyes were mirrored in the boy's, "…May I please say a prayer to Allah for the fallen princess?"

Covering Haneefah with the rough woolen throw, Rasheed lowly consented, the pain apparent in his voice, "Yes that would be nice—"

Ib dropped to his knees and placed his trembling hands together.

Rasheed continued, "…and later, I will make arrangements to have her soul delivered to Allah; for now I have work to do. For Princess Fahimah has been taken and is in need of rescuing."

"Princess Fahimah has been captured?" Ib shrieked incredulously. He positioned himself on his knees to face the amir. "Please, Sire, oh please, allow me to assist you on this quest. For, I have been training on the technique of the sword, and I have knowledge of the horses."

Rasheed considered this while laying a hand along the young lad's shoulder; then tilting the boy's head back, he studied his face. "What is your age now, Ib?"

"Fifteen! I have just turned fifteen!" Hastily, scooting on his knees across the wooden floor, he retrieved the book and held it up before the prince. "See! The princess gave this to me on my celebration day. She called it my birthday and even had it protected in this fine linen cloth and secured with a lovely ribbon. I believe, from her hair." He scuffled back to his straw mat and reached gingerly beside it, as to not disturb Princess Haneefah; and retrieving a shimmering opaque cloth of light blue, he then searched around to find a long black velvet ribbon. "See!" He held them proudly before the prince.

"*Aladdin*. But, this book is in English. You are unable to read this."

"Yes; but look Sire!" He anxiously opened the book and pointed to the pages. "There are pictures! And, Princess Fahimah, she reads the words to me!"

Rasheed shook his head in confusion. "Princess Fahimah? I thought Princess Haneefah gave you this book."

"Oh no, Your Highness," he stated with a grin from ear to ear. "It was Princess Fahimah."

"Well—ready yourself, Ib; for you shall accompany me on this quest to rescue her. Now, say your prayer and leave me with Princess Haneefah."

Ib shoved the book and its adornments inside his tunic. He folded his hands before his face and bent, near touching his chin to the dirt-ridden floor, and quickly muttered a prayer in Arabic. Then softly touching the princess's hand, he left the stall, closing the door behind him.

Rasheed slumped to his knees and laid his head upon Haneefah's quiet chest. He combed his fingers through her dark tresses and wrestled with the tears that brimmed just behind his stinging eyes. "I am sorry," the utterance was a fine whisper, "but, I cannot be here to send your spirit off to Heaven…please forgive me." Taking her hand, he rubbed it tenderly along his face, the feel of her touch heart-rending. "I will never forget you." He placed a gentle kiss upon her brow. Then, fighting back the flow of tears, he rose to his feet and rushed from the wooden cubicle.

Rasool had battled fervently till the last few gaggles of mercenaries had dispersed as the ground had begun to split and swallow a minute portion of Egypt. Then, as quickly as they had come, the earth splitting crags disappeared.

"Has anyone located the prince?" Rasool's annoyance reverberated within his voice, sounding above the remaining cries of war. The commander shouted again, to those men straggling around him. "Where are the prince and the princesses?" His temper flared red in his face and mixed with the heat of the noon day sun. "*Damn it! One of you insolent fools, answer me!*"

"Lateef, a young Egyptian sergeant, splattered with the red stain of war, trotted briskly toward the commander. "Sir—they were last spotted in the gardens." The sergeant drew his fidgety mare to a halt. She danced with a snort, the fire of battle still cursing flagrantly through her veins. "*Whoa Sheeba!*" Nodding his profusely sweating head in respect, he attempted to slow his rapid breathing.

"Commander Rasool...Sir...the enemy had broken through our barricade..." He breathed heavily, "...then did a reversal on us, Sir. They blockaded the men from passage to the southeast wing. The prince and princesses were trapped within the gardens."

"*Damn it!*" Rasool gauged the situation; a frown was broad across his swarthy color. His horse stepped in place at the sound of his roaring voice. "Are they still there?"

"No," Sergeant Lateef replied. "When the earth began to split, the enemy scattered. Someone said they then saw the prince heading toward the stables. There was no news of the princesses."

A hint of pleasure twisted within the commander's gut—a vision of blonde hair hanging from a wooden staff entered his mind. "So, where the hell is Captain Salman—*that idiot*—it was his job to inform me of the royalty's whereabouts. Where the hell is he?"

"He is dead, Sir." The young soldier replied solemnly. "His body has been seen just beyond the palace gates, lying deep within the sand. It looks as if he were drug there." He paused. "A few of the remaining men went to retrieve his body before the vultures have their way with him...Sir."

"*Damn it, all to hell!*" Rasool glared through a painted veil of rage; his blood seething in a boil steeped into his neck and cheeks, coloring them crimson. "Soldier—gather the remaining men. Take the injured to the infirmary and *find the amir!*"

The prince stood just outside the expanse of wooden corral; and placing his fingers to his lips, he whistled loud and long. A mild whinny sounded in the distance in response to his call; and Rasheed smiled. The white Arabian mare galloped strongly along the desert sand—her stride was majestic and powerful. Tossing her head in show—a natural blue-blood, bred from the finest of champions, she spied the amir with wide dark eyes while her affections were one of pleasing the prince. She whinnied again, as the empty saddle sat rider-less upon her back and the reigns fell free, leaving her open to resume control.

"Nefertiti," Prince Rasheed called to her. "Come to your master." Slowing to a trot, her ears pricked forward and she anxiously headed for the sugar cube lying within the amir's hand. "*Ahh, my beauty.*" Removing a glove, Rasheed stroked the fine blaze of her face while she gently nibbled the sweet away from his grasp, then chewed and nudged his forearm for more.

"Alright, alright," he smiled, "one more; but we shall not want to ruin your figure." He slipped her another and ran his hand along the taut of her neck, checking her for any battle scars. "We have more work to do; for Princess Fahimah has been taken," Rasheed spoke to the mare, as if she were a sworn mate, while tightening the girth on her saddle and securing her to a nearby post.

"*Prince Rasheed! Amir!*" He heard the unison of voices shouting out his name, while the two men's hollering sent the hairs on the back of his neck standing to attention, as they made for his direction.

"*Saheeb!*" Deverall, breathing laboriously, lumbered along behind Laddor who surged ahead by several lengths with ease.

Commander Rasool also emerged, arriving from the northern gates, and riding along the far fence row. He was followed by a near fifty battle-ready infantry soldiers on horseback. Moving at a good clip, they overtook the two men on foot, as he and his men approached in a thunderous assemblage. Rasheed's brow furrowed into a deep scowl and his normal congenial demeanor shadowed over in a cloud of displeasure as he watched Rasool through suspicious narrowed eyes.

"Who the hell is that?" Deverall slowed to a fast walk, sucking in buckets of air, as the horses galloped steadily past him. "Man, look out, Red," he shouted up to Laddor. "These bastards don't give a shit if they run you over, or not."

"*Harrak mahbul 'abiT!*" One of the soldiers sneered through gritted teeth at Deverall, as he galloped within a few inches of the tiring American.

Stopping dead in his tracks and panting heavily, Deverall hollered out, "Whadcha' say—you sand sniffin' jerk off! I dare ya' ta' say that ta' my face—whatever it was!"

The Egyptian soldier wheeled around and brandished a bloody blade.

"*Rasool!*" the amir commanded in Arabic, while Laddor and Deverall observed with their heads tilted in confusion, unable to understand the dialogue. "Restrain your men. These remaining soldiers may have defeated the foe in battle, but their victory was not so great that they could save their comrades from meeting a deadly demise."

"My sincere apologies, Your Highness." The commander bowed. His piercing eyes were directed along with his remark toward the inconsiderate soldier. "I assure you, Your Grace, that it will not happen again. Such forms of rudeness shall not be tolerated. Is this not correct…Nasser?"

Nasser quickly bowed with a half-hearted apology. "My apologies, Your Highness; I was completely out of line. Please excuse my insolence."

Rasheed eyed the commander and his officer with skepticism, wondering why he had continued to allow Rasool the position of commander to the regime's militia for this long a duration. It most likely having to due with the astute service the commander had afforded the previous amir—the Amir Nuri—Prince Rasheed's father. His father had loved and revered Rasool, it seemed more so than his own son. The Amir Nuri longing for power and a son who would follow in his footsteps, had desired the same thirst that cursed through the commander's veins—a devout Muslim dedicated to the cause, who craved power and control which was wielded with a strong hand to the point of being somewhat vicious. And, Rasool was that Muslim—strong, a champion of rivals—his sword technique impeccable. But, Rasheed was unable to fulfill his father's desire; *his* passion being one of peace and tranquility with all other kingdoms; his theory—rule with a firm but gentle hand and bring about unity throughout the nations.

Rasheed's gentleness stemmed from his mother, the princess; her beauty being beyond that of compare. She was an olive-skinned maiden with raven dark tresses and large warm eyes—an Egyptian jewel sent from the Heavens above. The prince loved and adored her; while she brought him warmth and happiness—a sense of contentedness—while his father, the amir, was determined to convert him to participate in his many evil doings.

One of his father's targeted rivals had been that of the western continents. Despising those beyond the Atlantic Ocean; his anger cursed through him like that of poisoned blood. And, though, Princess Adiva, Rasheed's mother, secretly loved the Americans, she never revealed that to Rasheed's father. His response being that of plotted betrayal on her part—the undeniable result—her death.

"Commander," the prince announced; the irritation visible in his tone, "I need to meet with you privately. There has been a loss of *great* magnitude; and we need to discuss the reasoning behind this, and how we are to approach the detrimental situation at hand." He glanced toward the palace. "And, with the entire west wing lying to the ground in a pile of rubble; I imagine the stables will have to do. Come with me." He turned to head back toward the barn.

With an outstretched arm, Laddor rushed to reach for the prince. A heavy leather boot immediately thwarted the front of his chest, blocking his intended passage. It was Rasool. Glaring at the red-haired American, the commander arrogantly sat upon his sweated horse and held his lifted leg firmly, just daring Laddor to advance.

"*Amir! What the hell's goin' on?*" Laddor shouted. Why aren't you on your horse in high pursuit of the girls?" Anger tinged his face quite the color of his hair. "Am I missin' somethin' here?"

Rasheed continued toward the barn, his grief choking slowly at his heart, as he struggled to concentrate on the task at hand—to have Fahimah and the American girl returned safely.

"Damn it, Rasheed! Call your dog off and answer me!"

Deverall secured his friend's arm with an understanding hand. "Hold up, Red—this isn't gonna' do any good."

"*No!*" Laddor yanked his arm away viciously—a twisted coil of disbelief and cursed rage filled his eyes, while the boot was still brazen to his chest. "You *bastard!* Don't you give a shit about what happens to Fahimah? And, they have Cherinne! They killed Princess Haneefah! *Don't you care?*"

Rasheed cringed—the cutting words invisible daggers piercing his back. Knots formed from his fists to his stomach; the thought of Haneefah lying dead in an animal's dirt-encrusted stable heart-renching. And, Fahimah injured in the hands of an enemy was utterly unbearable.

"*Ugghhh!*" Spinning about, Rasheed drew his fists as a raging cloud of agony and hatred crippled his sense of control. Breaking into a run, he lunged headlong into the detestable American. Rapidly, the shing of steel was heard as Rasool along with several of his men drew their thirsty blades while the heat of battle was still cursing through their racing veins.

"*Imshee, Imshee!*" the prince hissed detaining the commander, as his adrenaline pumping, drove him in a maddened state upon Laddor. Red hair crashed to the dry earth within inches of Rasool's stepping horse, nearly obliterating the American's face beneath heavy hooves. Rasheed threw one fervid punch after another, his breathing labored pants, while the thudding crack of fists was heard as he made direct contact.

"*Raahhh!*" Laddor bellowed, suddenly ramming a sharp knee into the amir's groin and sending a lightening bolt of stabbing pain exploding throughout the prince's loins. Crying out, Rasheed clutched himself and rolled defenselessly to the ground with Laddor quickly scurrying atop him. Laddor thrashed about wildly as his red flames whipped in a tumult about his head, attempting to paste themselves to the sweat dripping from upon his face and neck.

Deverall glared angrily at the commander, while the look upon the Egyptian's face was one of disgust; but the pilot thought, also, tinged with a hint of pleasure. He wondered why Rasool didn't stop this. Deciding to take action, Deverall reached for Laddor's collar. When suddenly the amir, grabbing a fistful of hair on each side of Laddor's head, curled up and swiftly cracked his forehead forcibly into the astounded American's face.

Laddor's skull instantly erupted into a burst of stars. "*Ooowww!*" He grasped his face with both hands while blood spurt between his fingers. "*Damn it! Not again!*" he garbled through the thick of blood and mucus. "*Damn you, Rasheed!*"

Rasool dismounted, shook his head in open disgust, then mumbled something beneath his breath. Securing his horse to the wood of the corral, he proceeded into the barn leaving the amir and Laddor to their ridiculous skirmish.

"Man, Saheeb, that was a *nice* move; if I should say so myself," Deverall noted avoiding the belligerent stare of his bloodied friend. He offered the amir a hand, assisting him to his feet.

Emotionally and physically drawn from the day's events, Rasheed collected himself, clapped his hands together and brushed the remaining dirt away. Weariness weighed as a wounded soldier upon his shoulders, as he glanced at Laddor, then turned and silently made his way into the stables.

Digging within his back pocket, Deverall retrieved a wadded handkerchief and handed it to his defeated friend. Laddor grudgingly accepted it as a steady flow of blood ran generously from his tilted head.

"Hey, Red…a little suggestion: always pin the arms tight and guard your face. Ya' look like shit."

"Oh, shut up," Laddor grumbled.

Leaning with arms crossed against a stable door, Rasool regarded the prince with an amused smirk as Rasheed entered the stables still shaking off the remnants of his altercation. "Your Highness, your performance was exemplary—my hats off to you." Rasool's tone was condescending as he bowed deep. "But…" he paused, "…does Your Lordship believe that you should be seen by the men romping around on the ground with some half-witted American, compared to that of a so-called bar-room brawl?"

"Oh, cut the crap, Rasool! I have had about enough today! Your niggling remarks are liable to lead to more than just a bar-room brawl." Rasheed pressed close to Rasool—his hot breath was inches from the large commander's face. Their dark eyes locked in a challenging stare. "Something tells me *you* had knowledge of this raid and didn't inform me. I should have you court-martialed." The prince searched the commander's eyes for the least hint of deception, then continued. "And, as a result, the Princess is dead; which I am holding *you* responsible for."

"Oh, she is?" The commander's remark was silky, while remote pleasure danced feverishly behind his eyes wanting to burst into a grin upon his face.

The amir's narrowed eyes slowly scanned Rasool's heated face certain he was responsible somehow. "It is Princess Haneefah, whose body lies lifeless within these walls"—the news that it is not Fahimah was sure to bring an apparent note of disappointment.

"*Oh, too bad,*" he stated with mock disappointment, "...Princess Haneefah was a genuine princess. What a shame. I had thought that maybe it was the Princess Fahimah. Now, *that*, would have been tragic," sarcasm slipped ungoverned into his voice.

"Now, would it—Rasool? Something just isn't right. Where were you and your men during the raid, while the royalty was left unattended? Answer me that Rasool!" The prince laid a hand atop the hilt of his blade, knowing that in a hand to hand altercation the large commander would easily overpower him. And, though Rasool was known throughout the land for his master swordsmanship, Rasheed thought that he could possibly match him.

"Ahh—so you want to scuffle. Eh, Rasheed? It has been many years since we have come to blows. And, if I recall correctly, you were getting beat till the guards arrived. But, that was so long ago; maybe your skills have improved since then. At least your father would hope so." The two men circled each other as the adrenaline flowed strong and the heat of the noonday sun began to slowly cool. Each surveyed the other while the air was thick with years of envy and mistrust.

"Yes, Rasool, you had had my father's favor, more so than I. For, you were a champion fighter and prayed to Allah as a devout Muslim ready to devour the western civilizations along with our neighboring countries. But, I strived for peace and unison between the nations; and that *included* the Americans."

"*The Americans,*" the commander stated as if a bad taste was within his mouth. "*Huh!* What a foolish people. You acquired that idiotic nonsense from your mother, Rasheed. She even purchased you that little American tramp that *you* entitled princess, whose every whim you beckon to."

Rasheed suddenly felt a tightening within his chest as the words the commander spoke echoed rapidly about the barn, words he has heard before; while his mind raced frantically, attempting to make sense of what Rasool was spewing with such assuredness. It was like trying to catch a puff of smoke or hold water within your hand as it easily spilled between the crevices of your fingers.

"No! You know nothing of my mother! She would never commit such a horrid atrocity!" the prince shouted. "And, *you* shall *surely* meet the rod, for your insolence and badmouthing of the princess!"

"*So*, you have forgotten our last skirmish then?" Rasool retorted with mock pleasure. "The one nearly four years ago when your father had informed you that the little blonde-haired girl, whose hand you held so tightly, running throughout the regime settlings, had been *bought and paid for*. Wake up—Rasheed! You have been asleep these past years! While you have been lying with that American girl your regime has become weak and your father would be mortified! His decision to make you amir was justifiably regrettable; and the day *you* so willfully destroyed him, he was making plans of another successor, which should have been *me!*"

Rasool unsheathed his hungry blade, still tinged with the dark blood of battle. While strength had drawn with every inch of steel as it had emerged from its leather casing. Fiery hate smoldered within the commander's blazing eyes as his enormous arms swung the mammoth-sized blade with practiced ease. In a fuming rage, he struck down upon Rasheed; each swing was a heavy, calculated, downward stroke.

Rasheed, wavering in a confused torment, was abruptly jolted into alertness. Swiftly dodging the commander's blow, he drew his own weapon. With tensed muscles, he held his sword firmly while trying to calculate his opponent's next move; and, avoiding the bludgeoning thrust of steel, he parried. His movements were slightly quicker, due to his agility and size. Sweat pitilessly beaded his face, streamed his neck and raced into his collar. His heart pounded loudly within his ears, like a big bass drum; it drowned out the sound of his labored breathing. Speedily, he swiped the back of his arm across his face, as the sweaty droplets rushed in rivulets to sting his blurring eyes.

A gutted roar resonated throughout the high wooden rafters; it portrayed the malevolence rising within the fuming commander and drove him forward. Rasool charged in an inexhaustible determination while his blade swung with demonic savagery and fiery flames licked behind his eyes and sweat burst from his glands.

"Rasheed, I shall kill you!"

"Your Highness?" Ib's feet shuffled along the sawdust floor, as the young lad turned the corner to be confronted by the two men consumed in the throes of heated battle.

"Ib, leave us!" The prince shouted between strenuous breaths, as the strength in his arms began to slowly diminish, along with the remains of his spent energy. "Get out of here!"

Ib tore his wide frightened eyes away and quickly hastened from the barn. Rushing through the metal gates, he ran along the fence line which encircled the section of sizable pasture nearest to the stables. The regiment was grazing their horses just outside the far gates, while awaiting their commander—along with Laddor and Deverall who waited impatiently for the amir.

"*Come! Come!*" Ib hollered as he waved frantically to the soldiers. All eyes followed his path, as the young stable boy raced across the field toward them. Quickly bowing, he caught his breath and spewed, "the prince, he is fighting with the commander! *Commander Rasool!*"

"*What?*" Lateef, the young Egyptian sergeant, squalled in disbelief, "the amir and Commander Rasool?"

"Yes, yes! Come quickly!" Ib turned and ran back in the direction from which he had just come.

"Omar, Maraat and Mahir—come with me!" the sergeant stated as he mounted his horse. "The rest of you remain here and await my orders. Come, Ib." Hurrying alongside the boy, he grabbed his hand and hoisted him quickly onto the back of his horse.

Laddor, pocketing the bloody handkerchief, rose from where he had been seated alongside Deverall in the rough grass. He started in the direction of the barn while wondering what all the commotion was about, when a soldier suddenly placed his mare between him and the gate entrance. A stern look of resolution was clear upon the man's face as he blockaded the American's entrance.

"*U'qud!*" The Egyptian pointed a finger to the dry grassy spot from which Laddor just rose. "*U'qud!*"

Anger flushed as lava from a volcano and streaked along Laddor's neck and face. Spinning to Deverall, he poked his thumb to his own chest and stated, "Is he telling *me* to sit down?"

The pilot reached up and grabbed his arm. "I think so. Just hold up, and let's see what's goin' on. Something's not right here."

"You think you're tellin' me somethin' new; and are the commander and the amir *fighting*? I can't *believe* they're not going after the girls! *What the hell's goin' on?*"

Deverall chose his words carefully trying to console his friend. "Look—if you've forgotten, we are out here in the middle of the blasted desert and the sun has just about done its thing for the day. Now—you know as well as I do, that to go out in the desert in the middle of the night is the same as committing suicide. We have to wait till morning. Also, we can't go alone. There is no way we could find anything out there without the help of the amir. *And*, last but not least—those goons aren't going to kill the girls—not just yet anyway. They came for the bracelet and apparently the princess's anklets. If they were planning on killing the girls they would have done it right then and there and just taken those things along with a wrist and an ankle."

The scruffy pilot removed his hat and ran a thick hand through his slick hair, sympathy thick upon his torrid face. "Look—I know you wanna' get Sweetheart back; and if I had a lady like that, I'd want her back too. And, you may not believe this, but the amir is heart-stricken. You saw—he wept like a baby when Princess Haneefah was killed. And, now Princess Fahimah is gone and injured on top of that. There may be some underlying stink going on beneath all this sand, but I believe that the prince will get it together and get those two back one way or another. Just have a little faith; unless, of course, the commander kills him first, then we have a *real* problem on our hands."

Rasheed fought back wearily, as the last of his energy was slipping away, with his earlier conflicts taking their toll.

"You cannot defeat me, Rasheed!" The sound of splintering wood rang throughout as Rasool thrashed helter-skelter and his plundering blade tore through stall doors like a knife through warm butter. The amir teetered unsteadily upon his feet while his boots scuffled backward along the dusty floor in the attempts to regain his footing. A thunderous crash of steel drove him into a waxing dullness where he was unable to escape; and his sword, suddenly being propelled through the air, landed several feet away. A wave of panic raced through Rasheed's being and his heart pounded to a furious uncontrolled rhythm. The stale air of the stables was thick within his nostrils and he suddenly thought of his father. An image of him as a young boy filled the inner crevice of his mind as he laboriously dodged the commander's relentless blade.

It was the same place—the inner floor of the stables—where the senior amir's revulsion at his son was made known. Rasheed's father, outraged with embarrassment upon discovering him hidden away in the barn from one of his mentors, had had about enough of his son's flagrant meanderings. Finding his son behind a stockpile of bagged grains, he heatedly drug him out to the open floor—a wide enough area to house a half dozen horses and then some.

Carrying two swords, the Amir Nuri unsheathed one and tossed it angrily at his son's feet; then he proceeded to draw the other. Rasheed looked at the sword in confusion, unsure as to his father's wishes.

"Pick it up, Boy!" He snarled.

With small trembling fingers, Rasheed grasped the hilt with two hands, and hoisted the cumbersome weapon, near his size, into the air. "Father…

"Keep quiet, Boy! You have disgraced this family! When we are finished I may even decide to put you to the Rod."

"But, Father," Rasheed's voice quivered in fear, "I just don't…

"Quiet!" His father rushed in a maddened flurry toward him while his robes flowed crisply behind him. Viciously, he sailed through the air and attacked his son. Rasheed, barely blocking his advance, shivered inwardly, while feeling that his father may actually have been trying to kill him. Tears welled in his eyes and he wanted to cry for help—call to his mother—anyone who would save him from a brutal slaying.

"Father….," he begged, "*Please…I am sorry!*" The amir charged again. His blade swung ruthlessly as a look of deviltry was behind his black heartless eyes. "*Father!*"

Rasheed slumped to his quavering knees as the weight of the heavy steel crashed down upon him and drove his shaking body to the dirt-ridden floor, while the only thing between him and a fatal death was the cumbersome sword, which shook violently within his hands. Tears flooded his eyes and ran freely along his flaming cheeks. Drawing his knees to his chest and gasping for a breath, he dropped his blade and sobbed.

His father looked upon him with disgust as he sheathed his blade and picked up the other weapon sheathing it also. "You are truly a disgrace, Rasheed. How can *you* be *my* child, a child of royalty? You will never be a worthy warrior." He smoothed his garments, made his way toward the exit, then paused and turned to his son who sat trembling upon the floor. "Rasheed, you were born to royalty and shall one day command troops—shouldering royalty is a heavy responsibility; so, grow up. Oh, and next time I have to come looking for you, you shall surely face the Rod." The bitterness of his words cast an unendurable burden upon the young boy, while the thought of the rod was cruel. It was a beating with that of like, a dowel, but long and smoothed—hard and unbreakable—with a leather laced handle made to be gripped by a large man.

Your hands would be secured, bound together above your head, while your feet spread, would be shackled by chains to the floor. An overly-eager guard would gladly unleash hell's fury upon you from the swell of your neck to the wrinkle of your ankles, many times inflicting broken bones and in some cases paralysis. His father used it to punish those who committed acts, not quite worthy of death, yet in need of severe punishment. Rasheed and the other children referred to it as the Torture Chamber.

Despondent, the young prince brushed himself off, wiped the remaining tears from his heated cheeks then ran to find his mother, making certain to never hide again.

Rasheed dropped to his knees as he struggled to return to his wakening senses. A look of triumph was on the commander's face as he raised his blade above his head, ready to deliver the final blow.

Suddenly the swish of an arrow was heard as it raced swiftly through the air. A sickening thud followed its resonance as it rapidly bit into flesh. Rasool pitched back then forward as the look of triumph quickly disappeared being replaced with a jarring stare. The feathered shaft, released from the sergeant's bow, protruded haughtily from his folded abdomen, sending blood gushing from the wound. Cursing, Rasool clutched at the arrow as the wound resounded with a ghoulish gurgle.

Rasheed immediately veered sideways as the glinting blade came crashing down, along with Rasool, who slammed headlong onto the floor.

CHAPTER 13

Slipping in and out of a restless slumber, Cherinne's head bobbed in a slow rhythm to the horse's dredging through the vast shadow of blackened sand. Flinching, she dreamt of riding within the golden chariot as its exterior was covered in wicked flames and it ascended toward the darkened sky. A battle ensued, engrossing her within its fury, while she was an all-powerful goddess fighting great beasts which had been produced from the bowels of the earth.

Cherinne was suddenly jolted awake by a firm hand which had wrapped itself tightly around the bracelet; while tiny flecks of color, striving to slip from between the fine cracks of the giant's fingers, quickly subsided into nothingness. Holding her wrist roughly, his grip covered the entirety of the armband.

"No sleeping," he snarled in her ear as he pulled his horse to a stop. "We shall camp here."

Quickly dismounting, he grabbed Cherinne's waist with two hulking hands. Large, broad and expansive fingers overlapped, while their grip was firm and unyielding. Placing her on the ground, her captor stood tall and wide—a mammothed sized man, while his tunic, spread, would be large enough to cover her king-sized bed.

Cherinne, removing her sandals, sunk her feet deep within the cool sand which wriggled its way between her flexing toes. Twisting, she attempted to straighten her back from the long strenuous ride, while a gnawing pain had settled upon her spine and ran just below her buttocks, into the back of her thighs.

Hafiz lifted Fahimah's limp body from his mare and laid her along the sand. Groaning, she painfully rolled to her side and remained still.

Rubbing the raw bite upon his neck, he shoved her with the tip of his boot. "Stupid broad," he sneered contemptuously. Then releasing the binding on his pack, he retrieved a woolen blanket which he tossed haphazardly over her. Then he unraveled one for himself.

Cherinne watched in envy as he grabbed his water pouch and took a big drink, not realizing how thirsty she really was until now.

Rummaging around in his saddlebag, the giant fetched a large water skin. A welcoming squeal was heard as he uncorked the top; while the swill of water, sloshing within the bag, was like music to her ears. Her tongue was thick, pasted to the roof of her mouth, and her throat felt like a clogged drainpipe, making it impossible to swallow or produce a mere drop of spittle.

She looked upon her abductor with pleading eyes, just to acquire the tiniest of sips as he pulled the shroud from over his lips and drank heartily. She could hear the glub of liquid as it made its way toward his stomach, while he observed her through narrowed leering eyes.

Droplets of water ran into the layers of his black shroud and quickly disappeared. And, swiping an arm across his mouth, he licked his heavy lips lavishly as if to tease her for the moment. Cherinne's shoulders slumped with disappointment, as he again, placed the water skin near to his lips. His eyes glinted with sadistic amusement and he lowered the leather bag and sealed it; though, to her amazement, he suddenly tossed it in her direction.

Quickly, she fumbled to release the cork, and, in a thirsting savagery, downed the water in an animalistic passion, licking at the few remaining drops as the water skin quickly ran hollow. The giant yanked the bag from her eager grasp then threw her a roughly stitched blanket whose smell and texture was compared to that of camel skin. She wrinkled her nose and grudgingly accepted it, while he prompted her to a spot just beyond his horse, and with a heavy hand upon her shoulder pressed her to the sand.

Cherinne cowered, uncertain of his motives; and drawing her knees within her arms, she pulled the blanket tight about her chilled body. Scrutinizing his every move, she inched slightly away, as his massive body settled down next to hers.

"Hafiz…" His booming voice cut through the dark thick of silence and startled her. "I'll take first watch while you rest; then, I'll wake you later."

"Alright, but watch this one. She is a real fighter. She is liable to cause more trouble, even though she is injured." He rubbed his neck and sneered, "Damn whore."

"Yes, she is a wild one—the one that wears the anklets of Semus. But this one, who looks to be her double, *bears* the bracelet. *She* is the one that possesses the power—the power to rain down almighty heaven and draw power from the earth." He chuckled deep within his shroud. "But, I do believe she is unaware as to how to utilize that power." Darkness loomed over Cherinne as his huge body leaned over her, blocking the illumination of the brimming moon which seemed close enough to touch. His breath was hot upon her cheek while the odor of sweat and horse filled her senses. Reaching across her legs, he grabbed her wrist and yanked it before him, while the force caused her to veer halfway across his huge lap.

Cherinne recoiled, as he held the bracelet in the light before him, the thought of him being so close making her nauseous.

"This simple girl—she shakes the bracelet as if it is a child's toy. How ridiculous. With all the power of Ra right here at her disposal she is ignorant to its use." He brushed away the strands of hairs that had plummeted forward and lay limp along his thigh; then releasing her arm, he shoved her away in irritation. He continued, "Though it begs to be unleashed as she battles in her sleep. So, wake her if she gets fitful while resting; for I would have to destroy her, and we cannot present her to the Lord Seth as a buzzard's fare—either of them."

The tension deflated like a popped balloon at the knowledge that she and Fahimah shouldn't be killed—not by these two anyway. But, what of this Lord Seth, she thought. She had heard the giant, during his confrontation with Laddor and the amir, mention something of him being a desert god. Who could he be—possibly a foreign leader? And why had she heard his name within her dreams and during the times she had been overcome by the bracelet? *Oh, Laddor,* her heart ached miserably.

Shifting her weight in the chilling sand, she tried to get comfortable and collect her thoughts, while weariness and fatigue were draining her every ounce of energy. Slumping into an Indian style position and pulling the blanket up over her head, like a makeshift tent, she sought to block out the world around her.

"*No!*" The giant suddenly jerked the cover from her head. "I must see you...and the bracelet!" Anger appeared in the dark of night from behind his shroud, rushing at her in a heated cloud of breath. Seizing a fistful of blanket and hair, he roughly yanked her toward him. Cherinne lurched forward while his blistering words were sneered close to her ear, "Don't even try to deceive me."

Thrusting his hand within her blanket and grabbing at the armband, he roughly grazed the inner flesh of her thigh. Fear raced throughout her body, choking at her throat as a wave of alarm weakened her stomach and she panicked.

"*No!*" She cried out in alarm as she scurried from within his grasp and crawled headlong out into the oppressing vastness. Sand sprayed in a gritty fountain, while terror marked any and all sense or reasoning she may have possessed. Her heart beat wildly, and her breaths were measured and deep as she scrambled to her feet and ran. The sand labored against her, while she had no idea where she was going, or in what direction.

Bolting to his feet, the giant moved quickly, as his large brawn drove him swiftly through the sand compared to that of a roaring freight train. Tears flared in Cherinne's eyes as she stumbled blindly along the arid land being steered by the light of the liquid moon.

"*Damn you! Get back here!*" The giant's booming voice thundered just steps behind her while his lengthy strides brought him within arms length of her flowing garments. He grabbed the whipping flaps of her tunic and brusquely plucked her from the sand. Sailing backward, her slender body careened through the moonlight sky spraying sand over them both, as she landed atop the giant, who in misjudging his footing, had toppled backward to the ground. Rapidly, he wrapped his massive arms around her in a vice-like grip and held her firmly to his rock-hard chest. Wrestling with her briefly and grabbing at the bracelet, he rolled her to the earth.

"*No!*" She seethed through clenched teeth. "*No!*" Cherinne thrashed about in a raving panic—the image of Fahimah fighting her abductor fresh in her mind.

Twisting, the giant landed atop her, sending her breath away in a spastic gasp. His monstrous weight crushed her frail body, as he pinned her arms and legs beneath him, making her all but paralyzed to movement. Grabbing her shoulders, he pushed her deep within the grit, while she strained to avert his wrathful gaze of yellowing eyes. Gusts of breaths panted through his shroud and Cherinne trembled uncontrollably in fear of what he might do.

Her thoughts turned to Laddor again—the times they had playfully wrestled and he'd gently pinned her to the carpeted floor. Desperately fighting his manly urges, he'd kiss her softly, then, disappointedly, let her up. Tears streamed her cheeks and she hopelessly called out his name.

"*Cherry?*" Laddor whispered her name into the flickering light of his oil lamp as he stood erect and strained to listen.

Huge piles of stone and concrete lay in a defeated heap upon the sandy dunes. Draperies, books, computer parts, clothing, any and everything from the amir's office all lay in heaps of dust, dirt, and sand. Threatening shards of paned glass protruded haughtily from the ruins, daring anyone to taste of their sharp edges. While exquisite pieces of furniture, normally cared for and polished, were crushed beneath the weighted mosaic tiled floors, no longer holding the luster of varnished cherry, but the splinters of firewood. Two of the crystalline chandeliers had broken loose of their chain mounts and had crashed forcefully to the floor, exploding into a billion stars of scintillating light and covering everything in glass.

Deverall made his way, toward his distraught friend, through the illuminating dusty dark and mass of rubble. "Whadya' say, Red?"

"Cherry—I could have sworn I heard her calling to me." His shoulders deflated with a warranted sigh. "I miss her, Deverall, and I fear something terribles gonna' happen." He cast his eyes to the ground—the sting of tears threatened to surface, but he refused to allow it.

Deverall laid a hand to Laddor's weary shoulder. "I know; and the amir misses the princess. He said that we're leaving just before daybreak, but we have to find that earring. He said it had been the commander's; and it doesn't help that we're searching in the dark and a quarter of the damn palace has crumbled to the ground." The pilot tossed a leather bound book to the heap of rubble and shoved a large filing-cabinet to the side. It creaked loudly, as he pushed it out-of-the-way and then clanged noisily as it banged against a stone pile. Reaching around, he grabbed at a handle of a desk drawer that lay broken and twisted beneath a large chunk of the ceiling.

His voice abruptly broke the deafening silence, "Boy, the amir sure was happy to find all the girls, or rather his wives, safe, along with the servants. Apparently, the sections of the palace that are the worst are: his office, the guest area and the commander's quarters. Damn, that big sonofabitch sure did some damage."

"Yeah, that's what I'm afraid of," Laddor replied, scaling one of the huge chunks of granite. Standing atop it, he peered out into the darkness and whispered, "Where are you, Cherry?" Then as anger, wrath, loneliness, and fear washed over him like a chilled wind on a winter's day; he shouted, "*Cherinne Havenstrit…. I'm coming for you!*" His voice echoed for a moment then was swallowed by silence.

"Hey, Red, besides you being a sissy an' all—I always wondered why you didn't just marry that girl. You two seem suited to each other and she does have a *great rack*. Why haven't you just tied the knot?"

Laddor's cheeks peaked crimson then his face knitted into a serious crinkle; he thought about the answer. "*Well,* I guess one reason was because Cherry always seemed to have goals—like becoming a well-established attorney. She's supposed to go back to school this fall and *I* certainly couldn't interfere with that. *Plus….*" he sighed, "I'm just not good enough for her; she deserves much better than me. And, besides, Reynolds hates me and he's kinda' like a father to her." He jumped down, his lantern swinging, cast eerie shadows before him; and, watching the light in a melancholy state he then continued.

"Cherry's special, Deverall. When I first met her, I was in the middle of high-tailing it from a couple of goons who were out for blood. A job I had taken had gone sour *real* quick and the situation was about to get worse. I was choking in the swell of uselessness. Well, she appeared outta' nowhere; and I'll tell ya', when I first saw her, it was like taking my first breath of fresh air. I ran to her, not caring about anything but escaping the fog of darkness I was surrounded in, to breathe of her wholesome light."

Settling himself upon an overturned wastebasket, he wiped a hand across the leg of his dirt-ridden jeans. "She was like this awe-inspiring angel coming to rescue me; and she did—reluctantly. She plucked me right from bad into good—hating the feat, as she unknowingly accomplished it."

A confused look furrowed Deverall's thick brows.

Laddor smiled half-heartedly, "Yeah, she hated me at first, even tried to Mace me; it was kinda' funny, now that I look back on it." He then chuckled low. "She took me back to that big mansion of her father's and worked me like a dog: cleanin' the pool, mowin' the lawn, cleanin' her car, all sorts of stuff. But, I loved her every minute—more than I could ever imagine lovin' anyone or anything in my life." Positioning the lantern within the crook of a broken shelf and a huge piece of mosaic flooring, he blew warm air into his cupped hands. Then reaching into his jacket pocket, he removed a small hand-carved wooden box.

Opening the lid, he gently took the small ocarina from the box and placed it to his lips. The soft melody wafted airily into the dark and reached through to the last crevice of night. Pausing, he then stated, "Ya' know, my mother gave me this flute when I was a child and I've carried it with me ever since. Cherinne has given me *everything* and I have given her nothing—nothing but grief. All I wanted to do was have her live large— larger than anything her father would have given her, except an empty house and an empty heart. But, instead, I gave her this." He waved his arm across the pile of destruction. "Why in God's name would she want to marry someone like me?"

The pilot seated himself on the arm of a couch which was snapped completely in half. A huge chunk of stone was wedged into its cushions. He studied his friend, "Well, Red, I think you may have already answered your own question. From what you say, you love her—really love her; and from what I've seen the last few days, she really loves you too."

Deverall glanced around at the dismantled ruin. "So, this is the amir's office or possibly Commander Rasool's quarters. Man, *what a mess!*" He released a low whistle. "It's gonna' take *forever* to clean this up. And we're supposed to be looking for an *earring?*"

"Yeah, that's what Rasheed said—an earring. Oh, and a journal of some sort. I think I saw it lying on his desk when we were attacked. Something tells me they have to do with the jewels I heisted from the amir."

"*Hey,*" the pilot grinned, "I think I just tossed a journal a few minutes ago. There are so many books scattered everywhere that I just wasn't thinking."

Leaping to his feet, Deverall shoved debris to the side, searching for the discarded book, while Laddor pocketed his flute and helped. The two men tore frantically through the rubble, like garbage routers hungering for a long over-due meal.

"I found it!" Laddor held the book up as he crawled out from beneath the other half of the sofa. Using the tail of his shirt, he brushed away the dust and flecks of glass from the amir's well kept secrets. With an itching nerve, Laddor turned the first page and skimmed through the jotted notes, as Deverall held his lantern steady to make out the wording on the pages. "*Ahh! Damn! It's in Arabic!* I can't read *this crap!*" Hope of discovering a way to help Cherinne quickly disappeared like catching clouds that drifted about in the wind.

Laddor angrily kicked the defenseless couch which silently took the brunt of his frustration. "Here," he tossed the book to Deverall who, in thumbing through the ledger, refused to give up the search.

"Wait a minute, Red. Look at this," he pointed a thick finger at sketches of ancient hieroglyphics inked upon the sheets. "*Look! It's sweetheart's bracelet!*"

"What?" Laddor stammered as he turned back, curiosity peaking his interest.

Deverall scanned the page, unable to decipher any of the entries. "Look," he turned the pages while gibbering with excitement as his heart raced with enthusiasm. "*There are two of 'em! Two females!* And, they both look like your Cherinne—*Cherinne Havenstrit! And, look!* The one that's wearin' the bracelet is ridin' in a chariot. She's holding the bracelet out and using it—it looks like—as a weapon; and the rays from the bracelet are shooting upon these warriors. *Look!*"

Laddor grabbed the edge of the sofa as his legs immediately grew weak. "*What?*" He squawked as his eyes rushed in a wave over the pages.

"And, look at this haul!" Flipping the page, the eager pilot pointed to another sketch of jewels, piled high as the amir and broad as the broken couch he leaned upon. He held the lantern high and looked disbelievingly into his friend's face. "This *isn't* what you stole?" he breathed.

"Yeah," Laddor's cheeks flushed as he croaked the reply.

The pilot's face broadened in a smile of admiration and amazement. "*Holy shit! You,* stole *this?*" His laugh was long and hearty as tears spilled down his full cheeks. "Well…"he wiped his eyes dry "…you've just moved up a notch in *my* book. *Damn man!* I'da never thought you'da had it in ya'." Slapping Laddor on the back, he then bowed and tipped his hat.

"Well," Laddor took the book, "don't go rollin'out the red carpet yet. Those jewels have cost not only me, but Cherinne, the amir, his princesses, you, and a whole lot of others more trouble than they're worth. If I had my choice, I'd give them back in an instant. I should've figured the whole thing was too easy; or possibly even a set-up." Grabbing his lantern and heading toward another mountain of destruction, he said, "Come on—I have some questions to ask Mr. Rasheed."

The burdensome weight of the world lay heavy upon Rasheed's shoulders, while the blood of both friend and foe stained the front of his white uniform. The harsh words of his commanding officer—an ugly possibility—were followed by the cold-hearted truth and difficult to swallow—like forcing down bile that rose from within. The cutting memories reached deep, bringing about old wounds that, through time, were able to remain somewhat repressed, but had currently blossomed into an aching torment.

Rasheed stood alone beneath the sparkle of the starry sky. In an all-knowing glow, the full moon shone down upon his miniscule portion of Egypt, which now lay in ruin—not only in structure, but in bodily vestige and emotional ruin also. He thought of Haneefah—her soul no longer amongst the living—drifting as a wispy smoke ring, as it curled its way up toward Allah in Heaven; while her wise words, so gentle and kind, would never be heard again.

He surveyed the damage, which would take weeks of clean-up and months, possibly even years, of rebuilding; and thought of the pride his father and grandfather had in the history and superstructure of the regime. The erecting of the main palace had taken near ten years and the remaining, surrounding buildings and structures, another five. It was a magnificent feat, accomplished by few, but now utilized by many.

Being a descendant of royal blood and very astute, Rasheed's grandfather had, many ages ago, made a pact with his blood relative, then, the ruler of Egypt. The pact had guaranteed sanction for the beginning construction and immunity of his grandfather's domain, in exchange for the aide of his loyalist's services to the Khedive during times of war.

Funding for the reconstruction would be of little concern, for the Tarun Regime flourished with ample funds from the investments of the present *and* previous generations, and needed not be a stumbling block now.

"Grandfather, you and Father always were bastards," Rasheed quietly spoke into the night. "I can just imagine your feelings of me now. Anything Mother did was understandable, being controlled by you two vultures; but I don't believe she had anything to do with the Princess Fahimah." His thoughts drifted to the blonde locks and the alabaster skin of his faraway maiden; and how she was now in the hands of an enemy without her injuries completely healed. "Fahimah, please do not give up hope. For, I shall search to the ends of the earth for you and return you home where you belong."

Rasheed recalled the sneering words Rasool had spewed at him during their confrontation in the stables; and Rasool's last words to him as his men bound and shackled the commander after plucking the arrow from his innards. Amazingly, the dastardly leader had lived; though his wound would need ample time to heal, and his days as commanding officer had come to an end.

A group of combatants followed by the young boy, Ib, sifted their way through the rubble, making their way toward the amir. "Your Highness," Sergeant Lateef, respectfully saluted, "the men and I have been unable to locate the trinket that you ask of. We have searched the ruins which we believe to be the commander Rasool's former quarters.

Briefly thinking, the Prince gazed out over the dust of the flowing dunes which rose and fell below the gleaming silver globe of the moon. Rasool, where have you put your treasure?

"Sergeant Lateef, bring your men and follow me. Oh, and by the way…" He turned to face the sergeant, "…It is no longer *Commander* Rasool. He has been stripped of his title. *You*," the prince pointed a firm finger at the young officer, "are now the commander. Congratulations on your new title." Rasheed quickly turned and headed in the direction of the stables.

Sergeant Lateef grinned at the genuine unforeseen act with a sense of gratitude. "Thank you, Your Highness. Thank you," He then turned to his men, "Omar, Maraat, Mahir—come with me."

"Commander Lateef!" Ib sprinted after the soldiers. "May I come with you, Sir?" he appealed through pleading black eyes. "Please, Sir—I wish to serve the amir."

"Ib!" the prince hollered over his shoulder! "Come, boy! You shall be my eyes and ears."

The young lad excitedly rushed to the amir's side. "Yes, Your Grace— I am at your service," he bowed generously as the sergeant nodded his head with certainty that *this* was the man to follow and *not* his former commander.

Rasool lay within one of the cubicles, gagged and shackled. And, though he had committed the worst form of insubordination, the prince could not find it in himself to destroy a man who had previously been so loyal to his father. He had even requested the services of a regime doctor to tend to the fallen man's wounds. Rasheed cursed himself for his weakness; knowing that though his father regarded the retired commander as a son, he would still have—without falter—destroyed him on the spot.

Ib hurriedly scurried about the barn to light the several lanterns in the section where Rasool was being detained. With a squeal of the hinges, Ib then swung the stall door open to reveal Rasool, his head slumped to his chest, restrained by shackles and chains. The restraints, normally used for unruly stallions during a mare's time of heat, now held a man with intentions worse than any stud.

Rasool slowly raised his head as the devil's glare ragingly drove heated daggers deep within the prince's chest; Rasheed attempted to avoid his deadly gaze.

"So, Rasheed—you have come back to face the truth," he sneered viciously.

"*Quiet! You insolent fool!*" Commander Lateef entered the cubicle and shouted, shoving Rasool with the toe of his black boot. "This is *The Amir* you disrespect! Lower your eyes and choose your words wisely!"

"*Ahh*—so, Lateef, you are now the new servant to his Highness's humiliating disaccorded shortcomings. Congratulations on your newfound placement; it suits you," Rasool remarked with contempt.

Lateef swiftly raised an angered hand to strike the belligerent officer.

"*No!*" The prince quickly blocked the strike. "Just have your men search his person for the jewel."

"*What?*" Rasool's eyes darted in disbelief from the prince's then to the others. "You have come to take *my* jewel? It is *mine!* I bore blood for that jewel; which I even dug from the earth with my own two hands!"

"I need the map it contains, Rasool," Rasheed maintained, as the soldiers barred his arms from movement and thoroughly searched his uniform pockets. Rasool growled angrily and cursed them all.

Maraat wriggled the velvet satchel out from within the outraged man's breast pocket. "Your Highness, would this be it?"

Rasheed carefully took the small cloth bag and unloosened the drawstring cord. And, turning it over, he emptied its contents into his hand. A beautifully polished golden pearl earring tumbled from inside onto his palm. "Yes, this is it."

Ib watched with wide wondering eyes, curious as to how the earring would aide them in the pursuit of finding the princess.

The prince held the earring up to a lantern and peered inside at the teeniest of compasses encased in the lower tier which would have only been seen by a trained eye. The prince quickly turned and glanced at the three men and the boy, wondering as to who should be chosen to wear it, while the ladies all rested peacefully within their chambers, distraught by the activities of the day. So, he wished not to disturb them.

Thinking back to his meeting with the Americans, as they shook in the guest area, Rasheed remembered the smallest of diamond earrings which had adorned the pilot's ear, *and* his offer to be of service.

"Commander Lateef, take your men and find Mr. Deverall. He may be of assistance to us."

"Red," Deverall panted to keep pace with his riled friend's lengthy strides as he searched for the Amir within several rooms of rubble. Laddor's flaming locks of auburn licked at his jacket while he moved quickly through the darkness lit only by his lantern. Then, he proceeded into those rooms which were filled with wreckage and ruin and completely consumed by blackness.

"What do you think all this means—those pictures in the book of Cherinne and Princess Fahimah?"

"I don't know. But, I intend to find your friend, the amir, and get a few things answered—even if I have to beat it outta' him."

"Ya' know, Red, one of these times the prince is liable to just have his men take ya' out back and remove that cherry-colored top of yours." Deverall took a deep breath. "He seems to be a ruler who believes in not asking his men to do anything he wouldn't do, kinda' like Alexander the Great. But I do believe he has his limits, and *you, I believe*, have pushed him to it. What's gotten into you?"

Laddor stopped short and the pilot nearly plowed into his friend. Abruptly turning to face the out-of-breath man, Laddor stated, "Look…" his face tighted in a scowl as every vein popped in a helter-skelter pattern upon his neck and ran into the rigidness of his shoulders, "I have put Cherinne in danger. And, I will exhaust every avenue there is to get her back safely. So, if that means I have to fight with the amir, then so be it. If he wants, he can kill me later; but, right now, she is more important than anything he could ever do to me."

Laddor whipped around to find the young Lateef, followed by three guards, glaring malevolently into his face. A staring contest suddenly ensued.

"*Ija ga!*" The commander asserted, motioning them to follow him toward the stables. "*Ija ga!*"

"Hey, I think he wants us to follow 'em." Deverall made an attempt at communicating by placing an imaginary crown on his head and repeating, "Amir, Amir?"

Pleased, Lateef nodded his head in acknowledgement.

"Come on, Red! He knows where the amir is." The pilot hastened along behind the commander and his men who disappeared into the darkness.

As they made their way toward the stables, the group of men, unfortunately, had caught the tail-end of the heated conversation raging between the amir and the chained ex-commander.

A bark of threats, sounding out in the Egyptian tongue, blasted from the cantankerous Rasool and drifted from inside the barn. Lateef held his gaze steady before him, while his men glanced uncomfortably at one another then at the two American's who were unable to decipher the content.

"*Rasheed*," Rasool snarled as he struggled in his bonds, "She doesn't deserve those jewels! They will give her the power to rule all of Egypt! And she isn't even Egyptian—she's an American! You dishonor Allah and all that the Muslim faith stands for! *RASHEED!!!*"

"*Ib! Bind his mouth!*" The prince hollered, turning to see the two Americans enter the stables as the others remained just outside the entrance. Laddor and Deverall's eyes swept the area ingesting the whole of the situation with surprised disbelief. Exchanging a glance, they then approached the amir who was engrossed in meticulously studying the pearl earring.

Gathering some nearby rags, used for saddle soaping the riding gear, Ib rushed to quiet the annoying Egyptian. Rasool thrashed about; and, releasing a series of skin-crawling hisses in the direction of the boy, he filled the barn with the pant of bombastic threats and the rigorous echoes of rattling chains.

Ib warily approached him and hastily shoved the rags within his gaping mouth. Suddenly, he screamed out as Rasool, exposing teeth, had clamped down and caught flesh. Blood seeped from his trembling hand as he quickly drew back and fought the tears that filled his eyes. Swiping his sleeve across his face, he turned to the amir.

"Hey! That wasn't very nice! You horse's ass!" Deverall yelled. Lateef and his men rapidly appeared as the amir, swiftly turning and briefly diverting his attention from the jewel, crossed the room and struck the ex-commander with a harsh blow. Blood spurted from a vessel within Rasool's throbbing nose, temporarily bringing his yammerings to a halt. Avoiding teeth and the flow of blood, Ib hastily stuffed Rasool's mouth with rag, being careful not to lose any fingers in the process.

Returning to his examination of the earbob, the prince again gazed fixedly upon the compass, which he had not seen since observing it and its mate so long ago.

"So, whatcha' got there, that seems to have you so enthralled?" Deverall peered over the amir's shoulder trying to catch a glimpse of the shimmering jewel.

Rasheed held the delicate earring up between two fingers. It shimmered beneath that of the lantern's flickering flame as the nine gazed at the glistening pearls in wonder. "So, Mr. Zeandre—you have this one's mate," he stated matter-of-factly. "You *do realize* that means we only have half a map."

"I'm not sure I follow you, Amir. What do you mean only half a map?" Laddor peered into the hues of color wisping through the white of the smallest pearl and his eyes suddenly grew to the size of a child's fist. "*Oh, my God,*" he breathed, as he saw the compass. "This is a map…? There's a compass in there!" He then turned to Rasheed, "Will it find the girls?"

"We certainly hope so. Fahimah had experimented, to some extent, with each of the jewels and I believe this is one that will lead us to the bracelet."

A congratulatory slap landed the amir's back, as Deverall laughed aloud. "*Holy shit, Saheeb!* You're just full of surprises!"

"Well, Mr. Busher Deverall—that's where *you* come in."

CHAPTER 14

Painfully, Cherinne lay beneath the giant, while her breath copped, came in short sporadic gasps, causing her head to swoon. She opened her eyes to a blast of dull-ache, racing as electric current from the back of her head to the heels of her feet, as she stared into the black of Nagid's clothing at the curvature of his collarbone. With each movement of the giant's massive structure, the sand beneath Cherinne's crushed body molded to her petite form, making it impossible for her to move or breathe.

Arching his back, he placed his weight on two hands; Cherinne lurched forward, grasping at a full breath of air. Then laying her head back to the grainy earth, she breathed deep. Shifting his weight and digging his boots deep within the sand, he restrained her with just his hulking mass, as he proceeded to press his groin painfully against her, bringing about a sting of tears. Angrily, he grabbed a mat of blonde hair and breathed into her face, "I told you *not* to deceive me!"

Fury, seeping from within the dark shroud, blazed as hatred and caused her to shudder; while her chest rose and fell erratically, with the certainty she was in the presence of pure unadulterated malevolence. The giant slammed her head to the sand, sending a milky way of stars exploding throughout her skull, which felt as if it had cracked.

She stammered in painful defense, through dry trembling lips, "I...wasn't..."

"*Shut up! You cursed wench!*" His shout reverberated close to her ear bringing with it a barrage of throbs aiming to burst her eardrum, while a waterway of tears clouded her vision, making the giant appear as liquid night. "I warned you!" He snarled through curled lips as he, maneuvering his legs, pried open her tightly clenched thighs and settled himself roughly between them. He stared hard into her face with eyes that had seen death a thousand fold—that looked upon women as objects to be brutally used and discarded, if not reverent and obedient. The blood of his enemy was imbedded deep within his skin and his pores reeked of their deceased corpes. Placing his lips just below her ear, his words were like that of poison.

"Do you have any idea how long it has been since I have had a woman?" The threat whispered into her neck, warranted her to vomit.

Suddenly her arms broke free to movement and slipped from beneath him, allowing her to strike out with all her afforded might. Her adrenaline soared, causing the blood to pound in her head and her heart to beat uncontrollably as she endeavored to fight him off.

"*NO!!!*" Cherinne screamed through horror-stricken tears. "*Noooo!!*" With every effort, she fought to get away.

The giant wrestled with her spindly arms that flailed about in a futile effort to stave him off. And, grabbing her wrists, he pinned the thrashing limbs, roughly grinding them into the dusty earth; while her fruitless efforts had caused her more grief, where she had gained no ground. "*Hold still!*" he shouted.

Cherinne turned her head, looking to anything but the dark of his face and the eyes of someone who was about to destroy her. "*Laddor!*" The croak escaped her parched throat while she trembled violently and her head spun. She gazed, through a blur of tears, toward the starless sky, while the moon watched in mockery the show below, seeming to draw upon it with pleasure. Mere flecks of colored light slipped from between the giant's fingers, as the bracelet slowly hummed upon Cherinne's skin; something she hadn't even noticed.

In a savage haste, the giant tore at the layers of tunic covering the delicate regions of her body; while his breathing came in shallow spurts of anticipation and he perspired in anxiety. Reaching his huge hand within the softness of her thighs, he roughly clawed at Cherinne in a heated state of frenzy. His calloused grip, a product produced through years of yielding a sword, scraped roughly against her flesh; while, with probing broad fingers, he searched out the purity of her body.

Cherinne's world plunged into a dark despondent grave, the only urge, to vomit. Unable to stave off the giant's cruel animalistic advance, she began to slowly whisper an unknown Egyptian prayer. It spilled as cool water from her dry cracked lips; light as angel wings, it ascended in a swirling mist toward the heavens, seeking for a miracle.

The giant's brutal exploration of Cherinne's open thighs was a harsh devourer of his attentiveness to the bracelet's slow coming birth. The cruel look of excitement abated slightly with the spewing of the milk and honey words, which spoke to him softly near his ear, and momentarily lulled his brutish behavior. His breath which was an assemblage of heated gasps upon her neck, faintly slowed and he buried his head within her hair. And, holding her securely with one hulking arm, he worked to loosen his throbbing self with the other.

Cherinne abruptly gasped as the power of the bracelet suddenly came alive. Ripping her from beneath the giant's startled grasp, it sent her body rushing headlong through a spraying fountain of sand, away from the giant, and racing toward freedom. She was quickly yanked skyward sending the plummeting granules of sand falling like rainwater back to the earth; the sound resounded within her ears.

"Oh no," she groaned in a tumult of added confusion, while she was grateful just to be released of the giant's clutches. Her aching body, shooting partially clothed into the moonlit night, somersaulted uncontrollably in a dizzying thrust, nearly causing her to heave. Ancient Egyptian spewed forth from her thirsty lips and the bracelet quickly responded by blasting away with a host of multi-colored rays.

Leaping to his feet, the giant angrily rushed along the sand, while hollering to Hafiz, "*MMOOVVEE!!!*" With several lengthy strides, he reached the horses, grasped their reins and steered them rapidly away from the blast of deadly rays.

Hafiz had been lying beneath the wool of his blanket observing with strained eyes, the attack his superior was inflicting upon the American girl. He watched from a distance with an irrepressible animalistic envy as he listened excitedly to the hiccoughing sobs of the female who fought relentlessly to keep her purity.

Adjusting himself, he shifted restlessly in the cool sand, thinking of the other blonde who lay unconscious just arm's length away. Eagerly, he licked his lips, a swarm of devilish ideas cursing through his mind, while the thought of invading an unconscious woman was unmoving. If he was going to take her, it was going to be sinfully wicked, especially if she liked biting. He would be more than pleased to repay her for the blood she had drawn upon his neck, with the notion of knocking her teeth out afterward. But, the proposal of looking after a woman with only gums turned his stomach cold.

Lumbering to his feet, he grabbed the water flask hanging from the binds of his saddle. He took a big swig in an attempt to cool the heat rising within his loins. "Worthless bitches," Hafiz snorted with another drink. "Only good for one thing."

He continued to observe from his horse, while the ravaging giant tore at the young girl's silky garments. Shimmers of white skin flashed before Hafiz's hungry gaze, accompanying the sound of whimpering cries which escalated his yearning for immediate gratification.

Moving closer to the skirmish, he had hoped to possibly share in some of the spoils; of course, after his superior, Nagid, had satisfied his enormous appetite completely. However, spying the glimmer of light slipping through the giant's fingers, he knew the bracelet had been provoked.

"*Nagid!*" He shouted just as Cherinne was ripped from beneath the giant's massive body and flung into the night sky. Thinking more, because of the surge between his legs, than his duty to the God Seth, Hafiz turned from the horses and grabbed the other girl, high-tailing it away from the bracelet's reach as Nagid charged in his direction.

The dry, thirsty land burst into flashing remnants of rainbow colored light; though their scintillating brilliance was a warped deception. In a mad frenzy, the horses, breaking free of the giant, scattered in an attempt to clear themselves of a fatal hit.

Cherinne battled the entity within herself, trying to control the tumultuous fit her body was enduring. Recalling the amir's struggle with the bracelet, while he had had her upon his horse, his shouted words, 'Control the bracelet!' still rang within her ears.

Dizzy—to the point of upchucking—she grabbed the armband with her left hand. It fought viciously to break free of her grasp, but, she was persistent. She shouted out words of an ancient language, commanding the bracelet to heed to her authority, while the power of the mystical armband surged throughout her veins. Determined to obtain control, she held her arm taut as the beams of light blasted about angrily, searing holes within the chilled sand below her and aiming for the giant.

"Hafiz! Use your crossbow! Shoot her down!" Nagid ferociously bellowed. The black tails of his robe licked the air in a flurry behind him as he dodged the helter-skelter of deadly rays. "*Shoot her!*"

Leaving Fahimah, Hafiz quickly ran down his horse where he snatched his crossbow and without hesitation aimed. The arrow ripped from the bowstring soaring speedily toward Cherinne; but her body suddenly somersaulted, steering clear of the thick shaft.

"*Oh my God!*" Cherinne gasped in the realization that the arrow was meant for her and that there were more where that came from.

Hafiz reloaded. Eyeing the girl within his sights he lavishly licked his lips; as the sight of her was exhilarating. Her silken garments, shredded to mere rags, revealed her lovely milky-white skin which was being presented before the entire desert world. And right now, that world was just him and her. The American female's beauty mirrored the image of a goddess as her long golden hair cascaded in shimmers before the moon and her arched figure screamed of magnificence. Hafiz wiped the sweat of his palms along his tunic, while a bead of perspiration traced his brow. Setting his sights again and attempting to concentrate on the task at hand, he outlined the curvature of her body with the aim of his weapon.

"*Shoot! You fool!*"

Suddenly, the light of the bracelet dissipated, as if swallowed by the night, and Cherinne plummeted with a harsh thud upon the sandy surface. Hafiz watched through his sights, as Nagid stormed feverishly across the terrain.

While the whole of the regime rested in a warranted slumber, an uneasy stirring lay within its core. Darkened shadows descended as autumn leaves upon the quiet stable, where the buzzing of anticipation mingled with the agonizing dilemma within its thickset walls. The spying creatures of Nephthys, the LaHm, listened intently to the whispers drifting from inside; the anxious plans being devised by the amir, whose voice of authority etched itself upon their immortal minds. Molding their forms to an oozing thick tar, they slivered along the wooden timbers, silently absorbing information through the translucent membrane of their beings—pertinent information to be delivered to their supreme being, Goddess Nephthys.

"Are you ready, Mr. Deverall?" The amir grinned reassuredly as he handed the pilot the pearl earring. "Now, you'll have to remove your shirt; for the map will be ingested as ink within your skin. Now, there's no need to worry; for, there will be no permanent marking or scarring, and from what the Princess Fahimah has told me it is *quite exhilarating*. She was able to make use of both earrings at the time, so the result was phenomenal."

Rasheed brought to mind the day she had first tested the pearl bobs. Having one of the guards take the Semus Bracelet and place it in any location he desired—within the regime of course—while Fahimah, with the aide of the earrings, had then hunted it.

He recalled the look of excitement she had displayed, as the drawings began to inch their way beneath her sheer garment. It was as if a master cartographer had been engraving the etchings within her ivory white skin, along every angle and curve of her front. His feathered quill, skillfully tracing her lovely shape, produced a map, which burst to life upon her flesh. Anxiously, she had removed the silken garment of clothing, following the markings of black ink from her neck to the tips of her fingers and along her torso down to her toes. A flickering twinkle entered her eyes, as she had sighed in wondrous delight, while spreading her arms wide and joyously twirling about the amir's chamber. He had applauded in encouragement.

"Amir? Hey, are you alright?" Deverall asked, removing his shirt and seating himself upon a low-set wooden stool. "You seem to be lost in thought."

Rasheed looked to his new-found American friend—a slight bit shabby, and a little more, than rough around the edges—but, still a friend. He glanced at the other four, believing them to be trustworthy. They watched in anticipation, eagerly awaiting a result, while Omar and Mahir had been directed to stand watch just outside the stable doors. And, though he had come to blows with the wiry red-head American on numerous occasions, he realized his haphazard actions were all for the love of a girl—the same love he himself had for his Fahimah.

"…Yes, Mr. Deverall—that thought is of my lovely princess."

Grinning broadly, the pilot stated, "Can't see as I blame ya' there. So, how's bout we get this party started." Removing his diamond stud earring, he dropped it into the side pocket of his Bermudas then slipped the golden pearl jewel into his ear. A fane smile crossed his lips mixing with bother lines upon his forehead. "*Well?*" He briefly scanned the hair patch upon his chest and puffed stomach with concern. His shoulders slumped in disappointment. He murmured, "nothin'."

"Hey, I think I see something, Sire!" Ib pointed to the pilot's gaping navel with six sets of eyes moving nearer to Deverall's bulge.

Laddor's expression quickly molded into a perturbed glower, as the boy was pointing to an over-sized clump of lint. Laddor rolled his exhausted azure eyes; his patience running thin. "Damn, Deverall! Couldn't you've at least dug that shag outta' *there* before you started this? Hell, we could've been lookin' for a carpet outlet!"

Pink flushed the pilot's neck to his broad cheeks. "Uh, sorry 'bout that Chief." The scruffy pilot dug within the large eye and with plump fingers removed the fuzz.

"Shaf! Shaf!" Maraat screeched as he pointed an excited finger and moved closer with his lantern. Anticipation was thick enough to cut as all those in the room held their breath.

Spidery veins of bleeding black ink gradually appeared from within the uncluttered navel and slowly crawled along Deverall's puckered skin. Broadening along his heavy torso, they climbed effortlessly along his hair-ridden chest, as if being guided by an experienced hand. Then, they proceeded to snake their way south. A Cheshire-cat grin forced itself upon his lips, and again his face flushed pink—yet brighter this time—as the lines disappeared within his shorts.

He sheepishly blinked and shifted in his seat as his chilled skin flared with warmth. "I think it stopped." Rising from the stool, he raised his bulky arms and gave his front the once-over. "So, how do I look?"

"*Well...*" Rasheed hesitated, rubbing the back of his neck with a slightly apologetic grimace, "I do believe the Princess Fahimah may have added just a touch of natural beauty to it. But, then again, she could do that to dirt."

"Deverall, this isn't a damn beauty contest!" Laddor snapped; his words were harsher than meant. His gaze rapidly dropped to the floor, followed by silence.

A full tense minute passed, while in the distance a horse whinnied, and the breathing and shifting of nervous feet, along with blood, pounded heavily within Laddor's ears.

"I'm sorry," the whispered apology ascended from amid the locks of red hair.

With a sympathetic glimpse, the pilot slapped the weary red-head on the shoulder, "Oh, its cool." Deverall then peeked into his shorts and his shaggy brows shifted unevenly. He chuckled. "Just wait'ill I take my pants off and ya' see this!"

"Your Highness," Commander Lateef requested the amir's personal attention. Rasheed motioned him to the side away from the hub of on-lookers.

"Yes, Commander...what is it"

"My apologies Sire for interrupting your lordship, but my men have been awaiting my orders, and daybreak is merely four hours away. I do believe that if we intend on leaving at first light, they will need to rest and prepare the horses, including provisions for our journey. Would you not agree, Your Highness?"

"Why yes, Commander—that would be a wise decision. My mind has been preoccupied with other matters, and I had not thought of the forces—normally that duty would have been overseen by Rasool." The prince ran a hand through his tousled hair. "Please exert your authority, Commander Lateef, and focus your attention on the needs of the men. We will require every man and horse battle-ready by first-light."

Lateef bowed his head with a tap to his forehead. "Yes, Your

Highness—my sincere apologies to you for my lack of discretion. I will see to it, to better serve Your Excellency." He promptly turned and hastened into the looming dark to assemble the small army.

Within arms reach of the amir, the LaHm slithered quietly and coiled themselves about the timber outcropping. Reaching from within the dark shadows, their slimy heads were just a whisper from the prince's ear. One by one they slowly opened their slitted eyes and blinked in the low flicker of a nearby lantern. Their slanted narrow irises, sensitive to any light, dripped secretion excessively, due to their having been molded and contained in darkness the entirety of their immortal lives.

Viewing the outlying destruction of the western wing—the void where grandeur structures had previously encased the whole of his office and chambers, fourteen restrooms, three enormous rooms for counsel and Rasool's headquarters and lodgings—Rasheed suddenly had fatigue sitting heavily upon him. With a warranted deep sigh, he closed his eyes briefly and wrinkled his nose at an offensive odor drifting nearby. Then, mustering the energy, he returned to the others and the map—unaware he was being watched.

CHAPTER 15

The wheezing puffs of breath and sieve of sand spewing from beneath the giant's boots were the single sounds heard, as his movement toward Cherinne was made in a blistering fury. Shaking her head, to eliminate the haze of cobwebs, she helplessly watched as he charged in her direction.

"*YOU!!!*" blasted from the belly of the raging giant; his word a mere sentence of death. The massive hands—able to snap her body in two—speedily locked themselves around her waist, thwarting the flow of air and causing her to gasp. Heatedly, he flung her, partially clothed, over his shoulder as the remaining remnants of her clothing, hung limply along his dark tunic. "I warned you twice! Now, you will be sorry!"

Cherinne hiccoughed with racking sobs, the hellish nightmare never-ending. Suddenly, she found herself praying for a speedy death.

The giant trudged heavily through the sand; and arriving at the meager camp sight, he tossed her roughly to the cold hard ground. Landing with a harsh, back-breaking blow to the earth, she moaned out of pain and utter misery.

Irately, he snatched a knotted rope from the back of his saddle, and bending to one knee, flipped Cherinne, as if she was ready livestock. She laid belly down, while her face already smeared with blood, dirt and sand, was shoved within the cool grit. Turning to her cheek, she stared blindly at the tip of a large black boot, scuffed with wear and days of dredging through the ruthless sand while being burdened with supporting the gargantuan man's weight. His hulk of shadow moved with his rampant breath above her, while her skin crawled with fear and she trembled—the pounding of her heart thundered in her ears.

"*Augh!* Cherinne groaned as the giant roughly twisted her arms back to meet with her now, completely bare legs, with the torn shreds of her clothing covering little. The bristly ropes dug deep within her skin, burning with every movement, while he hog-tied her as if she was mere butchering swine.

Finding her voice, she blubbered, "*please,*" through a bucket of enormous tears which flowed readily and streamed upon the dusty sand. "I didn't mean…"

Her words were abruptly cut short as she suddenly found a bulky elbow bent and blasting against the back of her head. The stabbing explosion—a blunt, yet jagged pain—plunged Cherinne deep into a bottomless pit of darkness.

"Hey—whatever your name is! Are you awake?" The harshly whispered words were spoken close to Cherinne's ear. Her body was jostled with a slight wrenching, while her muscles refused to respond in dread of awakening to the overwhelming aches and pains, which consumed every square inch of her being.

Without opening an eye, Cherinne muttered in a low, barely audible, tone, "please…leave me alone." Her parched lips cracked, and beyond numb, scarcely loosened the words. The tears that had flowed so readily were dried and lost to the sandy earth, as if the ducts had been sealed and forgotten.

"*Wake up!*" The female's saucy voice persisted in annoyance. "You've been asleep for three days, while I have had to gaze upon your repulsive presence, restraining myself from ripping every hair from your miserable head."

Three days! Cherinne thought, as her mind galloped in several directions at once. A compilation of reeking odors and deep, resonating, eerie sounds echoed and drifted just beyond her unopened lids, a sure sign she was not at home or even back at Prince Rasheed's palace. Attempting to pry open the heavy lids which kept her from facing the harsh reality as to her whereabouts, she openly grimaced. Her usually large chestnut eyes, now squinting slits, brimmed red in obnoxious swollen sockets; and, making an effort to focus in the dimness of the faded dungeon light, she regretfully sat up.

Scooting herself against the clammy wall, she placed a shaken hand to the swollen lump protruding from the back of her skull, which was now just a heaping region of headache, begging not to be touched. Carefully, she disentangled a sprig of straw from within a matted lock. Pink rope burns—temporary tattoos upon her wrists—stung willingly and she rubbed them each gingerly, while the whole of her body ached with all movement and each and every crevice screamed in agonizing throbbing soreness.

"Where am I?" She glanced around at the dank underground space, unable to make heads or tails of where she might be and the distance below the surface. Red clay layered the four damp walls plagued with potted crags, jutting root and various stone, while the floor, being much the same, was covered with a thin layer of yellow straw. The area could be compared to that of a large walk-in closet or possibly even a crypt, but with a slightly lower ceiling, barely high enough to stand in. To judge whether it was day or night was completely impossible, while only one escape led into utter blackness. It was a narrow hole cut deep within the earth which was guarded by four heavily steeled bars and secured with a weighty lock and chain.

An oil lantern sat idly upon the floor burning gently, as if with a small glimmer of hope. Its flame flickered quietly within the gray globe and its smoke billowed in a minute swirl toward the dirt overhead. Cherinne watched the calming dance of the tiny heated light and briefly recalled an image of Reynolds and his lighting of the candles in the winter cabin; their smallest efforts toward calm and warmth on a cold winter's eve. A roughly-stitched woolen blanket lay across her body covering to her feet. Torn and frayed, it carried the odor of wet animal and could've possibly have been used as a saddle blanket for either camel or horse. She drew it close to her chin.

Then, tearing her eyes from the frozen reverie of time which seemed so far from her reach, Cherinne looked squarely into the face of her double. Fahimah's features, normally polished and beautiful beyond compare were now smeared with a deposit of dirt and blood, stained from the battle fought days ago in the palace gardens. The puffy bruise inflicted by Hafiz, was now just a yellow-green splash of color, which highlighted the princess's coffee cup eyes. Eyes that speckled with flecks of green, gray, yellow, and blue; which accented her streaked blonde tresses imbedded with fragments of straw.

A brief staring match ensued; but being entirely too exhausted to participate in a game of cat and mouse, Cherinne lowered her gaze, completely unprepared for what she was about to see and hear.

"You are now in the hands of the Lord Seth, the God of the desert," Fahimah finally answered tersely as she gave Cherinne the once-over. "Serves you right—you thief." She stated coolly. "If Goliath hadn't gotten hold of you, I would have been liable to do worse. You have the bracelet—the Semus Bracelet—at your disposal and you don't even know how to use it. It is not a maraca to be shaken; it is a weapon to command *armies!*" Fahimah slowly rolled the small strand of yarn between her two fingers as she kept her eyes on the string, repulsed by the American. She then snapped a malevolent look in Cherinne's direction. "People have died because of you!" Gauging a reaction that never comes, Fahimah fumed, as her double lowered her chin to the rough wool and surrendered to silence.

Fahimah balled her petite fists, dirt and grime layered each and her shoulders tightened with tension as she shook with anger. "Did you hear me?" Quickly springing to her feet, she pointed an accusing finger at Cherinne. "It is because of *you* that Princess Haneefah is *dead! You!* And now, we are here—prisoner to the evil Lord Seth!" With labored breaths she found herself fighting back a sting of tears at the corner of each eye. "You have taken everything from me," she spat, "including the Amir Rasheed!"

Fahimah dropped to her knees before Cherinne, her troubled countenance hidden behind a counterfeit grin. "Maybe—just maybe—I shall take *your* man—the red-haired one," she whispered into the American's tangles, aiming to provoke her double into action. "Rasheed told me of how you never allow *him* to touch you. That you are still a virgin and that young man of yours screams out for you mentally and physically. But, *you*—being a selfish American female—keep him on a leash, like a meager animal—like a dog. Shame on you…didn't *your* God, *your* Almighty, make woman to serve man? Doesn't 'to serve' mean *anything he wants*, including the pleasures *you* withhold from him?"

Infuriated by a lack of response, Fahimah delivered another spout of menacing threats. "You're disgusting," she sneered, as the hairs upon her neck bristled, and the fire's light sparked in her eyes. Abruptly, turning her face toward the shadows, she angrily swiped away a menacing tear.

"I shall take him," she stated with finality. "When we get out of here, I shall take the red-haired American from you and I shall make him *mine*. He will no longer be your dog, to be turned to the curb when you see fit. I shall fulfill his every desire and man-given wish, bringing him to a rushing climatic peak, where he begs for me to cease the magic I possess, as I entwine myself within the flowing locks of his crimson hair."

Hearing more than enough, Cherinne slowly raised her throbbing head and looked through glazed, swollen eyes at the princess. She could feel Fahimah narrowly accessing her face as she confronted her. Fiery arcs sparked, amidst the close quarters of air, and in a throaty voice Cherinne stated defiantly, "No Fahimah—I'm afraid you won't. As long as I live and breathe, you will never touch Laddor; and I would shave his head clean, before his locks were ever entangled with the likes of *you*."

Electrical energy flared amidst the breathing space separating the two enraged females. Fahimah's twisting of the yarn increased with each and every bulleted word and wrathful glare. And while the span of the underground cavern was too small to spin her cocoon, she struggled to refrain from the attempt, making her bad mood even blacker. Her skills at hand to hand combat were impeccable, due to years of warding off *both* the hateful Egyptian children who ridiculed her American heritage, and the palace guards who both despised and loved the traits she bestowed.

A wave of emotion showered Fahimah as an attack played out carefully in her mind, brought about through years of conflicts, where she had engaged several opponents at a time, while fighting for her paltry existence. This disagreement with her double, brought to mind, one scrap she had encountered. One where she had hid in a drainage hole, beneath the ground, bleeding and crying in hiccoughing sobs, after being beaten miserably by a number she would never forget—five—five to one, till Grandmother Habbai had searched her out; and with a kind word had led her home.

Fahimah had been considered a *fellahin*; one of the group of poorest peasants who occupied the area east and west of the Nile River. More than half the Egyptian people lived in this poverty stricken rural area, while the others were chiefly desert herdsmen called Bedouins. The *fellahin* lived in crowded, unsanitary villages, largely along the Nile with the houses being made of sun-dried mud bricks, and most homes consisting of only one to three rooms. The lives of these people was one of endless toil: carrying water, raising chickens and selling meager amounts of butter and cheese at the distant market place, in exchange for the scarce amount of food they could afford for their families.

At the age of nine, Fahimah endeavored—with a young mind of determination—after years of being pelted with cans and sticks, to stand her ground. Her few years on this desolate part of earth had proven to be conflicting; while her extremely dissimilar appearance was significantly troublesome amongst the adolescent natives of this land.

She stood barefoot, sooty from head to toe, her tattered galabiyah torn to the knees and the pointed sleeves, then just frayed edges. Her long golden locks—streaked—were thickly braided, heavy and never remained neat or in place. They swung as weighty ropes about her head, outlining her ivory skin and rosy cheeks while her enormous dark eyes laced with full lush lashes were beautiful, yet despised by the other children.

Her eyes had darted from one child to another who stood before her. Their dirt-ridden clothing matched the hue of their faces, dark skin, hair, and wicked eyes which were black as tar. While the sun's heat, a relentless adversary, gave way to temperatures soaring well to one hundred.

Fahimah trembled in a sticky sweat; while her heart raced in the attempts to escape from her chest, begging for her to run. Her tiny fingers balled tight within the hand-sewn satiny dress of the doll clutched tightly to her chest, searched for comfort within the silk of the material, but unfortunately found none. It was a near replica of Fahimah and had been given to her on her Celebration Day; a present from the beautiful princess who often frequented their village home, bearing gifts and other goodies Fahimah never questioned receiving.

Tears had formed behind her large eyes, while she had been barely able to keep them abey; knowing that to show a sign of weakness only meant added offenders and a more severe thrashing.

'You are American!' The children spat, pointing short accusing fingers at the young blonde girl. 'You do not belong here! Go home!' A barrage of stones and sticks cursed through the air painfully striking Fahimah, as she held the doll before her, using it as a partial shield.

'*Stop!*' She screamed in the Arabic dialect; the earthly objects finally ceased, only to be continued with pounding fists, as the first child spanned the distance between them in a matter of seconds and knocked her to the dusty ground. The others then followed. She fought viciously, striking back with her clenched hands while her new doll took the brunt along with Fahimah's arms and face.

'*Stop it!*' She pleaded in alarmed fear, as she realized the children desired blood—her blood—which had already begun to spill, while the warmth slipped from her nose and swelling cheek into the collar of her tunic.

'*Waqaf! Waqaf!*' The command filtered through what seemed like an hour of snarled breathing, hammering fists and Fahimah's throated screams vibrating within her head and chest.

'*Leave her alone!*' An irate voice rang aloud seizing each attacker with a brusque hand and roughly tossing them to the side. '*Get home you meddling brats!*' Dust flew, as the elderly man kicked a sandaled foot in the children's direction then clapped his hands together in finality, as if cleansing his mind of the dirty deed his native people had committed. His shaggy eyebrows, thick as winter caterpillars, shifted as he assessed the damage done from behind a wrinkled façade and curled lips. He then turned; his meaningless life had been wasted for a few brief moments by a foreigner from a foreign land which he despised.

'Worthless American,' came the grumble as he made his way back to his shaded spot beside the pile of aged brick slowly giving way to a crumbling wall.

Fahimah lay with her eyes closed in a hazy fog of rippling pain. Her elfin, ski-slope nose instantly growing to the size of a large palm date, cast an unfamiliar shadow between her eyes and the searing sun; while blood quickly dried in red rivulets along her scratched face. One braid had been ripped free of its clasp, while catching within a boy's fingers, scattering blonde and flaxen tresses gleaming a honey-gold along the brittle dry earth.

With a gutted groan and the choke of blood thick in her throat, she coughed; and drawing her knees to her chest, she gingerly rolled to her side. Opening her eyes, she came face to face with her doll, which lay just inches away. Its lovely silken dress was torn and tattered, and its hair was plucked in spots from its delicate porcelain head which now claimed a gaping hole, devastating one whole side of kilned ceramic. Unable to fight the flood of tears rushing from her ducts—like a breaking dam— Fahimah burst into a convulsion of uncontrollable sobs.

Wearily, she climbed to her feet and rubbed her slender arms, now gouged deep with the marks of fingernails. She gathered the doll from the dusty earth, and, with trembling fingers, attempted to brush the dirt from its battered lifeless face. Seeing herself through a blur of freely falling tears, Fahimah clutched the doll to her chest and broke into a frantic run. Attempting to free herself of her miserable existence, she raced through the dirt-ridden streets, watching through misty eyes the grime of life passing her swiftly by.

Unfortunately, for her, a seemingly bad situation turned mostly for the worst, when one day the beautiful Egyptian princess arrived in the desolate village with the intentions of retrieving the young girl, who was, through time, becoming damaged goods.

Princess Adiva hurriedly entered the mud-encrusted adobe. The rich scent of the finest of perfumed oils was tingling to the senses as she entered the one room hut, seeming to the young girl, larger than life. Dressed in the grandest of wine-colored silken robes, ornamented with the most magnificent glitter of jewels, she filled the room with a thriving bloom of aura.

Fahimah stared in awe at the nervous energy radiating from the saucer-sized black eyes which peered from behind the brandy-colored veil.

'Rasool, unload my carriage in payment to the woman, and gather the girl. She shall need a blanket to cut the chill for the long journey.'

'Come, Fahimah, you are to leave here and never to return.' A slender but firm grip snatched the girl's small trembling hand as Fahimah's eyes darted wildly from the eloquent features of the princess to the aged face of the only family she ever knew.

'Grandmother Habbai?'

The elderly woman turned away, while the shadows, catching from the oil lamp, loomed about the room in a state of dim confusion and reflected off her graying thin hair.

'She is no longer your Grandmother, Fahimah. She no longer knows of your existence—isn't that right, old woman?' Silence ensued as darkness abruptly shrouded the princess's countenance; her eyes glaring with an unspoken warning.

'Any mention of *this* will result in the loss of your head.'

Princess Adiva turned to her henchman. 'Rasool, we have tarried long enough—the amir will be wondering of my whereabouts.'

'Amiri, shall I take the girl's few meager belongings?'

'No. She will have no ties to this previous life what-so-ever. She will leave with only the shreds of clothing on her back. And, as soon as you arrive at my brother's regime, you shall have them burned.'

'Yes, Your Grace.' He bowed seizing Fahimah and roughly secured her in a heavy woolen blanket.

'*Grandmother!*' Fahimah cried in a panicked fright as she struggled for a single glance at the chilly shoulder that never turned.

"*Damn you!*" Fahimah moved at a raging speed. The straw kicked out from beneath her feet and Cherinne was quickly pinned beneath her, unaware as to how she had even gotten there. Spittle sprayed from the princess's lips and spritzed Cherinne, while Fahimah's features contorted into a twisted torment, blazed with years of pent up anger, while she spewed one curse after another into her look-alike's face. "*Mat! Die!*" She half screamed, half cried, while hateful tears welled behind large vibrant eyes which now flashed with iridescent kaleidoscopes of greens, blues and browns.

Through an array of multi-colored flaxen hair, which whipped in an erratic wave of relentless energy, Fahimah clutched Cherinne's throat firmly with her two shaking hands. "You have taken *everything! Everything!*" The vision returned—a dark recollection—hidden within the deepest depths of a battered soul; the princess shuddered at the memory.

Rasool sat atop the large roving charger with Fahimah seated between his legs. 'Rasool, take the young girl to my brother, Lord Fineas Jamaine. Ride swiftly upon your steed and deliver her to him in keeping, till I am able to evade the gaze of the amir; he watches me as a hawk.' Rasool glanced at the amiri out of the corner of his narrowed eyes, with the knowledge that her secreted scheming would not only generate her death, but would also bring his.

'Now, Fahimah, you be a good girl and be mindful of the Lord. He can often times be quick to temper; but I will come for you soon.' Princess Adiva patted the young girl's trembling hand and gave her a wane smile, 'Such a pretty thing.' She brushed a straggly strand of gold from Fahimah's cheek. 'You have no idea how useful you will be.'

She hastily turned to Rasool, her expression fixed. 'Stop for no-one, Commander; and give my brother my regards.'

'Now, remember child—you are never to speak to anyone of me.' She took Fahimah's chin into her cool unyielding hand and pulled the young girl's face close to her veil which emanated the scent of lotus. She gazed into Fahimah's large kaleidoscope pools. 'Do you understand?' Fahimah shook her head, 'yes' while the scent of the Egyptian flower filled her nostrils, which brimmed with the bouquet. 'Good—now be off.'

Rasool spurred the dancing stallion onward, away from the princess who stood briefly watching at the far gates of the palace; while she had timed it just that the guards would be changing shifts. Darkness had shrouded the land as a broad palmed hand; and the waning moon, near to full crescent, furnished a minimal glow. Gathering her tunic skirts, she quietly made her way inside, slipping hopefully into the palace and undetected to her quarters. Arriving at her chambers, she quickly unlocked the door and disappeared inside.

'Amiri Adiva', the words oozed from the winged chair in the dark corner of her room. Her heart surged into a dreadful beating hammer, sending chills racing along her olive skin, now turned ashen. Fear choked painfully in her throat. 'Where have you been?' The whites of the amir's eyes radiated through the oppressing dimness surveying her countenance—judge and jury of her reply.

'I have been on an errand.' She attempted to control the quiver edging her voice. 'Where is Rasheed?'

'He is asleep, missing his mother's gentle hand, as he lay to rest his weary head. So, what, may I ask, was so pertinent an errand to have my wife outside the palace at such an hour with the commander of my guard? And, where may I ask is Rasool now?'

She trembled in cold shivers beneath the silk of her plum tunic, endeavoring to control her shaken tone. 'He has gone on to my brother's, Lord Jamaine's…' Her reply was abrupt, as her mind frantically searched for an answer. '…To…deliver a package.' She turned to leave, when suddenly, the Amir Nuri gripped her arm—his long thin fingers pressed sharply into her skin.

'No. You shall stay with me tonight. I will determine whether or not my beautiful wife has been unfaithful. Then I shall deal with Rasool tomorrow. And, for your sake *and his*, you had better be as untainted a flower as the scent you wear.'

Fahimah pulled the rough blanket snuggly over her head. The cool night air cutting through the wool brought a tremor of shivers painfully creeping through every part of her body; and her legs, uncovered, had long since turned numb. She inched closer to the heat radiating from the young man's large body who seemed unaware she was even there. His eyes followed the constellation of stars and the direction of the fading moon, while he urged his horse onward. The clang of the bit, the animal's thirst for air and mild squeal of the leather saddle were the only sounds resonating in the wallowing silence, as Fahimah gritted her teeth, attempting to silence the chattering.

The ocean of sand and desolate night slowly disappeared, with the tint of red, orange and blue-gray cresting the horizon, as the sun made forth for another scorching day. Fahimah's head bobbed along with the horse's step then slowly rose as they abruptly halted outside a great stone wall of concrete block.

Fahimah recalled the senses which were close enough to touch—senses that filled her head as they were cleared through the gargantuan gates at the Lord Jamaine's regime. The musky smell of camel and burlap bag, pots and pans banging as food was being prepared for the morning meal and individuals arising to the coming day commencing with morning prayer. Large stone dwellings constructed of thick granite, guarded by monumental statues of ancient gods and goddesses stood tall, carved to betray the authority they exhumed. Rasool dismounted his horse and dropped to his knees to murmur his dedication to Allah.

Never seeing anything other than the back alleys of their decrepit village, Fahimah's eyes wandered along every nook and cranny that she was able to absorb into her small person.

Rasool lifted her slight body from the horse. 'Come.' The blanket fell away from her face, revealing enormous eyes filled with wonder yet edged with fright; he glanced at her distastefully. 'Humph', a low grumble breathed from behind a wary façade. Fahimah teetered slightly as her legs ached miserably from the chill of the long arduous ride and had stiffened to mere flesh covered icicle sticks. She stumbled into the commander. 'Clumsy—keep to your feet.' Placing a weighty hand to her shoulder, he urged her forward through the doors of The Lord Fineas Jamaine's.

Fahimah's breathing became labored, as she struggled to obscure the haunting memories that flooded her mind, with the determination to drown her in a cesspool of agonizing recollections. She glared at Cherinne, despising the look of fear riddling her eyes, the reflection of her own trapped in a helpless misery from the past.

'Rasool—what form of jesting is this?' Lord Fineas raised a broad brow. My sister, Amiri Adiva, she has commanded you here with this child? An *American* child?'

Rasool bowed. 'Yes, M'Lord.'

'And pray tell; I am to welcome this child into my home?' A callous laugh roared forth from the Lord. 'Rasool…' His expressed amusement slowed to a subdued simmer, '…return to my dear sweet sister, Princess Adiva, with my apologies. I am in no position to house a child. What do I know of the sorts? My life is that of soldiering and weapons. I know nothing of children, and especially female ones that appear ratty enough to be fodder for the goats. She cannot stay here. Now, return to whence you came and take that wretched spectacle with you.'

The Commander's eyes darted hastily from Fineas to Fahimah as he recalled the words of the princess. 'Rasool, now Fineas will probably refuse; but inform him that it is a matter of life-or-death. He must do this for me—just until I am able to set the tides into motion. Do not bring her back here, Commander! The Amir Nuri will have both our heads!'

'I beg your forgiveness, Lord Jamaine; but the Amiri Tarun informed me that I may not return with this child. The princess begs that you allow her shelter till she can make arrangements to have her taken away.'

Fahimah glanced between the two men, realizing she was not welcome.

With a deep sigh, Lord Fineas's face, depicted as an open curtain, revealed his disgust at the pressing situation. He rose to his feet, from where he had been seated behind his desk, lined with an arsenal of weapons. He advanced toward Fahimah, scanning the entirety of her diminutive body, his eyebrows meeting in a full hedge. 'Not much to her. She will need to bathe and have a change of clothes. Have you those to supply?' He questioned the commander.

'No, Your Lordship, my instructions were to burn the meager rags she possesses. She has no other belongings.'

'Fine,' he stated, with a gesture of dismissal. 'I will send her to the servant's quarters. Someone there will know what to do with her. They will also take care of discarding the rags. Now, Commander, be sure to tell my sister that she has been graced by the hand of Allah for my kindheartedness, and that I shall expect this matter to be resolved quickly.' He spied Rasool attentively. 'I take it she is hiding this girl from the Amir Nuri. What a reckless game of deception. I pray to the Gods, she has taken into consideration the path in which she has chosen for herself and those involved. Now, see one of the guards out front and they will supply you with ample provisions for your return.'

Fahimah shook her head, struggling to keep the memories that were calling forth in abeyance, nightmares that were crashing upon her in an irrepressible torrent.

"*NOOO!!*" She screamed with a blood chilling cry; her face portrayed the marked sign of agony.

Cherinne thrashed about wildly, as yellow tufts of straw sprayed about the small space, discharging miniscule flecks of dust which briefly hovered to fill and choke the senses. Through no course of action she had committed, Cherinne observed the twist of blistering pain Fahimah was experiencing—a blinding pain, hidden deep, that was now rising to the surface, possibly being caused by the bracelet or some other source. And, while the princess's hands constricted tighter around her throat, she struggled fervently, oblivious to the flaring aches of her many injuries.

Puddle-sized tears formed in Fahimah's eyes and spilled like warm tea from a delicate china cup; she sobbed uncontrollably. With the vividness of the nightmare growing ever stronger, she could feel the bristles of the scouring brush roughly scraping along her near raw skin. The same warm tears flowed in pain and humiliation, as she, now reverting back to the past, stood shaking and unclothed, while two of the Lord's maidservants scrubbed relentlessly at her frail skin in an attempt to rid her of the accrued dark stains.

Fahimah flinched with each harsh stroke.

'Hold still, Girl.'

Suddenly Fahimah's grasp released from around her double's throat and Cherinne gasped for air. Fahimah then proceeded to run her hands along her arms and body, crying out, as she was now being consumed wholly in the clutches of the evil phantom recreating this haunting nightmare. It had her imprisoned between past and present; the vortex of reality and hallucination intertwined, while closing the gap for the princess's return to the present, weaving fact with fiction.

"*NOOOOO!!!*" She screamed out into the stale air of the clay walls; her weeping eyes shaded as they were locked to the past. Gasping for measured breaths, she now raked the flesh beneath her nails. Blood trickled from the deep trenches scraped frantically along her skin as she still sat straddled atop her double.

"Fahimah?" Cherinne watched in horror, the princess tearing senselessly at herself and her clothing as she dug her fingers deep within her long locks of hair in a maddened frenzy.

"*Fahimah!*"

'Fahimah? Your name is Fahimah? I am Rasheed,' the young boy stated as he peered into the alcove of crumbling rock, obscured by a thicket of brittle brush.

'Rasheed—Rasheed Daivyan Khalil Tarun,' he stated proudly with hands on hips and a broad glistening grin. 'I am here visiting my uncle with my mother.' Pushing the drying hedge plant to the side, he made his way in to seat himself near the young girl. The silence within the arid crevice suddenly grew heavy as he sat with his knees to his chin and twiddled his thumbs nervously.

Fahimah observed him warily from the corner of a red rimmed eye which had brimmed just moments earlier with a well of tears. Keeping her distance, she was ready to run. She flinched as he turned and attempted to grasp her gaze; she quickly averted her attention to the rocky parched ground.

'I heard you crying,' he whispered in a gentle voice. 'That is how I found you in here.' He paused, glanced at his moving thumbs then asked, 'Why were you crying?'

Her reply was soft, like that of butterfly wings fluttering in a warm afternoon breeze. Rasheed barely heard the stammered words, though she sat just feet away.

'I...I can't tell you.'

Tilting his head, he gauged the reply with uncertainty. 'Well...' he stood to his feet... 'I am a prince; and, I shall fix it,' he stated with determination. He glanced down at her as she kept her gaze to the ground, never meeting his eyes. 'I have to go now. My father has forbid me to hide.'

He scraped the dirt with the tip of his sandal. He then crouched down to exit the alcove, pulling back the tall grass to make an opening for his retreat. Then pausing, the young boy turned back to Fahimah, who sat with her head between her knees gazing toward the earth. 'I wanted to tell you—I really like your hair.' Then he disappeared.

'Rasool, you are under *my* authority—not the Princess Adiva,' the Amir Nuri's eyes burned black with a violent warning. 'Is this clear, Commander?'

'Yes, Your Grace,' Rasool evaded the amir's glare as sweat riddled his uniform collar and armpits.

'Good, you are like a son to me; and in being so you shall only receive eight lashes of the Rod. No sense in paralyzing my lead commander...' His smile was wicked—a dance with the devil. '...*Is there?*'

'There you are!' A forceful grip seized Fahimah as she wandered aimlessly through the back streets of the Lord Fineas Jamaine's regime, wishing with all her heart, she'd glimpse the young boy, Rasheed, who had been kind to her. She gasped and her heart raced wildly in a sickening panic, as the soldier grabbed her and roughly tossed her over a narrow shoulder. Her drying eyes, wide with fear, quickly returned to dripping pools with the knowledge of what was to come. 'We have been looking for you. Where were you hiding?' He ran a calloused hand along the back of her small thigh and slipped it between the folds of her galabiyah. Fahimah struggled for breath as her head swam and her stomach felt to retch.

"*STOP!!!* Please stop!" Fahimah cried, whimpering as a small child; her breathing was racked with uncontrollable sobbing. Her terrified eyes darted frantically about the cavernous enclosure as if looking for a way to escape and her hands grasped radically at her now matted hair, tearing at the strands that clumped within her fists which were now scraped raw by their frantic clawing.

"*Fahimah!*" Cherinne shouted into her face. She grabbed Fahimah's shoulders and violently shook her to rid the distraught female of this nightmare that had come full cycle.

"*NOOO!!*"

"*FAHIMAH!!*" The princess's pain, mirroring in Cherinne's eyes, caused a lump to form in her throat.

Fahimah's body suddenly thrust forward sending her face wrenching within the grottos clay earth, she turned to her side and wept.

'And what form of madness has come over you to perform such deviltry?' The Lord Fineas shouted at his sergeant-in-arms, as the sergeant stood partially clothed within the confinements of the battalion's bunkhouse. 'You have defiled my monarchy—*my* doorstep—with the filth of this heinous act! And, all for what…the defilement of a young female child? Take yourself a common whore and use her till your heart's content; but, by Allah, do not soil the hem of my garment!' Lord Fineas glanced angrily at the young girl, who cowered in the shadows of a darkened corner, away from the eyes of the Lord and his attending soldiers; while the lantern light danced along her alabaster skin, where the putrid odor of defilement hung heavy on the air. She shook violently, tears tracing the lines of her normally full cheeks, which were now empty and sallow as she attempted to cover her nakedness. The Lord tossed her a discarded woolen cover which lay across a hardback chair as the three men recoiled in fear that he may be reaching for his sword.

'You have brought shame to me and my house! And, for this black-hearted atrocity, *you*…' the Lord Fineas pointed a reproachful finger at one of the men '…Sergeant, shall be executed, while these two shirkers, which are in *your* command, shall be punished severely and imprisoned till I see fit.'

The sergeant dropped to his bare knees in lumbering shock; his face pressed to the floor, he begged in a broken voice, 'But, please your Highness—spare my life. I swear on all that is just before Allah, that I will not bring shame upon your head again. I will do all in my power to bring you honor; and, besides, Your Lordship she is merely an American.'

'No. That's where you are wrong, Sergeant…She is a child.'

Fahimah wrapped her tiny arms about the Lord Fineas, as he lifted her to him. Her tears spilled heatedly upon the stubbly skin of his collar as she shook violently and finally succumbed to the sequestering pain and grief.

It consumed her fragile being and she slowly slipped into the comforting darkness as the Lord carried her broken body to safety.

'Mother…' Rasheed trailed the skirts of her flowing tunic, as she hastily made her way around the room gathering the remaining few articles for their trip home from the Lord Fineas's. 'I found a young girl hiding behind some thicket brush today in Uncle's regime.'

Preoccupied with her task, the princess nodded. 'Oh?'

'Yes, and she was crying. I asked her why and she would not tell me. Mother…' he tapped his finger to his upper lip, '…as a prince, should I have forced her to answer…as Father does you?'

The Princess abruptly halted with Rasheed nearly colliding into her backside. She turned to face her son, just a young boy, barely coming into manhood. His eyes were wide, deep-set pools of darkest brown nearly filling the entirety of his face, while his hair of wavy ringlets cascaded gently about his boyish cheeks.

'Rasheed,' she brushed at an unruly lock on the crown of his head, the worry lines upon her face still visible behind a wane smile. 'You must follow your own path, my son. Do as your heart sees fit, not what the world around you supposes; and, you will make a fine lord someday. Now, run along and allow me to finish my packing.'

With a kiss to her lovely olive cheek, he turned to leave the princess's quarters. 'Oh, by the way, Mother—I told her I liked her yellow hair.' Then he quickly added, 'She said her name was *Fahimah*.' With that he closed the chamber doors, broke into a run, and made his way outside, where his father impatiently awaited him.

CHAPTER 16

The sweltering rays, of the Middle-Eastern continent's sun, slowly appeared, slipping unnoticed from behind the gray wall of night that gradually dissipated; while the cold-hearted terrain of the endless desert, beckoned to the blaze of torturous heat, readying itself for a drifting victim.

Egypt—a government reigned country—can no sooner rule the vast grains of white sand, than the corruption which befalls each individual regime. The regressive mentality of those who are in power and deathly cruel, some to the point of a barbaric nature, bring the full of the country's progression almost to a screeching halt.

Rasheed thought of his father as he fell to the white knees of his uniform praying just outside the confines of the stables—not to the greatness and wisdom of Allah, but for the safe return of the princess, Princess Fahimah, *and* the American girl.

He listened to the resounding echo of the many soldiers, who discontinued their packing for those brief moments of dedications, which transpired each morning, as the sun made its way over the horizon. He wondered of their prayers, whether they be in fervor to please their almighty redeemer, or, for one's own self-indulgence, like his own. Rasheed was unable to recall the last time he prayed fervently to the Almighty God. His thoughts turned to his mother, who knelt in prayer to a god—not the God of the Egyptian people, but to the gods and goddesses of the sky.

'Mother! Mother! Look what I found!' The young prince held proudly before his mother a bracelet, thick in gold and inlayed with a multitude of gems, mined from the earth's crusted shell. His excitement filled the whole of the room, with his boyish grin gleaming from ear to ear.

'Oh, this is lovely, Rasheed.' She took the golden armband, running a red meticulously manicured nail along the lovely gems and hovering just above the goddess's figure portrayed upon the crest. Her almond eyes were filled with awe as she hoarsely whispered, 'Close the doors, my son, and be sure to latch them. Then come, and tell me where you found this.' He did as she wished, then made his way to seat himself beside her on the grand bed—curtained with a flowing layer of lily-white sheers, embroidered with the papyrus plant in a magnificent shade of minted green. The flowing valances stroked with an array of lavenders, pinks, and creams intertwined to create a beautiful collage of infrequently seen colors; while the bed remained void of passionate love and affection, near to being, on occasion, an imprisonment.

The glimmering flames of her lighted lanterns carried the perfumed aroma of red jasmine and white ginger about the room in a swirling tuft of wispy smoke; while the candlelight revealed the trouble lines increasing upon her brow from years of foreboding unease.

'Isn't it beautiful, Mother?' Rasheed declared. 'I found it just beyond the ruins of the old Deir el-Rumi Monastery, beneath the ground, in an underground cave! There was a lot of other jewelry there too: earrings, necklaces, rings, all kinds of pretty stuff! I want you to have it all, Mother!' A squeaking note of soprano reached his adolescent voice and rang throughout the princess's chambers.

'Sshhh, my young one.' She placed a delicate finger to the soft of his excitedly moving lips. 'Rasheed, we must quiet ourselves, so as not to allow others to know of this, especially the amir. Have you told anyone else of your findings?' She glanced into the whole of his flushed face.

Guiltily, he looked to the cream color, carpeted floor and shuffled his bare feet nervously along the nap. 'Mother, you will not be angry with me—will you—if I told you I showed the boy apprentice, Rasool?' He anxiously grabbed her hand, and blurted out, 'I'm sorry! I did not mean to tell anyone; but, he followed me and the khamsin came, so he hid with me beneath the earth! I did not know, Mother!'

'Sshh, sshh, sshh,' she brushed a stubborn curl away from his troubled forehead and reassuringly smiled. 'Do not fret, my son. It shall be fine; for I shall speak with the young sword-smith.'

'Mother,' the look of guilt returned as the feet shuffling began again. 'I really like the bracelet. I would like to keep it for *my princess that I am to have someday*; but, I would like for you to have the rest of the jewels, *and*, I even brought you this ring.' He drew from within his tunic's inner pocket, a band of platinum, adorned with a single ruby stone cut into that of a heart. He held it before her. 'I thought it matched your nails. Would you please wear it, Mother?' His nose nearly touched hers and his eyes were wide as the Nile; he begged, '*Pleeaassee!*'

Princess Adiva carefully placed the lovely gift upon her right ring finger, then smiled warmly while embracing her son. 'Of course, I will wear this. It is beautiful, Rasheed. Now, remember, this is our little secret, and be sure to mention this to no-one.' She gave him a wink then sent him off with a friendly tap to his behind.

The Prince brushed the dust from his knees and clapped his hands to rid them of any dirt. He shielded his eyes as he observed the awakening sun, then turned his gaze toward the west. "Fahimah, I am coming for you," he whispered beneath his breath.

"Did you say somethin', Princey?" The pilot asked from just inside the stable doors. Yawning, he smacked mucky lips then shifted uneasily. His body was stiff as a board, while he had dozed in an upright position upon the barn stool still fully clad in his shimmery blue boxers. He twisted his large form impossibly while grasping for those hard-to-reach areas and nearly tumbling atop Laddor, who had dozed on the barn floor, propped against the pilot's cushiony side.

"Deverall, whaddaya' doin', man? That's *my* back you're scratchin'!" Laddor proclaimed through blood-shot eyes and a mouth that felt as if he had swallowed cotton balls. Leaning clear of the pilot's groping clutches, he irately stated, "Keep your grubby hands to yourself." Then, awkwardly lumbering to his feet, he undertook the chore of clearing his sluggish mind, dreadfully in need of additional sleep.

"Ahh, quit your whinin', Red. Besides, without the little Lady around I'da thought you'd be up for some physical contact." Deverall chuckled and gave the prince a hearty wink.

"Oh, shut up," Laddor retorted. "Rasheed—when are we headin' out?"

The amir turned to the American, whose clothes were unevenly creased and blood stained and his hair was like that of someone who had ventured to stick their finger in an electric socket. Rasheed briefly regarded those things and the American's mood which was one of sour grapes. Looking him squarely in the face, from behind tired eyes, the prince replied, "I don't recall my mention of 'we' to you at all, Mr. Zeandre."

Laddor's temper flared as an incensed dragon, while the hair bristling upon his head burned deeper tones of burgundy and red by the passing second. His ornery brow arced at an unnatural downward angle while heat raced to his cheeks pasting them with red flush. "So, what are you trying to say, *Rasheed*?" Laddor took a few steps toward the amir laboriously making an attempt to quell the trembling anger that flowed throughout the length of his entire body. "Are you insinuating that I am not welcome to join you and your men, while you all go hunting for the girls?"

"Yes—I do believe that is my decision," Rasheed answered, as his expression remained placid. "Do you have a problem with that, Mr. Zeandre?"

The young boy, Ib, quickly scurried within feet of the two men, busying himself with shoving a book into his cloth pack that he had clutched within his hand. Excitement at serving the amir clouded his senses as the tension was quickly rising in the shadows of the barn and he was eagerly preparing for the voyage.

"Ib, ready another horse," the amir called to him.

Ib paused briefly and quickly turned with a hastened bow, "Yes, Your Grace."

"We shall be departing soon." Rasheed turned to the pilot, "I expect you shall be joining us, Mr. Deverall, for we are in need of the map."

Deverall gave Laddor an apologetic shrug. "Sure, Princey—anything you want. And, I don't mean ta' question your authority or anything; but, don't you think ol' Red, here," he jerked his thumb toward Laddor, "should go along? He is *really* concerned about his girl. And, my motto has always been: *The more the merrier*. So, whatddaya say, Amir?" His statement was a partial plead.

Rasheed's response was flat. "No. Mr. Zeandre is much to blame for the predicament we are now in. His thieving of the ancient Egyptian jewels—which had been deemed as protectors of the regime, and those who reside there in—has caused a great detriment, in the death of my Haneefah, *and* the abduction of the Princess. In other words, Mr. Zeandre here, is a nuisance, and shall be dealt with as such. No—he is not welcome."

Laddor's ire peaked; he pushed the obtuse pilot clear of the scuffle he knew was about to ensue. "Stay back, Deverall, this could get ugly." Angrily, he shoved the sleeves of his crumpled jacket back and drew his clenched fist before his face.

"Not this again." The prince shook his head despairingly then turned as if to walk away. Abruptly changing course, he rounded about and landed a right hook to Laddor's unsuspecting jaw.

"OOwww! Why you, sneaky bastard, *Rasheed!"* Laddor placed a shaken hand to his swelling cheek. He drew back, ready to swing, when quickly, his clenched fist was snatched mid-air by Deverall.

"C'mon, Red…you guys need to exert more effort in searching for the girls than trying ta' kill each other."

Laddor angrily ripped his fist from the clutches of his friend; his heart pounded loudly in his ears while his stare never left the dark of the amir's eyes. *"Get off me, Deverall!* You and the Prince sure have gotten awful chummy!"

A fruitless attempt was made to smooth the wrinkles in his jacket, as Laddor aimed to compose himself. "I'll just have to go myself."

The amir shouldered a goatskin pack and stated with finality, "That would be very foolish, Mr. Zeandre. You are from a land that offers the comforts of a down-filled mattress and pillow every mile or so and the option of a continental breakfast. You will find none of those comforts here—not in the desert. You would be fortunate not to have your skin scraped raw by the course grains of sand that would accumulate within your garments, while you slept upon the unrelenting desert floor. And, if you are graced by the hand of Allah, a Pharaoh's chicken would make for a rather detestable meal—considering their choice of diet. That's if you are not possibly first killed by our Saw-Scaled Viper—or even worse, Scorpion—which will hunt you at night, while you are attempting miserably to get a few meager hours of rest."

"No, Mr. Zeandre, I do not recommend your traveling through the dunes of Egypt alone."

"*So, Amir*...what would you have me do, while the rest of you go bounding out across the Western Desert in search of the Princess and *my* woman—sit here twiddling my thumbs?"

Rasheed replied over his shoulder, as he was now just outside the stable doors. "Why no of course. You shall help to rebuild my palace."

"*What?*" Laddor's explosive response echoed off the pine walls, as he stormed toward the entrance and the amir.

"*Red!* Hold up!" The American's head snapped back with a painful screech as the pilot snatched a handful of auburn locks, preventing the fuming young man from engaging in another brawl.

"Let go of my hair, Deverall!" Laddor sneered in a winded breath.

The pilot maintained a firm hold.

"No! You two fight like my grandma's dogs! They were both males—stupid little long haired beasts." He scratched his head, trying to recall their breed. "Shit-zoos—or somethin' like that. Ugliest little flat-faced muggles I've ever seen, and *yappy*—bark, bark, bark; I'd like to strangle the lil' bastards! And, this one—well, he was the orneriest lil' thing—always horny, probably part jackrabbit. I think she called him 'Clinton'. Anyway—you two have gotta' quit this dog-fightin."

Deverall released his grip of silky strands and placed a solid hand on his friend's shoulder. "Hey, just think about your lady. You know as well as I do, sweetheart wouldn't want you scrappin' with the amir. She would want you busying yourself with gettin' her back, not gettin' yourself busted up. Now c'mon, I have a plan."

Goddess Nephthys, forenamed *Mistress of the House or Castle* was deemed responsible for the entrails and bodies of the deceased. She was the consort and sister of the evil Egyptian god Seth and a daughter of the earth god Geb and the sky goddess Nut, who created the Semus Jewels.

The almighty God, Ra—who had once been the ruler of all Egypt— had disapproved of the union of Geb and Nut. He commanded Shu, Geb *and* Nut's father, to stand upon the earth with his arms held high, separating his daughter Nut from her husband Geb. As the two were divided, this parted Heaven from Earth. And, while Nut wept miserably for her husband, Geb grieved immensely for his wife, as he lay beneath her heavenly being yearning to be joined with her.

As a result, Nut rained down the Jewels of War—the Semus Jewels. She, being the Goddess of the Sky, gathered all the stars about her, sweeping the blazing orbs into her arms; she drew them together and opening her mouth to the size of the sun, swallowed them within her life form. As the stars melded within her viscera, the essence of her immortal being intermingled with each fiery core crystallizing the tears that flowed freely from the ducts of her eyes. The dewy droplets forming all the gems of the heavens and galaxies tumbled generously upon the earth's surface in the form of diamonds, rubies, sapphires, amethysts, pearls, and other stones unknown to the peoples of Egypt—each jewel possessing its own power.

Preparations for a great war came underway by the brother and sister to free themselves of the desolation their lives had succumbed to. But, as the gems fell to earth to be collected by Geb to battle the almighty Ra, who had brought this detrimental decision upon he and Nut's head; no- one had considered the consequences of a curious little boy who searched beneath the dirt and soil, to discover the golden bracelet that commanded the jewels. So the precious stones, being in the hands of a mortal, were now no longer attainable by Nut who was locked in an arch across the Heavens, and, Geb, who was still trapped beneath Shu's feet. As a result, this was believed by some to be the cause of the Great Flood; as Nut wept continuously for forty days and forty nights and the tears no longer fell as gems but as great monstrous puddles of rain, drowning the Earth, Shu and Geb with it.

Goddess Nephthys, on the other hand, had her own purpose for the jewels.

Standing barefoot atop the crested peak of Mount Zubius, the glory of her preeminence shone brilliantly while her authority as a goddess rang throughout the shadowy nighttime spreading across the entirety of the Egyptian sky. She wore garments fashioned from the rudiment of the earth's elements, referred to as *Lemos Light,* a shimmering cloth which outshined the full of the satirical moon. It reflected the various hues of magnificent greens and earthy browns, created by the Goddess, Neith, the patron of weaving.

Bellowing in a shrill soprano voice, she summoned the LaHm to return to her person. They raced through the night sky, dark, slithery creatures, the scent of human flesh and bone was soaked within their slimy thin membrane; their eyes and slitted ears obeying their master's call.

"Heed my words…oh, Flesh of My Flesh. Come unto me and fill me with the blood of my blood and give me knowledge of those things which you have seen and heard this night!" Nephthys spread her arms and feet wide while arching her celestial creature—akin to that of the crescent moon. The tips of her long locks of everglade hair whipped frenetically, skirting just a breath from the surface of the dewy ground, attempting to grasp the rudiments of the terrain and rejoin the fruits of the earth.

The LaHm glided in rushing waves along the cool of the arid air, cutting through the midnight sky, while the moon watched, compared to that of a great overseer, as they slunk across the shadowy land. Reaching their destination, they effortlessly slipped beneath the silky green-brown cloth of Nephthys's long sleeves and flowing skirt. Screaming in raw, spine-chilling screeches that emanated from their mouth-less beings, the heated skin of the mistress received her racing worm-like sectors of slime into the pores of her moldering flesh.

"Speak to me, LaHm!" Nephthys roared into the cloudless night; her voice rushed as an ocean wave to be swallowed by the consuming dark. "Reveal to me all news of the Jewels—all news you have absorbed within your life blood and mine! I command you to fill me with the knowledge you have received!"

A maniacal grin spread her baleful countenance as the blood and cells of the LaHm raced at lightning speed to impregnate the full of Nephthy's body. While the paltry knowledge of the partial map and the location of the bracelet seeped in oily sanguine-black blood into her spidery veins. The meager vegetation beneath her feet withered in the presence of her deity and the light of the gleaming moon suddenly disappeared, as a bleak black hole, as she cried out in a fuming rage.

She balled her fists to strike the invisibility of the air with a heated anger, as her wrathful temper flared uncontrollably, with the realization she had obtained only part of the information she needed. "You worthless specks of vile flesh! You bring me this trivial gibberish, which you soak within my skin!" Her mood blackened as she scraped her putrid brown fingernails the length of her arms, gouging at the already failing skin. Trickles of blood rose to the surface, catching beneath the dirt-ridden nails. "How dare you!" She screeched as thunderclouds of fury masked her face.

Fahimah breathed shallowly as she attempted to return to herself. While Cherinne placed a quivering hand to the princess's sweated forehead, brushing the tangles of dampened hair away from her troubled face.

"Fahimah, are you okay?" The aching in Cherinne's heart was visible in her shaky voice as she tried to console the princess who was blanketed in a shroud of foreboding nightmare and sorrow. "Fahimah? Come on, it's okay."

She patted the princess's trembling hand while feeling a strange unknown bond with the female—a bond she was unable to explain. Perhaps, she thought, it was because she *is* a female; or maybe, because they were both trapped there together like animals and each had someone they missed very much. Or maybe, it had something to do with the bracelet. She pondered the bizarre feelings while running a hand along Fahimah's sweated arm…or possibly it had something to do with the fact that they looked identical—like twins.

"Don't touch me, American." The raspy words formed upon Fahimah's lips as she suddenly drew her shaking hand away. "Don't ever touch me."

CHAPTER 17

Commander Rasool's dagger tip pressed the taut layer of skin beneath Princess Adiva's cheek while she avoided the bludgeoning by a mere hair's breath. Watching out the corner of a frightened eye, she observed the Amir Nuri, her son Rasheed and the golden haired female, Fahimah, who Rasool had firmly secured about the neck within a clammy muscled choke hold.

'Come Rasheed,' his father's silty tone was sickening to the ear of his son. 'See the whore your mother has purchased for you, all in defiance of her husband. She has brought dishonor to me, Rasheed, and I wanted you present as we rectify the situation.

Rasool, here, has searched his heart diligently, and has decided to serve me instead of your mother who has committed such a traitorous act. The girl will die quickly; but your mother, she has brought me disgrace of which I will have to endure for eternity, so I shall repay her the favor.'

'Mother, is this true?' Rasheed trembled within the full of his boots, his young mind raced in uncertainty as his wild gaze darted from the two people he cared for most dearly, to his father and then Rasool. His quivering fingers reached for the hilt of his sword as he swallowed to choke back the lump rising in his throat. The walls of the room seeming to close-in around him, made him feel small and confined.

'Come now, Rasheed, don't be foolish. You cannot take Rasool in a duel.' His father's heinous chuckle was that of a honey-tongued demon—slow, yet sharp and assured; while his narrowed eyes, black as coal, were the gateway to the very depths of Lucifer's realm.

'You are incapable of *ever* being a man, a mere shadow of an eighteen year old sniveling coward; and how dare you even consider raising a hand to my authority.' Amir Nuri's countenance blackened as if the devil himself was present within the layers of his leathery skin. His words, cutting deep within the young male's heart, attempted to draw blood through no open wound, but from the very depths of the young prince's soul.

'Rasheed, don't listen to him!' His mother's cry gushed forth with a gasp; the blade of the dagger bit a little deeper just breaking the skin and bringing forth a drop of crimson blood. 'Get out! Get as far away as you can!'

Rasheed lowered his head attempting, without success, to bring the spiraling of the room to a halt. He raised his head knowing full-well that Rasool could easily take him in a matter of seconds; and meeting Fahimah's tear-ridden gaze, his mind drifted back to the day he had found her hiding in the brush of his uncle's regime.

'Fahimah.' Her name was a whisper upon his lips. *I shall fix it.*

As Nuri observed the eye contact between his adolescent son and the American whore, he snidely remarked, 'No, Rasheed, you cannot fix anything,' his father's snapping voice stung like a swarm of restless hornets and his black mood climaxed to a seething rage. A silver streak raced before Rasheed's eyes barely seen in the flickering flame of the three lanterns that burned within his mother's chambers. A strike of the Cobra, swift and deadly, the young prince never had time to react as his father's blade tore from its sheath and through the silk of the amiri's robes, burrowing deep within the flesh of her buckled abdomen.

'*MOTHER!!!*' The cry shrieked from Rasheed's trembling lips as his world suddenly collapsed around him. Stunned by his father's abrupt action, his feet were frozen to the floor while his knees weakened and his body suddenly began to shake.

Rasool's weapon dropped with a dull thud to the carpet, as his arm slipped beneath the princess's frail body which slumped within his quavering arms. A bewildered look turned his expression from indecisiveness to complete alarmed shock as he released his choking grip and dropped Fahimah to the floor.

'*Princess Adiva?*' the commander spoke to himself while blood soaked his gray uniform, dripping, seeping puddles of dark red upon the carpeted shag.

Fahimah's anguished cry drowned out the thick stillness of the room, while the odor of nervous sweat mingled with the blood of a newly bludgeoned victim behind the chambers locked doors.

Struggling for measured breaths, the amiri slipped from within Rasool's shaken grasp and crumbled in a weakened heap before his feet.

With a wave of dismissal, the Amir Nuri wiped the blood clean of his blade, creating a hair-raising *shing* as the deadly steel returned to its sheath. Irritation twisted with indifference, along with anger and loss which formed a peculiar look upon his craggy face—one which Rasheed had never seen before. 'Do as you will, Rasool,' came more as a thwarted sigh than an open command, while the amir turned to exit his wife's chambers.

'*Don't touch her! Get your hands off my mother!*' Rasheed's strained voice lunged forward, along with his drawn sword as he rushed across the room, closing the gap between himself and the captain.

Rasool reacted quickly; his enormous weapon ripped from its scabbard cutting the tension screaming between the two young men. 'Rasheed!' the commander shouted his voice roaring like that of a lion. 'You are about to meet Allah! Prepare yourself to die!'

'Get away from my mother!' the prince cried in desperation through the blur of dampness stinging his vision.

Fahimah watched with an aching heart the pain of the young amir; it mirrored in her own tears which fell freely upon her violently shaking hands, while she attempted to hide her face from the massacre that was unfolding before her eyes.

'*Rasheed?*' Fahimah fought back the nausea rising to her throat and positioned herself beside his mother, who clutched her seeping wound with trembling bloody hands while her royal silken robe was now covered in a stain of crimson red. '*Princess Adiva?*' the whisper slipped through the look of pain and sorrow riddling the golden-haired female's face as the amiri returned her gaze—a reflected look of fear and regret; while her eyes glazed with one about to meet their destiny.

Adiva reached for Fahimah with a shaking hand. 'Fahimah…help Rasheed,' the gagging words rose from the Princess's ashen lips; she coughed a spew of red then slumped to breath no more.

'Princess Adiva?' Fahimah shivered violently from the cold that breezed along her skin. '*NO!! You can't die!*' She turned to the young prince. 'Rasheed…' she openly cried'…your mother!'

'Fahimah, *RUN!!*' he shouted. 'Run and get the guards!'

Swinging his mighty sword in a high singing arc, Rasool had the determination to destroy the struggling prince. 'Rasheed, you have stepped beyond your bounds! You shall vanish as a puff of sigara smoke which is rancid and detestable.' His weapon, missing Rasheed by a hair's breath, slammed the princess's dressing table scattering perfumed oil bottles, nail colorings, herbal salves and hair adornments in a race across the floor. The crashing of Depression glass and the beautifully framed mirror, which his mother sat before each and every day, filled the prince's ears as he laboriously fought to avoid the thrashing raging steel.

'*GUARDS!! GUARDS!!*' Fahimah screamed the words with a corded throat while she raced in a blinding fright toward a set of chamber doors opposite the Amir Nuri.

The amir promptly spun, spying her through a narrowed contemptuous stare, like that of a hawk watching its prey. 'How dare you!' seethed through clenched teeth; his stone face shadowed with hatred as a leathery hand reached for one of many black rapier daggers secured within his sash. It twisted easily within his fingertips; then, spinning wickedly, it shot across the length of the room at breakneck speed.

'*LOOK OUT!!*' Rasheed shouted, fleetingly hurling his blade to block the dagger's heated rush toward the frightened American girl. The clang of metal rang sharply with a spark of steel meeting steel halting the course of the spiraling weapon. The young prince rapidly bound across the bed to engage his father, who had reached for another blade. Ripping from their brass rings, the delicate sheers entangled themselves around Rasheed and threw him atop the aged Egyptian. The force sent them both plummeting to the carpet's rough surface, trapping them between the bed and a solid wooden wardrobe.

'Rasheed, get off me, you fool!' The amir drew a sharp sniping breath, wrestling to regain his composure and clamber to his feet. 'Rasool! Kill *this* idiot *and* that girl!'

The Commander's sword, a silver blur of hot steel, raced through the poignant shadows slicing in a heated pursuit of the dodging young prince, who wheeled from his father to slam against his mother's clothes closet. Cornered like that of a hunted animal, he pivoted to and fro as the thrashing blade crashed in a merciless frenzy, slashing and destroying everything in its path. The steel hummed like that of the heavy driven wind of a *khamsin;* then a thunderous crack blasted within Rasheed's ears as the blade made contact with the dresser's wood, splintering the beautiful mahogany into numerous broken pieces. Tufts of carpet ripped from the floor, spewing in several directions the cream colored fiber which mixed with the feathers that had burst from the battered down mattress, fluttering about the room like that of a cascading snowfall.

The amir also scrambled to evade the wicked brutality that Rasool was unleashing; while the humiliation and pain of the Rod sparked fresh within the commander's mind.

'Rasool! You blundering clod! You're liable to bludgeon me to death! Watch where you're swinging that thing!'

The white of alarmed eyes flashed in the dimly lit corner, while the bustle of large hulking shadows leapt in wild contorted forms upon the bedroom walls. Their labored heaving breaths, echoed throughout the room, and the thick odor of sweat mixed with the sickening aroma of blood, red jasmine and white ginger. Fahimah fought to hold down the rumbling bile forming within her stomach.

'*GUARDS!! GUARDS!!*' She screamed again fearing they would arrive too late.

'You killed Mother!' Rasheed cried at his father in an anguished cutting pain while he fought back the tears that wanted to burst forth from his stinging eyes. 'I'll never forgive you!' He jerked forward and rolled as Rasool's weapon swung in a high piercing arc tearing through the remaining pieces of the wardrobe and barely missing him. Using his scabbard as a shield, Rasheed swiftly slid his body beneath the large commander, nearly five years his senior and twice his build, and disappeared beneath the canopy bed. The commander dropped to a knee and pulling the scalloped bed ruffle irately away peered into the darkness.

'You are not going to hide—are you, Rasheed?'

The muffled sarcasm of Rasool's voice filled the prince's ears as he shuffled quickly along the carpet. He recalled the times he had played hide and seek with his mother as a young lad—her lovely gentle voice calling to him while she hastened around her room looking in draws, under chairs and even in her jewel box to make him giggle, all-the-while, knowing exactly where he was—under her bed. A tear formed in the corner of his eye and ran to drop upon the shag's weave.

Rasheed appeared on the opposite side of the king-size mattress's framing and quickly, yet quietly, slid out from beneath the skirting, knowing he had only one chance of out-witting Rasool, for he was then completely open to any and all attacks from either him or his father. He scrambled atop the bed; his feet sinking deep within the cleaved mattress forced the feathers to plume in batches of white cluster clouds, making it difficult to see throughout the room.

Within seconds, Rasool quickly came to the conclusion that Rasheed was no longer hiding, but like that of a stalking lion, ready to pounce. Using his sword, he erected himself to standing position and turned just as Rasheed released a shrieking growl and sailed from the bed, to bombard the commander with full body mass. A staggered groan escaped Rasool as he toppled forward. His sword which he had used to hoist himself, drove before him into the Amir Nuri who was trapped between him, the flooring and the severely damaged clothes closet.

'Rasool? What have you done?' croaked from the aged man's weathered lips as the two young men lay heavily atop him. 'You fool.' A thin paltry breath escaped the amir as the shadow of death lay heavy across his gristly face.

'RAASSHHEEED!! Look what you made me do! You have put the curse of Allah on me!' Rasool heatedly shouted in an uncontrollable rage spinning and tossing the prince angrily against the shattered dresser. He bolted to his feet and bound upon the now dazed prince; his face contorted into a demented rift between vengeance and a foreboding alarm. I shall not be held accountable! You will!' he spat through gritted teeth. The fury blazing in his bulging neck muscles rippled into his flaming red cheeks as he gathered the prince's throat within his huge calloused grip. He squeezed with an immense inexorable strength from rock-hard arms, like that of sledgehammers, which had accumulated through years of soldiering and brandishing his weighted sword. The room spun in an uncontrollable vortex and Rasheed fought back fervently, wedged between the smashed wardrobe, the colossal-sized bed, and his father's dead body. He kicked his legs with all of his strength and thrashed his fists managing to make contact with the hulking commander. But, as the hold about his throat tightened, he began to drift into a welcomed blanket of darkness. And, as he wafted into that realm, he could hear the resonant screams of Fahimah, through that far-off dark tunnel, while the lily-white skin of her shaking hands shot before him in a hazy blur as she pounded without effect on the determined commander's back.

'*Release me you whore!*' A large knuckled fist flew from Rasheed's throat, twisted and drove within her abdomen, sending her frail body in an abrupt spiral to the now flattened mattress and exposed boards of the box spring. Landing with a harsh cracking thud, she released a taxed moan while her small figure lay limp—void of all movement.

'*Fahimah?*' the thought of the young girl dead raced through Rasheed's mind like being struck by a bolt of lightning and the words, 'I shall fix it,' hummed in his throbbing head as he finally succumbed to the enveloping darkness.

"Don't ever touch me again—or I will kill you."

Cherinne yanked her hand away from the princess, as if she had touched hot coals, shocked at Fahimah's remark. "I was only trying to help," she whispered, the hurt apparent in her voice.

"Well, don't. I don't need your help or anyone else's."

"But what about the Amir Rasheed—don't you want any help from him? I imagine he must be very upset because you are gone."

Fahimah slid to a sitting position and leaned her head back against the cool of the clay wall; she closed her swollen eyes and breathed deep. Her matted hair lay in ratted clumps about her shoulders and the whole of her front was soiled with red and brown dirt. She was not the beautiful princess of just days ago, but now resembling that of a homeless derelict, which Cherinne had seen on a visit to Ground Zero with her father.

"Our affair is none of your business. And if I'm not there Rasheed has plenty of other wives who can tend to his needs." The smallest twinge of pain and jealousy surfaced within her voice, then quickly disappeared.

Cherinne's mind raced back to the conversation she had overheard between the two princesses—Princess Fahimah and the now deceased Princess Haneefah.

"But…" Cherinne hastily stated; her tone was one of encouragement "He has chosen *you* to bear his child as heir to his regime."

Suddenly, she slapped a hand to her mouth, realizing she had spoken through 'slippery lips.' Her eyes darted madly about the underground cave while she knew she couldn't hide from the words she has just spewed—words that had been said in confidence. There was no way of getting out of this one. She now understood how Laddor must have felt those times he had blundered and was caught, like a small child caught in a lie who stood in judgment before an irate parent.

Fahimah's eyes sprung open, as the all-to-familiar flare of heated resentment boomeranged throughout the entirety of the grotto, then came to settle on the cowering Cherinne. "What did you say, American?"

The princess's face twisted into an unnatural form and Cherinne's skin rapidly crawled with fleshy bumps that raced along her smut-ridden skin. While she imagined that she sometimes may have looked at Laddor that same way when he had done something wrong. She shuddered at the thought that her features could ever be so frightening. Poor guy.

"*I'm sorry!*" Cherinne blurted out. "I was out of line. Please forgive me."

"I have nothing to do with 'forgiveness'! I want to know who told you this! Was it the amir?"

Fahimah shifted her weight causing Cherinne to flinch. "Don't worry, American—I will not attack you again as long as you answer me." While truthfully, she was too exhausted to really move.

"No…." Cherinne replied. "It was not the amir."

"Then was it Princess Haneefah? She always was too friendly with others—especially foreigners."

"No, it wasn't her either."

Fahimah wrinkled her small nose matching the frown lines gathered upon her puzzled forehead as she attempted to bring to mind who may have known.

"Then tell me *immediately* who would have told you! It could not have been Rasool; for, just the mention of my existence turns his stomach to granite! Now, enough guessing games, American; I am not in the mood!"

Gathering her wits for another blow, Cherinne drew an encouraging breath and answered. "I overheard you and Princess Haneefah's conversation in the gardens."

"*WHAT??*" The princess's prismatic eyes flashed with brilliant colors of greens and blues, chestnuts and golden yellows, growing to the size of tangerines. Despite Cherinne's fear of being pummeled she couldn't help but stare at the kaleidoscope of scintillating colors.

"Not only are you a thief, but now, you are also a *spy!*" Though still fatigued from her bout of nightmares, Fahimah quickly conformed to attack position, like that of a hunkering lioness.

"Hey! I resent that, Princess!" Kindness dissolved into an icy tone of animosity as Cherinne glared through her own eyes which had narrowed to dark chestnut slits. "I have stolen from no-one; and I was only spying because the *amir* asked me to! So, don't go around accusing people of something you know absolutely nothing about!"

A small tight-fisted grip wrapped itself around Cherinne's wrist and the Semus Bracelet, as Fahimah grabbed her double's arm and held it up before them both. "Don't go telling me who to accuse and who not to accuse, American! The proof is right here!" The ill-tempered princess angrily shoved Cherinne's arm away. Then suddenly, drained of all hostility and energy to argue, she roughly plopped back against the wall. "I am tired of you and I don't believe a word you say of the amir wanting to ease-drop. It is beyond him to do such a thing; and I am hoping that when my energy returns that I shall beat the truth out of you and make you pay for the lies you spread of him." She closed her eyes again as weariness called—the master of her body, mind and emotions.

Thinking Fahimah had fallen asleep; Cherinne lay upon the damp ground and closed her eyes. She drew the ragged blanket close to her chin and wondered if they would ever be free of this place. She thought of Laddor—the scent of his cologne and the silkiness of his long flowing hair, and of the estate and her warm comforter, Reynolds and his kind words. Her mind raced through the events that had lead them here, to this underground hole: The plane ride, as Laddor had drooled upon her white shorts and the attack by that ominous creature, the bus ride with her toppling into the Egyptian, the accident, and the dingy motel room, where she would now, more than welcome, the comforts of the single stained mattress, the feel of Laddor's skin beneath her fingertips as they had embraced in a kiss—a kiss for her hero. The Amir Rasheed, his dark full eyes as they had observed her during their brief conversation before the attack on the palace, the Bracelet, which he had commanded her to control, *and* the giant. Shuddering at the thought, she pulled the woolen cover tighter about her and drew her knees closer to her chest.

"Laddor." She whispered his name as she listened to the quiet consuming the whole of the underground cubicle and her.

A sharp gnawing pain prodded at Cherinne's back as she heard Fahimah whisper, "Hey—wake up." Realizing it was the princess's toe digging within her spine, she pried her crusted lids open.

"You sleep an awful lot."

Cherinne adjusted her eyes to the light of the lantern's flickering glow and regretfully sat up, while attempting to slow her spinning head. She smacked pasty lips, so wishing she could brush her teeth, teeth which she took pride in, which now suffered from the proper hygienic care she wished to give them. Resignedly, she laid back down. "So, what time is it?" she asked.

"How should I know? I am not a ticking clock," Fahimah retorted with disgust.

"Then, keep your filthy toes outta' my back, Princess, and let me sleep."

"And how am *I* supposed to sleep with your bawling and whining for that red-haired American? What is he to you anyway? I know he is not your lover, so why do you not want to share him?" Fahimah's tone was sultry, "I could think of all sorts of things to do with those long wine-colored locks..."

Cherinne yanked the blanket over her head. Embarrassment reddened her dirty cheeks and a muffled, 'shut up, Fahimah,' interrupted the princess's reveling remarks which had continued as a broken record.

"You do not wish to listen? Then, I demand that you clarify this situation! *You* have come between me and the Amir Rasheed and I wish to return the favor! So, I shall start with this *Laddor* you cry out for. So, tell me!"

Patience had never been Cherinne's strongest point and being with Laddor she had thought that maybe she had mastered it. But, being confronted continuously by a raving lunatic princess who drilled her constantly about her relationship, accused her falsely, and to top it all off, looked identical to her, Cherinne thought she would explode.

"*Fahimah! Shut up!*" Cherinne now completely alert shouted through the wool covering her head. "All you wanna' do is fight! And, I am *not* gonna' give in to you! Now, leave me *alone!*"

A whole foot, encrusted with dirt collected from a small portion of Egypt, planted itself within the small of Cherinne's back.

"If you don't come out from under that blanket and fight with me, I will be forced to eat and drink all the food and water, which they brought for us, while you were sleeping," Fahimah stated with mock pleasure.

A moment of silence passed with Cherinne absorbing this tidbit of good news; saliva quickened in her watering mouth.

"Food?" The camel-haired blanket quickly landed in a spiraling heap within a dark corner and she anxiously surfaced, shoving the princess to the side, who had it readily concealed behind her person.

"You were hiding this from me!" Hunger and thirst grabbed Cherinne within their clutches, like that of a starving victim, as she ravaged at the dried strips of beef—chewy yet flavorsome—while her craving taste buds exploded with the salty flavor. Hurriedly forcing a handful of cold glop, she thought to be beans, into her already jam-packed mouth, her jaws stretched thin, she gave the appearance of being a puffer-fish. Continuing to shovel the morsels of food into her overflowing orifice, she tossed back the flask of water sending the liquid splashing carelessly upon her famished lips.

Fahimah suddenly yanked the small metal dish from Cherinne's pawing grasp. "Hey, American, allow me some! I am also hungry and thirsty!"

Astonishment, riddled with disbelief and regret, shaded the bursting cheeks and wide chestnut eyes as Cherinne watched Fahimah through a completely different view. The princess carefully picked at the few remaining dry morsels, placing one gently within her mouth and the other two securely within a tuck of her tunic. Embarrassed, Cherinne handed the princess the flask of water, which she had nearly finished, except for a meager swallow and the drops that were now running in mortification to slip unnoticed from her chin.

Fahimah softly sipped from the leather flask, then again until the liquid was gone. She untied her sash, wrapping it snugly around the now empty container then fashioned it tightly to her waist.

Cherinne lowered her head in inexorable shame; a gluttonous beast danced as a reflection within the flickering flames of the oil lamp before her, while she could feel the lump of jerky choking in her throat. She forced the scratching bulge down, silent before what moments earlier had seemed an enemy; an apology could never replace the portion of food she had so rashly consumed. Yes, her western heritage shone like that, not of a lighted beacon, with the pride of the Statue of Liberty, but as insatiable covetous swine, with the image of herself and Laddor as they had practically rolled from the All-you-can-eat Buffet after they had gorged themselves on: baked chicken, carved roast beef, the white clam chowder, mashed potatoes, key lime pie and unlimited beverages. Yes, Fahimah, you are right; I am an American, and *yes,* I am a glutton.

"Fahimah, I'm...

Fahimah's hand quickly shot in the air—'the hand' gesture. They exchanged a look.

"Don't say anything, American; I would not have expected anything less." She pointed a slender finger at Cherinne. "For, look at the size of your hind-quarters. They look to be grain-fed stock, ready for market. I would be embarrassed to have even my mother see that, let alone a man; or is your red-haired *plaything* blind that he cannot see that obnoxious bulge?"

Sparking electric currents flared, ricocheting off the stale red clay of the cavernous walls; and Cherinne shocked and appalled at any mention of her buttocks being obese burned red with rage. She stood to her full five feet and clenched her fists; the tension snaking along her shoulders and back raced to tighten the chords popping along her neck and jaw. The cursing, she so desperately tried to avoid, spewed forth from her drawn lips like water rushing from a waterfall.

"Why you insulting little bitch!" Cherinne's lack of control amplified her fuming temper as another unbridled curse fell upon Fahimah who quickly clamored to her feet. "My ass is no bigger than yours! You whelping whore! And, I'll have you know that *most men* like my size three *hind-quarters—especially* my *plaything!* Who, you had best keep your slutty little hands away from, or I'll be liable to kick your scrawny little ass with or without the use of this stupid bracelet! I hate you, Fahimah! I hate your smirky little face! I hate your attitude! And, I hate the idea, that you look like me! Now—back off—or I'm liable to wipe up this grimy underground shit-hole with your stupid little shit eating grin!"

A burst of laughter gusted forth from the wicked-eyed princess as her eyes flickered and she tossed her head back and clutched her stomach. Cherinne, dumfounded by her reaction, scowled.

"What's so funny?"

Fahimah wiped her moist eyes as the boisterous laughter slowed to a girlish giggle. Her gaze suddenly locked with Cherinne's and the laughter ceased while the damp air rapidly chilled and Cherinne's skin suddenly puckered.

"It is hilarious, American," the princess's face shadowed and an icy stare proceeded. Her tone was cold as winter's fury. "It is hilarious; for now I know…you *are* my sister."

CHAPTER 18

Cherinne's brow creased markedly as she thought over the possibility that she and the female, she despised so greatly, could be sisters. "What are you saying, Fahimah?"

Gathering her blanket, Fahimah crossed her legs sitting Indian style upon the dirt. "You heard me, American." She gazed up into the shadow hiding Cherinne's puzzled expression. "*You* are *my* sister; and whether we detest each other or not, we are blood. Twins…identical twins."

"Wait! What are you telling me?" Cherinne stumbled upon the words, her head spinning in a vicious tumult of bewilderment, while her fingers raked nervously through the tangled strands of her hair. Time froze with confusion and the air of the small grotto was thick with uncertainty. Cherinne shook her head in denial. "You are my twin sister? I don't have a sister!"

"Yes, you do. Now, sit before me and I will elaborate."

Cherinne ran her hands along the length of her arms, as if she were warming herself; while her eyes darted wildly about searching the dimness for her past. She paced the few feet of the cubicle. The thought of Fahimah being her blood was atrocious; and though Cherinne had gazed upon her during her bout with a demon from the past and had jested of their likeness, the idea of the princess being her twin—identical twin—was absurd.

"I command you—sit down!" The princess's voice rang with an irate authority and she grabbed a remnant of torn cloth that hung loosely along Cherinne's moving calf as her patience was running thin.

"Wait a minute!" She stomped her feet to loosen Fahimah's hold. "I don't have a sister!"

"Yes, you do. Now, quit this childish outburst and sit. And, though, I detest it far more than you, I will explain."

A wall of tension had built in the small confines, making it nearly impossible to breathe. Suddenly the clanging of the heavy linked chain and lock startled the two females, cutting through the dissension. Hafiz's face emerged in the dim flame of the flickering lantern; and Cherinne, engrossed in their conversation, was abruptly taken aback. She gasped at the whites of his mismatched gaze which peeked from behind his black shroud and peered eerily through the iron bars. By the few lines etched across his dark forehead and the slight crowns forming at the corner of each eye, she guessed his age to be maybe thirty.

A cold shiver ran along Cherinne's body and red flush rushed to her cheeks with the realization he was staring at the bareness of her exposed skin. The torn soiled garment hung loosely upon her body, tattered to patches of rags and not leaving much to the imagination; mortification was apparent in her face. Her eyes raced frantically to the corner where she had hastily tossed the shabby blanket when the mention of 'food' had taken her from her senses. Spinning to reveal partial backside and hurriedly slipping into the corner, she grabbed the woolen cover, quickly secured it about herself, then slunk to the coolness of the floor.

The heat in Hafiz's groin had grown immensely, while he had gazed upon her from the darkened shadows of the tunnel. He had crept upon them quietly, in the hopes of catching one or the other exposing herself or possibly massaging the other's wounds; something he had dreamt of each night since their capture three moons earlier.

Watching the lovely American from just feet away, he had studied her every move. The softness of her alabaster skin, which shimmered in the flame's warm glow, making her appear as a goddess, as she moved within the shadows and before the lantern's light. He had observed the waves of her long golden locks, which had swayed with her every step. Her tense shoulders, jutting erect, had forced her firm breast taught against the silken translucent cloth of her feathery tunic as she had angrily spewed vulgar American words at her mirrored reflection, adding to his arousal. The thought of her screaming those same words, while he had heated unbridled sex with them both was maddening.

He licked his parched lips behind the cloth of the concealing shroud. The dampened fabric was now wet with a warm moist drool matching the sweat building upon his brow and within his robe which was just an added agitation, heightening with each quickened breath. While the words of his superior, Nagid, rang loudly in his throbbing ears. *Hafiz, the Lord Seth is ready to receive the maiden; prepare her for his majesty.*

And, what of the other female?

Glancing at the colossal-sized wooden doors separating them from the lord, he had considered his reply carefully.

Bring them both. But, be sure to bind the one who possesses the anklets; her fighting skills are that of a trained warrior and she may prove to be troublesome.

Complying with the order, Hafiz then turned to make the long tedious journey to the lower tunnels of the Lord Seth's domicile, where the many dungeons referred to as the 'Haush min maut', which meant *Courtyard of Death* in Egyptian, were located. They housed any and all prisoners of war before they were tortured then executed—a labyrinth far beneath the earth, with each tunnel leading to a different style torture chamber or hole to be left in to rot—a hell devised specifically to dissuade any regime of defying the Great Lord.

Blood rushed to every extremity of Hafiz's body in the uncontrollable anticipation of having the two alluring females alone, in the quiet of the earth. Where no-one could hear their low muffled cries, as he unleashed the dragon's fire cursing throughout his veins. Perspiration dampened his ruddy calloused palms as he shouldered his crossbow and a bundle of twined rope. His heart pounded loudly in his chest moving in rhythm with each accelerated step—the journey now a desired mission.

*Hafiz…*Nagid's words were one of warning. Cutting through the revelry, they were sharp, razor blades which slashed when shearing too deep; slicing painfully within his ears…*Don't allow the inferno that grows* *within your galabiyah to rule the hairs beneath your amami. The females' alluring beauty is one of craftiness; an evil which can drive a thirsting man away from water. They are the Lord Seth's possession now and he shall not want you touching either. Men have lost more than fingers for the mere thieving of bread; and his majesty will not tolerate his property being spoiled.*

Hafiz could barely control the anger rising in his voice. The tension hardened his shoulders as the crossbow irritably scraped the flaring muscles of his full frame and the words spewed from his mouth in haste—words which could have easily been considered insubordination and brought him death. *But, what of 'your' actions? Your intentions were not to be questioned, as you sought to fulfill your own needs? Why should I be so different?*

Stand down, Hafiz. A low boiling thunder sounded in his superior's voice. *I have had to account for my incompetence and I shall not have to justify myself to you also. Now, retrieve the females and notify me as soon as you return.*

Since Cherinne's departure, the weather forecast had called for more drought with little precipitation. But several severe storms had strangely materialized, taking the community of Key West by surprise. Monstrous up-roaring gales of fierce thrashing winds, which groaned in a howling rage made the skin crawl as they ravaged in frequented surges upon the land. Especially at night, when the dark thunderclouds that remained from the day rolled like steam engines across the midnight sky adding gloom to the already black air. A torrential downpour of rain drove the native inhabitants for cover; and those vacationing were forced inside to play Backgammon, when they should have been enjoying the sun and waters of the Florida coast.

The quiet of the estate was deafening, with it seeming like months, since the young miss had disappeared inside the Amphibian's hull with Laddor trailing at her heels.

Reynold's shaded his eyes from the water's glare, the lines deepened on his forehead, as he observed with skepticism, from Cherinne's balcony doors, the two men working below on the pool. The sun was a welcomed sight after the rushing course of floodwater rain and mysterious murky sky. Remnants of the beastly storms lay evident in the sopping grass and lazy puddles which loafed about in lounge chairs. Balmy rays shed heated warmth upon the pallid skin of Reynolds's cheeks and also upon the coffee colored faces of the pool men below. While the butler found no comfort in their presence. He dialed the seven digit number for 'Prestige Pools'—a pool repair company noted for their speedy service and affordable fees. The particular butler detested using their services, but the young Miss's funds were unfortunately being used elsewhere right now.

"Good afternoon—*Prestige Pools*," a nasally female sniffed into the line.

"Hello? Yes, I am phoning for Miss Cherinne Havenstrit at 2727 Highrock Drive. Two of your service men are repairing the pool located on the estate. I was just inquiring as to whether or not the men you sent here are…Middle Eastern. I don't recall ever seeing them before."

"Did you say Middle Eastern, Sir?"

"Yes, why yes I did—Middle Eastern."

The sickening sound of phlegm being drawn from within a sinus cavity soured the yogurt cup settling within Reynolds's stomach. A moment of throat clearing passed with a shuffle of the secretary's notepapers.

"Well—no, Sir. Doug and Travis were full-blooded American last time we checked, unless they made a quick stop at the tanning beds before your service call." She cackled at her own joke with a cough and long draw of mucus. "Is there a problem, Sir…?"

Bidding her 'good day', Reynolds rested the receiver upon it's gold and white ceramic cradle, disconnecting the call. Slowly, the balcony doors were closed and the latch bolted. Steadily making his way through the entire 25,000 square feet of living space within the estate, he devised a plan, in case *Doug* or *Travis* would decide to shirk their duties on the damaged concrete and attempt to make their way inside. Setting the alarm, he headed to his quarters—a small section of the north wing which provided ample living space for the butler, with complete liberties to the kitchen.

When Joseph Havenstrit, the master of the estate had left, Cherinne had offered Reynolds basically any area in the house to live. He had determined it to be a good idea *not* to have his quarters too close to the young female's due to their being alone. So, he decided on the large room closest to the guest's lodgings where he could relax in peace and quiet and fuss over his model of Columbus's Santa Maria. An intricately detailed replica, he had been absorbed in completing, for nearly a year.

Then, a day had come when the aging Reynolds had thought that possibly his eye-sight was deceiving him as a gleaming flash of red hair, lugging several battered suitcases and shouldering two over-stuffed packs, had quickly and quietly slipped within the guest room door, speedily closing out his confused scowl.

"What in God's name does that boy think he's doing?"

Reynolds rapped upon the large double doors while placing his ear hesitantly to the cherry wood.

The young male, named *Laddor*, who the missus had surprisingly appeared with three afternoons earlier called out from the other side. "Who is it?"

"It is I, Reynolds. Is Miss Cherinne about?" Worry lines added ten years to his middle-aged face—worry over whether she was occupying the room also *or* possibly engaging in activities suitable only for marriage.

"No, Reynolds—*Cherry isn't in here. She's out shopping,*" his answer was sung like that of a mocking bird. I will call for you if I'm in need of your services; but right now, Cherry is taking care of *everything.*"

A low wily snigger screeched within the butlers straining ears, followed by a groan of, "*Ohhh, Cherry,* you are an *amazing* woman! *I just love your tasty fruit!*"

The ashen skin upon Reynolds's face suddenly turned ghostly; and his chin, which had dropped in utter repugnance, quickly snapped closed in annoyance.

"*By Heavens! What in blazes is going on in there?*" His balled fist banged angrily upon the door. "Young man, you had best be talking apples and bananas! Or, I shall remove every hair on that God-awful head of yours with a pair of snub-nosed pliers!"

"Whaddya' say, Pappy?" The door flung open as the red-haired nuisance chewed boisterously on a succulent papaya. Its orange juices, filling the cracks and crevices of his long fingers, threatened to add spatters of color to the beige carpeting.

Grinning devilishly, Laddor's big eyes glinted with mock pleasure. His crimson locks outlined the smugness pasted on his messy face, while the hem of his faded t-shirt made for a wet-nap, as he sopped up the dripping juice.

Irritation bit through Reynolds's clenched teeth in a measured threat. "What do you think you are doing?" Imaginary darts flung in every direction mostly catching in long locks and a near hairless chest.

Laddor wrinkled his upper lip, while lavishly catching any left over papaya juice with his errant tongue. "Why, I am tasting of Cherry's succulent fruit! Would you like some?" He extended the half-eaten produce to Reynolds who attempted to control the rage reddening his features and running from his constricting shoulders within his tux to the tight muscles of his fists.

"*No!* I do not want to taste of Cherry—*Miss Cherinne's* fruit! *You obnoxious little twit!* But, I'm liable to bust your coconut if you ever refer to me as 'Pappy' again!"

The extended hand and papaya quickly disappeared behind Laddor's back as he shrunk away in alarm, his smile now replaced with an apprehensive stare.

Reynolds remembered that day as if it were yesterday. Opening his broad clothes closet, he reached between the pressed, meticulously creased black pants, occupying the far left corner of the wardrobe, followed by white button shirts, vests, then silk-lined black jackets. Spit-and-polished, black leather shoes sat along the closet's floor carefully aligned from presidential affair to every day butler service. He felt for the cool steel of the double-barreled shotgun which rested peacefully behind his trousers, hiding away while awaiting a day to stave off any undesirables with a blast of its bulleted fury.

"Ahh—so you have been asleep, my friend." Removing the weapon from within its haven he ran an aged hand along the smooth smoke-colored barrels. "It has been a long time. I prove that you will serve me well." Reaching his hand to an overhead shelf, he grabbed a box of Remington shotgun shells. "Come…we have work to do."

An abrupt ring startled Reynolds who bolted to an upright position, as he had apparently dozed while sitting in wait, within the confines of the northern living room—one of the four which was centered nearest the pool area. He grabbed the handset. A throated whisper raced from his dry lips into the darkness of night which had come during his slumber. Craning his stiff neck, he shifted clear of the shotgun which had been propped firmly to his side.

"Havenstrit residence."

…"Reynolds is that you?" A small far away voice screeched into the line.

With a scowl, he answered, "Yes, this is Reynolds. May I inquire as to who this is?"

An eager voice replied, "Its Laddor! Ya know Laddor Zeandre…with Cherinne!"

His middle-aged eyes rolled, the yellowing whites flashing in irritation; his tired remark was quite terse. "Of course I know who *Laddor* is. There aren't too many young men out there with a name the same as a set of two by fours fashioned together with spokes which are used for accessing areas out of their reach—you dolt. Where is Miss Cherinne? I should be speaking with her."

"I told ya' he was gonna' ask about her!" The squeak was barely audible through the long distance line. Reynolds, though his sight and body, at age sixty, weren't quite what they used to be, his hearing was impeccable. An argument ensued on the opposite end, while the other voice he assumed was Deverall's.

"Give me that phone, you chicken shit!"

"*Ooowww! That hurt!*"

A slight grin attended the scowl upon Reynolds face as he could hear the young male crying out in pain. And, though his dislike of the obnoxious pilot was a justified one, his dislike for the blundering Laddor was even greater.

Deverall panted into the phone, "Hey Reynolds! How's it goin'?"

Glancing at the shotgun propped within the heavy leather cushion of the swivel lounger, he replied with marked annoyance, "*It* is *going*, Mr. Deverall. I take it by the bumble-head's remark, that Miss Cherinne is not accompanying you."

"Uh…" Deverall stumbled for an answer, "…she's gettin' a perm!"

"Wha…"

Laddor's hushed whisper scolded the pilot, who Reynold's imagined, was wearing a foolish sweat-ridden grin. "You idiot, Deverall—Reynolds isn't *that* stupid! Umm…tell 'im she's gettin' a foot massage."

"Mr. Deverall!" Irritation snapped through several thousand miles of phone line while the butler's patience had reached its end. "I would appreciate the truth! Where is Miss Cherinne?"

A full moment of quiet passed; Reynolds tapped an age spotted finger along the receiver, while the effort to remain calm was becoming an arduous task—the thought of something endangering the young miss, nerve-racking. He inhaled deep, attempting to prepare for what he was about to hear. "Mr. Deverall—you had best spit out what I need to hear quickly or I may just reach my fist through this phone and knock some sense into you and that carrot-topped idiot. Have I made myself clear?"

Deverall's tone was one of an officer who arrived at your front door in the middle of the night with dire news and an apology.

"Well…Reynolds…there was a battle here at the palace—the Tarun Regime, the Amir Rasheed's—who is the owner of the jewels. Anyway…apparently the brigand that attacked had come for the bracelet—the Semus Bracelet—that's what they've referred to that bracelet as, the one that sweethe…I mean *Cherinne* is wearing. Anyway, they took both the girls and killed Princess Haneefah." The pilot was silent for a moment in respect to the deceased Princess and also to allow the concerned butler to absorb this information.

"What? Someone was killed? Good God in Heaven!" Reynolds hastily traced the sign of the crucifix upon his chest. The possibility of a death had crossed his mind, to promptly be erased, but, to actually hear of it was shocking. He ran a broad trembling hand through the salt and pepper of his thick hair. "Where is Miss Havenstrit? I demand to know this instant!"

"We don't know…actually," Deverall faltered, his voice somber. "One of the thugs—a huge guy, with this massive weapon, who we all fought against—including sissy-boy here—took off with her and the Princess Fahimah, who looks like her twin." He paused for a moment. "We tried to fight him off…but the giant did somethin' with his weapon…and the earth here was practically split in two. The amir's palace is in a shambles and…"

"Quiet!" Reynolds clutched at a breath, unable to absorb the distressing account. The knowledge of the young lady, he had grown to know and love as his own daughter, being in the hands of a Middle Eastern barbarian, was a grueling deliberation.

The whole of Reynolds's body suddenly grew weak, while his head spun with the closeness of the surrounding darkness of night. The one stream of light, breaking through a crevice of the heavy damask draperies hanging lifelessly at the enormous window, was the only ray of hope. He seated himself warily upon the leather of his chair, while the screeching and air of the upholstery, was a hollow reverberation humming in his ears.

Oh, Miss—how could I have allowed this to happen? He glanced at the shotgun; its black barrels glistened majestically within the crook of the lounger's arm, seeming to beckon for life.

Deverall's voice broke through the man's consuming anxiety. "Reynolds...ya' still there?"

Reynolds peered through the shady dimness at the receiver, as if it had suddenly appeared within his trembling hand. "Yes. Yes, I am here." His shaken words were evidence of his apprehensive self.

"Well, in that case, we need you to do us a favor...From what ol' Red, here, says, there's a truck full of jewels sittin' somewhere there on the estate. Is it still there?"

Reynolds, suddenly remembering the two suspicious-looking pool men, shouldered the weapon and swiftly headed en route for the hallway leading into Cherinne's bedroom. Feeling his way along the lightless corridor he reached the framework of her doorway and slipped inside.

The balcony drapes had remained secured back, with their lovely navy sashes tied in bulky cummerbunds, which hung from bronze leaf hooks adorned to the walls. *The young lady sure has impeccable taste,* he thought to himself, as the moon's light shone vibrantly throughout her room, as if someone had turned on a switch. It emitted a soft shadowy glow along several white shelves weighted with a vast assortment of books and college photos, making it appear lonelier than he could bear.

He crossed her room. The plush of the carpet's fibers were soft beneath his bare feet; the sensation an enjoyable one after the firmness of his own room's hardwood flooring. Keeping to the shadows, Reynolds stood with his back to a satiny drape while quickly peering over his shoulder through the glass French doors and down toward the pool area. The illumination of light rippled along the calming, dark water, bringing near a peaceful impression; though, from Reynolds's point of view, his dread of the situation could quickly become unnerving. He placed a slightly trembling hand on the security of the shotgun, while it anxiously awaited a squeeze of its heavy duel triggers.

Through the clear skies of the night, he noticed nothing out of the ordinary. The variety of equipment which had accompanied the two suspicious-looking men sat dormant as a hulking shadow, never seeming to have been moved or used. Reynolds scolded himself beneath his breath. The estate had been his responsibility; and only a shirker would have dozed during a period of uncertainty—like a knight resting lazily within his bunk while the lord's castle was under attack. He shook his head in disgust.

"Reynolds?" What's goin' on?" Deverall shouted into the phone, breaking through the overwhelming silence within the estate. "Are the jewels still there?"

"We have had visitors today," came his reply.

"*No shit?* Were they tan-skinned?"

Reynolds quickly shifted to the other drape and peered along the fence at a diverse angle along the pool's concrete decking. "Yes, they were— Middle Eastern. I'm not sure of their whereabouts at this time."

Deverall's fretted alertness threw Laddor who waited impatiently for an answer into a nervous frenzy. "*What?*" Reynolds could hear the faint howl in the background. "We need that earring to find Cherry! And, that hateful bastard, Rasheed, is gonna' leave soon! Are the jewels there *or not?*"

"Tell that imbecilic twit to settle down!" Reynolds's German-Scandinavian heritage fumed in an irate combination. "I need to check the garage, so just hold tight for a moment."

"*Hey!* While you're there, check to see if you can find the earring we need. That's what I called about. It has three pearls hanging on it and there's a compass inside one of 'em."

Unsure as to whether or not he had heard accurately, he attempted a repeat. "There's a *what* inside one of them? Speak English Deverall—I'm not quite sure I've heard you correctly; I could have sworn you said a compass."

A chuckle reverberated in the butler's ear. "Yeah, you're right." It became a laugh. "I did say compass. And, *holy shit!* You should see the artwork that's sprouted from my navel! It's a map! Covering everything but…"

Reynolds curled his upper lip, matching the curved slope of his two-toned eyebrows, while holding the phone clear of hearing distance, "Please, Mr. Deverall—if you would spare me the details." Still holding the phone from his ear, he stated slowly, "I'm going to put the phone down now—I will return shortly."

A broadened smirk was a pasted expression on Deverall's face as he held his shirt up firmly against his throat examining the cartography on his over-sized stomach. Placing a chunky finger to the drawing, he traced the black lines with childlike enthusiasm, his finger tunneling through the heavy patches of hair as his maniacal grin grew across his face.

"Man, Red—*this shit is wicked! Look!* It doesn't even come off when I rub my fingers against it! Boy, wouldn't Mirella love this! We could play *Candy Land;* and she could pick *Gumdrop Moun…!*"

"*Oh, shut up—Deverall!*" The pilot's pornographic revelry interrupted. "I don't need to hear any of your twisted remarks!" Laddor flopped his weary self back onto the palace's humongous guestroom bed, his achy body feeling twice his twenty-two years yearned for the comfort of his own feather mattress back home. He touched his multi-colored eye—one of the presents from the amir—which throbbed within its socket.

Deverall's steadfast conviction to have him accompany them on the tedious journey they were about to embark on, was a good one. How could the pompous prince refuse the knowledge he alone would possess, that contained the whereabouts of the princess and Cherinne? The knowledge conveyed to him by someone who was thousands of miles away—a place where he longed to be now with Cherinne, her smiling face, warm laughter and frightening scowl as she would club him for his dogged, lustful attempts.

He closed his eyes; the multi-colored one being an itchy puff of soreness. *Damn you, Rasheed,* whispered from his tired lips as he listened to

Deverall's steady breathing, as the tiresome pilot clutched Cherinne's cell phone to his ear and paced the carpeted floor.

Time drug as a ship's anchor trudging the bottom of the sea; the silence between the two men deafening as they waited for the butler to return.

Laddor traced his fingers along the flat of the scimitar's sheath strapped to his side; the scenes in the courtyard weighing heavily upon his mind. Mentally, he retraced his footsteps, wondering what he could have done differently as a hundred images raced before his closed lids: the battle, the attack in this very room by the irate princess, the exploding bus, all the way to Cherinne's closed eyes as she stood anxiously awaiting his gift—*his gift, the bracelet*—the bringer of death and destruction. Angrily, he struck his fist against the soft mattress. *Fool! How could I have been so foolish! Rasheed should just kill me; end this miserable existence of mine.*

"Yeah, I'm still here." Deverall's voice broke through laddor's silent rantings. "And, you have the earring…the pearl earring with the three bobs?"

Laddor leaped to his feet, no longer drowning in hopeless sorrow; while a new hope erased the suggestion of being be-headed by the amir or one of his lackey mercenaries. He placed his ear near to the mobile phone in the attempts to hear the conversation in progress.

"*No, shit!* It was glowing?" A hand disappeared beneath the excited pilot's outlandishly colored Hawaiian shirt as he caressed the full of his hair covered self. He grinned while pondering this new development.

"Well…we need you to put the earring on. No! No! Don't hang up! I'm not jokin', Reynolds! I have the other one on…and this cool lookin' map appeared on my chest. It's the coolest shit I've ever seen! No—that red-haired fairy didn't put me up to this. Look…"

Hearing enough of the one-sided conversation, Laddor yanked Cherinne's cell phone from within Deverall's grip. "Look—Reynolds, I don't care what you two may call me; and I don't care at this point what you think of me." His tone carried no desperation, but a note of genuine earnestness. "But, I do know one thing: We need the map contained in that earring to get Cherinne back. And, if you don't help us, she may die. Now, will you help us…I mean Cherinne—or not?"

The cool desert sand swirled in a dancer's delight, like the alabaster mare, Nefertiti, on which Rasheed sat; who, also, danced impatiently for his signal to proceed forward. He secured his yashmac, the white veil just beneath his eyes, to protect against the chalky granules that could possibly turn into a tidal wave of jagged glass. A force so powerful, containing billions of uncontrollable razor-like shards, it could shred the full of your garments, while effortlessly tearing away at your screaming, bloody skin. He gazed through the narrow slit of the cotton cloth at the endless sea of shifting sand, the rising and falling dunes of white that began just beneath his horse's feet. There were near three hundred kilometers of granules from the regime to the Red Sea Coast and trillions of tons of sand to the West, reaching to the Libyan border—a graveyard for those who had ventured beyond their means and their senses. Thousands of lives had been buried beneath the heated blanket of white; its warmth and velvetiness a deceitful ploy to draw its victims in. While it sopped the very moisture from your bones and left you as a brittle corpse, on which the eager buzzards could feed.

Meticulously etched upon the pilot's bulbous body, the map indicated that the location of the girls was somewhere in the western region of Egypt, between El Kharga and Mut, near four hundred kilometers afar. With determination, the adequate equipment and provisions, they could be there in five days time. Rasheed's concern wasn't so much the route traveled; but, that once they arrived there, what course should they follow then? The vast area of sand and blistering sun there covered a massive amount of dry arid ground; and, to wonder about foolishly would surely be the death of a thirsting man.

The remaining chill of night raced beneath the full of Rasheed's snow-white uniform. A chill he feared, not from the grayish-red darkness just before the sun's appearance at dawn, but the coming of the light of day that filled a man with an exuberating emotion of being alive, yet, also a dreaded conviction of confronting those things to come, of which he had no control. With great resolve he sheathed his sword and checked the entirety of his weapons.

"Nefertiti…" Rasheed leaned to whisper within the wispy white hairs of the mare's ear as he ran a hand along the smoothness of her firm neck. She whinnied softly at the sound of the amir's voice. A black hoof then pounded upon the earth, guided by the taut muscles of her long lean leg. "We have most tedious work to do; and, I do know how much you dislike the Princess Fahimah—the animalistic instinct within you both fights to steal my attention."

The attentive mare threw another hoof and tossed her head; as if just the princess's name, was an agitating fly. "Okay, okay," a smile broadened beneath his shroud. "I promise to give you extra sweet if you help me with this task. Besides, just because Fahimah can practically outrun you, doesn't mean that you still don't have favor in my eyes."

There's another toss of the head accompanied by an immediate snort. "Now—that was totally uncalled for." Patting her broad arching neck, he chuckled mildly.

The thunderous sound of hooves converged like a stampede of buffalo upon him as the small army Commander Lateef had assembled congregated in a mass with ample rations, equipment and weaponry. Anxiety filled the faces of his men—anxiety and strength of mind intermingled upon the faces they, also now, covered. Several loaded packhorses approached from the rear; their burdens were one of heavy artillery consisting of guns, ammunition, feathered shafts, crossbow bolts, blades and the Dragon—a four foot warhead missile able to be launched by a single combatant with the ability to destroy a tank or even a plane—in this case, possibly something far more powerful and treacherous.

Slowing his galloping mare to a trot, Commander Lateef pulled shoulder to shoulder with the amir as the prince gazed off into the ocean of sand and few rays of morning light.

"Excuse me, Your Eminence," Lateef quickly bowed his head. "The men are assembled and ready at your command."

Rasheed glanced through the rows of anxious men whose mounts, waiting patiently, had begun a restless stirring. "Where is Mr. Deverall? He is to be mounted and ready."

"My apologies, Sire. I last spotted him entering the east entrance with the other American approximately an hour ago."

A shout sounded from the rear of the brigade, "Amir! Amir Rasheed!" Deverall, sweat building upon his brow, bounded along the last of the grass terrain where the few remaining patches of green ended and the white of the sand began. While it was a god's miracle that the regime had any green at all with their location being so far from the Nile River. A god's blessing.

Laddor was a full stride ahead of the panting pilot; while his legs were closer to that of a racehorse. The possibility of outrunning the red-haired American had crossed the prince's mind—a hint of competition coursing through his veins.

"Amir! Wait for us!" Deverall shouted, nearly out of breath; while Laddor already stood just feet away from Rasheed, as he had easily skirted through the rows of soldiers and their fidgeting horses.

Rasheed's narrowed stare sharply ran the length of Laddor's full six-two. "Mr. Zeandre—I do believe you were informed of the fact that your presence is not welcome on this mission."

Laddor returned his hard-nosed stare, the knowledge he had of the girls' whereabouts aching to explode from his near quivering lips which he forced to remain sealed.

"Mr. Zeandre…have you not heard my words? You are unwelcome. Now, move along before you are trampled underfoot by one of my men's horses." He turned to the commander. "Commander, have you prepared a horse for Mr. Deverall?"

"Why, yes, Your Grace. The young boy, Ib, is bringing him now as we speak."

A rein in one hand and exuberantly waving the other, the young lad hastily trotted a fine gelding toward the convergence of battle-ready soldiers. He shouted to the amir through the dimness of dawn which was quickly approaching, "Your Highness, I am coming! Please wait!"

Rasheed was reminded of himself as a younger lad, and a battle that the Amir Nuri and his grandfather had intented of initiating, with a neighboring regime. As the men had sat proudly upon their mounts, including Rasool, who was positioned at the front of the regiment alongside his father; Rasheed had lingered behind to comfort his mother with promising words of his safe return. While the soldiers, his father, grandfather, and even Rasool had prepared to leave without him.

'I promise, Mother; I will return to you.' Rasheed placed a slender finger to a warm tear racing along her lovely cheek. 'Grandfather advises me to go. He says that if I fight, this will prove to Father that I am not a coward, and that I shall be able to rule the regime someday. Please, Mother, don't be angry with me.' He wrapped his arms around her trembling body while inhaling the exquisite scent of her perfumed oils. 'I promise to return. So please pray to the gods for me.'

Placing a kiss upon her cheek he quietly left her quarters; unknowing to either that his return would nearly be in a burlap sack with his father even more irate and disappointed in him than ever.

"*Hey!* Are you ignoring me now, *Rasheed?*" Laddor angrily spouted, annoyed at the silent treatment, which was unknowingly steered in another direction. "I was talking to you. *Hey!*" He rapped the prince's mare on the rear, which jolted forward, nearly tossing the unsuspecting amir to the ground. Lateef quickly drew his sword awaiting the command to strike.

"*Whoa! Nefertiti!*" Rasheed quickly collected himself and spun about. Rage poured from behind his white shroud, which fortunately covered the pinkish hue rushing into his cheeks from embarrassment. Hastily, dismounting he closed the gap between himself and the American nuisance. "How dare you touch my horse's arse! Mr. Zeandre, I believe you have now forced me to have you bound and shackled. Wasi waqqaf haadha…" Rasheed barked the order while pointing a finger at Laddor.

Deverall, panting heavily, drew a breath and stepped between the two warring men, like a mother hen coming between two squabbling chicks, but without the possibility of severe punishment being death. "Hold up now, Your Highness."

Rasheed notioned for the commander to hold as his eyes darted angrily to the interfering pilot.

"Red, here…" Deverall grabbed Laddor by the arm, "…has the other map—the map to find the girls."

The amir's narrowed eyes searched them both in disbelief. "What are you telling me, Mr. Deverall? This had best not be a deceptive ploy to remedy your friend from punishment. I shall not tolerate any such deception from either of you," his anger, at nearly being tossed, still brewing inside.

"No, no, Amir, I would never lie to you. He has the map. We just phoned sweethe…I mean Cherinne's butler in the United States…"

"You mean you have used one of the palace's satellite phones without my consent? What else have you poked your nose into that was entirely off limits to you?"

Deverall hurriedly interrupted the downhill path in which the conversation was taking, as the amir seemed to be more on edge than normal today, surmising that pressure and fatigue were beginning to take their toll. "No, no, Princey—we used sweetheart's cell phone; she has international roaming. We've touched nothing of yours."

He eyed them skeptically. "Good—then continue with this tale you are so certain will save your friend from any chastisement. It sounded as if you said you had a map."

"Yes, yes, we do—or rather Red does," Deverall stated shaking his head in agreement as he glanced at Laddor.

Laddor stepped closer to Rasheed and looked him directly in the eyes. Haughtiness, yearning to appear, slipped eagerly from Laddor's lips like throwing mud in the prince's face, which Laddor wished more than anything he could do. "Look, Rasheed—we, or rather *I*, have the other set of directions to the location of Cherinne and the Princess Fahimah. I know where they are."

Rasheed removed his yashmac—the shroud covering his face—and bluntly stated, "I do not believe you. You would say anything at this point to save your cowardly self from the punishment you so earnestly deserve."

Laddor pressed his nose within hairs of the prince, his angry breath breathing heavily upon Rasheed's face. His tone was low, seething through clenched teeth; it was barely a whisper, "Rasheed…if it wasn't for these men that you hide behind, I would surely hit you so hard, it'd knock that conceited smirk right off your haughty face."

As Rasheed listened to the American, who he had played out this scenario with before; his father's biting words surfaced painfully within his mind. 'Rasheed—you are a coward who hides beyond the curtailment of my hem. You shall *never* be a true leader, especially of this regime.' His father's steely stare had cut to his very soul. 'I resent the womb that gave birth to you; so wishing you could be returned to those few moments of pleasure and spat upon the floor to be mopped up by a valued servant.'

Rasheed searched the loathing eyes of the American that were mirrored images of his own; while seething rage tightened every muscle of his being. He abruptly tore his gaze away. "I do not have time for this nonsense, Mr. Zeandre. You are a mere speck, an eyesore, that I do wish would simply vanish like a smelly vapor in the wind."

"You mean a fart, Princey," Deverall volunteered too eagerly, as a few surrounding men snickered beneath their breath.

"Well, thank you for that brilliant deduction, Mr. Deverall. I'm sure the men appreciate your candid banter; since, unfortunately, some of them may actually know that vulgar American word."

Rasheed turned to gather his awaiting horse and remounted. "Mr. Deverall, please collect your gelding and make ready to leave."

"*Wait! Rasheed!* How dare you walk away from me? *I have the map!*" Laddor pointed a demanding finger at the prince. "So, this means you finally see things *my* way—that you *are* nothing but a coward?"

Rasheed looked beyond the sea of sand at the sun producing a ray just along the horizon. "No, Mr. Zeandre—this just means that my eyes have now been opened. You shall die at the next dawn. Commander Lateef," he translated in Arabic, "bound this insubordinate menace."

The color drained from Laddor's face turning him a ghostly white. "*What? But, I have the map! You can't kill me!*" he cried, as the commander, with a wave of his hand motioned to two of the over-anxious brothers, Omar and Mahir to restrain the young male.

Rasheed's eyes never left the crest of morning light. "No, that is where you are wrong, Mr. Zeandre. I am Rasheed—Prince Rasheed Daivyan Khalil Tarun, the lord of this empire and *I* may do as I wish. Commander Lateef," he spoke in Arabic, "have Mr. Zeandre secured on the back of one of your men's horses. If his claim is genuine and he has a map where the Princess Fahimah is located, then we will need this information."

Laddor glanced between the two, unsure as to their words. "I won't give it to you, Rasheed!" Laddor quickly shoved a crumpled slip of paper into his mouth and chewed exuberantly in the attempts to ingest the map. Omar and Mahir rushed him and slammed him roughly to the ground. A brief wrestling match ensued with the brothers attempting to retrieve the much needed information.

"I'm sorry, Sire…" Omar apologized as he rose to his feet and brushed off "…but, he has swallowed it."

"No need to apologize, soldier. I'm most certain Mr. Zeandre will be more than eager to volunteer the information once he is being interrogated." Without another word, Rasheed clicked his mare and spurred her toward the deadly waste lands of western Egypt.

CHAPTER 19

"You have been summoned by the Lord Seth," Hafiz's tone was set, while he wiped away a bead of sweat running from his brow to his tense jaw. "Come, you, who wears the bracelet. I shall prepare you first."

Cherinne's fearful eyes darted rapidly from Hafiz to Fahimah as she hugged her knees to her chest and drew the blanket to herself.

"No—take me instead," Fahimah volunteered, seeing the intense fear plaguing her double's face—certain she could take the militant in hand to hand combat and yearning to acquire the space needed to expand her yarn cocoon.

"Take me. I am the princess—the princess of Tarun Regime, Princess Fahimah; and I wish to address the Lord Seth and question him as to why he has so rudely brought us here."

Hafiz ran the length of Fahimah's body; his gaze being one of boundless seduction, as her sensuality seeped from the very eminence of her skin. Her clothing was unscathed, unlike her mirrored image's, who's revealed the delicate regions of *her* body. Yet, there was something different about the one who adorned the armband—an arousing bodily appetite which flowed from her very being, seducing the whole of a man's soul.

He fought the urge to defy his lord and master. An urge that sent bolts of electrical current throughout the whole of his body to the tips of his grasping fingers, one that drives a man to kill for the gratifying desire that only comes from a beautiful, sensual woman.

Angrily, he spat, "No—she is first." He nodded his head in Cherinne's direction as his heated senses were rattled and his fingers fumbled awkwardly with the intricate lock.

Cherinne drew further within herself, while the remembrance of the giant tearing savagely at her, trying to satisfy his animalistic urges, was sickening. It caused her head to reel and she trembled uncontrollably.

"*No!*" Fahimah stated more urgently. Not so much out of concern for her double; but, she itched dreadfully for the chance to inflict the insufferable pain of her needles upon this ignorant clod, who had participated in the events that had lead to Haneefah's death. And, for the detestable bruise, she had carried for days.

Hafiz suddenly disappeared from sight. The sound of a bolt being slipped within its grooved stock, and a bowstring being drawn and secured by its catch, rang within her ears. Watching through the dim lighting of the oil lantern, she wondered as to how she would stop a raging quarrel within such a confined space. She became annoyed, at both her double *and* the amir, for destroying her *Ryuho,* the remarkable emerald-gemmed choker which she could most certainly use in here, or, for that matter, anywhere. Fahimah cursed them both beneath her breath.

Hafiz spun about, with the glimmer of an arrowhead aimed in her direction. She flinched, while awaiting death that would surely come.

"I said, 'no'; *she* goes." He waved the menacing crossbow in Cherinne's direction; while a mere slip of his finger upon the trigger would send the bolt ripping easily through more than just clothing and skin.

Cherinne then quickly covered the entirety of her body with the foul smelling, coverlet while her heart pounded and she gasped for air.

"Now, come out from under that camel skin, girl, or this whore gets it!" The crossbow swung again in Fahimah's direction.

"*Don't!* I'll come out." Fear trembled within Cherinne's voice causing her teeth to chatter uncontrollably, while her terrified eyes never left the ground. With shaking hands, she removed the blanket, and drew the few torn remnants of clothing about her body. Her nearly exposed self trembled violently as she crouched to exit the grotto while a rough hand speedily grabbed her and immediately bound her hands. She wept openly, as they disappeared into the darkness.

Fahimah watched her double. A painful reminder of herself crept into her gut and left her shivering. She dropped to her knees before the small steel door, within the stench of the now rancid straw; and grabbing the bars, she angrily shook the steel as she cried out desperately for anyone to hear and release her. The ringing of the clattering lock and chain echoed loudly within the small cubicle, drowning out the immense quiet of the underground dungeon. Jumping to her feet, she forcibly heeled the door, without success.

The first break of dawn had come upon the horizon and passed; and Laddor had finally resolved to the fact that he wasn't getting free any time soon. Unfortunately for the assemblage of sixty men or more, his excessively annoying orifice could not be bound, in fear he would choke upon the unexpected tufts of sand spraying about from nature or Mahir's mount. His boisterous yammering which had lasted near miles of gritty white had finally fizzled out to a low grumble and seething curse. While, of course, he had been pelted a few times by a riding crop as he laid face-down, feet and hands bound, across the back of the Egyptian's horse. The repentant militant, attempting to make amends for his incompetence at allowing the map to be ingested, remained to the rear of the brigade, along with his blood brother and Deverall, in the futile effort to stave the amir from the screeching jargon.

"Damn, Red…" Deverall continued to scold mildly, "…I told ya' not to piss him off. See—now look at ya'. You look like a carrot-topped rooster ready for the henhouse chopping block. You pushed and pushed, regardless of my warnings, and now you'll be facing the commander's blade first thing tomorrow morning."

Laddor's face was red and enflamed, matching that of his hair, from the combination of rage, humiliation, and the oppressing heat. Having his elbow propped on the horse's hindquarter and his cheek resting in the palm of his hand he slumped his head onto the bulge of the horse's rump. His shadowed cheek lay against the short bristly hairs and he could hear the inward functions of the working mare as she toiled with the extra weight. Irritation filled his profound sigh, as he listened to the drone of the pilot's niggling voice itching within his ears; a continuous nag, heard only by a dopey insipid husband.

With great difficulty, he shifted his weight; while the binding cord, tight around his bare wrists, cut into the flesh as if eating away one layer of skin at a time. The aching in his torso and back was unforgivable; he groaned in misery. Finding the most comfortable position permissible, for a brief period anyway, he laid his face back down on the spongy swell of the over-sized horse. Fortunately, for him, Mahir's mount was twice the size of a normally sleek Arabian mare; where she was built more like that of a Budweiser Clydesdale than a sleek Arab made for speed. Big-assed females always were good for somethin', he thought—if nothing else, a place to prop your head.

The mare plodded along, one trudging step at a time, through the ocean of endless sand which appeared to multiply in size as a birthing enigma—growing not only in enormity but, also, in over-whelming strength. Its polished crystals, catching the rays of the searing sun, blazed like that of miniscule diamonds; their reflection was glaringly blinding.

Laddor's head bobbed in rhythm with the large beast's mulish stride as it clawed at the desert—quicksand beneath its feet—with a resolute determination to swallow them in.

The heat of the midmorning sun lashed out with a vengeance causing sweat to build in every crevice of Laddor's frying body and the sound of sifting granules of sand spraying from every hoof added unwelcome dryness to his already parched lips. Nausea turned his stomach, when suddenly a foul stench filled his nostrils coating the whole of his pasty taste buds.

"Ohhh, my God, I'm gonna' throw up! What the hell's that stench?" His curved brow arched high within his hair, while the rest of his face was set in a contorted grimace.

Mahir chuckled, tossing an amused glance in Omar—his eldest brother's—direction, who rode parallel, just at arm's length away. His dark shaggy eyebrows furrowed in mild confusion, while he was unable to understand a single word spewing forth from the obnoxious American's mouth. Mahir directed his brother's attention, with the leather crop, to the yammering prisoner and the raised tail of his own broad mare; they burst into roaring laughter.

"*Ohhhh myyy Goodddd!!* Don't tell me this *barrel-assed mule* is breaking wind! *Let me off here!*" Laddor's squawking demands brought tears to the brothers' howling laughter and Deverall, though knowing that his friend would be extremely irate, chuckled along anyway.

"Deverall—quit laughin' and get me outta' this." Laddor pleaded giving in to the heat, exhaustion and the excruciating thought of not being able to rescue Cherinne. Laying his head upon the rising and falling hump, he drifted into a restless edgy sleep.

Hafiz observed through the shadows, the easy sway of Cherinne's form as she staggered her way through the dismal, lantern lit tunnels. He trailed just far enough behind her to watch the movements of her entire body drifting in and out of the flickering lights; the crossbow locked and loaded, just centimeters from the base of her spine.

"You are a *fine* game," he stated; the sound of his voice startled her. "A succulent lamb to be slowly feasted upon then plucked from my teeth with the tip of my dirk." His tone was low and hushed, almost as if he was concealing a secret. It reverberated along the craggy walls in a sly silty manner which startled Cherinne into a dreadful panic. The nausea within her stomach rose to her scratchy throat; while the cool of the armband— the only aid she could possibly have now, here, miles beneath the earth— lay lifeless about her wrist. The bolt of his crossbow traced her outline. "What is your name?"

"*Cherinne*" slipped through her chattering teeth, which she attempted to control, but without success.

"*Cherinne.*" Her name was silk upon his tongue, laid heavily in the Arabic dialect; the sound of it was sickening to her ears. "Well, *Cherinne...*" he suddenly grabbed her around the waist with one arm and pulled her snuggly against himself; his rigid unyielding figure pressed firmly to her shaking body. She gasped for air at his roving fingers which pushed their way beneath the remnants of torn clothing to slowly caress the softness of her bare flesh. Her heartbeat ran painfully rampant at his forcible touch as his breath was hot spurts upon her neck just below her ear. "You are a woman who needs to be had." He ran his heated lips along her skin beneath her hair. "And, I will have you; but after you have been cleansed." He shoved her away. "For, your odor repulses me from days in the dungeon. So, prepare yourself; for I yearn for the flesh that signifies you untouched."

Shu, in separating the Egyptian sky goddess Nut, from her twin Geb, had hoped to appease Ra, the supreme Egyptian god of the sun, who being enraged at the secret marriage of the couple, demanded their disjointing. Terribly angered at the pair, Ra had also decreed that Nut would be unable to bear children during any month of the year. So, Thoth, the moon god, took pity on Nut because of his fondness for the scintillating glow of her flesh—a glow that resulted from stardust being encrusted within the nakedness of her being, which caused the light of her skin to radiate a warm luminosity which covered the entirety of the night sky.

Challenging the moon to a game of draughts, Thoth had hoped to obtain, as his prize, enough of the moon's incandescent light to create five new days to add to the month. With his clever strategy and master wit, he was able to succeed; and, on each of these new days—except for one to rest—Nut bore a child: Osiris, the eldest; Seth; Isis and Nephthys.

Osiris, son of the Egyptian deities grew into a tall and handsome deity and proclaimed the title "Universal Lord"; and when his father had succumbed to retirement, Osiris became the king of Egypt, taking his sister, Isis, as his queen. He civilized much of Egypt and the surrounding countries. While the people loved and adored their new God, they were immediately transfixed by his charisma; he became a great king and his name became a renowned whisper upon each and every tongue.

A glorious tale suddenly turned for the worse when Seth, Osiris's younger brother, had grown dreadfully jealous of his older brother's success and celebrated prominence. So crafting a devious plan, Seth invited his supposedly beloved brother to feast with him in commemoration of his accomplishments. Having a magnificent coffin brought before Osiris, he claimed that the coffin would belong to whom-so-ever fitted it—holding that individual's body in its magnificence till that person was resurrected in the afterlife. Osiris fell carelessly into his brother's devious trap and lay unknowingly in the coffin. When suddenly, the lid was slammed shut, nailed closed and the coffin tossed secretly into the Nile.

Isis, Osiris' sister and queen, was devastated to hear of the horrible act which had transpired between her brothers and was overcome with grief. She set about to search for her husband's body and finding him within the depths of the Nile, she fearfully hid the body in the hopes of reviving him through a series of mystical prayers. Seth became furious at her interference and, finding the body, sliced it into a multitude of pieces and spread them throughout the lands of Egypt.

Nephthys, the youngest sibling, also grieved immensely for the division in her family and helped her sister Isis search diligently till they were able to locate all of Osiris's body; for though Nephthys and Seth were both brother and sister *and* husband and wife, she was truly in love with Osiris.

Cherinne neurotically tapped her twisting forefinger against the cool of the golden bracelet, still secured behind her back, till the finger ached miserably and she was certain it would fall off. Her thoughts rushed in a multitude of directions, while the vile depraved words of her captor lay as thick, black bile within her gut. The dirt and stench of the underground grotto was a peaceful haven, compared to the filth and grime she now felt as the touch of the foul Egyptian turned her stomach, making her want to vomit.

It seemed an eternity since she had left the confines of the mud-encrusted hole in the earth; while the terror that plagued her now was far more detrimental than any of being face to face with the angered princess. Cherinne's head began to spin as her mind darted briefly to the conversation they had been engaged in, when they had been interrupted by Hafiz.

My sister; she momentarily contemplated the idea. No. It is impossible.

"Move along, quicker." She was startled from her bombardment of thoughts—the main one, escaping, while she flinched at Hafiz's firm hand which rested itself upon her shoulder urging her forward through the dank, underground tunnel. "My appetite increases while I observe you here, alone, in the dark; and I shall not be made to wait." Cherinne pressed on in the urgency to be somewhere, anywhere, besides here. The fear that shook her wobbly legs ran throughout the whole of her body as she stumbled forward over rocky terrain which tore at the bottoms of her sandaled feet. Her mind raced to her father.

"Please," she managed through chattering teeth, in the ancient Egyptian language mixed with modern day Arabic, "let me go. My father will pay you anything you want. Please…he will pay you handsomely."

He swiftly grabbed her to him and the air rushed from her body as he pressed his lips firmly against her ear. His heated breath was vicious, a low sneering whisper, "Your father has *nothing* I want. What I want is right here…" he ran the arrowhead of the crossbow along the curvature of her backside; her body stiffened, "what dances beneath the silk of your cloth." He roughly shoved her onward. "You are definitely *not* the Egyptian princess of the Tarun Regime. You *are* the American—trying to purchase your way through life, including your path to Heaven with the meager percentage of your coin. Revolting. You are a despicable nation whose value lies only in the abundance of your possessions. Allah would not tolerate such nonsense; and I would die a thousands deaths before I would insult him with the revolting acts that you Americans perform against your god. So, do not insult me with such mockery; for my reward is not in riches within this measly life, but in the assurance I have that I will obtain everlasting life in Heaven, a good meal every-so-often *and* the pleasures of a bed-wench whenever I so desire one.

Now, your boorish conversation has made me somewhat irate; and when I am irate I tend not to be so peaceable, especially when it is concerning the wench that is to appease me and, instead, she infuriates me."

The sharp tip of the bolt stung at the base of Cherinne's spine and she pitched forward with the unexpected jab; an insinuation that money was as useless a bribe to a desert rat, as a spoonful of water was to irrigate the sands of Egypt.

The trek beneath the ground became one of a grueling task and

Cherinne's chattering teeth and trembling finally slowed to a halt. Her weary limbs gradually began to give in to a dull ache, with her hands still secured, and her legs and feet paining from twisting and slipping upon the rough terrain. Words had not passed between her and her captor, as they continued to travel through the dimly lit tunnel that had snaked ceaselessly along the earth's innards. She listened to Hafiz's measured breaths, then tried to pinpoint the sound of his heartbeat with her extraordinarily fortified hearing, which she had acquired when she had obtained the bracelet. For that matter, she attempted to listen for anything that would give her a clue as to where she was or whether or not she would be able to escape. *Nothing.* She could hear nothing beyond the immediate sounds that were made by their echoing footfalls and the shuffling ground as they lumbered on for what seemed eternity. She puzzled over the fact that she had not heard him approaching the grotto where she and Fahimah had been imprisoned. Maybe she had lost the ability, which she wasn't sure yet whether to be a curse or a god-send. But none-the-less, the ability was nil down here.

Cherinne had begun to fear that there was no end to the passageway; that Hafiz's over-zealous urges had somehow distracted him of his path and he was steering them in the wrong direction, in the never-ending labyrinth. Fear of being lost for eternity beneath the sands of Egypt with this man sent her head spinning but she suddenly dismissed it as they finally reached a new tunnel that veered to the left leading them into a spacious clearing—a large underground cavern.

The cavern opened like that of a giant mouth, with rocky jagged teeth—stalactites—which had formed through centuries of water droplets, containing a variety of minerals, dripping through the many layers of earth.

The enormous teeth jutted downward in a threatening façade, in hopes of protecting the beautiful lake which lie below—like a mother safeguarding its child. The lake was a large expansive body of water filling the entirety of the cavern with smaller tributaries which flowed gracefully in departing branches that disappeared into the back drop of darkness that surrounded the whole of its beauty. The crystalline blue waters radiated with a lovely alluring glow, emanating a frosty mist resembling that of sparkling fairy dust, which flickered in a soft iridescent rainbow of color.

"Water," she quietly whispered through thirsting lips. "*Clean* water." Cherinne stared through wide, red-rimmed, tired eyes in awe of its beauty, never seeing anything that could come close to resembling its magnificence in all her years of travel or studies upon the surface of the earth. Her mouth hung open to her chin as she momentarily forgot the severity of her situation. But her brief moment of enjoyment was abruptly shattered by a harsh shove from Hafiz which nearly sent her toppling to the rocky floor.

"You shall bathe here," his voice was hoarse. The fatigue from the underground journey had now vanished with the near prospects of ravaging this female cultivating a surge of heated energy within his body, "...and I shall watch."

Cherinne threw a fleeting terrified glance about the expansive cavern, searching for a mere possible escape; while she struggled to suppress the reoccurring violent trembling which had briefly succumbed to exhaustion. Her mind scattered in a multitude of directions, as a frightened hare fleeing in a blind dash while endeavoring to save itself from a merciless hunter.

Hafiz roughly grabbed her arm, digging his long dark fingers within her flesh; and turning her toward him, he glared through a set of narrowed mix-matched eyes. A cruel snarl wafted into Cherinne's terrified face, "Do not even think to try and escape, for I shall not be easy on you as Nagid; his loyalties lie too strong with the Lord Seth—mine remain with Allah." He shoved her toward the water. "Now—remove those rags and bathe yourself."

Cherinne's heart pounded erratically in her chest as she took a wobbly step toward the pristine waters. They beckoned to her filthy limbs and torso; while the blood of battle and stench of the grotto was heavily embedded within her skin and matted hair. Fear rushed forward in a shaky voice. "But, I have no soap or shampoo for my hair." Her teeth began to chatter again, "...and my hands are tied."

Her heart leapt within her chest as he, with unseen speed, brandished his dirk and sliced precisely through the binding rope, which binded her hands and wrists, rubbed raw from the coarse binding. She gently massaged them, so wishing she could just place them in the cool of the sparkling blue water; but, without the massive amount of fear she was justifiably exhuming.

Hafiz then untied the sash secured about his black tunic and produced a small goatskin satchel which he tossed in Cherinne's direction. Slipping through trembling fingers, it landed at her feet.

"Everything you need is in there. Now—no more stalling or I shall have to bathe you myself." His eyes narrowed with a malicious glint, "...and you would not like the way that I would bathe you. You may drown in the process."

Cherinne quickly bent and retrieved the small tawny weather-beaten sack; shaking violently, she was barely able to loosen the leather ties that bound it. Tears formed behind her eyes creating an even more difficult task while her blurring vision made it near impossible to see to release the knot. She gasped in fright as Hafiz was suddenly upon her yanking the bag from her trembling fingers. Grumbling irately to himself, he unleashed the leather strapping, then grabbing her hands, he placed the contents within them. The anticipation was unrelenting and he needed the filth cleansed from her body for the experience to be completely rewarding. For, he'd had enough of women who reeked of camel hair and goat's manure; and with his estranged feelings toward them, he may as well have been knobbing a goat.

He led her roughly by the arm to the water's edge; his fingers dug deep within her already bruised skin which was purpling from his bearish grasp.

"*Bathe!*"

Cherinne cautiously stuck her foot within the cool water, while Hafiz observed in a cold-hearted manner. Beginning to remove the amami, which till now had covered his head, he harshly snapped, "Remove your clothing!"

Cherinne's mind whirled in a twisting cyclone of dreadful thoughts as she, beneath her breath, pleaded to the bracelet to awaken, to come alive, drag her, shoot her skyward—do anything but lie dormant while she compromised herself to this wretched Egyptian. Someone who could no-doubt overpower her and make her succumb to his brutally soulless wishes. No, she thought. I will not give in without a fight. I will not allow him to just have his way with me…even if it means death.

A tear ran the length of her face as she sniffled back the urgency to break down and cry. *I will not just let him take me at his own will.*

Wiping the back of a dirt-encrusted hand across her eyes, Cherinne turned to her assailant. She was momentarily taken aback at the sight of his hair hanging loosely about his face. Dark, choppy, lengthy ringlets layered in stacks upon his head accentuated the dark of his eyes and long lashes, making him appear somewhat striking. She studied his features for a brief moment while he removed his weathered boots and belted weapons, resting the crossbow upon the rock in which he sat and removing his clothing down to black trousers. Then, mustering the courage, she stated defiantly, "No."

The mix-matched eyes that had just seconds earlier appeared rather attractive stared at her in disbelief then quickly hazed over with dark thunderclouds of anger and rage. He moved quickly; while Cherinne was unable to catch a fleeting breath, as fury overtook the Egyptian and he was immediately atop her, his body suddenly slamming into hers. And, the last thing she remembered before hitting the water, was the ruthless look blazing within the black of his eyes.

CHAPTER 20

Laddor raised his sweated head, clearing the mesh of sleep cobwebs from his mind. While his wet body was pasted to the white froth layered between him and the mare; with the smell of damp soggy horse pungent, to near repulsive. Never in his twenty-two years of life had he ever felt this miserable; even during those bouts of rage, where his father had treated him with unjust harshness.

Laddor forced open his squinting red eyes then glanced over his shoulder to see Deverall slumped upon his horse, sleeping. The procession of sixty-two riders had moved along at a steady pace through the western desert of middle Egypt for the entirety of the day, finally coming to a halt at the setting of the vicious red sun.

"*NiHna mkhayyam haun*" resonated along the windless air, stirring the slumbering pilot from his rest. The regiment of men and horses parted as the amir, appearing worn and drawn, made his way toward the end of the procession, announcing this as the place to camp. He approached Deverall.

"Your Highness," Deverall nodded his head with a yawn, while rubbing the scruff upon his face.

"Mr. Deverall," the prince returned his formal gesture. "We will be camping here for the evening, then resuming before sunrise. I suggest you get some rest; my men will set you up with a tent and supplies. And, as for you, Mr. Zeandre..." he viewed Laddor with contempt through tired eyes, "...you will have your bonds removed to stave off any creatures that may threaten the rest of the meager existence you encompass till dawn. At that time, you will become feeding for the buzzards, which have trailed us for the entirety of the day."

Mahir sliced through the ropes which secured Laddor to his saddle and to the one binding his wrists. Shoving him from his relieved mare, he smiled maliciously, observing as the American thumped heavily to the ground.

Rubbing his fleshy wrists, Laddor then worked to untie the bindings about his feet; all the while, staring hatefully at Mahir and Rasheed. "And what about the map...*Rasheed?*" Laddor's tone was hard as granite as he bit at each word. "If I am to be ripped to shreds as buzzard food, then what of the information I contain? And, what about Cherinne?" He glanced at Deverall, who shrugged theatrically.

"Don't worry Mr. Zeandre...I have arranged for my men to retrieve that information from you." Rasheed's voice carried with it an ennoble authority as he then projected his words toward the front of the line, while Laddor listened angrily at the prince speaking in Arabic. "Commander Lateef, Sergeant Maraat, Ib...saiyid Zeandre mukafa ka-in khayin, walikeen huwa Hibal qala." Rasheed turned back to Laddor, a glint in his eye, "you shall not run far. And, as for Miss Havenstrit," his claim in English was made in absolute assuredness, "...she is now the administrator of the Semus Bracelet and shall remain at the palace with me." With that he circled his horse, clicked her forward and reversed his direction toward the front of the awaiting procession.

"*Damn that arrogant bastard!*" Laddor paced angrily then kicked the sand with the tip of his boot. It fizzled upon making contact with the flames of the small fire where he and Deverall kept their distance from the rest of the group. The smoke curled high into the cooling nighttime sky and disappeared into the darkness.

"*Hey—Red! Watch what you're doin'!* You're liable to put the fire out; then I'll hav'ta leave you over here by yourself and go join the rest o' the fellas. I'm sure that boy, Ib, wouldn't want the chore of restarting the thing, if you put it out. It was nice enough the amir had one built separate for us anyway."

Laddor's blood-shot eyes blazed red-hot with anger as he shot an irate glance at his friend. "Man, Deverall, why don't you just go over there with the amir! You seem to think he's so damn great! Go coddle with him! You *and* Cherinne! You both seem to like him better anyway!"

"*Hey! Hey!*" Deverall put his hands in the air as a sign of innocense. "I'm just along for the ride—pilot for hire—remember? And, as for sweetheart—you're the one who drug *her* into this mess, and it may not have been intentional, but it happened. So here we are. *And*, that Irish of yours is what's gettin' you into trouble with the amir, so don't go blamin' me for your troubles; and don't you dare put any of this on Cherinne."

Laddor's mouth snapped closed as the realization of what he had just blurted out sunk in. He trudged through the shadows of sand, away from the firelight and his friend who was right; enraged at himself, he threw his head back and glared at the clouded sky. "*UUgggbh!*" He raked at his hair and face. Then, dropping to his knees in the estranged desert, he remained consumed in despair and misery, till he heard the commander, accompanied by the sergeant, speaking his name.

"Sayyid Zeandre?"

Deverall's eyes affirmed it all as he glanced uneasily toward his friend who remained kneeling in the darkness, attempting to make sense of the direction in which his life had curved. The two Egyptian men followed his gaze to see their objective slumped wearily upon the desert floor. And pointing toward the darkened figure, the commander directed his sergeant to retrieve the despairing American.

Laddor's head began to ache with the realization that they had come for him, with all intentions of claiming the information they needed—with or without his consent.

He glanced toward the main assemblage of men who watched dispassionately as Sergeant Maraat, marched toward him in the dark and roughly seized him by the arm. The amir also observed from just outside the main tent, his arms crossed and a set scowl upon his face. Laddor's gut feeling instantly told him that this was going to get ugly as he noticed the amir turning and disappearing inside the canvas flap.

Several oil lanterns lit the inside of the large tent where Rasheed sat at a small collapsible table and chair, while he observed through the flickering flames a parchment which he had laid before him.

As Laddor was ushered in by the sergeant, with cold steel prodding the skin of his kidney, he glanced over the prince's shoulder to see that the document was a map. Laddor's gaze then quickly swept the entirety of the lodgings which contained a generously cushioned bunk, a few meager pieces of neatly folded clothing, and several weapons—including the prince's scimitar—a water flask and a flat tin bowl filled with food which lay cold and untouched.

"Mr. Zeandre," Rasheed stated without disrupting the undivided attention he was allotting the chart, "…have you decided on volunteering the information to me that I need or shall I be forced to retrieve it in the manner in which you treat a disobedient dog?" He turned to face the illusory fire of darts that shot heedlessly in all directions and reached the four corners of the slightly fluttering canvas.

Laddor, struggling with the impulse to unleash the animosity bristling upon his skin and flaring to every nerve within his body, lowered his gaze and restrained the notion. Remembering his friend's words, he simply stated through gritted teeth, "No." Then, raising his head to meet the amir's steady eye, he added, "And, I *will* rescue Cherinne and take her home—home where she belongs. And, nothing *you* can do will stop me."

Considering his words, the prince folded his arms; his tone was flat and impassive. "Have you forgotten the fate that is to meet you at dawn? Or, do you, Mr. Zeandre, plan to roam the sands of time as a spirited phantom, searching for a female who no longer desires the inconveniences of your childish ways? You so do resemble that of an immature adolescent; could be your father didn't strike you hard enough—eh?"

Laddor's anger crested to purest of rage, tensing every achy muscle which fought mercilessly to escape in flailing iron fists while his breathing was that of a labored task. Maraat's blade pinched through the fabric of his shirt causing him to flinch—just a reminder that he and the amir were not alone and one false move would bring death before his appointed time which was just a few hours away.

Laddor lost the battle to wrath and Rasheed suddenly drew back swiping a uniformed arm across his own cheek where he was removing a wad of spit which ran the length of his face. A swift blow to the back of his head sent Laddor buckling to the floor, as he heard the amir barking out orders in Arabic which *he knew* to be, 'take him away and be sure to retrieve the information we need before you kill him.'

A decaying pair of yellowish eyes blinked back the sting of the lantern's flickering light, as a gentle breeze built upon the sandy dunes unnoticed by those surrounding the camp. A slimy matter was deposited by the creature as it slivered atop the amir's canvas tent and observed, along with several other Lahm, the assemblage of men who, unknowing of their existence, sat below—their joking and preparing for the following day's crossing biding their time.

The creatures, snaking inside the royal tent, seeped within the amir's personal effects; and searched out the parchment which contained a rough sketching of the map which the pilot bore upon his chest. Finding the document rolled and tucked into a leather knapsack, two of the darkened creatures slipped their oily forms within the paper and absorbed every character of ink within the slime of their blackened rancid skin.

Then, completing their task, they slivered from beneath the tent's fitfully snapping canvas and rushed in a maddened haste past the sergeant they encountered earlier and through the murky night, racing the violent storm which was rapidly approaching.

Laddor's gutted cries filled the whole of the dark desert sky.

"*Mahir*! Haven't you silenced that American fool yet?" Omar yelled over his shoulder into the darkness. "He has been screaming like that of a girl for half the moon. My supper has not yet been able to digest properly, even after I said my evening prayers. Can't you handle just *one* worthless American who not only sounds like a girl, but also resembles one?"

The handful of soldiers seated around the fire near Omar chuckled.

Mahir's vaguely panting voice jested from beyond the darkened shadows of the camp. "I will be sure, Brother, to save a lock of scarlet hair for you to adorn the bridle of your horse when I am finished; though, it may be tinged with a quantity of blood. He bleeds like that of a virgin."

Laughing aloud, several of the men did not notice as the amir followed by Commander Lateef stepped within the campfire's hissing light, as Omar, chuckling, shouted back to his younger sibling, "Yes, maybe you could use him as a bedwench when you are through. I hear it has been too long for you and I will be sure to cover myself when bathing; for I also hear that you have been eyeing my horse."

"*Enough!*" Rasheed snapped angrily as the men scrambled to attention.

"Your Highness," Omar stammered as he and the other men quickly stood to attention, "…my apologies, Sire. I had no idea you were in our presence." He bowed low, his knee upon the ground. "My humble apologies."

"Where is Sergeant Maraat?" Rasheed's tone was short and clipped. He turned to the commander, "he is to be overseeing this assignment. I have had to listen to the prisoner's cries for the majority of the nightfall, while the information should have been retrieved long ago, as we will rest just past the midnight hour then resume our voyage. This is not a bludgeoning game we play—this is a matter of life and death for the Princess Fahimah!"

"My apologies, m'lord. I will locate him immediately."

The commander turned to make his way toward the darkened shadows of the desert where Mahir had Laddor bound, beating him bloody, beyond his senses.

The young boy, Ib, ran abruptly through the campsite, along the sifting sand, oblivious to the sullen mood of those standing to attention before the fuming amir. The mounting tension was thick enough to cut due to the obvious frustration and ill feelings toward the mishandling of Laddor's interrogation. Ib's shouts of urgency slightly severed the heated vibes of unease. "*Your Highness! Your Highness!*" The boy slowed to bow before Rasheed as he caught a much needed breath.

Rasheed placed a settling hand on Ib's shoulder and stated slightly irate at the interruption. "Gather your wits about you, boy; this is not a place to romp."

"…Your Highness, my apologies; but, Sergeant Maraat…he has been found. He is lying just beyond the campsite and…is covered in *slime*!"

Cherinne struggled just beneath the water's surface; her wide eyes, sated in the throes of terror, gazed skyward toward the craggy rocks threatening from above. They appeared as an irate mother disciplining those who have invaded the sanctity of the hidden child.

Dark inky shadows, floating in the water overhead, were the few remaining remnants of her clothing, torn to her underpants, which Hafiz was in the process of shredding from her body. The concern of being completely exposed was nowhere near that of needing a breath. And, raking at the dark steely arms holding her just beneath the air she so badly needed, her mother's face came to mind. The remembrance of her last dying expressions appeared within the dark surroundings that seemed to now be consuming her. Thrashing, with every last ounce of energy possible, Cherinne succumbed to the realization that she was quickly drowning. *Help me*, the words drifted through her mind like a leaf floating in an afternoon breeze; and awaiting death she closed her eyes. In answer to her lonesome self, she was suddenly yanked above the surface of the weighty water. Clutching at breaths that painfully gouged into her lungs, she was sure they are tearing her aching chest apart. She gasped at the sharp intake of air as a hard slap suddenly landed the side of her cheek and Hafiz shouted angrily into her tear-streamed face.

"Open your eyes, *you bitch! You shall service me before you die!*" He shook her violently as a low mounting fear began to creep into the back of his mind—the severe repercussions of this wench dying. His reprimand from Nagid would be detrimental; but nothing compared to the harrowing sentence he would receive from the Lord Seth—it possibly being death.

"*Wake up!*"

Cherinne blinked her eyes with the stinging pain as another slap cracked the side of her face, sending her crashing backward into the child's soothing arms—the cool liquid swallowing her was drawing her near to the water's bottom. Obeying the last words she may ever hear, she opened her blood-shot eyes and watched her hair which floated in long tangled ringlets like grasping fingers reaching for the surface. Her body sank toward the floor of the once lovely lake while the dim light above melded into a bleak darkness.

Time passed in chocking incremental lapses between painful consciousness and unconsciousness and Cherinne suddenly awoke spitting and sputtering upon the rocky terrain, unsure as to how she had gotten there. She rubbed the back of a wrist across her paining forehead; and barely able to move raw, nearly tangled portions of her body, she winced in excruciating grievous agony.

A glimpse of her surroundings and the diminishing flicker of the stones upon the bracelet informed her that she was still within the earth's core and that the bracelet must have come to life.

Rigorously burning sensations raced from her hair to her feet, while she achingly rose to a shaking elbow; and through a blurred vision, she swept the whole of the spacious vicinity, attempting to clear her mind and her sight.

"*Where is he?*" The throated croak surprised her.

Her eyes came to rest on his folded tunic, laying not feet away. Mustering the energy, she quickly scrambled to snatch the available garment.

Just as her fingers grasped the cloth, she jumped in frozen terror at the emergence of Hafiz. Bolting from behind a large jagged boulder which had been doused with the lake's water in the struggle, then blasted full of pin-size holes, he charged in her direction.

Through a clearing vision she could see the rage blazing from behind his black sinister stare as panic rushed in a lump to her throat. She scrambled to get to her feet. Her heart pounded mercilessly within her paining chest while she held fast to the tunic like that of a child's security blanket and ran along the rough surface of the lake's shoreline. Her bare feet screamed in protest as they skimmed along the uneven stones, while she briefly pondered what had happened to her sandals. Glancing back, she could see the darkened fury of the incensed Egyptian hot at the back of her heels.

"*Nnnoooo!!*" abruptly slipped from her parted lips as her bare skin skidded along the gravelly surface with Hafiz landing heavily atop her. She was shocked at the throbbing ache soaring along her torn breasts and abdomen and the lack of feeling from her hips down—numbed from the crippling pain and the driving force of the Egyptian on her back. Tears stung her eyes and her chest ached horribly, both inside and out, with the realization she couldn't get away—away from this nightmare and away from this man, whose incensed verve insisted on violating every faction of her being. His heated, panting breath was poison to her skin as he ran a hot acidy tongue along the rim of her ear.

"I have you now; and the terror reeks from your pores, exciting me more than ever."

A low groan escaped her lips as his roving tongue slipped inside her ear. "You will now experience the whole of my throbbing loins within every cavity of your beautiful American body, while I have you every imaginable way possible with an Egyptian male's pleasure. And though you are not bled and at first may not like it, you will grow to enjoy it— possibly begging me for more."

Tears dripped effortlessly upon the rocky ground as Hafiz drew back and Cherinne braced herself for what was about to come. Working to wedge himself between her stiffened legs, his body suddenly jerked forward. Immediately, he cursed and fingered the side of his wet hair, as a thick crimson, lukewarm substance trailed the tips of his fingers and ran along his arm, dripping upon Cherinne's cheek. The scent of fresh blood mingled with that of bodily sweat as she turned her head and could see that he was readily bleeding. His dark eyes clouded over in confusion, as a three inch sliver leaked blood from the side of his skull. Angrily, he shoved Cherinne away and speedily rolled to squatting position, just beyond the rock's shadow.

A cutting voice immediately cursed from the darkened tunnel entrance. "Let her go."

Fahimah's words were that of stone.

CHAPTER 21

Laddor slumped in a bloodied heap upon the gritty desert floor while the meager sound of the amir's voice, speaking in his native tongue, was a low droning hum which filled his head with more pain, if the possibility existed. His normally vibrant scarlet hair now lay as a blackish-brown sandy matt against the sides of his swollen face, and his body too sore to move, yelped in warranted agony as the amir shoved him with the tip of his black riding boot.

"Mr. Zeandre…" the words were muffled, incomprehensible as Laddor attempted to raise his head. His eyes, squinted to narrow slits, were blinded by the oil lantern which the commander dangled in his face. The amir's words, measured in monotone, boomed loudly within Laddor's ears. "Mr. Zeandre…I have…matters to…attend to. I will return shortly…to speak with you." Orders were barked at Mahir and the commander in Arabic and two men scurried across the sand and yanked Laddor to his bound feet. With his hands secured tightly behind his back, they drug him along the darkened terrain, while a heated tuft of sandy air breezed gently across his battered face.

"He is here! He is here, Your Highness!" Ib raced on olive-colored skinny legs through the bleak desert sand, his anxiety heightened with each pound across the terrain, while Rasheed's heartbeat increased with the uncertainty of the situation.

Reaching the location of the sergeant, they gazed upon the gooey substance which had settled thick within the Egyptian's nostrils and gaping mouth; while it looked as if he had been speaking or addressing a subordinate. His open eyes stared into the vast nighttime darkness, while an inquiring or puzzled gaze occupied their bleak expression. Upon further examination, Rasheed could see that the sergeant had sensed danger and had drawn his dirk; for, it also lay covered in slime, bent into the shape of a "U".

Rasheed bent to a slightly quavering knee examining Maraat through the quietly flickering flame of the lantern's light. Reaching out, he endeavored to touch the transparent layer of slime covering the sergeant from head to toe.

"Your Highness!" Commander Lateef placed his hand between the amir and the body lying before them. "Be cautious, m'lord. We do not know of this substance which is able to bring down and suffocate a sergeant-major. *And…*" he pointed a wavering finger in the direction of the mangled weapon, "…capable of bending carbon steel."

Rasheed glanced into the commander's uneasy eyes, realizing that the fright, Lateef was struggling to conceal, was fully warranted; while his own reservations drew a bead of nervous sweat to his brow. He rose to his feet. "Gather the brothers, Omar and Mahir; they seem fitted with indefatigable energy. Have them bury the body deep within the desert's belly; where the earth may partake of the corpse. And have the men paired in two's to guard the camp in rotating shifts; wickedness lurks within the shifting sand, so be prepared."

Bowing his head briefly, Rasheed whispered, "travel well." Then, while turning to retrace his steps back to camp, he wondered what course of action to take. And, running a hand through his glistening black hair he made his way in the direction of the American to handle the next dilemma.

"American—get dressed. The sight of your bottom offends me," Fahimah winced in severe pain as she snatched the spiraling anklet from the air as it whisked past Cherinne. Returning to the princess's outstretched hand the blade bloodied her fingers and palm on contact.

"*Lashr,*" she cursed as she limped from within the shadows of the tunnel in which they had just traveled. An expression of disbelief was apparent on Cherinne's harrowed face, as she stared open-mouthed at the sight of her double, who she was relieved to see.

"*Move it, Buxom Bottom,* before your boyfriend gathers his wits and does more than just throw you to the earth!" Fahimah shouted, dragging a bloody ankle along behind her. Scanning the shadows for the Egyptian, her sparking eyes darted from the shadowed area where he lay in wait, to the weapons too far off to hobble to.

Cherinne quickly slipped the black tunic on and snapped an irate glance in the princess's direction, "Hey, enough with the name calling!" Glimpsing down at the mangled ankle, she grabbed Fahimah's arm to assist her.

Hafiz made for the other side of the lake where his weapons lay, now, beckoning to be retrieved.

Fahimah quickly yanked her arm away, "I do not need your help." Irritation crackled in her faltering voice and she lurched forward in pain; while the ankle which had held the mystical rings bled effortlessly, and the flow of crimson increased with each afforded step.

The bracelets which had jingled haughtily with every movement of the princess, making it possible for her to run like the cheetah, had been torn from her ankle and remained silent. They had become weapons, razor sharp flying disks which sliced through skin and bone with the greatest of ease, then would reverse their course and return to their rightful owner. The problem being: how to retrieve them without losing several fingers or possibly a whole hand. This would be a task Fahimah would have to work on, but later, while the task right now was one of escaping. Escaping the courtyard of death, the *Haush min maut* used by the Lord Seth for those he wished to imprison and torture, then eventually put to death. Also escaping the Egyptian male whose heated desires rampaged in a black-hearted hunger to ravage the two females till his loins tired and he regretfully succumbed to exhaustion.

Cherinne grasped Fahimah's arm tightly, snapping back at the princess, "*Yes, you do! Now, come on!*"

She quickly scrutinized the several tunnels before her, fearing she would chose unwisely and lead them to a certain death, leagues beneath the desert floor.

Licking her forefinger, Cherinne held it in the air before her. And moving it slowly to and fro, she tested the mild differences in temperature coming from each of the tunnels. Sensing a slight amount of warmth from one, she urged Fahimah forward, "this way."

Fahimah eyed her double apprehensively. "What was that, American?"

Without hesitation or a glimpse from her appointed goal, Cherinne replied, "my weather gauge."

The dank, dimly lit tunnel seemed to extend forever. Fear rose in Cherinne at the possibility she and Fahimah were traveling further into the earth's belly; while the Egyptian, though he had tended to his wound, was still hot on their trail.

The rapid healing of Cherinne's torn skin upon her torso, breast and legs ached to be massaged or possibly even scratched. So holding securely to Fahimah's arm, she reached her free hand inside the black tunic, which served well as a cover, but reeked with that of Hafiz's bodily odor; she wrinkled her nose. Gently, Cherinne fingered the melding flesh upon her breast, which was healing at a surprisingly miraculous pace. She wondered of its power which could only be coming from the bracelet; and, while she had inquired of the many wounds being healed after her and Fahimah's battle, unfortunately, the amir had not been able to answer.

Cherinne removed her fingers and quickly peeked inside.

"No, they have not gotten bigger. Everything on you is south," Fahimah snidely scoffed at her double. She caught her breath as a jolt of pain rushed through her buckling ankle.

A wicked expression surfaced on Cherinne's face as she tightened her grip on Fahimah's arm and retorted with mock satisfaction, "Well, Princess...if you weren't built so much like that of a young boy, maybe *you'd have a little something south.*"

"*Humph!*" Fahimah tossed her head arrogantly; her petite nose shoved in the air, she hastily limped along, hating the idea of needing another crutch *and* conversing, even if cruelly, with the female she knew to be her sister.

Fahimah suddenly shivered slightly at the sound of Hafiz's deranged voice resounding through the tunnel in which they had just traveled. His low sinister laugh rose from within his gut and echoed within her throbbing ears; while his impeccable tracking senses were heightened with the scent of fresh blood which he had been trained rigorously for since a small child.

"Princess…I can smell the perfumed honey of your blood and it is tantalizing to my senses." He mused. "Come…let me partake of you and the American; and you can bleed together."

Nagid could sense the presence of the Lord Seth in the very air he was ingesting. It was like a chilly morning mist which lay heavy upon a frosty autumn's ground. Cool and crisp, it snapped and crackled, making contact with a scant amount of warm sand granules which had tumbled from the crevices of Nagid's boots. Upon immediate contact with the rocky surface, the white crystallized flecks of sand turned a beautiful icy hue of blue. Then, as if abruptly burnt by frost; they quickly withered into a deathly gray, like that of frozen meat; the granules, no longer a white and gently sifting personality of the earth, were now a pile of gray-blue ash.

"Nagid…I told you to never bring the white terrain from above within my presence, even to the door of my domicile!" Seth's voice reverberated within the giant renegade's head as he wondered of the iniquitous God's whereabouts. His yellow eyes, tightening to slits, scanned the whole of the murky, boulder-filled, underground cavern, which was decorated with a bizarre assortment of figurines and a mammoth-sized serpent.

The giant reptile, Apophis, one mark of supreme victory for the god, lay dead and coiled before his master's throne. While the throne was one of black and red mottled quartz, with a red velvet cushioned seat, large enough for several beasts—the main beast being the God, Seth.

Nagid warily observed the humungous stone pillars and graphite figurines for any sign of his lord. His thick, dark skin puckered slightly beneath his black, near plum, tunic with uneasiness at the knowledge he was being watched, observed like that of an insect.

Removing his gloves, he swiped a huge hand along his sweat beaded forehead truthfully enjoying the cooler temperatures of the territory below. While the hot, sun-driven sands above possibly sweltering to a near 120 degrees Fahrenheit were unbearable, with the entrance into the domain being the hottest location in all of Egypt, reaching near 140 degrees.

One of the unusually grotesque figurines, Nagid presumed to be a female demon, stared back at him in a riveting contempt, as if she was viewing him through the severed head she held proudly above herself. She was amongst a collage of perverted ashen-colored stone figures, each one displaying a mangled body part, representing that of the lord's brother, Osiris; who the lord himself had slain and butchered centuries ago. Then he had scattered the severed sections throughout the sands of Egypt.

Lord Seth's world was one of gloom and wanton deviousness; a brutal enemy of the gods, he had been associated with the violent storms of the desert and vicious defilement of both goddesses and mortal women. Son of Geb and Nut, he was rough and wild, with flaming red hair and chalky white skin; an evil god portrayed as a brutish animal.

"My apologies, m'lord; it shall not happen again," Nagid responded to the emptiness of the cool dark room. With no reply, he spun on his heels to leave.

"Nagid..." Seth's voice was silty while impatience was slowly mounting within his tone, "...where is the female?"

Despite the dank chill in the air, sweat prickled upon the back of the giant's neck. "She is being prepared for you, Sire...and, we have also brought the other, who wears the anklets," Nagid's voice echoed into the stony darkness, again, awaiting a reply which never surfaced. Certain he was through with his interrogation, he made for the gargantuan wooden doors in which he had entered.

"Nagid..." chills raced along the giant's flesh, "...be certain she is unscathed."

Footfalls were heard sifting through the sand and Laddor attempted to raise his head while excruciating pain raced through the entirety of his body. A shadowy figure made its way from within the campfire's flickering light; and, as the figure drew closer, he could make it out through blurred vision, to be the prince.

Laddor gently laid his swollen cheek to the cool gritty sand and for a moment wished for a speedy death. But, as the image of terror on Cherinne's face drifted into his mind, he rejected the thought, saving it possibly for sun-up.

Rasheed crouched down and with a gloved hand removed a matted tousle of blood-spattered hair away from Laddor's face. The words, 'don't touch my hair,' coursed from Laddor's lips in a muddled garble.

"What was that, Mr. Zeandre? Did you say you were going to give me the information I asked for?" Rasheed leaned in closer as Laddor mumbled something into the sand. "I'm sorry..." Rasheed remarked condescendingly, "...I didn't hear you. Could you repeat that?"

Achingly, Laddor raised his head and errantly replied in a single breath, "I said—go screw your horse."

Suddenly he grunted in pain, as he was struck with a swift backhand alongside the head.

"Sunset...Mr. Zeandre—you have until sunset."

The tent flap burst open with Laddor being tossed roughly inside. He lifted his head to see Deverall seated on the floor; an expression of shock and fear affixed to his raised bushy brows.

"*Man!*" He whistled low. "*You look like shit!*" He scrambled to his feet and assisted Laddor to a sitting position. "*Damn!* You look like somethin' from..." He scratched his head, "what was the name of that show I just watched....Elf lied....Elvis lied....*No! Elfen Lied!* What a bloody freakin' show that was! Anyway, that's what you remind me of." Reaching for a flask of water and uncorking it, he offered it to his friend who guzzled the cool liquid, oblivious to the pain he was feeling from his bloodied lips.

Finishing the last of the water, Laddor handed the container back to Deverall; and sighing deep, he dropped his head to his chest. "I don't know how much more I can take," he managed to whisper as his puffed eyes closed and he remained silent.

Panic rushed within Deverall's stomach. "*Hey!*" He placed a slightly trembling hand on his friend's shoulder. "You're not dead...are ya'?"

Laddor weakly pushed his hand away. "No," he muttered beneath his breath, "but I wish I were." Dragging himself onto an open sleeping bag, he slumped into the comfort of the nylon covered waffle. "Don't wake me till we leave."

"Hey…Red," Deverall's tone was a whisper and he rang his hands nervously. "I swear on all that's holy, I tried to talk to the amir, tried to get him to ease up and possibly just let you tag along. But his mind was set; and, come hell or high water, he wanted that information."

Deverall glanced out the tent's flap, "also, I heard that Sergeant Maraat is dead." Anxiety touched his voice. "They found him just outside the camp covered in slime. I wonder if it's the same thing that attacked the Amphibian." Deverall awaited a reply as he observed his friend with concern. "Well, I'll let you get some rest; just watch your back."

Laddor raised a hand in appreciation then shifted his position slightly. His thoughts retreated to the flight that had brought them there and the dark oily creature which had surrounded and nearly wrecked the aircraft. Now, he supposed, it was here, more than likely having something to do with the bracelet and the strange encounters that had been occurring since they arrived.

Cherinne, he thought to himself, I might not make it…I hope you can forgive me. Listening to the eerie sounds of the desert night he drifted into a pain-filled, fitful sleep.

The wind began to steadily bay, a dreary low moan which hummed along the shifting nighttime dunes. While, the sand, slowly swirling in windswept tufts, nervously danced to the similar melody as the methodic whipping of the tent flaps, which snapped as sails in an ocean wind.

Laddor bolted upright. Sweat-laden hair clung to his face and head as perspiration had soaked through to his clothing. His labored pants of breath were measured and deep, while his heart felt as if it would tear through his aching chest.

The low-flickering light of the oil lantern, within the tent, glimmered with a hypnotic sparkle before his swollen lids and he stared blindly into the light, attempting to awaken from this spellbinding trance. Gently rubbing the back of a hand across his eyes and shaking his head, he severed the hypnotic magnetism. Suddenly he became aware of the low droning wind, which was filling his senses, over the heavy breathing of his friend.

"Deverall—*man! Get up! Some shit's goin' down!*"

"*What?*" the pilot's question was garbled, while his mind was still in a fog of sleep.

"*Get up!*" Laddor shouted, while, despite the stiffness of his screaming limbs, back and head, he scrambled to his feet. The thunderous sound, of heavily pouring sand echoed in the not too far off distance, as he peered through the tent flap which flailed about wildly.

Grabbing the lantern, he limped from inside the tent toward the main campfire, while the rising wind had carried fresh sand which had covered the shadowy spot—the place where the palace soldiers had once been.

Twenty or so tents assembled and scattered about, determined to stand their ground, clashed with the mounting wind and sand. While the metal stakes and cables extended to full, were ready to snap from the shifting earth.

As Laddor shaded his eyes from the spraying granules of sand, he could hear a shout over the dull rumbling of thunder. Two alarmed sentries, the whites of their eyes flashing within the firelight of their passionately swinging lanterns, rushed from the oppressing dark as they yelled, "*Akhad RaTa! Akhad RaTa!*"

Rasheed quickly surfaced from within his tent dressed down to only white trousers. Shaking off a disturbed slumber and swiping a hand through his mussed hair, he strived to assess the situation. Shouting out orders in Arabic, he waved a directive arm at men who scurried from inside their quarters, while their minds were still clouded as they attempted to arm and cloth on the move.

As their eyes met, loathing and disgust were fixed in Rasheed's black stare; he shook his head. Turning, he started in the direction of the horses. Then pausing, and without looking at Laddor, he pointed across the howling dunes and stated, "Do you see that, Mr. Zeandre? *That* is '*The Mother*' sandstorm. You and Mr. Deverall had best make yourselves useful."

Squinting his eyes to the abrasive wind, Laddor turned his attention in the direction of Rasheed's concern. At first glance, he was unable to make out anything as the moon was being shadowed by the graying clouds and the earth was consumed in darkness. But as the surrounding geography of the desert unfolded and a faint flicker of ginger-colored light slowly came into existence, he caught a breath and his heart stopped within his chest.

"*Ohhhh fuuddggee*," the words slipped slowly from his puffed lips, as he viewed, with open mouth, the titanic wall of sand moving in their direction.

Laddor blinked, unsure if he was seeing clearly the four to five thousand foot barrage of dust, which was steadily sweeping the arid terrain, like that of a small continent driving forward beneath the orange glow of desert sky. He turned and raced back to the tent.

"*Deverall! Wake up!*" Laddor managed to spurt out in a rush of breath, as he burst through the whipping canvas flap and collided with the dazed pilot.

Deverall steadied himself and his friend. "Hold up—Red. What in tarnation's goin' on?"

Laddor's wide eyes and frightened stare exhumed the fear running from his head to his feet, as he stumbled breathlessly upon the words, "a…sandstorm…is here!"

"What the hell you talkin' about, Red?" Deverall shouted over the drone of converging wind as he stepped outside the tent. The staggered expression, '*holy…mother*' screamed through the canvas walls, as the whole of the desert shifted and transformed—the matrix of the approaching beast.

Fahimah wiped a bead of sweat from her forehead while her lengthy hair, which had loosened from her tightly woven braids, had plummeted about her face, causing the strands to stick to her heated cheeks. The searing pain in her battered ankle brought her near to tears, tears she would never allow her double to see—a sign of weakness in her country and weakness always led to more pain. Irately, she blinked them back.

"American," her breathing was labored and her skin was mottled with sweat. "The Egyptian is gaining. He will be upon us shortly and if there is any chance of surviving, I must fight." A groan wheezed forth from her chest as her ankle, torn nearly to the bone, buckled and she stumbled roughly to the ground.

"*Fahimah!*" Cherinne lurched forward nearly tumbling along with her. "*Oh, God!*" She kneeled to assist the princess and was shrugged away.

"Leave me." She rolled to her back while the lantern's firelight played off her face, which was pale as white paste; and the sweat, streaming along her cheeks, was able to be bottled.

Grabbing the princess's arm Cherinne attempted to help her to her feet. "No, Fahimah—I *won't* leave you here."

"No, American, you do not understand…I am trained to fight and…" their eyes met and Cherinne was consumed within the pain which hid behind their sternness, "…if need be…to die." Fahimah placed a slightly trembling hand on Cherinne's arm. "If I am not able to defeat this barbarian, I need you to tell the Amir Rasheed something for me." She looked away and wavered briefly; then taking a deep breath the words were a whisper upon her lips, "The Princess Haneefah was with child." She glanced into her double's eyes, studying her look-alike's response, "…and so am I."

She abruptly shoved Cherinne away. "*Now go!* For I feel the humming of the Egyptian's blood upon my skin, and he is near."

Tearing the hem of her tunic with the aide of her teeth, she quickly wrapped it tightly around the damaged ankle. Then bounding to her feet, she raced back through the tunnel and disappeared from sight, leaving Cherinne kneeling in a confused state as a flood of emotions darted throughout her body.

"Fahimah is going to have a child?" she mumbled beneath her breath, "…and the amir is going to be a father?" She jumped to her feet, as a moment of giddiness urged her forward, to get to the surface, to tell someone—*tell the amir!*

Breaking into a run, she hurried through the dimly lit tunnel, glancing at the firelight of each lantern that hung dormant from a heavy iron hook. The announcement of a child brought hope to her down-trodden heart and hope to the kingdom—joy and hope to the amir.

Suddenly, she could see within a fire's flickering light, Fahimah's pale and severely drawn face, the sadness in her multi-colored hazel-green eyes and fear not only for herself but for her unborn baby.

Cherinne stopped in her tracks, while her heart, pounding loudly in her ears, was unable to drown out Fahimah's cry that suddenly tore through the underground tunnel. "*Oh, no!*" The hairs on the back of her neck stiffened and her skin crawled with fright. "*Fahimah?*"

CHAPTER 22

"FAHIMAH!!" The chorded scream rose from Cherinne's throat as she spun on her heels and contemplated what to do. A cold shiver raced along her spine, as the scent of the Egyptian filled her nostrils, and her stomach knotted in fear. And, with no weapon, except for the bracelet, which refused to obey, her decision to search for the surface or rescue the female who could possibly be her sister, bore through her mind.

"Uggh!" Her hands grasped her skull in a vice like grip with frustration and fear cursing her very being.

She thought of Reynolds and his all-knowing wisdom and wondered what he would do. He had once said, when she had been forced to make the difficult decision to release the hired help, *'We all must make choices; and those that are made to benefit others are never futile, though sometimes they may be very painful to us.'*

"Yeah, Reynolds…you have no idea what pain is." The remark was sardonic; she touched her head in memory of the broken bus window and Nagid's elbow. Glimpsing at the cold gold band upon her wrist; she cursed, using the same curse as Fahimah, *"Lashr!"* Without the use of the bracelet and no other weapon, she reached up and removed one of the flickering lanterns from its hook, unknowing to her what purpose it would serve other than the feel of *something* in her hand.

Mustering all her courage, she drew a deep breath and forced herself back into the tunnel from which she just came, while a sense of strength pumped through her veins. "Don't you dare hurt my sister…you swarthy-skinned cretin; and don't you dare even think about hurting her baby!"

Hafiz's low monotone voice drifted eerily through the dank stone of the tunnel's winding encompassment. Cherinne rubbed her free hand along her arm, settling the rash of panic-bumps rushing along her skin. Suddenly, she slowed to a halt, as the sound of Fahimah's low whimpering cries surfaced from just a few steps away.

"I will gut you like the swine you are, Princess," the venom dripped from each word slinking through the moist air.

"You do not know me…" Fahimah drew through flared nostrils, "…you are the swine; and the amir will punish you as such."

Cherinne briefly listened to the acidy conversation, wondering what she could possibly do. Gradually stepping her way closer, she attempted to peer around the corner unnoticed; while anxiety and fright made it near impossible to control her trembling. She held her breath.

"*What the hell is that?*" Deverall shouted as he stumbled back inside the tent, his wide eyes portraying madness. "*Are you freakin' kiddin' me?*" He raked his heavy hands nervously through his hair. "We never even got past *mosquito bites* in brownies, let alone a *freaking sand 'mother' storm! What the hell are we gonna' do?!*" His bugged eyes hurriedly scanned the contents of the small unprotected tent, while his hands wrung in repetitive knots.

"Hey." Laddor tapped Deverall's arm nearly sending the fidgeting pilot from his skin.

"*Shit!*" He glared at Laddor, "*Don't do that! I about shit myself!* Whaddaya want anyway? I have to figure out what to do."

"First off…" Laddor remarked slightly more composed than usual as his insides twisted in fear; although, for once, he was more collected than his friend. "…it's the freaking 'mother' sandstorm; and secondly…you were in the *boy scouts*—not *brownies*—wake up. You're getting all confused; and one of the first rules of thumb, when a life-threatening situation arises is—never panic."

Deverall's brows intertwined unnaturally and the maniacal blaze within his eyes settled on Laddor.

Laddor cringed.

"Oh, shut up; and get outta' my way," the words were grumbled as he threw back the whipping canvas flap and disappeared outside. A shout wafted across the droning wind, "panic…my ass, sissy-boy…I'm just pissed because I was awoken from my dream: This red-head was smearing peanut butter all around my…" The last of his words were fortunately winked out into wind and darkness.

"That blasted Rasheed!" Laddor spoke to his surroundings. He touched the puffy swell of an eye; the various colors of the rainbow masking each skeletal casing melded into a blotchy patch of putrid yellow.

What'd the hell that guy hit me with anyway, he pondered briefly. Thinking that if they lived through this harrowing plight, someone was gonna' pay for all the black-eyes he'd taken. The amir's face entered his mind.

"Raasshheeeedd!" he bellowed out into the disconcerted night as he left the confines of the tent. While the now raging wind drowned out any chance of the amir hearing the belligerent tone, which carried along with his words.

A howling blizzard of razor-sharp sand drove along the surface of the earth covering everything in its blanket of crystallized granules, while Rasheed fought blindly in determination to secure his men and their horses as they scurried about adhering to his orders.

Shouting at the top of his lungs against the incessant storm, he was unwavering to the vicious stinging which coursed along his bare flesh, while the cloth of his trousers snapped angrily against his olive-colored skin.

"Secure the horses and tear down the tents! Small rations when wetting your yashmacs! Keep your skin covered—especially your face! And remain together!" Instinctively, he shielded his eyes with a forearm; while his red eyes, squinting against the burning sensation delivered from the torridness of sand, teared.

"Your Highness! Your Highness!" Ib shouted through his dampened yashmac as he shouldered, in a struggle, against the intensity of the driving wind to reach the amir; his slight weight near losing the battle.

"*Your Highness!*" He advanced slowly forward, while clutching the amir's uniform jacket tightly to his person. Finally he reached the prince, who remaining concentrated on the dilemma at hand, continued to shout out necessary orders through a harsh corded throat.

Grabbing the boy firmly by the collar, Rasheed attempted a thin, fatigued smile in gratitude. "*Hold to my trousers, boy!*" he shouted against the violent wind. Gratefully taking the jacket and slipping it on, he quickly secured it.

Commander Lateef appeared from the repressing dark, his lantern light swung eagerly in an effort to remain a lighted beacon in the consuming darkness. "Your Highness," his words fought against the driving force of airborne terrain; they were shouted in a broken distorted faction. "The men...have aligned themselves...with the tents and rope...storm-side of the horses." Handing the amir his dampened yashmac, the commander affixed his own in place, covering his dusky face which had already blotched red from the brutal sand.

Deverall trudged along, with heavy bare legs through the shifting desert, toward the trio. Shielding his eyes with a thick arm, he was trailed by Laddor who peered from behind his jacket which he used to cover his battered face.

Rasheed's eyes, narrowing to thin slits, observed him briefly from behind the dampened cotton; his hidden lips formed a slight smirk at the sight of the nuisance's battered features.

"Mr. Deverall..." Rasheed shouted, "...is the earbob secure?"

Deverall nodded his head, "Yeah—I have it right here." He patted the pocket of his blowing shorts. "...Unless this mother rips these from me," he cracked a half-hearted grin.

Rasheed turned to the commander. "Set Mr. Deverall and Mr. Zeandre up on the rope line," he bellowed; then glancing at Laddor regretfully, he included, "be sure they are tied."

"Yes, Your Highness," Lateef's reply was returned in a shout and a slightly laborious bow as he turned to leave.

The Commander paused as the amir, pointing to Deverall's bare legs, added in a bellow, "And, get him some trousers."

Training for the khamsins—the violent sand-storms, which have plagued the middle-east since the beginning of time—began for each Egyptian within the Tarun regime from the time that person was born. Simple measures could be taken to aide in keeping oneself alive as the desert sands would come to life carrying with them tons of sharp abrasive granules, which would effortlessly tear and burn at the skin, especially the skin of the lower extremities. Covering the exposed body was of utmost importance and also remaining together—if possible, while being secured collectively with a rope.

Rasool had trained the men to align themselves with the tents to their backs, fastening each tent together with cord—like that of a canvas wall. Rasheed had thought this ingenious, for not only did it aid in shielding the men against the coming storm, but it also helped to protect their transportation—the horses.

While using this technique for the monstrous storm which was rapidly approaching, Rasheed realized that the diminutive tents would be no match for the 4,000 foot of wall raging in their direction. Gripping Ib's arm tightly, with the driving winds carrying them toward the cluster of anxiously awaiting men and horses, he whispered a prayer of deliverance beneath his breath to the universal gods who had brought this storm upon them.

A colossal-sized slamming fist struck each man in an unrelenting blow, as Rasheed shouted upon deaf ears the words 'hold steady' which dissipated in a massive torrent of violently gushing wind and sand that crashed down upon his men in an avalanche of desert. The 'mother'—unleashing her bent fury—drove her massive bosom upon the men's screaming carcasses in the attempts to swallow their trembling beings whole within her ferocity.

"HOLD THE LINE!" Rasheed shouted, if only to himself, in an attempt to find reassurance in the soundless words being drowned out by the clamor, though their connotation urged him to stand firm. He held the rope tautly above his head, within his grasping numb fingers where the layers of raw skin were being pressed to the bone. The canvas slapped in a maddened frenzy at his body, trying to tear the only comfort from his hands; he pictured the Rod.

The horses danced wildly in a bonded cluster of desperation. Fear filled the whites of their blazing eyes as they pushed and shoved, like silver pin balls in an arcade machine, struggling to break free and run. Run from, and before the coming storm, till it seized them within its grasp and caused their hearts to explode from exhaustion and panic.

Rasheed, thinking that the commander was to his right, glimpsed in that direction. Emptiness occupied that sector of the line, which invaded the amir's optimism, while his arms felt to be ripped from their joints and he briefly counted the remainder of the 40 minutes that a sandstorm normally lasts.

Suddenly, he was slammed from behind—a sledgehammer effect—with every bone in his body feeling as if they had cracked. The terror-driven line of tents ripped from his searing hands and he was catapulted blindly forward, forgetting his men, his mission, the time and the boy still clutched to his trousers. His heart banged within his chest, and the scream that raced forth from inside his body, was hushed to his ears as he hit the ground and was covered by a heavy quilted blanket of sand.

Tossing his full mane of wild, flaming red hair back, in a boisterous, schizophrenic howl, the God Seth sifted the few remaining grains of sand within his hand, allowing them to slip through his nervous, itchy fingers to the barren ground beneath his feet.

"That will teach those meddling humans to tread upon *my* desert."

CHAPTER 23

Hafiz's blade played eagerly at the tip of Fahimah's sternum while his forearm, shoved to her throat, held both her arms firmly above her head. His damp rigid body pressed her petite form securely to the moist cavernous wall as he shifted his eyes to examine her bloodied ankle.

Fire spat from her kaleidoscopic eyes, burning first a blazing green then quickly raging near black. She held the anklets, which had returned to normal pieces of fashion jewelry, determinedly within a shaken fist; while, she, in a compromising position, was unable to unleash their blood-thirsting fury. Her heart pounded within her ears, drowning out the quiet of the underground tunnel and Hafiz's steady breathing as he grazed the roughly wrapped ankle with the ball of his foot. Flinching, she blinked back a warranted cry.

"Princess...you were supposed to remain *locked up*." His eyes bore down into hers observing the richly-colored pupils as they flashed in multiple levels of hatred.

"You have interrupted my work and as a result I have not been able to fulfill my duties."

The dirk bit at her taut skin and he continued, "You were supposed to wait till I came for you, but I see impatience has taken you hostage and you have rushed to accompany me, and in the process, have damaged yourself."

"I have not come for your company, but for your head." Fahimah spewed through clenched teeth.

Pressing his face closer, his heated breath mingled with that of her own. Their eyes locked, while he cruelly awaited the desired response as his foot pressed ever-so-sharply against her injury. A jolt of pain rushed from her buckling ankle throughout the whole of her body, raging in an unbridled grimace at the back of her steadfast gaze.

A leering smirk twinged at the corners of his lips while he was pleased with her pain. "Tell me Princess…do you look upon the amir with such hatred as he prepares to lay you upon his sheets? Or do you look to him with longing and desire—not the look of hostility that you give to me?" His cool lips brushed against hers and she promptly turned her head.

Angered at her rebuff, he ground his foot into her throbbing ankle.

Stabbing pain exploded, racing at lightening speed through her calf and thigh, bursting to the tips of her toes and shooting through the recesses of her body to her shaky fingertips. Fahimah's mind spun in excruciating agony as sweat poured from her pores; her lips parted slightly, as she uncontrollably gasped in pain.

"*I like it*," Hafiz breathed, forcing his lips upon hers. His acidy tongue plunged deep within her mouth causing her to gag as it shoved its way toward her throat.

Cherinne trembled as she quietly observed from just feet away, '*Oh my God!*' quivered in a whisper upon her breath; her mind raced frantically as to what she should do and she briefly thought of Laddor as being a saint compared to this guy. Tearing a strip of cloth from the hem of Hafiz's tunic, she cinched her waist and secured her damp disheveled hair, preparing herself for what was to come.

Fahimah gagged in a desperate attempt to retrieve air as she struggled to break her mouth free, while her lungs felt as if they would burst within her heaving chest.

Hafiz watched her reaction closely through an impassioned maniacal stare; the fear, pain and struggle within her flashing eyes drawing a raging power upon his loins. He removed his tongue. Then releasing the pressure from her neck she slumped just before the dirk's point. And glimpsing at the weapons grasped within her hand, he slipped the rope from his bare broad shoulder and prepared to bind her.

Nausea burned and rose from her throat, as she coughed and gagged, suddenly spewing the few morsels of food from within her stomach before her feet—nausea, which was caused by the excruciating pain, and, more than likely, her pregnancy.

In the confines of her misery and solitude, Fahimah had begun to feel the effects of the growing fetus within her womb: headaches, nausea, a maternal instinct, which could have possibly explained her fondness for the boy, Ib, and why she hadn't just allowed this lecherous Egyptian, *Hafiz*, to have his way with the American, possibly even kill her. She was becoming soft, and she despised it more than this worm before her. Weeks ago she would have slain the American—her sister—and her companions without a thought and possibly even the amir for visiting his wives' chambers. She had grown cold to his acts of bigamy which were wholly acceptable to the Egyptian world and especially for a prince, while something inside her ached miserably, wanting Rasheed's attention all to herself. But, that not being the case, she brooded in silence hoping that one day she could expel any and all feelings she possessed toward anyone, including her unborn child. And, with the agonizing recollection of her past, which had just recently haunted her, being brought back in a flood of suppressed memories, it made it near impossible for her to fight.

She winced in the remembrance of the Rod thrashing against her burning flesh; while the phantom, coming to life once more, attempted to draw her within its clutches.

'You shall be punished severely for the death of my son, the Amir Nuri *and* for Princess Adiva.' Anger raged from behind the deep set black eyes of the Amir Onslow, Rasheed's grandfather—a dark Egyptian, inside and out and well into his twilight years. In experiencing the gifts of growing age, like arthritis and rheumatism, and shouldering them reproachfully; it caused his already darkened disposition to turn black.

'Give this worthless whore 10 more lashes then send her before the blade,' he growled at the overseer, administrator of the Rod. Turning to leave, he paused and glanced his shoulder, 'then place her head upon the lantern's post before the gates, sending out notice for all in the regime to attend, so that they can witness the repercussions of an American invading an Egyptian empire.'

'*Nnooo!!*' The plead tore from Fahimah's lips as the Rod slashed at her exposed back and legs, taking the wind from her searing bruised lungs.

Amir Onslow's chief henchmen stood awaiting him at the dungeon door. 'Uthman, summon Commander Rasool to my chambers...I wish to converse with him over the unfortunate incident which has fated the regime. And, allow no-one to disturb my grandson Rasheed...he has suffered a horrific ordeal and needs time to examine his mindset. To suffer such an experience, as his father's death before his very own eyes, has to be extremely detrimental and heart-wrenching for the young prince. And as for his mother...well,' he threw a hand in the air, 'I never was too fond of her. She always seemed to me to be a scheming little whore, nothing better than for being on her back. Besides that carcass of hers, I never understood what Nuri saw in the wench.'

Shoving through the double-doors of his chambers, he settled himself behind his desk, placed his elbows on the mahogany and set his chin in his hands while Uthman waited to be dismissed. Amir Onslow's heavy graying brows furrowed as he noticed his aide's presence still within the room. 'Uthman—do you not have your orders?'His tone was condescending.

'Yes, Your Grace...' He chose his words wisely, '...I was just waiting to see whether or not there was anything else, and awaiting dismissal.'

'Oh—well, now that you mention it, also summon that young girl...' He tapped his forehead as if attempting to get it to work. '...I believe her name was Haneefah. Yeah—that's it—Haneefah. She is the lovely young daughter of Terlah, Amir Nuri's number three wife.' He tapped his head again, 'or maybe its number nine. *Oh, I don't know! He had so damn many!*' He ran his hand through graying hair, matching that of his now twisted brows. 'Anyway...have her sent to Rasheed's chambers; maybe she can help to console him.'

He eyed Uthman squarely. '*Now*, you are dismissed.'

Sweat broke upon Rasool's palms and beneath his armpits, despite the cooling system within the amir's chambers. 'You summoned me, Sire?' His voice had cracked slightly and he hoped the Amir Onslow had not noticed. While most times, the lord's demeanor could be even more wicked and unpredictable than his son, Amir Nuri's had been.

The aged Egyptian stood with his back to the commander, hands cupped behind him. 'Yes, I did, Commander. I'm not quite sure I have the complete picture of what happened today.' He turned to face Rasool, his piercing gaze causing the commander great discomfort. 'Now—when I arrived at the scene...' he paused while his eyes momentarily glazed thinking of the amiri's blood-drenched quarters and his son's bludgeoned body, dead before him. Rasool thought he may have, for a brief second, seen a flicker of sorrow or remorse, but suddenly the Amir Onslow smiled mildly and continued. '...My grandson swears that it was *you* who had slain my Nuri; that you were attacking *him* when you tripped or something.' He waved a hand as if shooing a fly. 'I just don't know, Rasool. Rasheed was in tears, crying like a baby...' he huffed, '...and can't get his weedy head outta' his arse to save his life. I had the physician give him a double dose of something to help him control that blubbering.' He grumbled, 'damned weakling.'

'Anyway, Rasool—I know that my Nuri loved you like his own son, if not more. And, I don't believe that you would have harmed him in any way. So—I am retaining your position and setting the blame on that American girl before the peoples of the regime. She is being subjected to the Rod as we speak.' He stood, smoothed his tunic and glanced the wall mirror behind him straightening a few strands of loose hair, as if preparing for dinner which had ended hours earlier. 'I will have her head displayed upon the first lantern come nightfall. I must prepare to attend...for this shall be enlightening.'

Rasool cringed within his boots—not that he had never seen blood or killed anyone, it was just the warped mentality of the senior amir was extremely disturbing.

Rasheed laid face down upon the bed; puffy, red eyes refused to close to sleep, as the image of his mother lying in a pool of blood, set heavy upon his mind and heart. The ducts of his eyes dry and swollen looked upon the young Egyptian female while they refused to shed another tear; the last of them spent. The medication running its course mingled within the young prince's blood causing the room to bend and twist putting Rasheed into another dimension.

'Haneefah,' his words were muttered in a low barely audible tone. 'I'm sorry I could not bring you pleasure.' His eyes momentarily closed as she ran her fingers lightly along the fine lines of his bronze back, occasionally fingering a silken curl which lay limp upon his shoulder.

'*Ssshh,*' she gently shushed his apology away. 'I did not come here, Your Highness for myself; I came here to comfort you. Please do not concern yourself with me.' She placed her lips to his heated cheek. 'And I know you are worried about the flaxen-haired girl, for I heard you call out her name—Fahimah—while you lay upon my breast weeping. You do love her—don't you?'

Haneefah smiled slightly crestfallen as she watched his eyelids flicker and he answered, 'I do.'

'I love you too, my prince.' Then she quietly, as not to awaken him, dressed and slipped silently from his room.

Amir Onslow observed Fahimah from behind contemptuous eyes as the attending guard opened the cell's gate—the rise and fall of her measured breathing, the only movement reflected within the lantern's flickering firelight. She lay crumpled on her side in the dungeon's far corner upon the damp and dirty ground, unable to move, if even her head, to acknowledge from where the animated voice was coming.

The amir slipped his slightly crooked fingers into the openings of his white gloves and waved away the attending guard. 'You may leave me with the prisoner. I have a few things I would like to discuss with her.' Stepping inside the cell and careful not to tread upon the fresh blood that lay upon the grimy clay floor, he knelt beside the young American female. Removing a matt of bloody soiled hair, once flowing and lovely, from her battered face, she mustered the energy to open her eye lids. He smiled.

'You know something...' his tone was set—shallow and unfeeling, like that beyond the grave, '...I love the scent of fresh blood; there is just something so tantalizing about it.' He turned his gloved hand within the fires light to see the crimson stain from her hair upon the white satin; a devilish spark beset his black eyes. 'Wild animals fight in a blistering frenzy over the scent of fresh blood, maybe I am part beast.'

Sniffing his reddened fingers, he then bent to stare directly into her glazed eyes. 'I honestly pray that every bone in your body is broken—broken as a fallen twig from the palm, and that you bleed internally; for I especially like the scent of your sweet smelling blood…' He glanced again at the red upon his hands. '…the blood of an American—it rejuvenates me and makes me feel young again.'

He stood to his feet and smoothed his galabiyah, briefly surveying her battered body. 'Now—while your head is hanging so grotesquely from the palace lantern light and the nerves within the back of your eyes stick in an unmoving clot of gel, unable to relieve themselves of the terror which stares upon my people; and your mind continues to race as to how it had come to this. While it feels as if your searing brain will tear through your every aperture and your soul has been sent to hell—remember this. Remember to thank that scheming bitch for what she has done to you.'

Removing the white gloves, he tossed them before her eyes, as a single tear raced down her unmoving cheek and he turned to leave.

Hafiz recoiled in disgust. *"What the—?"*

Fahimah retched again, her head spinning in the throes of the sickening past; she buckled before the dirk in dry heaves. *"Water,"* her thirst was implacable. She pleaded again, "I need water."

"I'll give you water—you foul-smelling cow." Hafiz reached for the shimmering anklets which she grasped tightly in her hand. "Now, give me these!" Wrenching her bleeding fingers open and removing the leg bands, he slipped them within his trouser pocket. "You came very near to removing my ear, Princess."

He shoved her face-first to the ground then bound her hands and feet. And, as he was securing the rope around the maimed ankle, the dirt-encrusted wrap grew to an enormous size of scarlet.

Fahimah panted at the pain which blinded her to any defense and caused the nightmares to pour upon her as an open dam breaking upon rock.

Hafiz's brow creased as he briefly ran his gaze over the bandaged wound, realizing she was losing too much blood and by her reaction, perhaps going into shock.

He roughly rolled her to her back, annoyance building upon heated pleasure; he tossed her limp body over a tensed shoulder. "Come on, you smelly wench; and don't you dare heave on me." Sheathing the dirk and retrieving his crossbow, he began his trek back to the watering hole; for his orders *were* to prepare the females and now he basically had them both where he wanted them—with this one searing in unbridled pain and the other just steps away.

"American," he shouted, his voice booming within the quiet of the gloomy tunnels, "...I know you are watching." His tone turned rather carefree, sending a chill racing along Cherinne's perspiring skin.

"Come and join us. We will be waiting by the lake."

The guard carried Fahimah's body like that of a sack of grain; every bone within her body splintered or broken. She breathed shallowly as the last remaining air within her battered body slipped through stale unmoving lips while she had been swallowed by oblivion, unaware of her surroundings. The echoing of his footfalls resounded loudly throughout the dungeon corridor, drowning out the slightest tinkling of her ankle-bracelets as he made his way toward the executioners shed—a roughly fashioned structure built strictly for the sometimes, not so swift, death sentences that the amir commissioned insubordinates. It sat just beyond the gates of the regime, with easy access for disposing of bloody corpses, quick to draw vultures and a putrid foul smelling odor brought about from the intense heat. Stocked with an array of various weapons from roping to sawed-tooth axes, it was styled just for those in defiance to the ruling amir—Amir Onslow—who had had the shed built along with the regime. A passionate fervor had flowed through his veins as he had waited anxiously of christening it, while receiving his meals there along with his objecting wives.

The first execution within the walls of the shed threw the entire people's of the Tarun Regime into a panicked frenzy; for the amir—beside himself—desiring the taste of fresh blood upon his lips, threatened to slaughter anyone who just glanced him incorrectly.

His three wives lived in constant terror, one of them being Nuri's mother, the first princess of the palace who the Amir Onslow treated viciously in secret while Nuri, as a small child stood by defenselessly and watched. His father took his mother to the shed often, maniacally running the various weapons and blades along her petrified skin; while small Nuri believed many times she would eventually not return.

When the shed wasn't being occupied as often as the amir had hoped he then deviously devised the Rod, which he had centered just below his quarters to enjoy the full effects of the vibrating screams just a board below his feet. It worked wonders in negotiations with other regimes; for the warranted sickly screams—planned during his meetings with other leaders alone—drifting through to his office—persuaded those meeting with him, to quickly succumb to his wishes.

With nightfall on the horizon and the skies turning a reddish-gray, Harim wanted to get his devotions underway. Irritably, he tossed Fahimah's limp body to the ground with a heavy thud and unlocked the shed's door. With a gruff, he scooped her up, shoved a hip against the heavy wood and stepped inside the cooled dark. Harim laid her slouching body onto a blood stained wooden bench of the 20 foot square cubicle and reached for a nearby oil lamp. Grabbing a tinderbox and oil pot, he lit the flint, caught the wick and briefly eyed the flickering light, then hung the lantern on a nearby hook. The lamp's light swayed methodically as he heaved a sigh and closed the door.

'This is a fool's errand, meant for a fool,' he grumbled slipping on an apron, splattered with the dry remains of a number of previous victim's blood. He shifted his gaze to Fahimah who laid unresponsive on the aged-worn bench while trying to decide on the weapon best suited for the unproblematic job. 'Great Allah, she's half dead as it is; it doesn't seem worth the effort to use my tools. Should certainly save myself the time of cleaning up and just snap her neck. Except for the fact, that the amir wants your head atop the blasted lantern post,' he complained to Fahimah's occasionally blinking eyes. 'Well, *Bint*—what shall it be—the sword or the machete? It doesn't matter much to me; still have to clean one or the other *and* my apron. Let's just get this over with so I can get your head mounted—give my alms, and feed my appetite. I haven't eaten all day.

He turned to retrieve the machete. 'I think this will do—short and sweet.'

Suddenly, the shed's door burst open, nearly knocking the lantern from its post; the light danced wildly casting racing shadows throughout the cubicle.

'What in Great Allah!' Harim's voice cracked. Gripping the machete's handle, his eyes darted about the single room, along the shelves of weapons, the washing bins and to Fahimah who hadn't flinched. He stepped toward the door and peered out toward the coming night.

Immediately, his head exploded into a shower of gleaming stars as a foot made contact with the side of his fleshy face, sending him dazed and plummeting backward into a wall of weapons that crashed upon him and to the floor.

Haneefah hastily slipped inside the confines of the single, death encroached room; and grabbing Fahimah's weakened, lifeless body, she lugged her outside. Fastening the lock, with Harim unconscious inside, she hauled Fahimah, step by laborious step, back inside the palace while the majority of the regime was on their knees, their faces hidden between their hands, occupied with giving their evening prayers.

Rising from before the prince's chamber doors, Uthman brushed himself off and stepped around the corner briefly, stretched and helped himself to some water as Haneefah panting heavily and nearly spent of energy, slipped with Fahimah inside Rasheed's room. Darkness filled the prince's chambers as he laid quietly in much needed tranquility, the medication he had been administered making it possible for him to rest.

Haneefah listened to his steady breathing for a brief moment—her love for him insurmountable. She then proceeded to lay Fahimah on the floor between the king-sized bed and the wall.

Uthman! The name bellowed along the empty hallway, as Rasool, followed by Omar and Mahir, paused in front of the prince's chambers. Uthman set his glass down upon the cherry foyer, his thin brows set in a downward furl. He hastened around the corner.

'What in the world are you shouting about—you ignorant clod? The prince is resting and I have strict orders from the amir that he is to remain undisturbed!' Uthman's words were whispered between clenched teeth. 'Now, remove yourselves, before you wake him!'

'No.' Rasool glared down at his senior—by possibly fifteen years—their rank one and the same while Uthman was half his build. 'The American prisoner has escaped and we believe it was Princess Terlah's offspring, Haneefah, who has assisted in aiding her. And someone has reported seeing Haneefah wondering about the vicinity of the prince's chambers.' Rasool grasped the door handle in a firm grip, 'I want to take a look.'

'No...' Uthman removed the commander's hand. '...Haneefah is to be comforting the prince in his time of sorrow...I will.'

Haneefah rapidly removed her tunic, mussed her hair and slipped beneath the prince's blankets; Rasheed groaned and rolled to his side.

Uthman opened the door ever-so quietly and peered into the dark.

Rubbing her eyes, as if she was groggy, Haneefah raised her head and met Uthman's stare. And, placing a finger to her lips for him to remain quiet, she directed her gaze toward Rasheed.

Uthman raised an apologetic hand, then paused. The scent of fresh blood and sweat tingled upon his senses while they drifted heavily upon the air. He sniffed deeply and his eyes narrowed to darkened slits. 'I smell blood; it intertwines with sweat.' His gaze swept the entirety of the room then settled again on her. 'Explain this, Haneefah.' His tone was set.

She lowered her head in feigned embarrassment, then returned his gaze and whispered softly, 'This was my first.'

Eyeing her skeptically, he quietly closed the door.

CHAPTER 24

Deverall shoveled his way out from beneath a canvas tent covered by a cargo of sand. Stumbling to his feet and removing the yashmac—the cotton cloth covering his face—he shouted into the peeking yellow rays of the morning sun, *"I'm alive!"* Breathing deep, he coughed to relieve his throat of wondering granules, then shook like a wet dog freeing himself of water as the sand sprayed about, sounding like that of falling rain. Quickly, he evaluated the situation, while others tunneled their way out from beneath the tents and more of the same—sand.

"Red?...Amir?" He shouted watching while two horses struggled to their feet; bucking and kicking, they neighed and whinnied as if also thankful to be alive.

"Over here!" Laddor returned his call. "I need a hand."

Deverall trudged through the extra foot of off-white granules; a brief memory of him as a child tramping through the snow of a massive blizzard and pulling a toboggan to meet his friends, entered his mind. He grinned vaguely to himself. "I'm comin'; just hang on." A shifting mound stirred before him and he quickly dug to retrieve the commander, pulling him panting from the sand.

"Shukran," Lateef managed through a drawn breath while brushing himself off and removing his yashmac. Attempting to focus, he apprehensively scanned the shifting surface as others rose to their feet and horses ran a-muck.

"Il Amir?" the commander inquired as their eyes met.

"*Deverall!*" Laddor shouted impatiently. "*I need a hand!*"

"Hold up, Red. Is it the amir?"

Laddor grumbled beneath his breath, "No—it's his horse."

Lateef urgently shouted out to the emerging men as they rose in a fog, like vaporous zombies from the earth. "*Al amir! Al Laqa al amir!*"

Inspiration charged through the eager pilot's veins with the amir's recovery far greater than that of the man's horse. And, slapping Lateef on the back, he hollered with a ready grin, "*Let's do it!*"

Rasheed lay with a cheek against the cool of the enveloping mass of sand, breathing painfully, in shallow choppy breaths with the aide of his yashmac. Darkness, black as midnight on a new moon, surrounded him as he forced his sand-covered lashes open to peer into nothingness; while his body lay completely immobile beneath a small portion of Egypt. Spurts of air flittered within the hair just behind his ear and he felt an ever-so-slight movement. Searching his memory of the storm and where he might be—the tent tearing from his hands, the horses fighting in a panicked frenzy—he remembered—the boy.

Rasheed closed his heavy lashes allowing his thoughts to drift from his mind, from beneath the earth and from the present. He returned to his bedroom so long ago, where Haneefah had laid in the dark, perspiring in worried anxiety beside him while her eyes were wild with apprehension and the scent of blood was thick in the air.

'Your Highness! Your Highness!' She had pleaded in a panicked whisper, '*please wake up!*' She gently jostled his shoulder.

'*Fahimah?*'

'No, Your Highness...it is I, Haneefah,' she answered lowly, slightly dejected. 'But, Your Highness...I have brought Fahimah here and she is desperately in need of a physician.' She then noticed the blood staining her hands, most certain that Uthman had not seen.

Rasheed attempted to rub the groggy sleep from his eyes while the medication was still heavy within his system. Rising to a sitting position, he ran a weak hand through his mussed hair and glanced around the darkened room—the draperies drawn tight and his lantern light extinguished—he tried to affix his eyes to the dimmed light. '*Fahimah?* She is here? Where?'

Haneefah slid to her right, allowing him access to the floor. 'She is there,' Haneefah pointed—a look of dismay heavy upon her countenance. Her eyes met Rasheed's, as she barely whispered, 'she may be dead.'

Rasheed, barging through his grandfather's study doors, startled the aged Egyptian from his examination of a half-eaten chicken leg, while the cracking wood, vibrating, sent a portrait crashing loudly to the parquet floor. Fire brimmed upon his brow, shooting deadly sparks in the direction of the senior amir, as hatred toward the man emanated from his angry measured breaths and raced along his heated skin.

'Rasheed. My *gracious,* boy…you startled me. Didn't that mother of yours teach you any manners?' He returned his gaze to the cooked fowl within his grease-laden fingers. 'I'm surprised to see you up and about so soon.' He reached for a snifter of liqueur before him, and poured the golden liquid into his empty glass. Swirling the goblet within three fingers, he nonchalantly inhaled the bouquet and took a drink. 'So…' his dark stare locked with that of his grandson's flaming eyes as he set the goblet and fowl down and wiped his hands, '…what has you so unnerved?'

The young prince shook with rage, attempting to control the anger exploding throughout the entirety of his body. His fist clenched in knots and his words spewed forth venomously, each one bitten through gritted teeth. 'Don't be coy with me, *Grandfather.* You ordered your men to put Fahimah to the Rod—then had orders to behead her.' His eyes glazed with emotion as his feelings wrought to explode in infuriation or send him bolting across the aged Egyptian's desk to beat him senseless. 'You are a *monster!*'

'*Rasheed!*' Onslow stood to his feet and slammed his hand to the mahogany wood; the prince flinched. Onslow then snapped his fingers and Uthman stepped from within the shadows.

'Now—listen to me…' the amir's icy stare darkened; the same devil raging inside as that of Rasheed's father, festering within his black heart. His tone carried a deadly ring. '*I* am head now—the amir. I will rule *my* regime as *I* see fit. And, the releasing of my prisoner really has me—how shall I say it…' he tapped his head, '…piqued. I am very tempted to bring forth both you *and* that Egyptian girl to the Rod for releasing my prisoner, while I know she was hidden within your room.'

Candid surprise leapt upon the young prince's face while he struggled to suppress the shock overriding his irate expression.

'The flooring was stained beneath your bed,' the amir continued, 'but unfortunately with you being my grandson and Harim being extremely over-anxious to pay *someone* back for his swollen jaw…I've just decided to have *both* the American female *and* the Egyptian female taken to the shed.'

His furrowed brow suddenly molded into a look of triumphant satire with his stare intent; he smiled then chuckled maniacally.

'If only your father could see your expression now—the look of simpleton terror upon your pathetic face. He'd readily strike that useless wench that spawned you.' He flicked his hand as if waving away a nuisance, 'Now, leave me boy. I would like to finish my meal then go and watch the execution. Harim won't tarry too…

Rasheed suddenly shot through the air, in spite of of the lingering remnants of calming medication flowing through his veins. His heart pounded furiously drowning out the remaining words of his loathsome grandfather, as he determinedly bounded across the heavy desk with dirk in hand. Slamming headlong into the amir, the desk chair flipped sending them both toppling brutally to the floor, along with plates of half-eaten food, the crystal goblet and the near empty snifter of liqueur. An explosion of crystal and china rang loudly throughout the room and into the corridor as they crashed upon the variegated colored parquet floor sending a maidservant running for aid.

Papers fluttered lazily about, riding upon the heatedly charged air with anger and wrath consorts of the men's demeanor, while Rasheed struggled atop his grandfather attempting to stick him through.

Uthman moved swiftly as he drew his sword and slashed upon Rasheed with fiery conviction. Conviction to himself alone, while the final result would be the prince's head or his own, if he did not accomplish his duty to the satisfaction of the severely demented Amir Onslow.

The glistening blade slashed at Rasheed, being a mere extension of the mighty hunter's body. While the skilled commander, who had drawn blood with the aide of his military support for near all time—driven by the amir's whimsical sadistic pleasure—had thrived upon the battlefield.

Catching Rasheed broadside, the incensed cutting edge tore through cloth and skin sending him tumbling weak and dazed to the floor—the stabbing pain rendering him useless as he buckled in agony and dropped his weapon.

Uthman rapidly stomped a foot to the prince's heaving chest and raised the gleaming steel above his head—the rising and falling, terror-stricken heart his main objective.

'No!' the amir shouted scurrying to his feet and quickly brushing himself off. He irately discarded a chicken leg which was shoved within a fold of his lapel then grabbed a fistful of Rasheed's hair. Onslow yanked the prince's sweated head back to meet his gaze. His breath was laced with the smell of fowl and liquor while his words were breathed as fire upon his grandson's face.

'How dare you come against *me*—you sniveling weakling.' His eyes bore through to Rasheed's soul. 'I shall not let you die here, not until after you have witnessed the beheading of those two females. And because you have defied me, their deaths will be prolonged and painful, torturous till the end.' He yanked Rasheed to his feet, 'Now, come with me—Grandson; we shall watch together.'

Blood slipped warmly through Rasheed's fingers coloring the side of his white bed-shirt a bright crimson. He held the injury with a shaking hand while his breath raced within his raspy chest and pain rushed to every part of his body. Wearily, he looked into his grandfather's aged face, the craggy lines etched deep within his swarthy complexion added insult to his harrowing features while Rasheed determined him to be the very spawn of Satan. He closed his eyes momentarily and breathed a much needed breath, then spoke with words of noble authority.

'No, Grandfather—I won't be going anywhere with you; and you will never speak of my mother again.' His gaze locked with the man's. 'Because right now...*you* are going to Jahannam.'

With the miniscule amount of energy still within his body, Rasheed spun. And, avoiding Uthman's rapid reflex, which readily delivered a massive blow, Rasheed dodged, sending a dinner fork directly into the leathery skin of the amir's throat.

CHAPTER 25

"*Dig!*" Deverall shouted in a sweaty pant. Sand sprayed behind him in a fountain as he dug into his work with a fervent passion. Using his hands and arms like that of a steam shovel, he plowed within the never-ending expanse of sand, while his back ached miserably, and it felt as if his weighty arms would fall off.

"*Ajal! Ajal!*" Lateef bellowed with urgency, the minutes turning into hours as the sweltering sun rose for an appearance bringing forth an unmercifully scorching morning, while the army of men tunneled in various spots along the surface, with no sign of the amir.

Even Laddor assisted with the back-breaking endeavor; his face puckered and bruised, he continued to grumble, wondering why he would contribute to such a ridiculous feat—digging up tons of hot sand looking for someone who probably was dead.

"Hey, Red…" Deverall shouted over. "I bet Princey will be happy that you saved his horse," he grinned wearily. "You'll have to tell 'im all about it when we find 'im."

Laddor's grumbling halted. "*Yeah,*" He replied dolefully, while the rescuing of the horse had been a small miracle. He pictured the amir atop the Arab mare; then thought back to just hours earlier as he had lain beneath a sand covered tent entangled with Nerfertiti.

She had lain on her side beneath his outstretched legs, which had somehow gotten intertwined within her halter and the cording of the canvas tent. Fortunately, her nose had stuck just above the desert's surface and he was able to uncover an eye. The long black lashes, covered with sand, fluttered in a heated panic as she had struggled beneath the weight of him and an enormous amount of antique colored granules.

'*Ssshhh*,' he had coaxed her gently, stroking the white blaze just above her large nostrils. 'Lie still, we'll get out soon.' His words fell upon deaf ears as he dug to uncover one.

He had scooped the sand, handful by handful, to keep it from totally encasing her flaring, drippy, pink nostrils and suffocating her as her single bulging eye watched him in wide terror. Then, assisted by two of the commander's men, who quickly severed the tangled, knotted ropes, they observed happily as she laboriously struggled to dig her way out from beneath the heavy sand. Afterward, a small applaud went up, and as they clapped with a whistle and a holler, a slim bond of comradery had formed between Laddor and the amir's men.

Laddor wondered in thought, as his cracking, sore hands dug deep within the endless granules. It reminded him of being on the beaches back home; where he and Cherinne had playfully made it a contest to build a large wall of sand along the water's edge while attempting to keep the determined waves from seeping through. Of course, they had lost the battle. Shoveling the mountain of sand was like stopping the ocean. Impossible.

Suddenly, a shout went up, parting him from his revelry—the amir.

Laddor's heart beat grew in rapidity, as he left his appointed excavating post and hastened toward the group of men heaving—not one, but two—bodies from the sand, while he had completely forgotten about the boy.

Lateef roared out orders in Arabic—one of the words, '*doctoorra*', which Laddor recalled as being 'doctor'. His gaze quickly ran to Deverall and their eyes met. The ruffian physician suddenly emerged and stepped arrogantly through the parted men. Waving his free hand in an annoying manner, he clutched his black leather bag within the other. His tone was vicious, like that of an irate cobra whose tail had accidentally been tromped on. The men scrambled—beside themselves—possibly fearing for their lives from being subjected to his cruel and brutal treatments or possibly fearing for the unfortunate amir. Doctoorra Raghib hissed out his orders.

A roaring growl echoed just outside the entrance to the tunnels of the Haush min maut as Nagid angrily threw back the heavy iron door and stepped inside. He glanced the row of lanterns leading miles within the earth, while his eyes adjusted to the low flickering lighting, which was somewhat dimmer than that of Seth's outer hall. A number of weapons adorned his thick leather belting, while he used the Swaheel like that of a large over-bearing walking stick, as he began the long arduous trek into the labyrinth of tunnels. The resonant pounding of his heavy black boots upon the gravely surface and his weighty inhaling and exhaling were the only sounds heard within the passageway. Pausing briefly, he peeled back the massive hood of his broad-shouldered cloak and pricked his ears to listen attentively for any hint of Hafiz or the two females—nothing. He cursed to his shadow hulking upon the damp walls—a giant beast hovering about him—while his huge frame nearly filled the passageway's cavity.

"Hafiz—I shall sharpen my blades upon your bones, *you insolent fool!* Our lord sits in wait for his trophy—the female with the mystical bracelet. And his greedy appetite grows to immeasurable heights while his army of Jabali ascends, arising to the audacious occasion." He drew his hood and pressed onward.

The 'Jabali' are great beast, derived from the dry earth, with a head of a boar and the body comparable to that of an ass. They are measured to that of an eight foot man, with large curved tusks and deep-set, beady eyes while their teeth, long and likened to that of sharpened spears, are meant strictly for tearing at raw bloody prey and the defeated enemies flesh. Their dull skin—coarse and deeply wrinkled—dowdy brown in color, is slightly tinted with a hue of greenish-gray downy, giving the creature the appearance of being covered in mold, while their pores emanate the odor compared to that of goat manure through the cloth of their garments—hooded course cloaks.

Forged from the strongest elements of the earth, their large array of weaponry is fashioned in the elitist armaments of crossbows and swords, while they also use catapults, maces and clubs—all the weapons absorbed throughout time within the continent's battlefields from those who have engaged in past war. Their command is one of simplicity—defeat the Goddesses Nephthys and Isis for their god, Seth's, freedom. For him to ascend to the floor of Egypt and above, return to the throne, while he had been imprisoned beneath the broad desert by Isis's heavenly powers.

Cherinne's heart leaped within her chest while the lantern jingled within her shaking hand. "Bastard," slipped from her lips in an irate murmur. Hafiz's footfalls became a diminishing echo as she could hear him departing in the direction from which they had just come. Stepping out from the curvature, she decided to follow, despite the anxiety racing within her core.

Hafiz made it a game, knowing that she was just steps behind. "*American...*" he called, "...so this female is your sister...your identical matching? So then, tell me—why do you squabble with her so? Is she not from the same loins that birthed you—the same blood? The scent of your milk is akin, like that of the cedar and hemlock, apart from the fact that one is poison and the other is not."

Anger, fear and apprehension cursed along Cherinne's skin, while she bit back the urge to holler, scream, cry or even fall down on her knees begging for him to stop—stop talking and let them go.

"*SHUT UP!!* You make me sick! And, she is not my sister!" The enraged request gusted forth in a breath from her lips, as she ran a sweaty palm along the sleeve of Hafiz's tunic, in an attempt to warm the chill that dampened her skin.

"*Aahhh*, so she speaks, Princess." He noted to Fahimah who laid in quiet upon his shoulder as her chest rose and fell in shallow breaths. "And, I can hear the anxiety within her voice. Fear which causes her to tremble within my galabiyah as it caresses the smooth of her taut skin— the same skin that you possess." He ran a hand along the firmness of Fahimah's thigh sending her head spinning in a tumult of memories.

'Rasool...you *must tell me of my past!*' Fahimah implored locking eyes with the immovable commander. He ran his thick finger upon the grain of his desk as she leaned across it, out of breath and out of patience, while persistently requesting information that had been locked away by him alone. Information that held his position secure, safeguarded against those who could possibly dispute his unwarranted allegiance to the Princess Adiva and have him dismissed or possibly even executed. Uthman would be the first to lay claim to that right, with the reasonable intent of remaining alive after his attack on the now present amir—Amir Rasheed.

'I told you, *Fahimah*...' her name was acid upon his lips, '...what the Amiri Adiva did was unforgivable in the Egyptian world—the whole middle east, as far as that is concerned. And, I would be putting myself at risk by letting you even glance the names of those involved. So, leave me, girl. Just the sight of you draws heat upon my blood.' He waved her away, returning to the stretch of documents spread before him.

'No—*Rasool!*' She slammed a small palm upon his papers, her eyes suddenly burning with tempered wrath. 'If you do not show me the information I request of you, I shall bring the amir...and not the *dead one* either—either of *them*. I shall bring Rasheed. And you know, as well as I, that he will tear your entire quarters apart in search of what I ask.

Now, I ask you again, Commander...where is that information?'

He eyed her with contempt, knowing that what she spoke was true— Rasheed would go to any lengths to assist this meddlesome, western filth in retrieving the documentation she so determinedly requested; and now that both senior amirs were dead, the young prince was in command.

He unlocked the bottom drawer of his desk. Sliding out a narrow wooden slat, which concealed a hidden compartment, he removed the undisclosed documents—documents which held the names of those who were higher-ups in the Egyptian world and the American government, guilty of the purchase and sale of American children. The children, who were brought to the country in secret, were privately disbanded to gradually infiltrate the Egyptian government and eventually the entire Middle Eastern continent. Being placed in powerful homes with powerful positions, they would hopefully, one day, control the Arab world. The process was a dreadfully slow one, which the United States government had foolishly devised out of desperation to retain control of the massive amount of oil drawn from the continent and also to sieze the continent's many weapons of mass destruction.

Both the Amir Nuri and his father, Onslow, had despised the western nations, as their hatred grew with each passing day. Becoming deeply involved in armament agreements with neighboring Arab nations, who were devising a plan to destroy the western world, they had been organizing a massive attack.

Princess Adiva, abhorring her husband and the Amir Onslow, had contacted her brother, Fineas, and, despite his disapproval, had requested the names of his contacts. While she planned to purchase Fahimah for *her* son, Rasheed, who would, one day, rise to power and befriend the western world.

Regretfully, Fineas had stood before her and handed her a folded white slip as his eyes searched hers for an answer. 'Adiva—you are my sister and I do care for you so. What you are about to do will place you in grave danger—you *and* Rasheed. Please reconsider.'

'No, Fineas. I must do this, for I am trapped within this land with no escape and the Lord Nuri would hunt me as a dog if I were to try and ever flee. Also, his lust for the American soil's blood has become stronger and he will stop at nothing to see it annihilated. I must try.'

Rasool angrily tossed the stack of papers at Fahimah, while she hastily grabbed for the fluttering documents as they cascaded about the floor. Shoving his chair back, he rose from his desk, grabbed his artillery belt, cinched it and strode to the door of his chambers.

'I will give you till the next bell tolls.' He reached for the door handle, his gaze locking with hers. 'But remember this—*you are not exempt* from this quandary and shall suffer the same punishment as I for your involvement if anyone were to discover the truth. Now, I must leave this place; for the sight of you makes me sick.' He stepped outside his chamber doors and Fahimah could hear the jiggling of a key within the latch; he had locked her in.

She dove into the pieces of parchment with a maddened fervor—her eyes scanning one document after another while the Arabic writing bore into her mind and burned along her fingertips. Names unknown to her buzzed by, places she'd never even heard of before: Torrance, Woodsburgh, Key West—all locations in the western world. Her brow creased as she searched diligently, digging deeper within the jumbled words that careened before her mind—many incoherent to her.

She fidgeted with a heavy braid, recalling the biting words the Amir Nuri had spewed. 'See the whore your mother has purchased for you'—the words bit into her mind and tore at her heart.

Edging the documents with a finger, she shifted to lie upon her stomach, then dug in again as the moments were quickly running away. Line after line she read, accounts of children who had been taken from their parents and those who had been involved in the scandal—names of high elective officials swam before her eyes, officials from both worlds. Running a slightly trembling finger along the list, she froze at the name Tarun—Adiva Tarun of the Tarun Regime, and their physician Raghib. Her name was there also—Fahimah.

An avalanche of feelings raced as a thoroughbred throughout her body and her heart jumped within her chest causing her to quaver and her focus to blur. Shaking her head as if to revive herself, she read on, trying to contain the tears that splashed at the back of her eyes. She bit her lip.

The account told of a young couple who, many years back, had visited the continent from the United States and had been unknowingly selected to partake in the scheme—that being Julianne and Joseph Havenstrit. Being informed of the beautiful beaches and lovely resorts of some of the Far Eastern countries, and wanting to explore the world of the Egyptian pyramids, the young couple had ventured to Asia on a long needed vacation.

Julianne, in her third trimester had insisted on taking the trip, despite the various warnings of traveling outside the country so late into her pregnancy. The documents noted that she had gone into early labor and as a result was rushed to the nearest hospital which was governed by the American Embassy. There she gave birth to, not just one child, but two. Two baby girls—identical twins. Spaces were available for names with one left blank and the other x'd and being scribbled in as 'Fahimah'.

Fahimah gasped as the breath rushed from her body, while she held to the oval braided rug beneath her. The room began to spin and she suddenly became ill.

Laying her head upon her folded arms she attempted to measure her breaths, but the feelings crashing upon her from the unspeakable information available at the tips of her fingers brought anguish to her very soul. She laid her face upon the floor and wept.

Hafiz tightened his grip, securing Fahimah to his shoulder, while her jerking and twitching had become an annoyance as she lowly moaned.

"Stop! Or you shall be tossed upon the gravelly floor. I have had enough of your jerking about."

"Then put me down," she breathed through paining lips.

"Ohhh, I shall put you down, but not upon your feet." He licked the sweat beads above his lip and ran the back of an arm across his damp forehead. "But, I believe I will have you bathed first; your scent is compared to that of camel dung. And, it will not be by me, but by your sister while I watch."

Cherinne had heard enough. "She's not my sister, *you idiot! I don't even know her!*"

"You are lying, American—how typical."

She quickened her step, while the intense fervor to scream at him eye to eye was over-whelming, then possibly bloody his lip with a small clenched fist.

"No! She is not my sister!"

A whisper slipped from the shadows before Cherinne as she could hear Fahimah's voice speaking lightly. "Yes—American…yes, I am."

Silence weighed upon the dank tunnel, with the scuffling of feet, being the only sound faintly echoing upon the walls; while Cherinne's mind shuffled through the pages of her life, in a mad panic, to piece a shred of evidence together that might lead to the truth of Fahimah's claim.

The passageway finally opened to the awaiting lake, while remnants of Cherinne's clothing lay strewn along the water's edge with items of Hafiz's left upon the rock where he had been discarding his garments.

Setting Fahimah upon a large boulder, he contemplated his best course of action—one that would be most satisfying. The princess's chin slumped to her chest and she sagged as a cloth doll ready to be lobbed to the fire's flame; Hafiz smiled.

Pausing within the shadows, Cherinne awaited his actions while a nervous sweat built upon her body.

His voice sounded as a chime within the quiet, echoing off the cavernous walls; its ring was taunting, screeching at her ears.

"American—why don't you come out here, where I can observe you? I imagine you look lovely within my cloth. And, please do not attempt to douse me with that lantern's oil which flickers within your shivering hand, for I shall have to kill your sister and we wouldn't want that—now would we."

Cherinne carefully stepped from within the shadows, determined to stand her ground and somehow free her and Fahimah. *Lashr!* She cursed at her uncontrollable trembling body and chattering teeth as she observed Hafiz busying himself with gathering his things.

He turned to meet her gaze and she colored under the stare. "Aahh, *you do look lovely* within my attire." He noticed her hair cinched back and the belting of her waist, "...*and* you have also adorned the ensemble with accessories. That is quite the charming endowment. I believe that after the Lord Seth has had his fill of you; I shall keep you for myself."

Returning his attention to Fahimah, he rapidly removed her bandages and discarded the bloody rags. The ankle was raw and the bone exposed; she winced at his touch.

"Come—we shall get you within the water," he stated, hoisting her upon his shoulder as she groaned. "American..." he called out, "...draw near and tend to your sister. We shall get her cleansed and then I shall repair this ankle." He added, "...but not before I have had my way with you both."

Regretfully, Cherinne progressed forward while despising every hair upon Hafiz's head, unsure as to what course to take while Fahimah was in such a weakened state.

Surprisingly, Fahimah spoke; her tone was soft, yet set. "Please, Sister—I would like for you to come and bathe me."

Hafiz stumbled upon the words which the injured princess had spoken while his loins were building to a frenzied heat. Quickening his steps toward the lake, he licked his lips.

CHAPTER 26

Doctor Raghib threw back the flap to Rasheed's tent, darting a threatening glare about at anyone who might be watching as he exited. Deverall and Laddor hurriedly spun on their heels and listened with half an ear as they feigned involvement with their tent and gear while Lateef strode to meet the physician.

"Doctor Raghib," the commander placed his hands on his hips, the feel of his hilt beneath his palm delivering strength to approach the hardhearted, partially maniacal physician. It was not so much that he feared the man; he just, one day, may be in need of his services. He repressed the quavering within his voice. "What is the condition of the amir...and, also, the boy?"

Raghib eyed Lateef with a smoldering stare. "He and the boy are stable, though they are severely dehydrated and the prince's sniveling for the princess has been persistent."

"So, how long before we are able to travel?" The sun had begun to disappear in a pinkish-red hue beyond the vast sky, while they had lost a day of journeying.

Raghib tossed a towel, on which he had been wiping his hands, at the commander. "Morning," he replied coolly. "Now—I shall retire." His gaze snaked along the horizon as if he was somewhere in the distance. "Do not disturb me till then. Oh—and have someone bring me some food."

All eyes observed the physician, and they collectively released a sigh, as he made his way back to his tent and disappeared inside.

"Man—that guy sure does give me the creeps." Deverall wiped a stream of sweat from the length of his face. Poor Saheeb—I imagine he's regrettin' the day they hired that bastard on."

"Yeap, he sure is up on himself," Laddor noted. "His head's so high in the clouds; I imagine they have to use a scaffold to wipe his ass." Laddor laughed and Deverall slapped him good-naturedly on the back.

"Hey, that's a good one!" Deverall chuckled; enjoying a few moments of easiness while the tension truly had been taking its toll.

Laddor suddenly ceased his jesting, embarrassed and ashamed he had even laughed. Dropping his head, he glanced at his hands as if they contained a magical cure for any ailment, while he thought of Cherinne and what may be possibly happening to her—if she was still alive.

"Hey…" Deverall laid a weathered hand upon the young man's shoulder; sympathy flickered across his eyes, "…it's okay to laugh. You're tryin' your best and that's what counts at this point. And I'm sure sweetheart knows that. Now, c'mon—let's go see how Nefertiti's doin'."

Darkness had descended in a heavy cloud upon the camp while most had retired for the evening. Rasheed suddenly charged into Laddor and Deverall's tent, panting and dressed down to khakis; his shadow was large against the canvas wall reflecting from the low oil lantern's light. "Mr. Zeandre…"

Laddor lay with his backside to the prince. Unable to sleep, he continued to remain quiet and unresponsive, just waiting for two of Rasheed's sentries to wrestle him from the comforts of his sleeping bag and thrash him senseless.

"I have been informed that you saved my Nefertiti. Is this a fabrication or is it truth?"

Laddor watched the distorted image upon the wall, as the dancing shadow ran a phantom hand nervously through its hair. "Yes—it's true."

"Well, if it is so, then I owe you a debt of gratitude and I shall relinquish the sentence I have placed upon you," Rasheed announced; then he hastily spun about ready to depart. "Again—I thank you."

"Rasheed…" Laddor spoke to the lulling silhouette, "…do you think we'll find 'em?"

The black inky shadow remained quiet for a brief moment while mulling over the predicament. Then, Laddor watched as the dark form's orifice moved upon the canvas wall. "I believe we will find them, with the aide of the earbob and the information that you possess. And, as you have witnessed, my Fahimah is a fighter. She will not allow herself to be put down easily."

Rasheed then stepped outside the tent into the oppressing darkness, watching the lanterns flicker to low as the men settled into the night. He whispered beneath his breath, "I hope."

"She'll drown if you don't release her binds!" Cherinne rushed after Hafiz as he carted Fahimah toward the lake. "*Remove her ropes!*"

"I believe you take me for a fool, American. Now go! Tend to your sister!" With a labored groan he tossed Fahimah, with hands and feet bound, into the center of the lake. Cherinne's heart leaped within her throat and she found herself frozen in time as Fahimah splashed broadside into the water sending a wave rippling across the surface. Her eyes flashed in multi-colored terror while she thrashed about then quickly sank beneath the surface.

The baby! Ripped through Cherinne's mind and the words were caught on her restraining lips.

Hafiz's gaze narrowed along with the grin spreading his cheeks as he keenly observed Cherinne's reaction—a reaction of alarmed horror which sent his heart and mind racing in a maddened frenzy to meet with that of his aroused loins.

"What are you waiting for?" his tone was silty and his stare unnerving, while he settled himself upon a nearby boulder, placing his elbows on his knees and his chin in his cupped hands. "Bathe her."

"*You bastard!*" Cherinne raced toward the water; and drawing a deep breath, dove in. The cool of the water slapped her into warranted action while she was reminded of school and swimming for the aquatic team. It seemed a million years past, and everything up until the day she received the bracelet, unimportant and trivial.

Opening her eyes to the crystalline water, she searched frantically for Fahimah, and discovered her rapidly sinking toward the darkened bottom, while struggling to break free of her binds. Cherinne forced herself through the dimming waters, the many flickering lantern lights from above just a faint hue of white upon the surface of the shadowy lagoon as she descended nearer to the floor. Slipping an arm within Fahimah's, she hurriedly rushed her toward the surface—the urgency to get her air, harrowing.

They broke through the water's face, both gulping for a much needed breath. Wading nearer to the shallower faction of the lake, they sat waist high along the rocky bottom while attempting to gauge the rising and falling of their heaving bodies.

"*Aahhh!*" A twinkle beset Hafiz's eyes as he regarded them from just steps away. "The sight of you both dripping and wet is intoxicating, as your long damp hair clings to your features and your lovely frames, while the cloth is tight to your wet skin. I am invigorated and most tempted to join you; but, first, you must bathe."

A viperous glare blazed from Cherinne's eyes and she shook with rage. Anger flushed her face to crimson, as she struggled to remain seated and not race upon this sadistically lecherous clod who was being pleasured at her and Fahimah's expense.

"No!" Cherinne yelled through grinding teeth. "Her ankle is bleeding and she is pre…"

Fahimah suddenly shoved her with a shoulder and exhaled, "no."

Cherinne glanced at her, while her eyes portrayed worry, fearing she had said too much.

"She is what?" Hafiz leaned toward them, his brows rutting in curiosity.

"Uhh…she is pretty bad off…maybe going into shock," Cherinne staggered upon the words, attempting to rectify the blunder. "*Leave her alone!*"

"No, American…" Fahimah whispered from behind strands of hair while her head rested against her chest, "…it is okay; take me into the water. It will revive me and cleanse my dirt-ridden pores." Her kaleidoscopic eyes imprisoned Cherinne within their sporadic display of color. "Please."

"Okay," Cherinne replied hesitantly. "If that is what you want."

Fahimah's tone was set, "yes, that is what I want."

Throwing a spiteful glare at Hafiz, Cherinne gently pulled Fahimah within the water, only to where she was able to touch; while the buoyancy of the princess's petite body made it easy to maneuver her. Blood streamed along the surface turning the water's cerulean blue to a deep sanguine as her bloodied ankle trailed along behind her.

"Are you okay?"

Fahimah nodded her head, yes, while never taking her eyes from her sister. Feeling the coolness of the water seeping within her skin she laid back and tried to relax, to concentrate on the sensation of being clean after days of dirt and filth. Briefly, she closed her eyes and listened to the sound of her own measured breaths, as her ears had become closed and she was consumed within its hollow vibration. A splash beside her drew her attention. Turning her head, she could see a small goatskin satchel surrounded by a burst of ripples, quickly sinking beneath the surface.

Cherinne hastily grabbed it, already knowing of its contents.

"Please wash my hair," Fahimah whispered, cracking a thin lined smile. "I hate when my hair is dirty."

Cherinne replied with a weary grin, her tone was soft. "Yeah; I think I'll wash mine too. Removing a bar of lye from within the pouch, she drew soapy bubbles within her hands and ran them through Fahimah's grainy hair. Then Cherinne proceeded to suds her own, while the feel of clean hair would be refreshing.

"Enough with the hair!" the Egyptian declared, while he had risen to his feet to watch as his palms sweated and the rousing tension absorbed the whole of his body. "Remove her garments! I want to see her flesh!" His mismatched eyes bled with desire; and his frenzy for visual gratification mounted with each passing moment. Hatred sparked the gap between him and Cherinne.

"It is okay…" Fahimah whispered, "…just slide my garment within my hands so he does not tear it from my body—I will want it back afterward."

Cherinne nodded distantly, continuing to focus on the princess's emblazoned eyes as she carefully slipped the tunic from Fahimah's bare shoulders and beneath the water. With a quavering hand, Cherinne then slowly rubbed the soap along the princess's silky taut torso and abdomen, realizing she was cleansing the sanctuary for a child—a child that may never have the chance to be born. A sudden dam of tears broke behind her lids and she blinked in astonishment at their fury.

"Do not cry," Fahimah's voice was tender. "I shall get us free of this…just be patient."

Cherinne continued to bathe the princess—closing her eyes as she neared parts, she herself hated to even think about, let alone bathe—knowing that the nursing field would never have been her preferred field of expertise.

Fahimah began to work diligently with the ample space she now had to accomplish her premeditated task. Holding the tunic tightly within her hands, she slipped her fingers within the hidden fold of the garment's cloth and removed the small water-logged piece of yarn. Careful not to drop it, she rubbed it heatedly between her forefinger and thumb causing the fiber to quickly come alive. Fahimah instantly spouted, "*Dive!*"

"*What?*" Cherinne's face wrinkled in uncertainty.

"*RABBA!*" Fahimah commanded. The echo bounced sharply off the cavernous walls, and Cherinne suddenly understanding, disappeared beneath the water.

Hafiz's sadistic revelry was broken as he had been totally enthralled at the sight of the two twin females submerged within the water touching one another's wet skin. While his appetite had increased to its fullest potential and he had been ready to unleash his blistering ferocity.

At the shout, he angrily raced to the edge of the lake. "What is the American doing?"

"Just watch—*you vermin!*" Fahimah sneered as fire brimmed within her flashing eyes and a vicious grin crossed her lips. Rapidly, the yarn snaked its way around her arching body while producing a vortex of blustery howling wind; and moaning, she disappeared within her cocoon.

Hafiz was transfixed at the sight, while it was just as exhilarating as the bathing pageantry he had just beheld. He licked his lips lavishly and stepped within the water's edge, watching with heated intensity the astounding spectacle unfolding before his hungry eyes.

Suddenly, a look of shocked disbelief shaded his face, as his legs became weak and his chest pained beyond compare to that of any bulleted injury. He slumped to his knees, unaware he had been blasted with hundreds of needles.

Four days of arduous riding brought the amir and his men to a halt as they looked upon Deverall's slightly deflating stomach to see they had reached the end of the map, which disappeared within his shorts in a patch of scraggly hair.

"We have come to the end of the map," Rasheed announced after observing its contents and remounting Nefertiti. He left Deverall to smooth his shirt, situate his straw hat and settle into a dark pair of sunglasses. "Commander, Lateef—please have Mr. Zeandre approach the front. We will be in need of his services."

"*Whoa Horse!*" While his riding skills were none of bragging, Laddor wrestled with the reigns of his sorrel mare, who had belonged to the deceased Sergeant.

Rasheed chuckled mildly behind a hand while feigning a cough, then clicked Nefertiti to slow and quiet Laddor's mount. Leaning, he grasped the mare's halter and stroked the full of her firm neck. "*Ssshhh, sakit,*" he soothed the sorrel in his native language while running a gentle hand along her blaze.

"Her name is *Nakia*, which means *purest girl.*" Rasheed spoke without shifting his gaze from the mare's large almond eyes. "She is a fine mare, bred from the purest of stock. I'm sure the Sergeant would appreciate your care of her, as she was very special to him."

While trying to compose himself Laddor nodded, as his relationship with the prince, fortunately, had grown to civil.

Rasheed continued. "She is missing her master and will attempt to adopt you as such; but, you also have to remember that she is *female* and needs to be treated with a gentle hand—though, sometimes the species may be temperamental."

He inspected her twitching ears and scratched gently behind them. "Somewhat like my Fahimah, who restrains the internal beast, yet occasionally allows it to unleash." Turning from his thoughts, he addressed Laddor who watched as if entranced.

"Mr. Zeandre, the evening sky is upon us; and we shall travel in the direction of the Acryptic Star—the brightest star which burns beneath the desert sky. Due to its intense luminosity, you can observe it throughout the entire continent's life cycle. But we shall need to consider the directions from that point." His gaze locked with Laddor's. "Can we depend on you for this?"

Laddor briefly studied the amir's face, "Yes. Yes, you can…since you've asked."

"Good, then let us proceed. The men are in much need of food and rest; it has been a long tedious journey."

Deverall lay quietly, exhausted after days and nights of treacherous heat while Laddor sat upon his quilted bag and held his silver ocarina within his hands. He turned it methodically between his fingers while the yearning to hear the notes of its melodious tune was something afar from his aching heart.

Placing the instrument within its cradling of red velvet, he opened and closed the lid slowly. He thought of the times he had attempted a tune for Cherinne, while she sat and listened intently, with a broad smile added to her exquisite features.

"Mr. Zeandre? May I enter?" Rasheed stood just outside the tent in the now present dark, patiently awaiting a reply.

"Sure, Rasheed—the door's open," Laddor's response was one of weariness, while Cherinne's absence was becoming a heartfelt weight.

Rasheed entered in his usual attire of just trousers—an overly-handsome individual, even to the male eye. Laddor figured the prince as somewhat of a Romeo, getting more action than deemed necessary for one man. Nah, you could never get too much action, he concluded; he shoved the thought from his mind.

Rasheed, quickly running his eyes around the small confines of the tent, noticed the small wooden box setting upon the American's lap. "What have you there?" he inquired. "Maybe a keepsake?" Kneeling, he examined the box closer and Laddor opened it to reveal its contents.

"Yes. It was a gift from my mother." He rubbed a meditative finger along the polished silver, skimming over the small holes which produced its sound; while a slight tinge of sadness prodded at his heart each time he gazed upon it.

"Ahh, so it is a *shabbabi*. May I?"

Laddor placed the flute in Rasheed's outstretched palm and the prince pressed the small instrument to his lips. And, seating himself crossed-legged opposite Laddor, he felt for the notes and commenced to play.

A sweet melody rose from within the canvas walls as Rasheed's dark eyes sparked to life. Then he closed them as the gentle music wafted into the oppressing darkness and disappeared into the night—like a small trickle of hope reaching for an answering star.

Laddor also closed his lids and listened closely, attempting to remember the notes, so he might one day be able to play them for Cherinne—the tune being quite lovely.

Rasheed brought the melody to a close and handed the instrument back. "Thank you—your shabbabi plays nicely."

Laddor nodded in agreement and placed it back into its velvety encasing. "What do you call that tune, Rasheed?"

"It is a melody for the weary traveler; it does not possess a name."

Their gaze locked and Laddor wondered whether or not Rasheed was going to ask about the map.

The prince then grinned warily and directly stated, "You know why I am here. It is imperative that I receive that information you possess. Can we discuss it civilly?"

"Of course, Rasheed—as long as there's no more beatings, where I'm the object of aggression," Laddor replied, recalling from days past, the twisted battered face staring back at him from the ocarina's metal. "You and your men seem to have it in for me; and all I wanna' do is find Cherinne and get her home. And, knowing her, she'll never agree to staying here with you. She has a life from all this and plans…*and*, I wanna' marry her someday.

So, I'll give you the information; but you have to swear to me that things will change—that I won't receive anymore black and blue eyes from you *or* your men. And that Cherinne will be able to leave and go home where she belongs." Laddor's mind was set to only reveal the information upon shook agreement. He put his hand out to the prince.

Rasheed's dark brows creased as he eyed Laddor and briefly pondered his reply. "Well…" Rasheed finally conferred, "I will agree to one condition: You must show me respect—as an amir *or* even as a friend; then, I shall call off my men. *And*, concerning Miss Havenstrit—she is capable of selecting for herself. So, *she* will decide."

The prince's open palm shot confidently into Laddor's; the terms not quite what Laddor had in mind, but near enough. He firmly grasped the prince's outstretched hand. "Done."

.

CHAPTER 27

Cherinne's heart pounded along with her feet, which ran along the gravelly floor of the tunnel. Sweat, building upon her face and neck, streamed between her breasts and onto her stomach; she swiped a damp arm across her beaded forehead and shifted Hafiz's pack which banged against her back.

The ever increasing tunnel's passages seemed to go on forever; however, Cherinne pressed onward. Fahimah was cupped within the crook of her arm, moaning with each pounding step. The bleeding of her ankle had finally slowed and as Cherinne had wrapped it, she questioned the princess as to whether-or-not Hafiz was dead. Fahimah just snorted and answered, "probably—unless Seth finds him and decides to look kindly upon his rotting corpse and revive him."

"*Revive him?*"

"Yes," Fahimah had answered, "The Lord Seth *is a god.*"

Suddenly, Cherinne froze in her tracks, as if she had been cemented in glue. She quickly glimpsed upward, listening to the faint sound which was sifting through the rocky terrain above.

"What is it?" Fahimah, panting, leaned against the dank weathered stone while she loosened the crossbow from her shoulder.

Cherinne searched the dimly lit structure above her. "*Sshh.*" Her eyes diligently explored every crack and crevice of the cavernous passage. "I can hear it," she muttered still observing through the dark high ceiling above. "I can hear Laddor's flute!"

"What?" Fahimah retorted in uncertainty, her face wrinkled in disbelief. "I thought your hearing was limited within the earth?"

"It was; it is! I mean *it was* when we were deeper in the tunnels. We must be close to the surface!" Her face beamed in a show of absolute delight and her mind raced with excitement. "I can hear the ocarina!" Carelessly, Cherinne lunged forward in a fervent embrace and grasped Fahimah within her arms. "Laddor is here!"

"American—you are crushing me." Fahimah breathed through a stiffened jaw. Grabbing Cherinne's shoulders she pushed her away. "I do not want you touching me."

Cherinne tilted her head in confusion as the joy sagged from her features like a deflating balloon.

"What's up with you, Fahimah? You keep claiming that we're sisters; but, yet, you act as if I'm a leper. I just don't get you." She shifted the pack which was supplied with a few rations: lye soap, dried jerky, rope, and Hafiz's canteen, which they had collected while he lay panting covered in a painful layer of needles. Then, they fled.

Anger cursed between Cherinne's shoulders and she roughly grabbed Fahimah's arm to pull the princess along. Silence weighed as a black cloud around them, the tension thick enough to choke the heated breaths from their tired lungs. Cherinne continued to listen for the flute; and, no longer hearing the melodic sound, she briefly thought she may have imagined it. Sadness, along with the weight of the pack and Fahimah suddenly became a torturous burden.

Coming to a fork in the tunnel and confusion adding to her frustration, Cherinne abruptly spun to face Fahimah. Their eyes locked in a disputed embitterment and breaking the deafening silence, Cherinne, with set determination, demanded, "I wanna' know, besides the fact that we are mirror images; I wanna' know how *you know* we are sisters. And, I'm not helping you along *anymore, Fahimah,* until you tell me."

Fahimah's eyes began to flash with color and the corners of her mouth twitched as she attempted to subdue the violent irrepressible memories blazing through her mind. Emotion raced throughout her veins in heated droplets of blood and she tore her arm free of Cherinne's.

"Why should I tell you? You do not know of the pain and anguish I have suffered. *I am your sister!* I knew it the moment I saw you. And, Rasool has documents that confirm this!" Tears suddenly burst to her flashing eyes and she shook at their rage. "*My mother is your mother, Julianne Havenstrit!* And, my father is Joseph Havenstrit!" Her eyes rimmed red while her face was twisted in a tumult of blistering pain. She angrily shoved Cherinne away. "I was taken from them—*purchased* by Princess Adiva—and they never came looking for me! *NEVER!! I was their daughter too!* And, *you...*" She pointed a shaking finger at Cherinne, "*...you* were the one they held, the *one* they loved and protected! While I was treated as an object, secretly taken from one place to another beaten and tortured, raped by armies of filthy men! *I hate you!*" The words spewed as venom from her quivering lips, "And, now you will take the amir and any shred of good I have had in this miserable life!" She slumped to the tunnel's floor, tears streaming her paling cheeks as she suddenly began to retch.

Shocked at Fahimah's outburst and unable to absorb the diminutive amount of information she had just received, Cherinne reached a quavering hand toward the princess. A flood of sentiment tore at the very depths of her soul at the realization that Fahimah was definitely her blood and sibling. Feelings of loss, compared to that of someone's passing, cut as a double-edged razor at her heart—a life with her twin sister gone as a puff of air in the wind—never to be returned or treasured. Puddle-sized tears rushed from her burning eyes onto a hand which endeavored to maintain the dripping liquid, but, lost mercilessly, while an apology could never buffer the tormented female from the damage that had already been inflicted.

Cherinne's legs buckled from weariness and she was unable to stay to her feet. Images of Fahimah as a small child splashed before her as drops of rain and the sound of her crying voice, searching out for someone, struck her like a fisted blow. She fell to her knees, attempting to draw air; while her head spun in a vortex of time trying to remember something—anything—that would have told her of Fahimah's existence. And, while she was enveloped within a paining reflection and her sobbing was that of her sister's, Cherinne was too late to hear the swinging swaheel's blade as it swiftly careened through the air, just missing her, as she had plummeted to the tunnel's floor.

Deverall had been listening to the conversation which had transpired between Laddor and the amir. Slipping his dark sunglasses to his sparse hair line, which he wore to block the lantern's light, he remarked on his friend's over-achievement at making peace, possibly even going as far to making a friend.

"Hey, Red—I thought you handled that fairly well; I'm impressed. Now—the real question I have is: Do you remember the directions? You're the only one who knows 'em, except for, of course Reynolds, who's a million miles away; and for some reason," he scowled, "I can't see Reynolds gettin' 'em the way you explained. Now—why don't you explain it again? A good laugh surely would help with gettin' some well needed rest." He lowered his shades, crossed his arms over his slowly diminishing belly and shifted to get comfortable. "Please afford me this tale."

Laddor settled back and began the tale that the butler had growled into his ear.

After Reynolds had retrieved the earring, he had stood within the estate's large kitchen, wondering as to what he should do. Turning the earring between well-aged fingers, he glanced at the slowly ticking clock, realizing that the only individuals awake at that hour were derelicts and mobsters. He reached for the local directory, knowing he had to find someone to don the earring.

"*Those two idiots!*" he grumbled. "They were supposed to watch out for the Missus." He glanced at several pages in the phone book with no success; thinking that possibly he could bribe some female from a local tavern or all-night convenience store to just sport the earring for a brief moment while a map, the two idiots had referred to, appeared upon her body.

"Oh, good Heavens! They'll have me locked up for even suggesting to some roly-poly, little half-witted girl that she remove her attire to show me a map! They'll think I'm insane!"

He thrummed his fingers along the marble-veined blue-gray counter and finally turned to the 'M's' for massage parlors. Forming the crucifix upon his chest, he selected the number for *"Big Boy Massages"—Open 24 Hours, Seven days a week.*

'Father, please forgive me; fore I have sinned…' breathed through his mouth and flaring nostrils.

He dialed the number. 'Big Boy Massages' the sultry voice spoke through the line, the female's tone is smooth and saucy.

"Uh, hello, Madam…oh, I'm sorry, I…uh…didn't mean *Madam*," Reynolds choked upon the words and whispered to the empty kitchen, "I'm gonna' *kill* those two!"

"Uh, I'm in need of service." His voice cracked.

"Yes, Sir—what can we do for you?"

"Well, I…I…" the choking words let loose and spewed forth from him nearly in a shout, "*I need serviced at 2727 Highrock Drive!*"

"Its okay, Sir," she expressed from a sensual tone. "We are a very discreet company—you need not worry of any type of exposure. I will make arrangements to have Cookie come over; she is very professional."

Reynolds slammed the receiver to its cradle; he measured his breaths. "Someone's gonna' pay for this."

Time, seeming to freeze, drug throughout the empty estate, like a weighty cement block. Lights finally flickered and pulled into the circle. The vehicle's high beams blinded Reynolds, as he watched from behind a damask drape of the front sitting room.

"Turn off your lights, you twit! Someone might have seen you coming in the drive!"

A mild breeze wafted through the open window as a dark silhouetted figure slinked from inside the auto. Reynolds reached for his handkerchief, ran it along his sweated forehead and dabbed his flaming cheeks. His heart banged as an angry fist against the inner lining of his chest to the point it ached. "Good Heavens, I'm liable to have a heart attack!"

The chimes rang, startling the butler to smooth his jacket and compose himself. Failing miserably, he unlatched the heavy vestibule door and opened it; sweat poured from beneath his armpits and collar.

"Good evening, Sir," a young—possibly 23 year old—scantly attired female, exhaled through breasts the size of cantaloupes. They pushed through her silky camouflage button-blouse, which she had tucked into a simple short black-velvet skirt. Refusing to glance below the hemline, Reynolds was unable to notice the shoes—*if* she was wearing *any*. Her mid-length chestnut hair, pulled back in a single black tie, hung with loosened strands, framing her average features and *earrings*! In all his confusion, he had forgotten to request a girl that wore earrings. *Thank you for small favors*, he glanced toward Heaven.

The young female flashed him a card through long polished red nails. "Big Boy Massages sent me over; said you were in need of some service." Toting a large lengthy strapped bag, she gently pushed her way inside. "Are you the one who called?" She scanned the foyer attempting to see into the other room lit only by streams of moonlight seeping through the crooked drape. "Sure is dark in here." The white's of her eyes grew as she inched toward the sitting room.

Reynolds rushed to secure the drape as his stomach turned and his skin grew ashen.

"Can you please turn on a light, so I can see—or are you just one of those who like it completely dark? It's a little more difficult for me to work if it's completely dark. So it'll cost ya' a little more, bein' my eyesight's at risk and all; but, seein', by the size of this place, *you can* afford it." She sat her bag down. "Can you be a doll and get my table from the car? We can set up in here if you like or somewhere else; it all depends on how far you want to carry it." She placed herself upon the sofa and ran a petite hand along the brocaded fabric—every finger except one containing a cheap, imitation stone or metal.

"Uh," Reynolds stumbled to a brass reading lamp and switched it on. "Uh…Miss…"

"Cookie. My name's Cookie; but, if you wanna' call me somethin' else that's fine too. It'll just cost ya' another twenty bucks." She smiled through large crooked teeth behind bright pink lipstick and gloss.

"Uh…I…" he wrung his hands nervously, for the first time in his life desiring a cigarette, while his head felt quite puffy.

Her gaze narrowed and her hazel eyes flashed in sudden acknowledgement. "*Ohhh*, so you want *something else*. I thought so. You seemed a little nervous 'bout just gettin' a massage. Well, that's fine; it'll just cost extra and I require a hundred dollar deposit up front."

She stood to her feet. "So, that's why you kept it so dark in here. Well, the couch is nice and all, but wouldn't you prefer one of the big bedrooms upstairs?"

Reynolds head spun and he clutched at his thumping heart, the words caught in his throat while he desperately needed a drink of something—possibly scotch.

Cookie, getting impatient, began to unbutton her blouse.

Reynolds grabbed the lamp to steady himself; while the walls of the room seemed to be collapsing around him. "Heavenly Father…"

"Gee, you're uptight." Her dark silhouette meandered toward the shaken butler as her silky top slipped to the floor. "Do you mind if I call you 'Daddy'?"

"*Good Heavens!*" Reynolds ran a shaking hand through his damp hair and his arthritic knees grew weak—an image of Cherinne entered his mind.

"*Put your clothes back on!*" He blurted, rushing to retrieve her garment and shoving it into her hands. His parental instinct kicked in. "Young Lady you should be ashamed of yourself! I am old enough to be your grandfather!"

The whites of her eyes gleamed within the lamp's low light and he wasn't sure whether she would cry or fly into a temper tantrum. She stood with her hands on her hips, the top dangling loosely within an arm while indignation crept color into her already rosy cheeks.

"Then *what do you want? Kinky* will cost you double and the deposit is *five hundred dollars!*"

Reynolds knew he had to get this situation under control before she ran from the house crying hysterically or mad, without him having even seen the map. He took a well-needed breath.

"Look—first off, I do not want anything that has to do with you removing your garments for *my pleasure*. Secondly…" he pulled the earring from his slacks pocket, "…all I want is for you to put this on." He held the pearl earbob before her. "That's it—nothing else."

"Yeap, that was how it happened," Laddor chuckled along with Deverall. "I can just imagine the look on Reynolds face when she removed her top!" They both burst into a gutted roar, tears streaming from their laughing eyes.

"Yeah, and don't *you* have to cough up the five hundred bucks it cost for something…*kinky?*" Deverall rolled to his side, holding his stomach to keep from busting a gut.

Laddor growled, "Don't remind me."

Glancing at his extremely optimistic friend whose encouragement had made things somewhat bearable and had kept his morale from taking a complete downhill charge, Laddor laughed until his belly hurt.

The steady ticking of the large grandfather clock was a therapeutic remedy for Reynolds as he laid the phone receiver upon its cradle. While his experience with the *free-spirited* maiden had been quite exhausting, his dealing with the two idiots, thousands of miles away, had become even more of a burden. And, with dawn quickly approaching and anxiety at the Miss's circumstances streaking through his aged veins like scalding milk, attempting to sleep, was a waste of time.

Figuring he would search the internet for any information pertaining to this so-called prince—Rasheed Daivyan Khalil Tarun—Reynolds made his way into the estate office. He would also aim to contact someone at the United States Embassy who would be able to assist him in bringing Cherinne home—if she were still alive. The mere thought ran cold along his matured skin.

"For your benefit, Mr Zeandre, she had best not have had a single hair touched upon her blonde head," he grumbled beneath his breath to the laptop. Looking upon its materializing screen, a picture of Cherinne and the bubble-headed idiot appeared before his eyes. "*Blasted red haired buffoon.*"

"Let's see—I'll try *Egypt* first." He quickly typed in the country's name and scanned through the various scads of information. He paused in mild confusion as the estate chimes suddenly echoed throughout the hallway and slipped beneath the closed door. "Who is God's creation could that be?" Checking the time on the screen, he grumbled, "It's nearly five a.m." Grabbing the rifle that sat idly by, ready and loaded, he headed toward the front vestibule, hesitated briefly and glanced out the closed drapes.

"What in God's name does *she* want?" His forehead wrinkled, along with his peppered brows, as he noticed the young female—*Cookie*—fidgeting about out front. "Good Heavens I've already payed her! She can't be back for more!"

Propping the rifle alongside the doorframe and switching on the light, he irritably swung the door open. *"Young Lady*—do you have any idea what time it is? You had best be..."

"IrtaH! Dil-waqt wiSil baTin!" One of the poolmen from earlier suddenly emerged. Barking orders into the butler's blank face, he shoved the screaming young female into Reynolds, sending him stumbling backward in an awkward stupor. As Reynolds shook his head, aspiring to collect his bearings and quickly assess the situation, a second shadow appeared in the doorway—the other Middle Eastern poolman. Reynolds rushed for his gun. The sound of thunder suddenly exploded within his skull as his surroundings immediately streaked white then black and excruciating pain blasted through the back of his head.

Goddess Nephthys lay idly upon the mountain top's peek, overlooking the formidable sands of Egypt. The seared terrain beneath her lengthy form shifted and stirred in a heated covetousness, grasping at the thatch of grainy everglade locks which plummeted and snaked along the kindred ground. Combing long putrid nails through the coarse strands, she yanked them irritably from the gluttonous earth. "Leave me," she hissed; her glowering eyes smoldered with annoyance—the pupils, large black spheres, filled the whole of their deep-set gloomy sockets.

A Scarab beetle hurriedly tunneled its way out from beneath her sludge-colored skirting in an attempt to evade the goddess's shifting stare. It, unfortunately, being much slower than that of her fleeting reflex, was seized beneath her thumb and the rocky surface. Squeezing it ever so steadily, with an aide of a finger, she took note to the impairing fracture of its hard protective shell as the massive pressure ruptured its coat of arms and its body easily burst within her thumb and forefinger.

Holding the green-brown cadaver before her, she inspected its trodden skeleton, as if considering it for the first time. A twisted, fanatical grin broadened her blood-red thin lips as she slowly parted the crimson bands and leisurely inserted her thumb while the beetle promptly disappeared.

Licking her forefinger, she examined the nearby terrain for another; while the LaHm, feeding off the tidbit of needed nourishment, awakened to their master's feeding. Rushing beneath her sweltering layers of skin, they raced in a crazed frenzy to be unleashed.

"Quiet, my festering serpents; your time shall come when you are able to aide in the retrieval of the bracelet and squelch the obnoxious taunting of the Lord Seth. His bombastic threats of ascension, to ruler of Egypt, shall perish along with him and his army of Jabali." Snorting, she rolled to her narrow stomach and searched the few dried and withering sparse patches of foliage for another bite.

"*Lord Seth*—my loathsome husband," she spoke to the foreboding night, the whispering of her voice swallowed by the churning aura. "I shall crush you as the Scarab. You have been the undivided root responsible for my disconcerting transformation to *this—this abomination*—some may refer to as a body." She pushed at the near gray-green sludge-colored skin upon her exposed forearm, "My *loving brother*," the testament was acidy upon her breath, "You shall pay."

An eerie stillness combed the warm terrain as Laddor knelt before the pink streams of sky appearing to be the approaching of morning light. Sifting the granules of antique-white sand between his fingers, he noticed that the heated grains had slight more warmth to them than the surrounding area. Pacing the perimeter of approximately one hundred square feet, he occasionally bent to retreat another handful then discarded it for a new. The same result: sand which was warmer—much warmer—than outside the boundary of which he had just traced.

Glancing toward the campsite and the horses which lingered idly by for their master's bidding, he surveyed the far-off vicinity, watching for the slightest indication of Rasheed's stirring. And, without the least hint of the amir's presence, he searched his pant's pocket feeling for the earring which he had confiscated from Deverall, while the exhausted pilot had been imitating that of a riled grisly. Grasping it tightly within his fingers, he removed it gingerly from its safekeeping.

Laddor held the trinket at arms length, against the vast, still dark, sky. Away from the first peaking beams of coming dawn and toward the Acryptic Star, the brightest star in the entire eastern world.

"*WORK!!*" he shouted. Uncertainty and urgency sounded in his commanding voice, while a shiver of anticipation raced from his fingers to his feet. "*Show me the way!*"

Rapidly awakening, the quiescent star caught the milky-white melding of colors within its grasp and the earbob suddenly exploded. Millions of blazing, miniscule stars burst in the sky before his eyes, as the luminary brilliance of the many lights, ruptured into a gigantic mushrooming cloud, which hovered in the nighttime sky. Then, the sparkling flecks appearing as snow, tumbled toward the ground.

Laddor stumbled backward as the blazing white light, which had burst before his eyes, seered into his pupils. "*Ugghhh!*" The warranted reaction brought forth a dreadful cry as he raked at his closed lids in harrowing agony. "*Sonofabitch!*" Dropping to his shaking knees, he panted in enunciated breaths as hot tears flared at the corners of each eye. "*Oh my God, I'm blind,*" he whispered desperately between winded draws of air. "All this—and now I can't see! I can't even see if there *is* a map, or an arrow, or something telling me where she is!"

"*CHERINNE!!!*" The grief-stricken wail echoed into his cupped hands and he covered his face in a rush of overwhelming frustration and pain. "*I can't see!* I can't see to find you!"

Slowing his rapidly racing heart to steady, Laddor stayed to his booted heels, wondering what fate would behold him now if he was to remain a captive to blindness.

"*Damn it!*" he slumped to the gritty surface and rolled to his back. "I'm no good to anyone like this," the words were spoken to the black which registered through his open lids. While the pain, surprisingly, began to slowly diminish behind the rush of white light still blazing within his head. "Rasheed *should* just kill me."

"If that is what you wish," the abrupt quip brought Laddor to sitting as Rasheed's voice, reverberating within the darkness of Laddor's throbbing head, brought him utter embarrassment.

"Mr. Zeandre—I see the entirety of your over-zealous intentions has gotten you—how shall I say—into deep camel droppings again. Eh?"

Laddor acknowledged Rasheed's presence and arrogant remark with a masturbatory gesture.

"Now, now; that's not very nice," the prince remarked. "You have caused quite a commotion with my horses," he stated while kneeling, "*and I see you were trying to command one of the jewel pieces without my knowledge.*" Rasheed viewed the area where the earbob had burst into fireworks of white light. "I see there is nothing that insinuates you even used the jewel; are you sure you administered it correctly?"

"I don't know," the retort was wearily snapped.

"Well—I see nothing; so, we will have to review your steps again, but first after I take a look at your eyes." Observing his pupils with fascination, Rasheed then pressed firmly against Laddor's tensed shoulder guiding him to the sandy ground. "Now, just lie back."

"Whaddaya doin'?" Laddor squawked, awkwardly pushing the prince away.

Avoiding suspended, flailing arms, Rasheed continued with more persistence. "You are facing the direction away from the light of the sun and I need you to lie in the direction that I may see."

Laddor reluctantly complied while Rasheed chuckled, "You did not think I had other intentions for you—*did you*? With all my lovely wives, I would never even consider such a thing." Thinking of Haneefah, the prince suddenly became silent, while he had lost more than a wife but, also, a cherished friend.

"Hey, Rasheed—I'm really sorry about the Princess Haneefah," Laddor spoke from behind a veil of darkened spots. He rubbed his eyes with the back of a closed fist. "She was very beautiful—I'm sorry."

Rasheed gazed toward the dimly lit horizon as the pinks and grays were mixing in a marvelous harmony of temperate color. His thoughts, miles away, were of the olive-skinned princess with her soft skin and kindly words.

"Yes, she was 'life' within her own right—a woman and friend beyond compare and I shall miss her each and every sunrise." The memory of Haneefah brought an awful ache upon his mourning heart; he forced himself from the recollection.

"Now—let's take a look at your eyes. I take it, they are still paining you?" Slowly running a suspended hand just above the reddened sockets, he watched the pupils which had shrunken to mere, tiny cobalt-blue vertical slits.

"This is very interesting," Rasheed's breath was warm upon Laddor's face. Laddor turned his head, uncomfortable at the situation. Rasheed continued, "I believe your pupils have become quite…how shall I say…*dragonesque.*"

The small slits stared into the coming of light and Laddor blinked as the pain was somewhat subsiding. *"What! What does that mean?"*

Rasheed rose to his feet. "It means that your pupils have taken on the shape of minuscule slits—like that of a fairytale dragon. I shall retrieve the doctor and have him take a look." He turned to leave.

Laddor speedily grabbed Rasheed's leg with a shaking hand. "No! Whatever you do, don't get the doctor!"

The prince tapped a pondering finger to his upper lip. "Ah, yes—I do believe I understand your hesitation. Doctor Raghib *is* highly qualified, but quite heartless; plus, with his dislike of you, he is liable to be a bit more insensitive—possibly even quite rough. I shall go and see about retrieving some salve—maybe that will help. Then, we will take a look at the area in which the earbob's starry remnants blanketed. There is no evidence that it even existed," he stated glancing again at the sea of undisturbed sand, "so we will investigate it when I return."

CHAPTER 28

The raging swaheel gouged at the tunnel's craggy walls, tearing at the rocky construction in a hazardous, downward swing. Nagid's monstrous form, filling the whole of the tunnel, moved awkwardly as Cherinne's scream was drowned out by the thunderous sound of crashing granite and sandstone which plummeted in uncontrollable heaps upon the ground.

"*Oh my god!*" The words spewed from her mouth as she scurried away from the massive weapon's blade and stumbled to avoid another harrowing blow which had blasted above her whirling head.

"*Fahimah, look out!*" The fiery swaheel blazed through the curtain of black, while pitching lanterns, were obliterated to fragments of glass and smoking oil. The taste of sulfur was strong and burning to the throat and Cherinne gagged for a fresh breath. Clumsily, she felt her way through the thick sooty air and along the dusky wall. Loosing her footing, she released a startled grunt, as she tumbled to her knees.

Tears dripped from her full eyes as she gazed back through the pluming dust and dark to stare, in disbelief, at the massive wall of granite now separating her from her sister.

"*Fahimah?*" the name lodged in Cherinne's chest as she rose to her trembling legs—legs which ached miserably to run from this place, this horrid place of death and destruction, evil and ill-will. Her fingers throbbed to claw at the obtrusive rubble blocking her from saving the only sibling she would ever know—a lost treasure just recently discovered, one that, no matter what, she would always cherish. And, though it was too late to mend the damage that had already been done, she had hoped to start the relation anew.

Wiping away the dirt-ridden tears that streamed her cheeks, she glanced at the wall of solid rock, vowing she would not allow death nor time, a giant or an evil god, to take her sister away. Cherinne turned on her heels and ran toward the surface in the direction in which she had heard Laddor's flute.

"Commander Lateef—have we determined yet what has caused the earth tremors which have occurred just beneath our encampment?" Rasheed questioned as the shifting sand had uprooted several tents and stirred the horses to a riled tizzy.

"No, Your Highness," the commander stated while bowing. "I have several men accompanied by Omar and Mahir investigating the area. And I hate to inform Your Grace; but, the satellite phone is not receiving reception at this location; for I had attempted to contact a local regent to see if there had been any underground testing in this area of weapons of any sort.

Also, I'm not sure how to put this," he scratched the hairs just beneath his amami, the cloth turban covering his head, "the young boy has stated that he had heard a female screaming beneath the sand. We were under the impression it was the American, Mr. Zeandre, he was hearing. For his appearance is somewhat feminine with the way he fashions his hair and all." He paused briefly, "Also, I was curious…has his eyesight returned?"

"Yes, it is returning slowly, but the pupils have remained odd in shape while gradually enlarging, and we have administered a salve to help with the pain and irritation.

Also, you made mention that the stable boy, Ib, had heard a female *screaming?*"

"Yes, Your Grace. It occurred during the same time as the American's accident and the tremors. Do you think they are associated, or one in the same?"

Rasheed considered this news carefully while his brow twisted in uncertainty and he tapped his finger above his lip, a habit he had acquired from his late grandfather Onslow. Attempting to keep his excitement at abeyance till they were sure it was one of the girls, he asked, "Where is the boy now?"

The commander pointed toward a dark patch lying horizontally in the sand, where Ib lay, with his tunic blending in with the surrounding terrain. While the color of his dark native skin and hair was a distinct contrast to the light-colored granules.

"He is over there, Your Highness, with his ear to the sand. He is listening for the female who he believes to be Princess Fahimah."

"Gather all the men, Commander, and have them continue to comb the area thoroughly; and tell the boy to continue to listen for any sound that he may consider to be the princess or Miss Havenstrit." Spinning in the opposite direction, Rasheed remarked over his shoulder, as his heart was quickening in his chest with the thought of Fahimah being near, "I need to speak with Mr. Zeandre and Mr. Deverall, then I will assign further orders." He then made his way toward the giant patch of ground, where Laddor sat beneath the blazing sun watching, through hazy eyes, the shifting of sand before him.

Deverall quietly stood behind his friend, listening to the heavy sighs that escaped Laddor's grievous body.

"Deverall—I know you're back there," Laddor's voice was melancholy. "I can see your lumpy shadow in the sand which, by the way, has deflated slightly. I suppose this trip was good for *something*."

"Aww, com'on Red—we've come *this far*," Deverall's tone made an attempt at encouragement. "How're your eyes doin'—any better?" He slipped back his dark shades. "Let's have a look-see."

Laddor hesitantly removed his sunglasses. The brightness of the blistering sun was nearly unbearable, as the intensity of its bright yellow rays burned into the abnormal, dark blue pupils, forcing them to decrease again in size.

"*Ugh!*" He barked, quickly replacing the black lenses over his red-rimmed sockets. "This isn't gonna' work! I can't even take my sunglasses off!"

Deverall stretched, and removing his hat, scratched his sweaty head. "Well, at least you can see now—*right?* That's a good sign, 'cause you'll hav'ta be able to see the huge smile that's gonna' be on sweetheart's face when she's grinnin' from ear to ear in appreciation that you've come to rescue her. She's sure gonna' be happy to see ya'."

"Yeah, or really pissed. Remember—I'm the one who got her into this mess and she's liable to never forgive me…"

"Mr. Zeandre…" Rasheed hastened toward the two, who, pausing in their conversation, noticed the grin of assurance spreading his face from ear to ear along with the rising excitement in his voice. "…I just received news that the young stable boy, Ib, has heard a female just below the surface of the sand and my hope is that it is one of the girls. He believes it to be Princess Fahimah."

From behind dark shades, the two American's, eyed the prince skeptically and Deverall's lips curved into an arch. "Uh…maybe I'm missin' somethin' here, Princey; but how would that boy be able to hear someone through tons of sand? He doesn't have one of them there jewels does he?"

Rasheed considered his previous encounter with the youngster in the stables and reviewed, in his racing mind, the few meager items the boy had possessed. Suddenly, his eyes flashed open in a staggering revelation. *"The book!"* He rapidly tapped his forefinger to his lip. "The book contains a jewel! I saw it pressed into the eye of Jasmine. I had seen it briefly, not thinking much of the colored stone; but, now that I think about it—it is a collection of the Semus Jewels!"

"Now, hold up, *Saheeb*…" Deverall placed a solid hand to the amir's shoulder. "How is it *you* know of Jasmine?"

The prince rolled his eyes toward Heaven. "Surely you jest; there are very few who are not familiar with the story of *Aladdin*."

"Welp, that's good enough for me," the pilot retorted.

Rasheed quickly knelt beside Laddor. "Mr. Zeandre—I really need to know what direction was contained in the other earbob." His eyes sought out, through the tinted glass, the unusual pupils which gazed outward in a fixed unnatural stare. *"What did it contain?"*

Laddor hesitated, still slightly wary of the agreement imparted between himself and the amir—his desire: to have his eyes healed and go the search alone.

Rasheed bowed. "I swear on my honor to keep my word, that I will not have you flogged, as soon as you convey this information to me—not only as an Egyptian, but also as a prince."

A heavy sigh from Laddor, conveying an exhausted 'okay', brought both Deverall and Rasheed in closer, with a giddy expression riddling each of their faces.

Laddor wearily reached into his pant's pocket and retrieved a small slip of notepaper.

Both male's mouths dropped as their look suddenly became one of shocked astonishment and Rasheed fumbled, "You had them the entire time in your trousers pocket? Then what was it that you swallowed?"

Loving the dumbfounded look upon the prince's face, and being as he had tricked the entire lot, Laddor produced a large, well-needed smile. "…It was Cherinne's bus ticket."

Sitting upon his enormous throne, Seth reveled in the churn of the spiraling vortex that surrounded his impish, vile being. His massive, smoking cloak, rode upon the blistering winds, encompassing the dark aura which smoldered about him like a water-doused fire. While his immortal being released a crimson-gold vapor, which wafted about the murky, dimly-lit cavern of his immense, underground domain. The long flaming-red locks of his head, blazing in a majestic glory of their own, screeched along the blistering current in a hastened madness, while attempting to rip from their master's skull. The full wild strands, screaming to be released, whipped about in an incensed frenetic mania.

Seth eyed the Jabali commander through a narrowed azure view; while his irritation mounted at the disruption of his self-satisfying ritual and the absence of the sacred bracelet, along with the female who possessed it.

"What is it?" he gnarled through the gusting gale, irate flames cursed from his blue-black gaze, while he spoke through the face of a cherub— a trait passed down through generations of his family—beauty given to his sisters Isis and Nephthys, and significantly to his older brother, Osiris, who he despised and hated.

His hatred and jealousy, obsessing him to the pinnacle of an impassioned frenzy, had driven him to destroy his brother, Osiris, by tricking and mutilating him. While his wife, Nephthys, had loved and adorned their sibling more so than her own husband, turning her back on Seth and preparing for a full-scale war. But, while she had been scheming to take revenge upon her brother and husband for Osiris's death, Seth had swindled her also, by calling to her from beneath the layers of earth, pretending to be Osiris raised from the dead. Rushing to her brother's side, Nephthys had become ensnared in a putrid squalor of living swill which engulfed her decomposing, altering carcass, transforming it into a mere casket of repugnant growth—the LaHm—abominable creatures which implanted themselves within her skin.

Seth confined her there, weeping for a thousand years—her pleas to be released falling upon deaf ears till finally, Isis, their sister, was able to locate Nephthys's utterly deformed body and free her from the horrors of the fetid, rotting pit.

"M'lord, the human intruders have arrived at the entrance to your kingdomship, My Grace," the Jabali commander, Gulzar, announced in a deep, throaty grunt, through flaring wrinkled nostrils. His beady eyes remained to the ground in a submissive reverence, as they hid behind large obtrusive tusks which curved in an upward half moon, supported by a great beastly head upon eight feet of solid body, comparable to that of a two-legged ass.

Slowly rising from his reigning seat, Seth advanced forward and appeared from inside the wind-driven vortex; while it, being controlled by an unnatural power within his mind, continued to rapidly gyrate behind him. A malicious leer encased his face as he stood with his hands clasped behind his back in observance of the two legged creature. Displeasure edged the tone in his voice as fury seethed like a festering boil, evolving rapidly within his sadistic thoughts.

"So—my blistering heat has not deterred them and my gigantic mountain of sand did not annihilate them. So, then, *Commander*," the lord curled his upper lip, annoyance apparent in his barking snarl, "what would *you* suggest I do from *down here?*"

He angrily grasped an ivory tusk and drew the great beast down to eye level. Seth's icy stare reached deep within the monster's soulless being, searching the inner crevices of his fusty brain possibly for an answer or a sign of acknowledgement. His maniacal gaze narrowed as he observed the great beast's façade. Curiosity, like that of a child, then persuaded him to press a rigid finger, adorned with a long manicured nail, against the green-gray, moldy skin of the beast, to insert the sharpened fingernail deep within the coarse, wrinkled hide, just below the marble-like eye. A sadistic smirk riddled the lord's face and he prodded deeper, his inquisitiveness mounting along with a strange sensation which raced throughout his senses. Their eyes locked and Seth slowly wedged his finger to the knuckle, like an adolescent exploring the forbidden.

Gulzar blinked as a trickle of fresh blood seeped from beneath the thick coarse layers of flesh, increased in flow and became a small oily black puddle at his hoofed feet.

The monster's dark, oil colored blood traced Seth's palm and ran along the white of his skin, disappearing within the sleeve of his wine-colored cloak. "Your facade is repulsive," Seth suddenly grimaced, his desire quickly subsided. Rapidly, removing his blood-soaked finger, he shoved the giant beast backward, sending him hurtling feet away where he crashed with a droning thud upon the grotto's rocky terrain.

"Shall you enter my domain again—the stench, of the swine you are upon you—I shall separate that revolting appendage, you refer to as a head, from that hideous deformity you label as body." He promptly inserted his dripping finger within the spinning vortex and withdrew it clean.

"Now—you are supposed to be the *Great Commander* of the most vicious army that ever existed throughout time; and until I have possession of *that bracelet, you* shall be held accountable for ridding me of those pesky humans, so that I may concentrate on the task at hand—my formidable wife."

The commander achingly rose to his hoofed feet. Brushing himself off, he bowed slightly, the flow of dark-purple traced his long snout while he warily swiped the back of a brutish five-fingered, hair-ridden claw across the leaking hole and turned to leave. He paused, his keen sense of hearing pricking to the resonating sound of Nagid entering from the

Haush Min Maut. Gulzar's curiosity peaked and he deliberated his pace desiring to know the result of Nagid's retrieval of the female and the Semus jewel.

The pounding of Nagid's heavy footfalls echoed along the creviced walls, along with a reverberating anguished sigh which released from his stout chest. Closing the tunnel door behind him, he turned to face the Lord Seth, whose glaring stare magnified, as he noticed the female Nagid was carrying, was injured and without the bracelet. Nagid bowed humbly and laid her, unconscious, at the angered god's feet.

Gulzar quickly exited, leaving Nagid to face the malevolent deity alone.

Plumes of heavy gray smoke rose from beneath the layers of earth with the crackle of fire and brimstone thick within the air and choking to the nostrils. Jabali soldiers scurried about hungrily; the tantalizing taste of fresh blood and flesh, humming upon their watering pallets. They busied themselves in preparation for war, each selecting a weapon of choice, which varied from a broad leather belt, lined with the sharpest of dirks, to a threefold bolted crossbow used to annihilate three unsuspecting victims in one precise shot.

Gulzar entered the tunnel which descended to the lower levels of the lord's realm. Beating the terrain beneath his stomping feet; he waited to be out of earshot of the lord to release an enraged, earsplitting roar. Then, shoving through a group of soldiered beast, awaiting their weapons which were being hand forged for each one's chief ability, Gulzar unleashed the constrained fury burning like raging fire within his gut. The humiliation delivered so brazenly by his lord, impelling his thirst for blood. Grabbing a hot soldering rod he swiftly rammed it into the nearest soldier, sending his massive body crashing to the dusty ground as the stunned Jabali howled in alarm and pain.

Gulzar's heated draws of air matched that of the erratic rhythm of his large pounding heart. Tossing his head angrily with a snort, he aimed to clear his mind and rid himself of the debasement that he—*the commander of the Jabali*—should never have had to endure. Rapidly, he turned that anger to bloodlust.

He abruptly spun on his thick two horned hooves while rage seeped from his beady black eyes and a shout roared from his chest, "Ready yourselves—warriors of Jabali…" he struck a clenched heavy fist into the air; the command thundered throughout the underground warren, "…For, come daylight, we go to *wwwwaaaarrrrrrr!!!*"

CHAPTER 29

"*Laddor?*" Cherinne whispered, hearing him call her name as it rode along the wind like a dandelion seed upon a summer's breeze. Her heart raced in excitement driving her exhausted body to a hastening jog. The low lantern lights whisked by as she increased her speed and hurried through the tunnel toward what she was certain to be the surface.

"I'm here!" she shouted anxiously, as her skin puckered through the building sudation which clung to her body. "I'm here!"

Cherinne's name, like a breath of air, suddenly disappeared as if it had been swallowed by the gloomy depression that attempted to swallow her brief moment of hope. She continued to push forward, perking her ears to listen for Laddor's voice or any indication that he was still near.

Searching the darkened void above her, she cried out, "Please—don't leave!" The appeal progressed into nothingness, ingested by layer upon layer of white sand. She quickened her step to a hastened run, growing frantic that she would be left behind.

Laddor clasped the small slip of paper, his only link to where Cherinne might be, tightly within his hands. The heat of day was quickly rising, casting his large shadow upon the piece of stationery. Scribbled words, like that of a five year old, appeared before their eyes, which were barely decipherable. Rasheed shook his head in disgust, questioning as to *if* and *where* Laddor may have been schooled.

"Shut up!" He squawked, crumpling the slip into a wad, and returning it to his pocket. "I know what it says; and *besides*, I was in a hurry when I wrote it!"

Rasheed rose to his feet and began to pace; frustration, annoyance, defeat, and loss mounted upon his wit like thunderclouds slowly roving across a summer's sky just before their fierce storm.

"*Aarghh!!*" He irately kicked the hot, dusty sand with a boot, then continued his repeated trek while running a fretful hand through his glossy hair.

"*Com'on guys*," Deverall mildly appealed. "I know it's hot and we've been out here for days; and that Red here," he motioned in Laddor's direction with a nod of his sweat-beaded head, "doesn't have the penmanship of Lassie, but at least he knows what the directions say.

Now—how 'bouts we pull ourselves together and get this lil' party over with; cause I'm desperately in need of a cold one, and my ass is bout' as raw as uncooked prime rib, from bouncin' round on that there damn saddle. *And*," he glanced from Laddor to Rasheed, "the girls may be just below us in need of our help."

Rasheed discontinued his pacing then warily returned to seat himself at Laddor's side, his prospects of finding the princess slowly depleting. His manner was set, while he attempted to obscure the reservation in his tone. "Yes, Mr. Deverall, I do agree and I respect your candor. So, Mr. Zeandre, if you can decipher for us, that would be greatly appreciated."

Laddor floundered to his feet, slightly teetering, as his hazing vision, which was slowly clearing, still inclined his head to whirl uncontrollably when rising too quickly. He put his hands out to steady himself; then, through the vertical slits which comprised his eyes, he stepped within the area in which he had previously traced.

Speaking, with the use of his hands, which seemed more a benefit to him, than to the amir and Deverall, he repeated aloud his conversation with Reynolds and the method used for the earbob.

"Okay—he said, 'the girl inserted the earring; then while she giggled and twitched with delight, a very small map appeared just above her left breast'." Laddor paused, glancing at Rasheed and Deverall to ascertain they were still listening.

"Then," he continued, "Reynolds said that while she oohed and aahed and pranced around, he attempted to decipher the tiny markings upon her chest."

Sitting crossed-legged, Deverall hastily shifted his weight onto his thick, straggly-haired knees; while the skin, covering the reverse side, was completely bare. *"Com'on!"* he crowed impatiently, while Rasheed raised a thick brow, a peculiar frown riddling his normally striking features with him swimming in a sea of wonder as to *what girl* they were referring to.

Rasheed quietly folded his hands in his lap in the attempts to remain patient.

"Anyway—" Laddor began again. "The map pictured a bright star which, I assumed, was the *A cryptic Star* with, what I *also* assumed, was the earring depicted just below it, with a ray shooting from the star to the earring."

"Was there anything else?" Rasheed questioned, smothering the anxiety choking at his throat. His heart raced within his chest at the realization that the American actually did know what was contained in the other earbob; and, his finding the princess may not be just an optimistic endeavor now, but an actual success.

Deverall sweated in anticipation, while he wrung his hands and enthusiasm blazed through his dark shades. Removing his hat, he swiped a hand through his wet head and fanned himself with the straw Panama hat.

"No—there was nothing else."

The prince pondered Laddor's reply, his lip tapping neurotic; he hurriedly scrambled to his feet. "I have an idea."

"Ib," Rasheed bent to a knee beside the boy who continued to lie upon the sand, his ear pasted to the off-white terrain. Gazing through fixed eyes, his auditory perception was gripped within the earth's many layers, as he was listening intently for a voice.

"Your Highness," he spoke quietly without blinking; Rasheed barely heard his hushed words above the rustling of horses and men, as they scoured the territory for anything that could signify they were in the correct location. "I can hear the American female. She calls the name of her male, while her footsteps echo in intensity, as if she draws near."

Removing his hands from beneath his stomach, he laid them palm side down before him. Slowly sifting the sand away from his head, as if he was clearing another layer of dusty earth, he listened with more acuteness. "And, though I beckon to the Princess Fahimah…" he blinked, "I am unable to hear her voice. Your Highness—do you think Princess Fahimah still lives?"

Rasheed quickly turned his head as a tear threatened the corner of his eye. He forced it away and returned his focus to the boy as the harsh truth of reality slapped him hard. The reply was but a whisper, "I don't know."

Shifting his body and rising to a sitting position, Ib apathetically brushed the sand from his clothing and hair and removed a book from within his galabiyah. It was the fairytale book he had had in the stable— *Aladdin*.

The prince extended his hand; "May I?" Rasheed promptly thumbed through to the picture of Jasmine, where the smallest of jewels was pasted within the princess's eye. He ran his forefinger over the miniscule diamond, which in catching the rays of the sun, burned bright with fervent zeal. Placing a hand on the young boy's shoulder, his gaze gripped the large, dark blinking eyes.

"Tell me, Ib…is this," he pointed to the jewel, "how you get your acute power of hearing?"

"Yes, Your Grace—Princess Fahimah gave it to me so that I would always hear her voice if she called to me.

Rasheed removed the tiny jewel from its safe haven, feeling a mild tingling within his fingertips.

"I am sorry, Ib; but, I need this jewel, for it may help in the aide of finding the amiri. The young boy, slightly rueful nodded his head in agreement, while his bind to the princess was now slipping as water through his fingers.

The blistering heat of the sun was disheartening; and the arid terrain rippled in a hazy throng of waves soaking any sign of moisture from the thick choking air.

Rasheed shaded his burning eyes as he searched the blazing white sky for the Acryptic Star, while the small gem vibrated gently between his finger and thumb as Laddor and Deverall watched intently.

Covering his eyes, so as not to suffer the same fate as the red-haired American, Rasheed held the precious stone toward the star. Using his utmost commanding voice, the voice of a supreme leader and astute ruler, he shouted, "Acryptic Star—*deploy!!!*"

The quiescent star exploded to life and clutched the miniscule gem within its grasp. The tiniest of diamonds ruptured upon impact and burst into a million lights within the heated sky. Hovering above the men momentarily, it then fell to the ground and disappeared, much in the same manner as the earbob.

Rasheed was tossed backward, landing bewilderedly upon his haunches.

"No!" Ib raced along the sand with his arms out stretched to the remaining trickles of light that quickly sprinkled as fairy dust to the ground; his only bond to the princess gone.

Rasheed hastily collected himself, rose to his feet and shook off the dizzying effect the mere explosion had caused. Swiftly, he surveyed the area in which the affects of the small jewel had blanketed and saw there was no alteration, only billowing waves of skimming heat hovering along the sand.

"*Lashr!*" He curled his fists, as the cords of his neck expanded into iron bands, while red flashed upon his sweated body and face. With defeat and rage deeming as superior, his self-control peaked to its limit.

Spinning on his heels, he began a jog that rapidly became a race against time, against destruction, against the blistering heat which was causing his brain to swell in a paining ache. Rasheed was a child again running from the hurt inflicted by his father; while yet, he was still unable to hide.

The weight of his leather boots, kicking up patches of sand, was a mere annoyance, more so than a deterrent as he raced toward the hot noonday sun. He ran toward nothingness and no-one while all in the vicinity stood to attention and watched.

Deverall nudged Laddor. "Hey—maybe you should go get 'im, before he drops from heat exhaustion."

"*Me?*"

"Yep," the pilot retorted nonchalantly as he raised his shades. "Cause I know I can't run that fast; and at that speed he's liable ta reach the Atlantic by the New Year or drop dead."

Laddor frowned; then blinking in an attempt to clear his eyes, he nodded and quickly broke into a run. While his sight was still somewhat hazy, he was still able to make out the dark form as it raced toward the scorching white light of the sun, into the heated depths of hell, which consisted of mile upon mile of man-eating desert.

"Rasheed! Wait up!" Laddor stretched out his lengthy legs, not having run like this since his perilous flight through the city, when he had been running from the three thugs who, in being misinformed, had believed he had swindled them. That was the day he had met Cherinne. His thoughts turned to that day and how she, with determination had eluded the men. Then, he thought of her now, being trapped beneath the earth in harms way, injured or worse; it drew unbearable pain upon his pounding chest. Listening to the steady inhale and exhale of dry desert air, he felt a surge of energy and determination envelope him. It increased his speed, like a racehorse whose ability was unleashed, and was left wide-open to run.

Laddor's camel colored boots dug deep within the sand, while the collection of heavy granules sucked at his legs and feet, endeavoring to pull him, exhausted, to the earth. The tightness in his quadriceps flowed to his calf muscles and into his grasping toes, while spurted tufts of sand spit from behind, as he closed the gap between himself and the prince.

Rasheed glanced back, his earlier days of running through the cobble stoned paths of the regime returned to him rapidly and his sense of competitiveness heightened. Pressing onward, he gauged his breathing and narrowed his eyes from the searing sun, while the American approached quickly and they were now running neck to neck.

"Amir—where ya' headed?" Laddor quipped between breaths as their gaze locked in an unspoken rivalry; his stare was still that of azure vertical slits hidden behind black shades while the amir's silent reply came forth through a resolute, deep-brown stare. Laddor removed Cherinne's thin black hair tie from his wrist and quickly secured his damp mop of flapping hair, then surged slightly forward.

Rasheed feeling somewhat ridiculed, was truthfully unable to answer as to his destination—his intention, not to race, but to release the frustration building within himself.

Increasing his speed, he glanced competitively from Laddor to his inadvertent path and pressed onward, surging slightly ahead.

With a grin, Laddor positioned himself alongside the prince and observed the regent from the corner of a sweated eye. Feeling as a feline in the game of cat and mouse, he was most certain he would be the winner in this round.

Panting slightly, Rasheed persevered, resolving to be the victor and not allow himself to be beaten by this American who had indisputably brought anarchy and pandemonium to his regime. Gathering every ounce of energy within his rapidly exhausting body, he intercepted his opponent and flashed Laddor a weary grin as he surpassed him. And, feeling a sense of coming triumph and urging forward, he hadn't noticed the shifting landscape, which was rapidly pouring as a waterfall within the earth.

Rasheed's face coiled with surprise and fear, as he suddenly, without warning, dropped as a lead weight within the ingesting sand and disappeared.

"*Holy Shit!*" Laddor stopped dead in his tracks, teetering on the edge of a massive sink hole which steadily nursed at the area of terrain surrounding it. Collecting his footing and wiping away the streaming sweat soaking his face, he shook off the shock and bewilderment then slumped to his quivering knees.

Plunging his arm deep within the desert's living vacuum, he felt for a hand, clothing, skin, hair, anything he could grasp to yank the amir free. "*Raasshheeed...*" he growled, "*com'on!*" It was like searching the hat for the longest straw; his heart pounded not only from running, but now, from the anxiety and fear that he would come up short, while the sand flowed like water beneath him, gliding into the hungry pit before his cloudy eyes.

"Al-Feyn Al-amir?" Lateef shouted as he, racing along the hot landscape with several of his men and Deverall, quickly approached.

"Help me! He's in the blasted ground!" Laddor snapped from exhaustion, while his limbs felt as if they were melting from the scorching heat and roughness of the rushing granules.

"*HAFAR!!!*" the commander's voice boomed, sending soldiers—as human digging tools—ravaging at the very ground before them. Mounds of sand sprayed through the thick, smoldering air as the intensity to find the amir mounted and desperation again built upon their shoulders.

"*NAAAGGGIIIIDDDDDDDD!!!*" Seth's voice bellowed, filling the whole of the underground kingdom while the shattering vibration stirred within the rocky terrain itself. All life within the vicinity shuddered at the reverberating roar as it tore through the Haush min maut and raced through the labyrinth into the lovely lake's crystalline waters and into Cherinne's ears.

"*Oh my God!*" Cold chills rushed upon her skin as terror gripped at her raspy throat. Shifting the pack upon her back, she ran in fear for her life.

"Nagid…" Seth wrapped a tight fisted grip, seeming to amplify in size, around the giant's clothed throat, inflicting immense pressure on the thick bulging chords which constituted the giant's esophagus. "…I specifically warned you." The lord's stare cut through the giant's glazed eyes as Nagid's air was rapidly depleting and the massive force was burning the heightened senses from his collar to his ears, causing his skull to thrum at the very film of skin which covered his expiring brain.

Seth viewed the female that lay unconscious just beyond his feet. Running his gaze the length of her motionless body, his eyes came to rest on the crossbow, normally wielded by Hafiz. His icy stare darted back to Nagid. "Where is Hafiz?"

Incapable of drawing a breath or assessing the damage being done to his slowly bursting lungs and barely able to lift his broad massive shoulders, Nagid laboriously raised them to a slight, insignificant shrug. While his nostrils flared and his gaping orifice wheezed with a reverberation of sounds from his collapsing esophagus.

"*You blundering disgrace!*" The stolid stone of the cavern floor cracked and moaned as Seth slammed the giant's body effortlessly to the rock encrusted ground, splitting the surface in two.

Fire and ice blazed and intertwined within the lord's eyes, giving his cold stare a sadistic radiance; while his sandaled foot thudded upon Nagid's chest, pressing piercingly on his paining ribcage as it rose and fell in an erratic gulp for air.

The flames which flickered atop the many burning torches, spread throughout the grotto, danced in a feverish attempt to remain lit as Seth's aura quadrupled turning from a crimson-gold to a rotting green, filling the underground cavern with an eerie pungent smog. His insatiable locks whipped in a heated agitation, stirred by the omnipotent power of their lord's elemental control; and as he stooped, the screaming tresses reached for the still giant. Slivering like viperous reptiles, they ran along his clothed body in search of bare defenseless flesh while the nervous sweat of the frightened giant reeked through the pores of his thick swarthy skin, drawing the red, blood-thirsty beasts nearer. And, reaching within the open crevice of cloth along the giant's jaw bone and ear, they rapidly slipped beneath the black fabric in a hastened rush to feed upon the now ashen flesh.

Seth observed Nagid's intrepid stare, searching the black pupils for the slightest hint of fear, while the stench of anxious sweat was tantalizing to his senses and he feasted in its rancidity.

"M'lord."

Seth's revelry was abruptly broken and the tresses screamed in angered annoyance as they swiftly withdrew, leaving Nagid panting for air. While he had been holding his breath, ready for the detrimental pain in which his lord would so easily inflict upon his now pallid skin.

Seth's icy glare tore from the giant to Gulzar. "*What is it?*" Venom coated each biting syllable.

"Your Excellency…" he bowed low, "an intruder has breached the royal empire's shield. We believe they are somewhere in the Haush min maut."

"*WWHHAATTTT!!?*" he roared, rising to his feet and heatedly shoving the giant with his foot. His rigid stare darted from Gulzar, who warily awaited a deliberated blow to Nagid, who was slowly lumbering to standing. Curling his fists in knots, Seth ran a hand through his jangling hair. He pondered the situation while attempting to slow his engulfing rage, slow the dark aura swirling and building about his ill-tempered body.

Seth glanced at the two subordinates, as he suddenly felt an odd sense of energy rush upon his skin. A slight chill entered the air and his countenance abruptly altered, returning the murky haze to golden. His gaze darted to the lovely female lying defenseless before his feet—Fahimah, who had been pelted upon the head by crashing rubble which had rendered her unconscious.

Seth bent to a knee, and with an elongated fingernail, swept a strand of golden hair away exposing her features. The wicked tresses upon his head quickly came to life ready to strike the full of her exquisite ivory skin. But, raising a commandeering hand to the screaming devils, he halted them in their intended tirade upon the princess.

"No." He ran his nail along her faintly rising and falling cheek as she breathed shallowly through parted lips. "I shall keep this one." Rising, he then continued to observe her through flashing eyes, as he instructed his commanders.

"Nagid, go and hunt that intruder; destroy him on sight. And, after you have finished, retrieve Hafiz; for he is a valued asset with his crossbow. And, Commander—"

"Yes, Sire." Gulzar stepped forward and bowed humbly.

"Send your men to the surface and destroy anyone or anything that you deem a mere agitation to your lord. And…" a baleful grin etched his face, as he perceived the shimmering iridescent glow of the anklets which Fahimah had concealed within the silky, paper-mache' thin material of her garments, "…. as for that lecherous bitch—my wife—I shall deal with her. For I see now that we have a meager collection of the Semus Jewels within our possession, so I will shortly be rising to the exterior."

Bending to a knee, he scooped Fahimah within his dark claret cloak, obscuring her completely from sight. His rock-hard physique vibrated with a resonating thrum, a spirited current which heatedly flowed against her delicate paled skin. She shuddered lightly and her eyes fluttered in the attempts to painfully open. He whipped about and the tails of his broad shouldered mantle rippled gently in the reverberating gust. And, nodding a notion of dismissal, he headed to his bedchamber.

CHAPTER 30

"Where is he?" Laddor crowed. His face was centimeters above the hot sand and his head ached from the glare surging off the white terrain which bled through the rims of his dark glasses.

Rolling away, his arms tired and body spent, he allowed another to endeavor the treacherous digging in search of the amir. He was accompanied by Omar, Mahir and the commander, whose white robes were laid out like sheets for a pressing, encompassing the hole, their arms burrowed deep to the shoulder joints.

A leather water-skin speedily sailed through the heavy air from an unknown source, landing clumsily in Laddor's lap. Hastily unscrewing the cork, he greedily gulped at its remaining contents; the few drops tingled upon his tongue, while the dampness hadn't even moistened the parched skin of his thirsting mouth.

"Rasheed! Don't do this!" he groaned beneath his breath. He wearily stood, while the enormity of their circumstances fell like an avalanche upon his scrambling mind. Sand showered the ground before his feet from his drenched clothes and skin as he irritably brushed it away.

"I don't care how *freakin' cold* it gets in Joseph's cabin and if we get ten feet of *freakin' snow*. If Cherinne and I get the hell outta' here I don't wanna' *ever* see another blasted grain of sand or feel that wretched hot sun on my back again," Laddor mumbled. Exhausted of all energy, he left the digging to the Egyptian soldiers, whose swarthy weathered hides could endure the blazing rays of the devilish Middle Eastern sun, more so than his white western world skin.

He watched as Deverall took his round at the excavating, as men rotated in shifts and dug in desperation. Water skins were tossed to those temporarily used up and awaiting another turn—sixty-two men in all including himself and the spicy, slowly deflating pilot whose rotator cuffs, biceps and triceps would be screaming in protest the entirety of the following day.

Shoving his dry, cracking hands within his jean pockets, Laddor headed to his tent where he would lie quietly for a short while and think of how he was going to explain the circumstances to Cherinne's father *and* to Reynolds. Then possibly muster the energy for a solar shower, which would be the highlight of *this* day, whereas others had been in the hopes of finding Cherinne. That hope had now completely vanished, along with their only jewels, any contact with the outside world and the amir.

He was convinced this was the devil's lair.

Laddor raised his smarting head while the whole of his eyes felt quite puffy and drowsiness clouded his muddled mind. After his shower he must have dozed, ending up sleeping the entirety of the miserable day away. He heard Deverall enter the tent and lumber wearily to his sleeping bag. Pushing up on a panging arm, he inquired through a slightly garbled voice, "Did they find him?"

"No." The reply was short, unnatural for the normally upbeat, optimistic pilot, who, in shifting his over-exhausted blister-skinned body, closed his eyes and cursed the very maker who created the sun's intense heat. "He's gone."

Laddor lay quietly, his draconic eyes alert to every minute shadow and movement within the tent's darkness. He listened to the sound of Deverall's lumbered shifting and mild breathing till it became an all-out growl. In utter frustration, he dug his fingers into the small stiff pad— referred to as a pillow—then placed them to Cherinne's hair-tie which still secured his damp hair. He clutched her black camisole firmly to his chest—one of the few remaining remnants of her he was able to fit into his pack, and, of course her cell phone, whose battery had died long ago.

Struggling with the flow of tears which stung at his slatted eyes, he, finally succumbing to their fury, turned his face into the unyielding pad and wept himself back to sleep.

"*Raasshheeeedd*," the prince listened to his name through a faraway humming in his mind as the gentle sound was whispered upon the wind.

"*Fahimah?*" He answered to the darkness filling the whole of his throbbing head while his body was a heavy weight—unmoving—a foreigner to his personage and inner self.

Her milky-white features appeared before him, searching his face with wide kaleidoscopic eyes which danced before his fingertips as he gently touched her cheek. "*Fahimah*," the whisper fell upon Rasheed's ears, muffled and soundless to his auditory sense. Sadness filled her quiet, settled pools of color and she warmly placed a trembling hand upon his face.

"Rasheed—you must wake up," her soft pink lips murmured tenderly as he, thirsting for their touch, slowly drew them to his, their warmth and tenderness burning with fire through his entire being.

"No—Fahimah...I've missed you—come to me," he beckoned. Her sweet breath was upon his as a feathery lock of her hair plummeted against his face. "Come to me." Slipping his aching arms around her petite waist, he lurred her to him as he drank of her body, mind and soul.

"*Ammiirr.*" Cherinne gently tore herself from within the prince's yearning arms while the passionate kiss was still fresh upon her mind and lips. Her happiness at having discovered him there, lying within the tunnels, was an overwhelming unconsumable joy, while she slightly embarrassed and weak, had welcomed it freely.

Awakening from his revelry, Rasheed's thick lashes, heavily laden with sand, gradually began to open, as his sweated body and clothing were covered in the tides of Egypt. Slowly rising to a sitting position as granules flowed from his body, like rain, he glanced at Cherinne in the attempt to focus his foggy mind. Flush crept to both their cheeks, in the sudden realization as to what had just transpired between them.

"I can't believe you're here! Is Laddor with you?" Her voice bubbled with excitement and for a brief moment a smile covered her weary appearance. Cherinne's features were so comparable to that of the princess, it ached Rasheed to look into her tear-brimming brown eyes, while the image of Fahimah still stirred within his mind and loins. He answered 'No'.

"Are you okay?" he then anxiously asked as he ran a hand along the sleeve of Hafiz's black tunic, pausing slightly as his fingers traced along the bracelet. He then quickly inspected the length of the tunnel behind her for any indication of the princess.

"No—I'm not okay," the words suddenly burst through a barrage of dripping tears as she slipped back within the comfort of his arms. "I'm so scared..." her dreaded words flowed like water, "...and they've taken Fahimah! My sister!"

Rasheed pulled her from him, searching her red, teary eyes which leaked like rain from foliage leaves, "You are sisters?" He didn't give her time to elaborate. "Where have they taken her?" his tone was slightly harsher than intended. "Who?"

Sniffling, she slid an arm across her face. "The giant took her. *I'm so sorry!*"

Quickly shedding the last of Egypt's sand from his sweated skin and clothing, he observed her weeping. His heart pained as he could see the princess through Cherinne and his abruptness had aggravated the situation.

"We have been searching the desert for you for days." He drew her trembling body into his open arms and stroked her hair as her tears dripped and traced the curve of his neck.

Swallowing the large lump forming in his throat, he surmised, "Well at least she has the anklets and the aide of her thread."

Collecting her emotions, Cherinne wiped the tears away with a dark tunic sleeve. She searched the amir's harrowed face as anxiety poured from his dark eyes. Days in the desert had been an arch enemy with his worry for the princess beyond compare; and nothing could have prepared him for the words that poured softly from her lips as she silently calculated his reaction.

"No, she was forced to remove the bracelets. *And...*" her eyes never left his, "...she is with child."

The full of the sandy Egyptian terrain rumbled and quaked at the rising of the first Jabali who ascended from the coolness of the dark, dank underground realm to the agitating heat of the coming day. Shaking the sand from his massive form, his leathery hide thick and wooly, he released a thunderous roar while beating massive claw-like fists against his large obtrusive chest. His beady black eyes scanned the whole of the shifting surface from behind his enormous jutting tusks; and, throwing his head about in irritation, he snorted.

An array of weaponry filled the whole of the camel-skinned over-sized scabbard mounting his back; and unsheathing a giant poleax, he shook it angrily at the emerging sun.

The morning star, seeming to cower in mild trepidation, briefly shaded to nearly black—an eclipse—caused by the immense amount of wickedness rising from the near pits of hell, with thousands more Jabali breaking through the coarse layers of earth.

The shifting sand, wrenching and contorting like thunderous waves of the ocean, spawned them as rancid fruit in the attempts to spew them from within its bowels, where they had rotted and festered as a molded growth. They brought forth massive deadly weapons, ranging from sharpened blood thirsty dirks to colossal-sized catapults, supplied with blocks of jagged rock, broken from the earth's inner core.

The Jabali Commander Gulzar appeared upon the surface; his seething gaze followed that of the darkened horizon while he was mildly contented at the disappearance of the detestable sun. A blaring roar escaped his large thick-skinned mouth, lined with razor sharp teeth. It scaled across the parched, bone-dried land while the ten-thousand beasts about him bellowed in unison and the continent shuddered at its vibration.

Turning on his horned hoofs, he eyed his regiment of brutish creatures. And in a thick, booming tone, he eagerly asked, "Who's hungry?"

"Al-*Hayya' Al-isliHa!!* Al-*Hayya'Al-isliHa!!*" The words screamed through Laddor's foggy mind from an alarmed soldier just outside their tent. Suddenly, Ib barged his way inside the motionless canvas flap. The white's of his eyes loomed in unreserved terror about the bulging black irises as panic dripped in sweat from his crinkling brow. The only English word, Laddor had ever heard him speak, raced from his trembling, fumbling lips while he pointed a shaking finger outside. *War.*

"What the hell's goin' on?" Deverall mumbled irritably, still absorbed in sleep's quietude. Shifting his bulky body, he lazily rose to sitting. "And, what the hell's all the shoutin' about?"

"*War! War!*" Ib shouted. Spinning on his sandaled feet, he hastily ran from the tent; while the commotion of men and horses clamoring about outside brought Laddor wearily to standing.

"Who the hell is there to go to war with? We're out in the middle of *nowhere.*" Deverall shook his head. "Maybe it's another khamsin or sandstorm, or whatever they call it. Hey…" he nudged Laddor's leg, "…Or maybe, we're gonna' battle all those sand-bunnies collecting in our shorts." Chuckling weakly, he grabbed his hat and glasses then smacked his pasty lips. "I'm gettin' too old for this shit."

Ib rapidly returned, and seizing Laddor's arm, pulled him from the confines of the tent, practically dragging Laddor to his stiffened knees.

"Hold up, Kid." He brushed the boy's grip away, attempting to adjust his eyes to the few paltry rays of the red morning sun cresting upon the desert's brim. Men and horses raced through the camp hurriedly preparing their few meager weapons, while the commander was frantically shouting out orders Laddor couldn't understand.

Babbling in his native tongue, Ib pointed a shaky finger at the dark ant-like specks slowly roving across the horizon. Shaking his head, to clear his mind and his sight, Laddor peered through vertical slits at the massive amount of black moving along the terrain.

"What the hell is that?"

"*War! War!*" the English words abruptly collided with rushing Arabic which spewed forth easily from the boy's quivering lips.

"Sonofa…" Laddor abruptly turned to see Deverall already outside the tent staring, with a spicy curse already escaping his gaping mouth in a stutter, "…bitch."

"*Holy Mother!* Where'd the hell those guys come from?" His gaze darted to Laddor's and their eyes locked. The insanity of the situation quickly settled upon their now alert minds, sending a rush along their abruptly perspiring skin.

Scurrying back inside the tent to retrieve the resting Mauser and Laddor's new sword; they cringed at the resounding call of the enemy's blaring horns which raced along the desert in preparation for a war—a war they knew they could not win.

Airborne Nephthys screamed along the red-rim of the arriving morning sky while her festering skin puckered at the heated waves of the nauseating sun. Glaring angrily at its coming intensity, she arrogantly threw her nose to the arid air then pressed onward in pursuit of the resonating war horn which had awoken her from her darkened slumber.

The impatient LaHm squirmed restlessly beneath her scaly pelt in a feverish animosity to be released, while their master's thirst to destroy the Lord Seth was a parched perception upon their mouth-less palates.

"Ready, my pets," she hissed from behind crimson lips and blazing eyes which scanned the horizon to see the insect-like Jabali rising to formation just below her.

The fervor within her blood boiled with the realization her beloved brother and husband, Seth, had acquired a piece of the jewels, leaving her no choice but to obtain the bracelet.

"*Ridiculous swine*," she sneered, while her senses raced along the baked terrain in search of the armlet she so desperately needed to defeat the being that had destroyed her sibling and love, Osiris.

"I've come for you, Husband." A twisted maniacal laugh screeched from behind a vicious smile. Suddenly, she noticed the small militia of humans below.

"Hmm," her upper lip curled as she circled quietly above, assessing the situation beneath her, while her garments flapped gently in the light breeze rising from the assembled beast's movements. Curiosity peaking upon her brow, she swooped in for a closer look, inquisitive as to why Seth would send such a massive armament against such a mere weak adversary. Then, the supposed realization dawned upon her—*they* possess the Semus Jewel.

CHAPTER 31

The walls of the grotto seemed to extract and warp, causing the blood to rush to Rasheed's head while the words the American female had spoke seeped inside his staggering senses. My Fahimah is with child? He reached for a craggy wall to steady himself as the news brought a sensation of much needed warmth upon his heart, yet also a dreaded fear.

An image of the princess appeared before his tired eyes—a vision of her as she had, not so long ago, lain with him within the comfort of his quarters. He could remember the soft touch of her skin and the scent of her lovely golden hair as it had cascaded gently upon his pillow. And, being careful not to awake him, she had moved about lightly beneath the satin sheets.

Exhausted from a rigorous day of training, he had begun to drift into a state of well-needed sleep, while the sound of his breathing had gradually filled his senses. He had steadily wandered into a condition of vagueness and uncertainty, a disorderly mistiness; and when Fahimah had whispered into his ear, the delicate words, 'Rasheed, you are going to be a father,' they never registered. And, while his mind was foggy and he had thought it to be a dream, he had unfortunately drifted into a deep slumber.

"Amir, are you okay?" worry echoed in Cherinne's voice as she viewed the mixed expressions upon his face. And, while she had decided to reserve the news of Haneefah till another appointed time, to give the beset amir time to absorb the information, she fretted as to his state of mind. Cherinne placed a caring hand upon his arm.

Tearing his mind from the memory, Rasheed glanced at the female who claimed to be Fahimah's sister—a sibling, a blood sibling who was linked directly to the princess. And, seeing that her apprehension was one of genuine concern, he suddenly grabbed Cherinne's wrist, and held the bracelet before her; and, looking directly into her eyes, he stated firmly, "You *must* use *this*."

"*But I don't know how!* I can't get it to work!" Tears formed in her eyes and gently traced the length of her cheek, "and I could've gotten us outta' this mess and saved the Princess Haneefah." Her eyes, melting as chocolate drops in summer's heat, looked to the prince for an answer.

Slowly slumping to her knees, she suddenly felt the weight of the world upon her quavering shoulders, while her life which existed just weeks ago, had become a frivolous notion—a meaningless beginning to an end. *She* had been deemed 'administrator of the bracelet', and *she* was now responsible for the protection of *all* who depended on its remarkable power. Her only thought slipped as a mumble through her trembling lips, "Where's Laddor?"

Rasheed bent to a knee and brushed away a lock of hair which had plummeted to her face. "I am not sure." He searched the darkened void overhead. "I assume he is just above us." Blush reddened his bronze cheeks. "We were in the midst of a race."

"A race?" Bewilderment encased Cherinne's expression and, through tear-blurred eyes, she observed the prince skeptically. She wondered whether it to be another dream, like he had been having of Fahimah when he had passionately kissed her, or whether there was more to the account than what he was actually conveying.

"Never mind that," he brushed it away as lint from a fine woolen coat. "We must concentrate on the detrimental situation at hand—finding the Princess Fahimah, and supplying *you* the information you need to activate and command the bracelet. I do not have my journal available here to show you, but maybe as we search for her, I may explain what knowledge I possess." He viewed the many tunnels separating into the complex labyrinth just before them. "Now—which direction would you suggest we go?"

Rising slowly to her feet, she perked her auditory sense in the direction of the splitting paths which divided into numerous directions, like spider legs within the earth. A strange sound of sifting sand filled her ears and something she assumed to be an animal's roar. Suddenly, her legs buckled and she tumbled forward, nearly colliding face-first with the stony surface beneath her.

Rasheed struggled to stay afoot as rock and soil crashed in a thunderous roar from the surface above partially closing off several of the passageways ahead. Dust and dirt plumed as a thickened cloud about them, filling their eyes and lungs with a smog of particles which cascaded like rain from the exploding debris. They scurried from the enclosed tunnel in a desperate need for air.

"*Rasheed!*" The sound of Cherinne's cry filled the prince's ears along with the distant sound of blaring battle horns.

"Great Gods!" he whispered harshly, grabbing her hand and rushing from the underground passage which had crashed in a massive cluster of rock and soil behind them.

"What's happening?" she screamed from a chorded throat, while her heart leaped within her chest and cold chills raced upon her skin. She thought of the giant as she ran along behind the amir.

Shouting over his shoulder, he replied, "I believe we are going to war."

An unnerving quiet settled upon the land of Egypt as Lateef assembled his nervous uneasy men, who attempted to remain vigilant, while fear poured from their many sweated glands. Awaiting the order to proceed forward into the dire clutches of the enemy, they knew the possibility of escaping was improbable.

Reigning in his dancing mare, the commander narrowed his cynical gaze to the blackness advancing along the desert's rim, which blocked out the daylight's coming stream of light. In an attempt to conceal the mild trembling of his fisted hands, he clutched the leather straps tightly, while hindering his mount from racing headlong to a deliberated suicide. The full of his royal blue uniform clung to the sudation building upon his chest and back, and he tugged at the folded collar with the feeling he was being suffocated. Taking a well-needed breath, he slowly drew his sword while attempting to bury any fear deep within the resonating of its blade. His steel rang with assuredness, something he himself surely did not possess. And, though various weapons lined his right and left flanks with a man stationed at each appointed position, he swallowed hard the lump within his dry throat.

Mahir, stationed to his right, checked the vast array of weapons lining his affixed, thick, leather belt while eyeing the crossbow which he gripped tightly within his hands. He glanced over at his older sibling, Omar, recognizing his eldest brother of five's stare as he sat sternly upon his mount. The same austere stare he had possessed years ago when they, being small boys, had during archery practice accidentally shot a bolt astray, sending it to pierce the family's only milking cow. Omar had also stood firmly then, his eyes set before him in much the same manner he was now, while Mahir had sat trembling and weeping, as they awaited the severe lashing from their father who was due to return home from toiling away in the hot, parched fields the entirety of the day.

Sensing his brother's apprehension, Omar turned; and, holding his younger sibling's gaze, he nodded a silent readiness while Mahir saluted in return.

"Commander," Omar then addressed Lateef, whose mind was trapped in the outlying terrain, a faraway expression upon his face, "what are your orders, Sir?"

The commander glanced at the gold band encompassing his left ring finger, thinking of his wife and the small infant that remained behind: how his service to the Amir Rasheed had been brief, but most intriguing: and how his abrupt promotion from sergeant to commander had been with honors.

Turning in his saddle, he briefly settled his eyes on the Dragon—the four foot warhead missile capable of destroying a tank or small plane in one fatal shot. A slight feeling of steadfast resolve inhabited his stirring wits and he replied to his new sergeant-at-arms.

"Sergeant Omar..." he spoke to the distance, as the enemy's trumpets pealed through the heavy, choking air and the clangor of death was thick upon its sound. The shifting terrain billowed in a cloud of hazy dust, as thousands of Jabali combed the sand with two-horned hooves while the earth shivered at their massive movement. "…Have the men hold till my signal." His gaze shifted to the weapons and men aligning his left. "I wanna' take out as many of those bastards as possible before this day is over."

Deverall was seated to the rear of the small militia. Shielding his eyes, he stared toward the sky which had gone from crimson yellow to near black then back to crimson again. Suddenly, he squawked at the sight of Nephthys hovering just overhead, "What in hell is that?"

"What?" Squinting, Laddor followed his gaze to the wisp of garments flapping gently upon the wind above them, unsure as to what he was seeing. "What is that?"

Nephthys's long skirts flowed gracefully behind her with ankle-length foliage-colored locks pressing to her sleek form as she descended toward the assemblage of men who awaited the deadly driving force of the ferocious beasts before them. Spying the full of Laddor's long red mane, her queer smirk abruptly transformed to a baleful wicked stare as a rush of enraged thunderclouds covered her face.

"*Brother!*" she screamed the word through a blistering façade while the Lahm whipped wildly beneath her constricting skin with the intentions of overtaking the male beneath the crimson mane.

"No! He is *mine!*" the irate shriek cursed from her snarling lips. She swooped in for the kill while the scent of human flesh and horses was fresh upon her senses. It was a bouquet she hadn't smelled for a thousand years, while she had been deemed long ago, by the almighty god, Ra, as keeper of the entrails and bodies of the deceased.

"Sonofabitch! It's my mother!" the jaded pilot jested with a shout as he reached within the waist of his shorts and drew his Mauser. He eyed Nephthys's slender carcass as she neared their position.

"*Seeettthhh!* You detestable wretch!" The seething words slipped through clenched teeth; and fire brimmed in her smoldering eyes with the locks of Laddor's red-head an open loathsome target. Rushing in a fierce bluster of raging force, beyond Deverall's slow perception, she slammed into Laddor and his horse, sending them both crashing to the sandy turf.

Deverall fired off a shot with a number of soldiers around them spinning from the harrowing situation before them to the fuming deity who had appeared from out of nowhere. The aligned formation of horses danced in an agitated frenzy while the situation had gone amok.

"*SheTan! SheTan!*" Laddor heard the word cried over and over as his body struck the unyielding terrain, sending his air rushing from his chest. Shaking his head, as if something were loose, he scrambled to get to his quivering knees.

Nephthys rapidly rose to her feet and rushed upon him, screeching a compilation of curses from red sneering lips. "Seth! I have come for vengeance, my detestable black-hearted husband! And I shall not leave till I have torn your foul depraved skull from your decrepit vile body!"

"*What?*" Laddor stuttered as he stumbled to his feet. "I don't even know you!"

Deverall sent off another shot which ripped along the full of her skirting and sent her tumbling to a defensive position.

Her anger raged with intensity and her eyes which were cloaked in blackness scoured the men assembled before her. Confusedly, she settled her gaze on her target who had attempted to obscure himself from sight, realizing it was not that of her husband. Severely frustrated and irate, she cried out to the abominable flesh which snaked its way passionately beneath her skin in a disgruntled frenzy to break free. "*LaHm!*" the one searing word sent the creatures ripping from her crusty layer of tissue in a hastened madness toward the men.

Raashhheeedd...Fahimah's mind twisted and gyrated in a sickening torrent of agony while she was unaware as to where she even was. Darkness filled the whole of her surrounding world while pain was the only awakened sense forcing her to remain conscious....*I thought you would come for me.* His face, as a young boy, appeared before her and the words *I shall fix it,* trickled as a lost memory before her inner self.

"I shall fix it," the words formed, barely audible upon her numb parched lips and she slowly began to slip back into the meager comfort of oblivion as a tear traced the length of her face.

"You will fix *what*—my Dear?" Seth's silky voice abruptly slunk as poison within her ear as he once more slipped beneath the ebony sheets.

Seth had viewed the flaxen-haired female lying naked and silent beneath the coverlet of his enormous bed, somehow hoping she was not dead. For, while she had fought valiantly, but was unable to overpower him, he had enjoyed the touch of her alabaster skin and her lovely façade and had even healed her injuries absorbing them from her trembling flesh into his.

His thoughts suddenly turned sour and he grimaced with the thought of his wife just overhead.

Slipping the last button through the eyelet of his black silken shirt, he irately snatched the sanguine colored cloak resting upon the cushions of a large velvety sleigh back chaise. He whipped the mantle about him in a hastened flurry. Glancing his shoulder at the female, he plowed through the eloquent chamber's doors to address the militant standing at arms, who glimpsed beyond the open entry to see Fahimah lying near incapacitated and vulnerable. Listening to the clipped orders being deliberated, to secure the room and allow no-one in or out, Hafiz smiled behind void, lifeless eyes, the only evidence he had perished within the tunnels.

He licked his dry lips recalling the immense pain she had deliberated upon him. The sense of being torn and swallowed within the blackened pits of Jahannam, while his slit puckered flesh had been feasted upon by eager worm-like maggots, and his heart, which would live on for all time, ripped from his chest to lie before his thrashing feet. He cried out for another judgment—any other judgment—than to be consumed within the pits of hell, while the meager span of time had seemed to him an eternity.

Then suddenly, he was unexpectedly awakened to an electrifying consciousness that reached in and snatched his body from the clutches of death. The Lord Seth, so graciously had spoken the words of life upon him and had returned him to his normally fiendish self—minus his heart, which had been left behind. Then, brazenly reproaching Nagid for his incompetence and barking out a set of deliberated orders, Seth had turned in a fluster to revisit his sultry quarters and the female who lay barely conscious, spent from hours of struggling and hours of the god's ferocity.

CHAPTER 32

Smoldering ash and dust rushed in a billowing cloud upon Rasheed and Cherinne as they raced through the tunnels away from the crashing rock, debris and sand, which plunged to the earth and enclosed the passage behind them. The desert moaned, with the dunes of its surface tossing to and fro, like that of turbulent ocean waves, pitching upon the sea.

Holding tightly to Cherinne's hand, Rasheed pressed onward, while the blood pounded in his head and rushed through a body that was exhausted. An unnerving, chilling sweat broke upon his anxious skin, as his legs feeling like elastic bands, seemed as if they would snap. He shouted to Cherinne, "Come on!" while he was determined to escape from these treacherous underground tunnels, rescue his princess and return his men safely to the palace.

Shifting uneasily, the earth slowly began to settle and quiet itself; though the land creaked eerily and a steady methodical pounding, rose from the massive driving force plowing its way through the stirring sand.

Panting for air, Rasheed slowed each achy step. Then coming to a halt, he bent to retrieve a breath. Cherinne followed suit while she struggled slightly to keep the dark fuzziness, which had entered her brain, from sending her plummeting, unconscious to the gravelled floor.

The prince observed her from the corner of an eye, amazed at her uncanny likeness to his Fahimah—her mannerism, assuredness, walk and even the scent of her perspiration; the moistness glistening upon her damp lovely skin. The task was becoming quite arduous not to embrace the American as he would have the princess. Suddenly, he tore his gaze away with the realization she had noticed him staring.

"I am stunned as well." Blush crept into her cheeks as she brushed the fragments of dust from her garments. Her eyes locked with his as she gauged her breathing. "But I am not Fahimah; and I cannot battle as she does." She glanced away. "And, knowing that she is my sister—and even though she despises me—I will fight to the death to try and save her."

Rasheed studied her closely. "And, how is it that you are so certain you are blood? What proof do you possess?"

"Fahimah told me," her large coffee eyes locked again with his. "She said that someone named *Rasool* had the proof—some kind of documentation."

Rasheed's eyes sparked open as if a light bulb had been switched on in his head and deep frown lines rapidly lined his brow. Pondering the circumstances briefly, he abruptly spun about and silently made his way in the direction toward what he hoped was the princess.

An unsettling quiet, along with a measured distance, had grown between Cherinne and the amir, while the sound of steady thrumming above had taken on a low dull roar. Cherinne struggled to keep pace with the prince and a mild agitation began to settle itself upon her with the feeling he was displeased at her. Finally she called to him, having to slightly raise her voice above the escalating sound from above, as he was trekking steadily at a good pace ahead.

"Rasheed…you have not told me of the bracelet. I need to know how to use this thing."

He suddenly spun to confront her, while he had realized that her presence in Egypt was severely detrimental to Fahimah. And, he was, also, being forced to swallow the large, very foul tasting pill of Rasool's ranting, which, in all actually, had been truth. The documentation the commander possessed, of her being taken from her parents and involved in a scandalous plot against the Egyptian empire, along with his abhorring her, was surely a sentence of death for Fahimah. Not by his hand, but by those of the government.

Mother, what were you thinking? Rasheed nearly conveyed aloud while also contemplating the notion that Fahimah may want to leave the Tarun regime and go home to her family—a family which she had been torn from and had never gotten a chance to know. Those thoughts, compiled with: her being taken captive, she no longer adorned the anklets, *and*, she was now with child—his child; his stomach suddenly retched and he had to bite back the bile.

"I will tell you of the bracelet and of its history, and we will use it to destroy those who are holding the princess against her will and also to defeat those who make war upon my men. But..," his aristocratic demeanor instituted itself within his set eyes, "...you must remain silent to the claims of Rasool and to the fact that you and the princess are siblings until I am able to figure a course of action deemed best suited for Fahimah *and* the whole of the regime."

Cherinne nodded her head in understanding, while she had worries of her own—ones that concerned Laddor and Mr. Deverall being involved in a war that the amir continued to speak of. What war? Apparently, there was a war in progress—and with whom? *And*, was Laddor in danger?

"Rasheed...I promise not to tell a living soul...but, I also want you to promise *me* something." She lightly touched his arm. "I want you to assure me that Laddor will make it home—back to the estate—also, Mr. Deverall. Please."

Rasheed turned, unable to uphold her pressing gaze. "I am sorry; but I am unable to keep that promise; for..." he continued his trek through the tunnel, his chest tightened as the air was thick with disappointment. "...Your Mr. Zeandre and Mr. Deverall are most definitely in the midst of the oncoming battle as we speak; and we were only a small militia of sixty-three, minus two—me and my sergeant. So, the odds of anyone surviving what is slowly advancing across the sandy terrain above are slim or next to none." Without turning he stated dryly, "I am sorry."

"*No*," the whisper achingly slipped from her closing throat. "*No!*" she shouted to his back, frustration bringing forth a barrage of tears which glazed within her eyes. She forced them away as she rushed upon the amir and grabbed his arm. The pounding of her heart drowned out the thunderous march from above as she turned him toward her. "No Rasheed!" Her paining eyes searched his in a frantic desperation. "I won't let anything happen to Laddor! Tell me how to use this thing!" She yanked back the sleeve of Hafiz's tunic, revealing the omnipotent bracelet which remained dormant within a will of its own and glistened proudly as if in mockery. "There are so many people depending on me; and I can't even help them!" She released his arm and her gaze dropped to the dirt and rock encrusted ground. "*Please.*"

Firmly grasping the wrist which adorned the armband, he held it up before her, his tone was set, almost lifeless. There was no sentiment in the marked earnestness of his eyes, just an intensity that burned with the power which the armband possessed.

He drew a breath; and as if speaking with one of his men he stated, "First and foremost…the Semus Bracelet was created by one of the most eloquent goddesses that ever existed—Nut, she being the goddess of the sky. I am not going to go into great depth as to why and how, just that she created it to fight, fight a battle against the supreme god Ra, to be with her true love from whom she was to be eternally separated. This bracelet…" he turned it within the lanterns low flame, observing the small flicker of multi-colored lights which danced from the array of jewels lining its edges; "…this magnificent piece was created to control armies and defeat unconquerable deities. And *you*…" he placed her arm to her side and gauged her reaction while his eyes and tone sparked with life. "…You possess the power of the gods *right here*, right here at your fingertips. And all you have to do is call upon its strength; call upon it as a *goddess*, a *supreme being* and command it to your will—whatever *you* wish."

Doubt cast its shadow upon her face, while not a single college course had prepared her for this, she shuffled uneasily.

"*Cherinne Havenstrit*…" with a forefinger he stroked a long lock of platinum hair which had plummeted to her shoulder, "…*you* are now the administrator of the bracelet—*its owner. You* have become that deity and no-one else can claim that title."

Then, cupping her chin within his hand, he gazed long into her wide attentive eyes, "…*and you* have the power to move mountains. Search within yourself and you will discover that power to not only save Fahimah, but also to save your friends."

His thumb traced the contour of her cheek and she numbly nodded in accordance, while her pulse raced from a body which screamed in protest at the massive amount of responsibility which had suddenly been placed upon her, and also from the amir's gentle touch. A distant gaze encompassed her face as she considered the information Rasheed had just conveyed to her, with the knowledge of the power she possessed at her mere summoning—mind-boggling.

Snapping from her foggy daze, she hastened along to keep pace with the prince, who in turning from her, had again pushed ahead.

A slight incline in the geography of the tunnel's floor compelled Rasheed to quicken his step, while his heartbeat increased along with his footing, placing him near to a run by the time he reached the casing of granite steps which ascended to a large door.

"Cherinne!" he motioned impatiently for her to hurry along while she was completely absorbed within the futile attempt to command the armband. "I believe we have reached the end of the tunnels."

As the earth quivered and shook, Rasheed presumed himself to be hearing the sounds of livestock, the gruntings and various snorts from within the Jabalis' drying nasal cavities which filtered into the desert atmosphere, drawing at the waterless air.

"I am your master. *Work!*" her voice lost its strength in the midst of the thunder overhead as pebbles and rocks severed from the ground's quaking solidity to plummet to the passage's base. "Holy crap!" the loosening of the earth around her startled her into shaken awareness and her eyes darted about the shifting tunnels to see the amir eagerly awaiting her. "Oh, thank God! The words slipped from her gaping mouth to be swallowed by the loud roar which echoed in a thunderous clamor above. "We're near the surface!"

Rasheed's shout of '*come on*' became that of a mere gust of unheard breeze as Cherinne, shifting her pack, engaged the incline and ascended the steps two at a time. Hastily grabbing her arm, he yanked her beneath the granite alcove as larger sections of earth crashed within feet behind her. Rolling his eyes, he wondered as to how she had made it this far.

Turning, Cherinne observed the intriguing etchings carved within the heavy wooden door before her. And tracing with the tips of her fingers, the intricately detailed hieroglyphics, she shuddered at their depicted message. Carved deep within the rugged door's grainy face was the image of a gruesome deployment of senseless slaughter being committed upon a man—or possibly god, by the looks of his attire and the crook and flail he was using to ward off the harrowing blows being thwarted against him.

"It is the God Osiris and his brother, Seth," Rasheed explained while running his hand over the deity's figure who was the aggressor. Seth's depiction was being portrayed as an immortal human with long unruly hair which was wild and likened to that of live serpents. "He is attempting to carve his brother's body into pieces."

Grimacing Cherinne asked, "Does he succeed?"

"Unfortunately, yes," the amir answered, negativism was heavy in his tone and his eyes met Cherinne's. "*And*, he is the one who has Fahimah."

"Oh my God, he looks like a monster."

Rasheed took her hand and slowly opened the massive door; it creaked and grinded upon its burdened hinges. "You don't know the half of it."

Hafiz observed as the remaining tails of Seth's dark cloak disappeared from sight with the lord en route for the surface. Wiping a bead of chilled agitated sweat from his forehead, he slowly turned the lock securing the master's chambers, while listening for the *click*, as the dead bolt released.

A number of oil lanterns adorned the quarters. Gently they flickered with a soft iridescent glow, casting shadows, bending and warping, upon the few elaborate pieces of furnishings set about the room. The scent of sweat and human secretion was thick upon the air—a tantalizing tang to the militant's senses. Hafiz inhaled deeply, feeding of its vigorous bouquet.

Glancing around nervously, with the risk of getting caught increasing the electric current of blood racing through his veins, he stepped ever so quietly within the room. His flesh crawled with the rancidity of the lord's aura which settled lightly as a fine mist upon his face; its condensed energy was smoldering to the touch. Hafiz drew the hood of his cloak.

He entered the silent chamber, its location separate from the rigorous activities of the outer realm and the lord's throne room where the congregation of vile, contemptible, blood thirsty men and beasts assembled to heed the will of their god. He silently closed the door and secured it behind him.

The aged wood, beneath his feet, creaked. Hearing a strange sound advancing from the outer hall, he thought someone was possibly approaching. Pausing briefly, he quietly drew his crossbow and licked the sweat which had beaded upon his upper lip. And crouching in a defensive stance, he watched the many shadows as they danced upon the dimly lit walls. Then, most certain he had been hearing things, he shouldered his weapon and made his way toward the bed where Fahimah lay in a semi-conscious state—her mind and body lost to that of another dimension. Her slight breathing drew forth in mild sporadic spurts and she moaned lightly beneath her breath, like that of a maimed animal that had been injured beyond repair, alone and awaiting death.

A malicious smile crossed Hafiz's face as he recalled the searing pain which had sent him crashing to the unyielding earth and the horrible depths below. For, he had once been that animal—weak and severely injured, awaiting his demise. I will enjoy this immensely; the thought stirred within his sadistic mind and loins. And, even if what he planned, killed her, the lord had already had his fill and would just assume it had been his own brutality.

Hafiz slowly removed his crossbow and cloak; anticipation at revenge surged like wildfire throughout his tense swarthy flesh. Yearning through dark, impassive voided eyes, he reached an eager hand toward the coverlet, while bending to Fahimah's ear and whispering, "I have come for you Princess; it is time for me to collect."

CHAPTER 33

The powder blue sky rapidly turned to azure then dark gray as a massive collage of vicious thunderclouds rolled as a steam engine across the desert sky. Flames of white lightening grabbed as electrified fingers at the men and ground below. Gulzar glanced upward, while his disturbing perception as to what was to come next, caused his musty self to perspire in anxiety. The Lord Seth, after thousands of years, was rising to the surface.

Drawing a breath within the hair-encrusted openings of his sinus cavities, he smelled the odor of fetid flesh which was rankly infesting the stirring air. The stench sent a tingling through his senses and into his brain. "Nephthys, has come," he exhaled through thick bulbous lips which looked as if to be smiling, their appearance never changed, even while being reprimanded or tearing at a succulent Achilles tendon.

His view shifted to the few meager men settled restlessly across the dunes; their mounts danced anxiously in an unruly ballet where the music had suddenly lost its rhythm and the sound screeched across one's paining eardrums. The scent of terrified sweat was pungent, like a roving fog it drifted along the dimming sky; its sweet aroma caused his stomach to growl while an awaiting meal was tantalizing. He smiled.

Suddenly, the blanket of sand advanced then receded and Gulzar shifted his footing along with the thousands of other Jabali who endeavored to keep their massive bodies upright as the earth unexpectedly quivered and split.

"Hold steady, men!" the commander bellowed, as his booming voice was swallowed, by the ear-splitting, screaming and tearing of the cracking earth. The white terrain suddenly collapsed, drawing a small portion of the darkened horizon within its belly. Jabali beasts teetered upon their wobbly feet and roared in a thunderous din then plummeted headlong into the huge gaping breach.

"Blast it!" Gulzar growled, as the unnecessary loss of his men was infuriating. Irately, he spun about to suddenly see an enormous ogre-like beast exploding from within the earth's crust and sending a torrent of grainy sand raining upon his men. It was an immense creature, heinous in character and appearance, with a large obtrusive head fashioned with huge jutting horns and eyes that blazed yellow with fire. Its massive size was comparable to that of eight Jabali.

A large bloodied iron ring secured within the beast's puffing snout, attached to a long heavy-linked chain, controlled the creature and its combating will. Its muzzle dripped readily with a mixture of secretion and blood as it snorted in protest and its jaws opened to release a hair-raising roar. It was a vile, wicked beast from the sheer pits of hell, and Seth controlled it effortlessly, like an adult with a child's toy.

The smog of the lord's crimson-gold aura flowed about him in a wispy furling haze and his wine-colored cloak snapped as a hung sheet upon a stirring summer's wind. While his locks of flaming hair screamed about him in a frenzied lust and his gleaming azure eyes were set, as he heatedly searched the open terrain for the one he referred to as wife. Finally spying her amidst the assemblage of humans, he wickedly snickered to himself. And, seeing she had chosen to reveal herself, not as her normally exquisite person, but as the squalid creature she now was, he grinned.

"*Oh, this is rich.*"

Circling the vicinity, he scowled at the hundreds of Jabali that were falling heedlessly into the giant fissure and being swallowed within the hungry sand pit, consumed by the earth as bone meal. Pursing his lips, Seth drew upon the parched hot air surrounding him and forcibly blew a massive tidal-force wind from deep within his celestial being. The shifting ground, gorging upon sand and howling creatures, abruptly halted its ravaging and immediately heeded its master's call.

"Very good. Now for the wench."

The LaHm, squealing in a high-pitched scream, tore free of Nephthys's paltry skin in a hastened frenzy to assault the few men upon their mounts who warily stood their ground. Rapidly brandishing their weapons, they swung wildly in an attempt to ward off the attacking slime-like organisms which rushed at lightening speed to blanket their faces.

"NEEEPPPHHHTTTTHHHYYYSSS!!!" the sound of the goddess's name billowed in a thunderous roar across the entirety of the arid land sending it warping and bending in a tumultuous rumble. "I have come to defeat you—you worthless *whore!*"

"*Aaarrgghh!*" Nephthys angrily spun about, an irate scowl worming along her graying forehead, as she glanced confusedly from Laddor to the detestable god. Flames of hatred blazed in her flashing eyes, and turning, she contemptuously stared up at the depraved deity. "*Ssseeetthhh!!* You loathsome coward—I shall rip your manhood from you and feed it to the fish of the Nile!"

The lord's crackling guffaw sent an enraged chill racing down her spiny back. "So, this is personal—oh, mere bedwench. I had forgotten that our brother, Osiris had unfortunately lost *his* to the fish." His heinous laughter filled the whole of the darkened sky.

Deverall exchanged a queer glance with Laddor. "What the hell's goin' on?"

"I don't know—but I don't like it," Laddor grabbed the reins of Nakia as she, entangled in her gear, stumbled to her feet. "*Whoa*, Nakia—it's okay girl." He turned again to Deverall and his tone was solemn. "He's the one who took Cherinne."

The whole of the underground sanctuary was pungent with the stench of blood and death. Yet a sickening sweet smell, tangy to the senses filled Rasheed and Cherinne's nostrils as they had entered the sovereign's underground domain.

"Oh my god! What is that?" Cherinne gasped at the sight of the humungous serpent lying as stone upon Seth's throne room floor. Its scales faintly shimmered iridescent in the dusky lighting of the few torches nearly burned down to the stalk joints, and the large vertical yellow eyes flashed with the appearance of still being alive. Cherinne hastily grabbed Rasheed's arm as a troubled feeling had immediately settled upon her chilling skin.

"That was the evil serpent, Apophis, who was also defeated by Seth," Rasheed lowly whispered.

A number of perverted granite figurines eerily stared through voided sightless gaps of stone. They seemed to watch and observe while the two made their way cautiously through the main corridor of the evil god's lair. Their distorted forms cast an uncanny array of darkened shadows along the cavernous walls and Cherinne cowered at their benevolent gaze. She readily kept pace with the amir as they quietly exited the main hall.

She glanced at the prince, whose face was exhibiting that of a troubled expression; while fear for the princess was evident in the glassiness of his eyes. "Rasheed..." she stared back at the giant beast displayed as a prize upon the cavern floor, "...I will do my best."

"I know," he touched her arm. "So, listen closely for any sign of the princess; if my calculations are correct, that last tremor was the lord rising to the surface. For, if he were *here*, there is no way we would have gotten this far."

Cherinne nodded, "Yes, I have heard him on the surface shouting to someone named Nephthys." Suddenly she paused and placed her finger to her lips, "*Ssshh,* I hear something." And perking her ears toward a chamber door exiting away from the main throne room, she motioned with a shaky hand, "They're in there."

"Who?"

Cherinne began to tremble and her face rapidly turned ashen. "I think it is Fahimah...and Hafiz."

"*Nnnooo!!*" Fahimah cried frantically into the gloved hand which firmly covered her mouth, while her energy was spent and her painfully abused body struggled in a frantic desperation to escape. Hafiz's intensity mounted at the unexpected resistance she was putting forth, while the lord had placed her temporarily in a near comatose state to extinguish her hostility.

Suddenly, he yanked her naked body from the bed and roughly slammed her to the cold hard floor. Her head exploded in pain from the harsh, abrupt contact, while the cracking of her achy skull sounded loudly in her throbbing ears.

"Now you will know, Princess, what it is like to enter the very pits of hell," Hafiz sneered vehemently.

"*No!*" Fahimah breathed between labored breaths, her head whirling in a sickening monotone thrum. The flickering lights of the lanterns cast a multitude of dimly lit shadows before her motionless eyes, while their glistening kaleidoscopic sparkle was gone and had been replaced with a dull lifelessness. Enveloped in the searing pain which rushed from the side of her head to the pit of her boiling fetal-bearing stomach, Fahimah retched.

"*Ugghh!* You rotting pig!"

The tip of his boot shoved her away from the spew of bile and he angrily yanked the jumbled sheet from the bed and crossly tossed it over her.

"What is the problem with you?" He turned, repulsed at the sight of her continued vomiting; the odor was foul and disgusting. "You are not consumed with fever and yet you have heaved before me in the past." Abruptly spinning, he eyed her suspiciously in the low light, as the oil lantern's flames wavered upon her pale drawn features.

Realization at her condition suddenly dawning upon him, he bent to a knee and removed a dirk from within its calf sheath. Using its tip to remove, from her panting body, the satiny black sheet which slid along the sharp gleaming blade, he gauged the look upon her drained pale face. Fahimah trembled and clutched her stomach while laying in a fetal position—not a princess of royalty now, but a frail female who aimed to protect what was slowly growing inside her.

Curiously, his devious mind grasped the notion of seizing the only thing from her possession which would bring her dire remorse and severe unrepressed pain and eventually her death. The thought was intriguing. And, while she would scream in unbearable pain, he would swallow the piercing cries within his gaping mouth, absorbing her weeping, panting breath within him. He needed some rope.

Rapidly glancing around the darkened room, he noticed the golden braided sashes, securing the ebony sheers back at each corner post of the oversized bed.

Perfect.

Hastily retrieving each one while keeping an eye to Fahimah who lay dazed and nearly unconscious, he returned to her side. Securing his dirk between his teeth, he speedily bound her arms and legs, then removed the knife and swiftly swiped it along his pant leg.

"Princess…" he fastened the final knot as she lay defenselessly on her side. Running the tip of the gleaming blade along her small nearly flat stomach, his gaze narrowed and he stated suspiciously, "…you do not look to be with brat." She gasped at the slight poke of the blade within her skin; her heart pounded fiercely and her eyes flashed with renewed horror. For, while she had been ravaged upon by the Lord Seth and her spirit to live torn from her very soul, she had managed to hold onto the one thing that had bonded her to the prince—their unborn child. Frantically, she searched her muddled mind for any escape.

"Seth will destroy you if you kill me." It was a murmur in desperation, "…especially if I am carved open."

His grin was malicious. "Oh, I do not plan on scarring your lovely skin *or* killing you right away. Ya see—Seth has appointed me guard over you and this room while he is busy tending to another wench." He slipped the blade between her trembling legs and the stare of his white-less eyes observed the terror upon her face. "I plan on making you suffer immensely, like you did me, Princess. So prepare yourself, for this is really going to hurt."

Rasheed listened with his ear, at the heavy wooden door, to the muffled cries of Fahimah. The fear so pungent upon his senses, he could taste of its rancidity. "What is going on in there?" He hastily grabbed Cherinne urging her to listen. "Can you tell how many people are in there?"

Trembling, she pressed her ear to the door, the sickening cries of her sister drawing nausea to her throat. "I think it's two," she replied through quavering lips. "Rasheed…" her eyes were wide with terror, "…something terrible is happening! Hurry and help her!"

Quietly drawing his blade he back stepped several paces, then charged full-force to shoulder the massive doors. The contact sent them creaking upon their hinges and crashing to the adjacent walls.

His mind could never have prepared him for the horrific scene he observed, as the doors swiftly cracked open, and he adjusted his eyes to the dim quarter's lighting. In the few lanterns' remaining glow, he could see Hafiz atop Fahimah. A dripping bloody blade was held before his engrossed sadistic eyes, with an oozing puddle of crimson blood spreading quickly upon the grainy lines of the wooden floor and easily slipping between the cracks.

An image of Princess Adiva, Rasheed's mother, briefly entered his pitching mind and his sword, drawn and ready, suddenly felt as an immense weight within his shaking hands. The scent of fresh blood was thick upon his nostrils—nearly suffocating—along with the evil presence of the lord's remaining aura which had settled itself along the air.

"*Great Gods!*" he barely whispered from a choked throat as his head spun and terror rose from his roiling stomach to his burning cheeks. Fahimah's eyes now flashed, not in their luster of shimmering color of blues and greens and various colors of the earth, but in a demented shock of agonizing pain and horror, as her body shook in an uncontrollable spasm. Her wild gaze briefly met Rasheed's, unaware as to whom he was, and her teary eyes suddenly closed.

An icy shiver rushed through Rasheed's body to the souls of his frozen feet and a sickening feeling raced upon his sweated skin.

"*Fahimah!*" The echo of Cherinne's shrill scream resonated within his pulsing ears, abruptly rousing him from his inert state into one of exasperated action.

"*YOU BBAASSTTAARRDD!!*" Severing the clutches of foreboding shock, he heatedly rushed upon Hafiz with the hilt of his blade clutched firmly within the tight grip of his shaking hands. "*I WILL KILL YOU!!!*"

Hafiz rapidly raced to retrieve his crossbow, then rolled with precise ease to obscure himself behind the velvety chaise, while his heart quickened with anticipation as he drew the first bolt—two on reserve. And, while his weapon had been forged for the use of three, he generally preferred the precision of one. Placing his itchy finger on the trigger, he would restrain himself and use them wisely.

Rasheed's fiery blade crashed down upon the cushioned furnishing sending plumes of white stuffing, like cotton-candy bursting into the air. A cold callous guffaw escaped the mind-twisted militant with his realization as to who had interrupted his sexually sadistic entertainment. The amir.

"Amir Tarun," Hafiz's silty voice rose from the darkened shadows, his sneer was mocking. "I see you have come for your princess. Well, as you can see, she is now no longer carrying that of your loins…"

"*Uuuggghhhh!!*" Rasheed manipulated his steel as an incensed mad man and sent it careening through the thick air in a high screaming arc, while the words of Fahimah's aggressor were making him sick.

The lounger cracked and split bringing Hafiz tumbling from behind its protection and swiftly kneeling in a darkened corner to fire off his first shot. At the speed of light, the bolt discharged sending Rasheed hastily diving from its path and landing upon the darkening puddle of Fahimah's blood. It smeared like oil upon the sweated skin of his heaving chest. Fire burned as ice in Rasheed's eyes, and immediately rising to his feet and touching the sticky remnants of his unborn child, he released a bone-chilling cry and charged toward Hafiz.

Hafiz narrowed his gaze while his lifeless eyes gauged the amir's movements. Rapidly, he slipped in another bolted arrow as his heartless ranting was quickly silenced by Rasheed's intense ferocity.

Scaling the smashed chaise, Rasheed sailed through the heated air while its electrifying energy gave him strength he was unaware he even possessed. With his sword extended before him, he feverishly bounded upon Hafiz and plunged the sharpened blade deep within the fiendish villian's shoulder. The rush of searing pain threw the howling militant off-balance and sent the discharged bolt screaming haphazardly through the air while he grasped at his seeping injury. Irately, Hafiz then sent a booted heel smashing into Rasheed's unsuspecting jaw. Then quickly scurrying to his feet he fled, dashing toward the open doors.

White hot pain raced from Rasheed's temple to the iron bands of his snapping neck. "*Arrgghh!*" He immediately shook his head to clear his mind and raced after Hafiz.

A cold chill rippled along Cherinne's skin. And trembling violently, she hastened to Fahimah while remorse and immense fear at her sister's condition brought a host of raspy sobs.

Fahimah's paled face, drained of all its natural vibrant color, was drawn and haggard. Her appearance was gauntly, possibly from the lack of nourishment and nutrients, which her body would have absorbed for her now aborted infant, *also* from the immense brutality her body had suffered.

Cherinne quickly wrapped Fahimah in the coverlet while the satin sheet had absorbed a large amount of the princess's blood. And dropping to her knees, she grabbed Fahimah's frail hand and rubbed it gently against the flow of uncontrollable tears she wept, which were accompanied by a spew of apologies.

Returning, Rasheed rapidly wiped the blood from his blade and sheathed his sword. Oblivious to the weakened state of his bruised body, he dropped to his shaking knees beside Fahimah, while fearing he would worsen her injuries if he were to touch her. His heart pained with an ache that was worse than any cut of a deadly blade. And, fighting back the sting of tears exploding in a flood of rage and pain behind his eyes, he gently gathered her damaged body within his arms.

"Cherinne..." he breathed the words through a heaving chest, "...hurry—search for her garment. Hopefully, the yarn will still be concealed within the inner lining, and it will aide in her healing; though..." he searched Fahimah's sallow face, "I do not believe there is anything to be done for the..." his eyes left the princess to settle on the dark stain of blood tracing the floor. The magnitude of the loss gripped him as a vice.

"*Rasheed...?*"

Cherinne scurried to her feet in the awareness that the amir was becoming absorbed within the horrific tragedy before his eyes. She prodded his arm.

"And what of Hafiz?"

"He got away," he exhaled, painfully averting his glance which then met Cherinne's.

"No, Rasheed...Hafiz will lay in wait."

His tone was unyielding, without recourse or falter, as he then stared into Fahimah's pallid face and inhaled deeply. "Then I shall kill him."

CHAPTER 34

The few golden rays of the obscured sun slowly emerged through the layer of gray opaque clouds then gradually disappeared into the desert's horizon. Arriving for a brief début, they cringed as Seth's gaze irately darted in their direction and transformed them to shriveling streams of red.

Nephthys threw her nose to the air, annoyed that the unmannered brute had actually done something she approved of. For while her barbarous condition forced her to obscure herself from the daylight's intense heat, her original lovely, majestically regal state had loved the sunshine, relishing in its warmth and presence each and every day. As she viewed the bruised-colored skin upon her arm, the brief expression of contentment upon her deteriorating face rapidly turned ugly. Narrowing her spiteful gaze, she glanced upward at the pompous oaf.

"Seth! Come down here—you *mangy parasite!*" Her ear-piercing icy scream sent Laddor, Deverall and the amir's men buckling in pain. They covered their ears from the shrill cries she shrieked forth from her dual-channeled throat while their terrified horses reared and struck at the very air before them in an attempt to extinguish the reverberating raw force. Nephthys's incessant fury toward her eternal husband had created mistrust and anger toward all men; except, of course, Osiris who she had cherished dearly. So now, they would all pay.

"Holy shit—Lady!" Deverall howled as he pressed his heavy hands to his aching ears and his mare danced wildly in determination to pitch him.

A hateful glare flashed the pilot's way as he suddenly cocked his pistol and aimed for her immense screaming orifice. "Shut the hell up or I'll shoot your ass—you stupid bit…"

A loud obnoxious laughter broke through the assemblage of chaos and Nephthys turned to see her bad-mannered husband, his angelic face alit with delight at her bothersome confrontation with the humans. Rage boiled as acidy liquid, flaring within her hateful eyes.

She immediately spun. "LaHm! Transform!" The infuriated goddess raced along the sand and suddenly dove beneath the desert's surface while the black oily elements of her fusty flesh rapidly turned from their attended targets and hastily slipped below the soil behind her.

"*What the hell?*" Deverall squalled as Nephthys disappeared from sight. A full moment passed. "Where'd she go?"

Lateef, settling his skittering mare barked, "Sergeant Omar…I want a full report as to what is occurring at the rear of my infantry! And do not hesitate to shoot *anything* that *resembles* a threat!"

Grunting in assent, Omar spurred his horse, circled the men and headed toward the rear of the brigade. He briefly observed his brother, Mahir; anxiety seeped from behind an unwavering façade while his resolve to remain steadfast was failing miserably.

Mahir gripped his weapon tightly.

The thunderous steps of the moving Jabali had nearly reached their doorstep and the men held steady to heed their commander's signal. And, with the sickening sensation of death heavy in their hearts, they knew they could not survive this massive attack.

Before dispatching the signal to engage, Lateef spun to momentarily take one last look at his men, their faces were drawn and impassive; the stench of terror leaked from their very pores. His gaze was then abruptly gripped by the raining hailstorm of screaming arrows released in their direction.

"Laugh at me—*will he!*" Nephthys snarled contemptuously as she blazed her way through the gray layers of sand just below the white surface. The secondary levels remained cool and unbleached by the searing rays of the vicious desert sun.

"*LaHm! Transform!*"

Eagerly, she mounted the oily creatures as they slithered obediently beneath her slender form, her fingertips thrumming at the direct impingement of her own putrid flesh while she sank her fingers deep within the coal black slimy membrane. A reverberating squeal prickled along her pulsating skin, as the LaHm altered to the desired figure of her vengeful mind, casting a wicked smile along her parted red lips. She shrieked out another command. "*Make haste—Great Beast*; for, I have rancid blood that needs to be drawn!"

Racing at breakneck speed she suddenly blasted from within the earth's surface which sent a torrent of sand atop Lateef and his men. Resolute determination to bring death upon that of her awaiting brother cursed through every fiber of her celestial being.

"*IINNCCOOMMIINNGG!!!*" The commander bellowed, aware there was no escape for his men who struggled relentlessly upon their nervous steeds. Chaos at the abrupt attack sent both men and horses into an exasperated frenzy.

Suddenly, Nephthys exploded from beneath the layer of heated terrain with the black gelatinous figures now transformed into that of living creature, which were exaggeratedly contrary to that of their normal form. Nephthys sat atop the great fawn-colored beast, unlike that of her depraved iniquitous husband's mount which was grotesque and obnoxious, dark and unruly. The LaHm, now fashioned into an imperial picturesque beauty, a qateefa—part mammal, part fowl—blasted into the arid air. Haughty conceit was prominent upon their newly-formed highly majestic head fashioned with a lovely coronet that impressively adorned flashing emeralds, topazes and garnets. It was a scintillating dazzle of radiance.

The creature's resemblance was likened to that of an Arab charger. Immense, snow-white angelic wings, encrusted with flecks of crystalline gems, carried it skyward, while the faintest twinkle of the many miniscule jewels imbedded in the beast's fine taupe fur, shone brilliantly. The previously hideous, mouthless LaHm—now distinct in their own renowned glory—were lovely beyond compare, a fraction of Nephthys inner-self which had remained unscathed by the warping, torturous pit where Seth had concealed her to rot.

The creature's wide emerald-colored eyes scanned the terrain below as they ascended toward the desert sky. Nephthys spied the barrage of bolted arrows aimed in her direction and the assemblage of Jabali now moving as a massive freight train along the horizon.

"GGUULLZZAARR!!! You worthless swine! Shoot at me, *will you!"* She abruptly spun, spread her decaying arms wide, and again screamed from the dual channels of her fusty throat, *"LaHm Aaeeggüss!"*

The shriek ripped from her open orifice along with the remaining worm-like sectors of slime which rushed from the pores of her decomposing flesh. An ear-splitting screech cut through the air, as the gigantic mass of black oily membrane, shot through the stock-still sky and formed an immense shield. Enveloping the majority of the fiery arrows, the LaHm then landed atop the few hundred Jabali compiling the front lines of Seth's forces.

A grin spread Nephthys's red lips, as she slightly fatigued from the extreme usage of her inner carcass, observed the collection of exasperated Jabali beasts as they stumbled and staggered about in desperation to rid themselves of the suffocating gunk. Using their clawed hands, they tore at the blanket of sanguine-black glop covering that of their large nozzled snouts; their efforts were futile.

"Ggggrrrrrrrrr!!" You slimy wench!" Gulzar shook his huge fist at the sneering goddess as he pounded heavily along the quavering terrain in a solid run with sweat drawing readily upon his fleeced brow. Surrounded by his remaining vast force, he charged onward toward the amir's regiment; while the thunderous hammering of hooves pounded loudly in his ears. "We will ingest *you and* the humans!"

Seth irately spurred his enormous beast. It tossed its giant head angrily while fire blazed from its red demonic eyes as he steered it in the direction of his menacing wife.

The obsessed god spread his curled lips paper thin and opened them to the entirety of his angelic face, from hairline to chin like that of an expanding elastic band. And, drawing in the parched desert air, compared to that of an enormous vacuum, he inhaled deep. The colossal suction swallowed a massive quantity of bone-dry atmosphere, till he had absorbed his fill within his enlarging chest.

Abruptly turning toward his despised wife, he exhaled sending a violent rush of tornadic wind swiftly racing through the upheaval of scarlet sky. It delivered a slashing torrent of cutting gritty sand, likened to that of an explosion of glass fragments—a khasmin.

"*LaHm!!*" Nephthys shouted as she hastily drove her baying beast, the qateefa, away from the surging storm of wind and sand that raged as a massive wall behind her.

"*TAKE COVER!!*" Lateef bellowed as he turned his mare and spurred her in the direction of Nephthys as she raced through the sky above him. With a shaking hand, he speedily secured the yashmac across his sweated face and glanced to observe Mahir whose face portrayed that of steadfast alarm. The soldier rapidly shouldered his weapon, affixed his shroud and followed suit. For a brief second, the commander wondered as to the young boy Ib's whereabouts, as he urged his horse forward while waving his men away from the swelling gale.

The single man, who had been commissioned the post of manning the Dragon, scurried behind the weapon in an attempt to shield himself from the oncoming onslaught of raging earth and atmosphere.

"*Let's go!!*" Lateef extended a hand to the Egyptian soldier and swiftly yanked him to his dancing horse. The commander's heart pounded wildly within his chest and fright ran from the nerves of his outstretched arm into his fingers. Men and mounts scurried in a harried turmoil and sweat poured cold from beneath Lateef's constricting uniform. Attempting to observe his battalion through the uprising dust being skirted into the statically charged air by the horse's hooves, he heeled his horse to run.

"*Holy shit!!* Did you just see what that lunatic did?" Deverall crowed as he fervently kicked his chestnut gelding. "I've only ever seen crap like that on T.V.!"

Laddor rolled his eyes; then for a split second, observed the wide frightened stare of Ib who was seated on the back of Deverall's mount.

He spurred Nakia. *"Come on, Deverall—let's move!!"*

"ItHarrak barra!! ItHarrak barra!!" Omar's baritone voice boomed in a struggle to override the reverberating sound of the blasting winds and sand. And, though his dislike for the Americans had been instilled within him from a child, he nodded in accord at Laddor and Deverall, in appreciation for their assisting the Egyptian boy.

With a quick return of the gesture, Laddor swiftly urged his mare away from the wall of sand which was rapidly raging in their direction. He smiled onerily. "Hey, Deverall..." he shouted over his shoulder, "...ya' think he likes us now?"

"Who?"

Laddor pulled the scarf, dampened with sweat, about his face, his words were slightly muffled. "That big Egyptian sergeant—his younger brother, Mahir's, the one who kicked my ass...I'd like to return the favor to the *little bastard* someday."

Despite the circumstances, Deverall chuckled and Laddor threw him a nasty glance. "What's so funny?"

"You," he retorted in a shout, then continued with a wide awry grin. "Here we are in the middle of a bloody war with a sandstorm pounding down upon us, and two insane deities who are trying to not only kill *us* but each other, and all you can think about is kicking some poor Egyptian's *ass!*...Sweetheart definitely needs to straighten you out." Deverall pushed his gelding onward, following the path of the withdrawing sergeant.

"Com'on, Red—you can kick ass later."

CHAPTER 35

Cherinne frantically searched the dimly lit room, while her chest ached miserably at the unnecessary loss and she needed desperately to cry. Trembling, her mind galloped in several directions while a cold shiver rushed upon her skin, as the thoughts of what had just recently transpired within this eerie room, drew nausea to her stomach. *Oh sweet God!* Her eyes fleetingly glanced the bracelet as it caught the minute flickers of lighting that glimmered from the lit lanterns about the darkened room. Sorrow rapidly turned to anger at her inability to control the armband's divine power and she grumbled aloud.

"What is it?" Rasheed questioned, averting his gaze from Fahimah, whose pulse was slowly diminishing to nothingness. "You need to hurry; her condition is failing."

Cherinne scurried about within the shadows then checked the large clothes closet. Quickly shuffling through the silken shirts and other apparel, she drew a much needed breath. Seth's vile aura was soaked within each and every article of clothing's fiber, and she cringed at the energy's revolting vibe. Searching the single shelf above, she found a white garment folded and pressed, as if it had been carefully laundered. The remnant of Semus yarn lightly thrummed within the inner fold; she was certain it to be Fahimah's.

"I found it!"

With a wrinkled forehead, she returned to the prince and the princess. Fahimah's drawn face was paled to the color of milk and her shallow breathing was sparse and irregular.

"What is the matter?"

"I don't know," Cherinne stated opening the refreshed garment, wondering as to why such a depraved, wicked god would decide to keep the garment *and* even have it laundered. Maybe he knew it contained a fragment of the jewels, she thought, or maybe he was just planning to keep the princess like 'a pet', to use or caress when the desire so arose—the Beast. The thought caused her to feel quite ill.

Gently taking Fahimah's arm, she snapped, "Turn your head."

"What?"

Locking large coffee eyes with the prince's dark stare, she stated again, slightly gentler this time, "*Please*, turn your head."

Rasheed rolled his eyes. "It is not as though I have not seen her unclothed before."

"Yes," she snorted, "but you are not *married.*"

"*What?*" His forehead wrinkled as he reproachfully averted his gaze.

Removing the coverlet and placing Fahimah's arm through a sleeve, she retorted, "From now on, no more peeking without commitment. Besides—you have wives for that sort of thing and from what I understand—Fahimah *is not* one of them. And, since *I'm* her sister, I need to start looking out for her best interest."

"And, you are insinuating that I do not have *my Fahimah's* best interest at heart?"

Cherinne finished dressing the princess in the simple garment, the one she wore the day they had been abducted in the palace gardens. "I'm sure you do, Amir; but what I don't understand is why *she* is not one of those wives—*which is called bigamy in my country*—and why *she* had *not* been given the bracelet. "…I'm finished."

"With what—your lecture or your dressing?"

Cherinne met his gaze. "Both."

The reverberation of rousing earth was suddenly loud within Cherinne's ears, mixing with the march of beast moving more swiftly over the shifting terrain. "What is that?" She listened closer. "It sounds like heavy rain."

Rasheed viewed the shadowy ceiling above them, his brows creasing at the familiarity of the massive hum. "It sounds to be that of a khamsin—a sandstorm. I need to get to my men; I am sure they are in need of my assistance. But, more important, we need to leave this place and get Fahimah to the physician."

Fahimah moaned lowly as her pulse increased and her eyes fluttered lightly; she stirred within Rasheed's arms, and the sense of her closeness was a mild comfort to the amir's aching heart. Brushing his lips along her pale cheek, he gently gave her a squeeze. Then, turning to Cherinne, he motioned with a nod of his head.

"Come—"

The sound of Nagid's footfalls, running along the graveled tunnel floor of the Haush Min Maut, resonated within his ears along with the steady breathing escaping his enormous chest. Biting back the many curses which spewed forth from his seething mind, he continued through the dimly lit passage in pursuit of the one who had invaded the lord's realm. While he, in truth, craved the heat of battle, the itch of annihilation which burned as fire through his throbbing veins. He gripped the hefty weapon—the swaheel—his armament of choice which had been customized for his own utilization. The hilt, seven feet in length was thick, substantial in his huge fisted hand. It melded into a three foot slightly curved tree-splitting blade fashioned with carbon steel razor sharp teeth. He rapidly spun the weapon within his long, thick fingers then angrily struck the tunnel wall sending dust, granite and sandstone crashing to the passage floor.

"*Meddlesome humans!*" He snarled through coiled lips. "I will kill the whole lot!"

The tunnel split as a crow's foot and he decided quickly to continue straight, toward the deepest dungeons where prisoners had been housed and left to rot. The stench of human waste and death was thick within his expanding nostrils, and covering his shrouded nose and mouth with his free hand, he continued onward. The sting of rancidity was burning to his leering eyes; and passing the open cells, he tossed a sidelong glance toward the grotesque remains of several human bodies. Maggots heavily coated the lingering corpses, while white hair grew persistently in a straggle upon the bony skulls and the carcass's nails curled near to that of fishhooks.

Increasing his step, Nagid swallowed the knot of bile rising in his throat and released another faction of curses aimed at the rotting skeletons; then turning westward, he concentrated his anger toward the intruder and the humans above.

His route encompassed the entirety of the eastern sector of the Haush Min Maut; and, with no a trace of the intruder, he was rapidly tiring of this insignificant task. He changed course and headed in the direction of the lord's throne room contemplating his accountancy to Seth and the repercussions of his failure to locate the interloper. Grunting, he pursued his destination while his renowned skills as a battle-ready warrior were being squandered, misspent on searching for those who could hardly do any damage to the royal reign from down here.

Suddenly, he paused; his heart pounded loudly in his perked ears. Holding his breath, he quickly crouched within the shadows while spying Hafiz, just beyond the next bend, hunkered down, with crossbow in position. Nagid could also see that Hafiz was injured.

Sweat poured from Nagid's sweaty brow; and removing the coverlet, he swiped a rock-hard arm across his face. He surveyed the situation.

Suddenly, the Egyptian male, who he remembered to be the prince of the regime where they had attacked and taken the two females, appeared within his sight. In his arms was the princess, who he himself had retrieved from the tunnels and presented to the Lord Seth along with the mystical anklets. Through slitted yellow eyes, Nagid continued to observe as the American girl also appeared. Exiting the passage they were leaving a section of the lord's quarters. Frowning, he gripped his swaheel in a tight fisted anger; while the thought of receiving another humiliating series of blows from his master, for these three miscreants, was enraging.

Hafiz, sensing his comrade's presence, abruptly turned. And seeing the giant lying in wait, he motioned in the trio's direction. Nagid acknowledged with a nod of ascension and moved into position.

Rasheed stayed to the shadows while anxiety flowed thick, like molten lead, choking at his pulsing veins. Carefully observing the area just outside the throne room, he whispered to Cherinne, "Come—the coast is clear."

"Rasheed—I have a bad feeling about this; and I can hear breathing."
His brow wrinkled, "Over the noise above?"

"Yes," she whispered close to his neck while she trembled and clung to his arm. "There are two of them—one is Hafiz. I can tell by his irregular spurts of breath due to his injury. And the other, I believe, is…the giant."

"And, how do you know this?"

Her worried eyes filled with insurmountable fear. "He has a slight hiss to his breathing, like he has swallowed gravel. Rasheed…please…he tried to force me…"

"Sshh," his eyes conveyed kindness. "I understand." His mind raced in several directions while he contemplated the best course of action. "It is an ambush. We need to find another way out of here—any suggestions?"

She grinned warily, anxiety heavy in her voice, "only one—the bracelet. It shoots me skyward when it activates. Other than that, I don't know how to get to the surface unless one of the tunnels leads that way."

He sighed deeply. "Well—since you are unable to activate the armband, then we must choose the later of the two options."

A cold chill suddenly raced along Cherinne's skin as Hafiz's silty voice, abruptly cutting through the passageway, eerily drifted along the walls and dark, seemingly endless, ceiling above them.

"Amir—surely you do not believe that you will leave here with what is now the Lord Seth's possession. That female you now hold within your person belongs to the lord; and he will not look kindly upon your actions. In fact he will slaughter you."

Rasheed observed Fahimah's paled face, then glanced at Cherinne.

"And as for that American girl, her identical who bears the bracelet, she is as open game, while the lord possesses the anklets of the princess. She may be had by anyone." Hafiz paused and the silence was pungent.

"…Unless, of course, you wish to…*exchange*? Regardless of which you choose to leave behind—one must remain for the lord's pleasure."

"*No!*" The word spewed forth from Cherinne's lips in a low whisper as her frightened stare darted to Rasheed. Her body stiffened at the mere thought of remaining behind; her trembling worsened.

Rasheed searched his racing mind, like pages being rapidly shuffled through a book.

"No!" He shouted determinedly. "Your Lord Seth shall have *neither!*"

Nagid motioned with an outstretched hand for Hafiz to remain in position. Holding steady to his swaheel he kept to the wall within the outlining shadows and crept along closer to the three, nearly the length of his large weapon away.

"Oh—but I beg to differ. See—the lord has taken the princess's body and mind…" Hafiz's tone reeked with self-satisfaction and a smug grin wormed its way along his swarthy features, as he attempted to rid the amir of his sanity, "…then *I*, carefully removed her spirit." His empty eyes slightly sparked with life and he continued. "The sweet scent of her blood still mingles with that of my dirk's blade."

The malevolent words, the cold malicious militant so eagerly spewed, tore at Rasheed's very soul. He shook his head in the attempts to clear the horrific scenes weighing upon his fraying wits while a picture of his grandfather briefly entered his mind. Drawing a deep breath, he momentarily closed his eyes to block the icy words and concentrate on escaping with their lives.

The giant's hissing breath suddenly scratched within Cherinne's ears. "*Get down!*" she cried with the realization it was too late and he was upon them.

The massive weapon's blade immediately crashed in a thunderous explosion just above her trembling body, sending rock exploding in a cloud of dust and rubble and she and Rasheed scattering from the burst of flying sandstone and granite. Her ears resonated with a ringing aching throb and the taste of ash was thick within her throat. Choking on the plumes of rising soot, she staggered disoriented on her quavering legs out into the open. And, attempting to blink back her distorted vision, she stumbled unknowingly within Hafiz's view.

Hafiz licked his lips, while his throbbing gloved finger itched dreadfully upon the trigger of the crossbow, yearning for revenge. And, observing a flash of clothing through the uprising dust and rubble, he gently squeezed the cold metal of the weapon's trigger, taking his last shot.

The feathered shaft sprung from its cradle and raced through the cloud of dust enveloped air. And, with a sickening thud, the whirring bolt struck Cherinne deep within the chest.

The force of the loosened arrow drove her body backward; and, in shock, she stumbled about awkwardly in the chaos of the cavern. Numbness clouded her mind and she was unaware she had even been hit. Suddenly, becoming engulfed in the throes of excruciating pain, she staggered forward and plummeted to the rough hard surface. The tearing of her muscle and flesh was agonizing, while she gasped for anguished spurts of air and placed a shaking hand to her burning heart. Red quickly seeped the black of her garment and the touch was warm to her trembling fingers. It pained her to draw a breath.

The armband thrummed steadily upon Cherinne's wrist, voicelessly beckoning to her in the haze of her muddled mind, coinciding with the rhythm of her racing heart. Quietly she listened to its extraordinary sound while blocking out the shout of her name and the noise about her. And, as her heart gradually began to slow and she closed her glazed eyes, she succumbed to the increasing darkness. Tears burned along her cool cheeks, while her pulse, like a drying tributary's flow, suddenly ceased.

"*LaHm aaaaeeeeggggiiissss!!!*" Nephthys blared the command through her dual throat as she anxiously raced before the blast of cutting sand. Rage smoldered in her blazing charcoal eyes, while her dark, slithery sectors of slime rapidly rushed from the several hundred exterminated Jabali to coagulate in the form of another shield. They screeched in a heightened wrath of tempered fury attempting to hold steady while Seth's enlarged orifice continued to discharge the tornadic coil of air—an obliterating wall of earth and current. It crashed headlong into the squealing screen of worm-like creatures, driving the massive pliable shield across the twisting terrain.

Nephthys's worn body suddenly slumped upon the qateefa and she layed her haggard cheek along the curvature of the great beast's neck; as her decaying cadaver, weakening at the immense amount of energy being utilized, needed the power of the bracelet. Listening to the resonating of the beast's steady heart matching that of her own, and the sound of the raging wind surging upon her flesh, she refused to be beaten. A resolute whisper of determination rushed through her clenched teeth. "Seth…you will not defeat me…Brother." And, urging the snorting qateefa onward, she swooped in low, just above the Jabali army. Her dark gaze locked with Gulzars.

Gulzar observed Nephthys from below as he continued his thunderous trek toward the humans. While the large swine-like beasts, swarming about him in droves, moved along the dunes of arid land, grunting and snarling, releasing a thunderous roar.

Spying a single Jabali roving dopily along the vibrating terrain, brain damaged by the loss of oxygen inflicted by the LaHm, Nephthys dove in his direction and stripped him of the long leather bullwhip attached to his side. Haphazardly, he swiped at the thieving goddess then clumsily plunged snout first to the rumbling ground.

Nephthys wrinkled her nose at the agonizing grunting of the beast as the surrounding Jabali, heedlessly continuing their callous flight, crushed the unfortunate monster beneath their two-horned feet. The aroma of spilled, fresh blood was a bouquet, heightening the bestialized senses of the flanking creatures. Immediately, an orgy of feasting ensued, while the howling beast was abruptly torn to pieces and devoured as the army continued on its way.

"Revolting," she scoffed, heeling the qateefa with crusty bare feet and turning in the direction of her dastardly husband, while the warm desert wind burned at the corner of each drying eye.

"Nephthys…you big butted trollop!" Seth sneered with a sidelong glance as he spurred his snorting beast away from her, while the sandstorm could wait, with him loving the heated sensation of a riveting chase. "You never were good for anything, so I shall feed you to my swine as pig fodder!"

"*SSSSEEETTTTHHHHHH!!!* *Come here!* Or are you also suffering from premature *phallocrypsis,* like that of your manhood?"

His haughty demeanor suddenly twisted black, as the game had now abruptly ended. "How dare you defame me…*you cow!*"

Deverall's brows entwined in marked confusion, as he watched from below. "What the hell does that mean—phallo…crypsis? Is she *tryin'* to piss that lunatic off?"

Bullwhip coiled in hand, Nephthys steered in the direction of Seth's riotous beast. Her eyes blazed with blistering fire as she suddenly whipped the snapping cowhide, sending it snaking along the sizzling air. The sleek leather cracked and popped, eagerly lashing at the raging god, and catching him along the swell of his cheek.

"*You bitch!*" He speedily grabbed at the flicking scourge while the welted slash trickled with beads of fresh blood.

Racing through the air, Nephthys snapped the whip again, this time along the hindquarters of Seth's obnoxious beast. The incensed creature thrashing and snorting, pitched into a riotous buck, nearly sending Seth toppling to the earth.

Infuriated, Seth shortened the creature's chain in an attempt to settle its heated fury. "*Nephthys!* It's time for you to *die!*" Angrily, he heeled his mount, and veered through the blustery sky, while the lust for his wife's blood surged through his pumping veins and he was determined for a victory.

Closing the gap between him and his sister, Seth suddenly catapulted from the detestable creature and sailed through the statically charged air crashing atop her.

The frenzied battle of entities ensued.

"*Holy Shit!*" Deverall yelled from below. "*Kick his ass!*"

CHAPTER 36

The convergence of Jabali collided headlong with Lateef's men sending the small militia into a state of mass confusion. The commander, swinging his raging sword in a high screaming arc, brought it down upon the first Jabali's huge grouted head, while he rapidly recalled the odds he had figured as he sat eyeing the barrage of beasts roving across the horizon—approximately, *one hundred and sixty to one*. He swiped an arm across his sweat beaded face and heatedly slashed at the horde of beasts swarming upon his horse, as the pealing sound of clashing weapons rang within his ears.

"*The Dragon!*" He barked through a clenched jaw at the soldier mounted on the back of his horse. "Release the Dragon!"

Gripping his blade with a perspiring hand, he evaded the coming onslaught, while the soldier slipped from his frantic mare and headed in the direction of the sand-covered missile.

Fighting through the horde of Jabali beasts, the determined combatant reached the location of the buried weapon. Hurriedly, he swiped away the layers of sand from its casing, and positioned it to obliterate as many of the hideous creatures as possible. His hands trembled, as he sited the short-range surface-to-surface missile, speedily primed himself and mumbled a quick prayer to Allah. Taking a deep breath, he fired.

Each moment seemed a slow deliberated tick of the clock, till the resonating squeal of the deadly warhead sounded as music upon the combating men's weary ears. Discharging as an incensed inferno, it screamed just feet above the shifting terrain, blasting with fury through the barrage of stupefied creatures and tearing beasts in two.

The swarthy soldier, aged in years, grinned inside; while the feeling of raw power surged along his thrumming fingertips at the sight of the torn creatures writhing and shrieking in excruciating pain upon the now red-black desert floor. A slight smile crested his hair covered lip, while, for a brief moment, satisfaction were all he felt, his minimal usage of the Dragon meriting temporary pleasure.

Suddenly, his sense of perception shifted like that of the stirring desert and confusion shrouded that of his previously gleaming eyes as he, without warning, was watching the bloodbath before him, from a head that now lay severed at his spastic feet.

"Playtime is *over*," Gulzar snorted; irately, kicking the tri-pod over, he shoved the still carcass with his two-horned hoof. His giant poleax ran with the stain of the soldier's tantalizing blood, while the curse of hunger and thirst were merciless upon his palate. And hearing the convergence of his surrounding men, Gulzar hastily ripped an arm from the corpse's socket, took a bite, and moved along to his next victim.

Lateef repressed the vomit rapidly rising in his scratching throat as he observed, in shock, the horrid scene before him. The senseless onslaught of his man being torn to pieces, then ingested within the moldy slobbering snout of a grunting swine.

"*You Beast!*" he hollered from a banded throat, as malice burned hot within his exasperated personage causing him to tremble with rage. Weapon drawn, he spurred his mount and charged upon Gulzar.

"*Deverall! Look out!*" Laddor's eyes loomed with terror at the flood of Jabali charging upon the insignificant amount of men who sent off one round of ammunition after another. Their cartridges clicking empty, they resolved to draw their swords.

Keeping in close proximity to the warring Sergeant Omar, Laddor brandished his blade to the best of his ability, striking out at one atrocious beast after another. Buckets of sweat pored from his perspiring body soaking that of his clothes, face and hair. *"Whoa Nakia!"* his terrified mare danced wildly, nearly flinging him to the waves of lurching sand before the path of the raging monsters.

Suddenly, the sky, which had burned in flames of pink and scarlet, shaded the color of stirred pitch. Cracking with a thunderous bellow of vibrating electricity, it swallowed all specks of light which existed in the whole of the Middle Eastern continent. While a squall of freezing wind unexpectedly blasted upon the warring men and beast, sending a thin layer of ice rushing along their sweated pelts and skin.

"Red! Where the hell are ya? I can't see!" Deverall's voice trailed through the peal of clashing weapons and streaking lightening which flashed within the dark. "What the hell's goin' on?"

Laddor momentarily shuddered, as he grasped his chest, which was chilled with a thin layer of ice. While the silky camisole secured inside his shirt, which had mildly thrummed against his racing heart, suddenly quieted itself.

Gasping at its significance, he swallowed hard and replied to his friend. "Something's wrong with Cherinne…we have to find her."

"Chhheeerrrriiinnnnnnneee!!!" Rasheed cried through a choking throat while his distraught gaze darted the full of the underground cavern. His body trembled as he watched the horrific scene unfold before him—the recoil of Hafiz's crossbow as it discharged its last bolt then screamed eagerly through the air and fervently drove into that of Cherinne's chest. While the brutal force, impelling her petite figure backward, had slammed her body with a sickening thud to the rocky surface, where she now lay completely still.

Frantically searching his frazzled mind for a course of action, Rasheed was aware he must protect the one treasure he still held within his arms. Panic ran the length of his quavering legs to the soles of his boots as he fought the warranted desire to rescue Cherinne. His thoughts turned to the celestial power contained within that of the Semus Bracelet, the supreme power of healing that it possessed. And, while Cherinne lie motionless, the thick bolt lodged deep within her chest, he was unable to fathom the notion that she still lived.

Suddenly, Rasheed caught his breath, as he noticed the tiniest of lights flickering from the many brilliant gems of the rousing armband, seeming to come to life.

"*The Semus Bracelet!*" Nephthys exhaled the words, as Seth endeavoring to pry the bullwhip from her scaly decaying hands, commanded the thrashing vicious locks of his head to gouge into the goddess's festering flesh.

"*Dabah hiya!*" he seethed through clenched teeth. The snarled order sent the nasty tresses into a heated frenzy as they quickly slithered and entangled themselves within the long everglade mane of the infuriated goddess. "*Nephthys…I will kill you!*" His cape snapped incessantly to the jolts of electrified air, cracking with sparks of light, and sending flickers of heated sparks raining upon those below.

"No, Brother—*you won't!*" Abruptly, Nephthys lashed out at the elongated fibers of her dank weedy hair, slicing through the strands with a brittle hand, like a sharpened sickle through pasture weeds. Freeing herself of his dominating grip, her head instantly snapped back, enabling her with momentum and accuracy to bring a dirt encrusted foot crashing alongside his surly face.

Immediately turning, she swan dived from a thousand feet—plunging into the vast bleakness of the earth before her, leaving the infuriated god to ponder whether or not to follow. And, without hesitation, she plowed through the layers of quavering sand toward the summoning of the Semus Bracelet.

"Oh no you don't, *Witch!*" Seth's icy stare wildly searched the terrain beneath him and he irately shouted to his mount, "*WuHush!*"

The great beast bucked and snorted sporadically, shouldering with that of the qateefa; Seth lept upon its coarse, bristly haired back and rapidly seized the harnessed chain. Yanking the resisting beast in the direction of his now departed wife, he curled the bullwhip about his arm, while the fervent hunt was to the death—her death. With a thunderous crash, he tore through the thick of gritty earth, while the beasts of Nephthys's fetid carcass, rushed in a hastened zeal to reunite with their master. The swell of ear-piercing cries, released from their mouth-less forms, filled the now stagnant air, as soldiers, men and beasts, wondered about in a mass confusion of blackness endeavoring to locate the enemy in the dark.

Rasheed collided with the cavern floor. Desperately, he attempted to cling to Fahimah as she plummeted from his arms and roughly skid to the ground now covered in sandstone, rock and soot from the descending deity's entry into the kingdom below. Through the rising clouds of dirt and ash, the incensed goddess materialized before him. Choking back the coat of soot and particle gathering in his chest, Rasheed crawling on all fours, again gathered Fahimah within his arms and rose to his shaky legs.

Fahimah lowly moaned, as the slits of her eyes revealed only the somersaulting whites. While the minute fraction of yarn filament, barely maintained her condition to stable, as she was in desperate need of medical care.

Suddenly, the ceiling exploded into a mass of bursting rubble, with the enraged Seth blasting through the structure of his own domain, sending the bastion into a heaping pile of wreckage. The immense reeking beast, which Seth reined, bellowed out an obnoxious snort, sending runny secretion airborne in a shower of slime.

"*Ewww!!*" Hafiz mewled as the beast's secretion had sprayed that of his broadcloth cloak. Favoring his injured shoulder, he swiftly rose to his feet. Briefly, his eyes locked with Nephthys's, then darted to that of the thriving bracelet. And, catching a glimpse of Nagid carefully moving into position, to take the goddess by surprise, he readied himself to run.

Nephthys whipped about to face that of her vile, dastardly husband.

"*Nephthys…*" Seth's tone was sickening, silty upon his devilish tongue, while his leering stare sent a chill racing along Hafiz's spine as the curious militant observed the confrontation of husband and wife—deity against deity—through wide, slightly amused, eyes. "…I see you have come to visit me in my chambers—though, *dear wife*, I am quite sorry to disappoint you. You see, I have taken another, not quite so *crusty* as you or wildly demonic, but a fighter just the same."

Nephthys glanced out the corner of an eye at the bracelet which hummed upon the still female's wrist, wondering whether Seth had noticed its presence at all, while his concentrated efforts were more on the destruction and defaming of *her*.

The cavern's air was charged with vengeance and her retort was terse—a vial of smoldering wrath. "Seth—if Ra were aware of your goings on, he would ban you to the souls of the underworld then spew you out as secretion. So—*dear sweet, Brother*—spare me the adolescent insults, for I have no interest as to who you have had in your bedchambers. Frankly, I pity the poor wench."

Rasheed also observed from the shadows. While the sweat weighed heavy upon his furrowing brow with the realization that the scoffing satire, pouring from the insipid gods' viperous lips, was in reference to his Fahimah. Suddenly feeling nauseous, he wavered upon his stiffened legs, which sent loose gravel skidding along the grotto's floor. Catching his breath, he shuffled to speedily conceal himself and the princess, but unfortunately was too late. All eyes immediately darted in his direction which gave Nagid the opportunity to strike.

Swaheel in hand, the giant rapidly charged upon the unsuspecting goddess. A roaring growl rose from his steely throat, while his slimmed, yellowed eyes gleamed from behind the black of his masking shroud.

Nephthys abruptly spun about, while irritation and fury flashed in her curt stare at the giant's ridiculous attempt to accost her.

"*LaHm!*" The inky slime-like sectors which had previously been fashioned to that of an alluring celestial creature, quickly formed to that of their original state. Screaming, they raced in the direction of the charging giant while Nephthys seized the opportunity and darted toward the beckoning armband.

Seth snapped the flailing bullwhip, sending a heated crackle resonating along the granite ceiling and crumbled walls of the shattered throne room. It snaked along the dusty air aimed at the determined goddess who speedily dodged its flogging clips.

Rasheed took the opportunity and ran.

Seth abruptly turned, as his deadly sidelong glance sighted the amir attempting to escape with the female—his female. Orgasmic malevolence rushed upon his sullen brow; and while he, being the theoretical god of Egypt's desert could take *any* maiden he so desired, the one he now preferred most, was being stolen from beneath his nose—like that of honey bread from a market stand.

Without delay, he steered the massive beast between his legs, in the direction of the fleeing prince.

"COME BACK HERE!!!" Rage reverberated in his booming voice, causing the remains of the underground kingdom to bow and shudder. Rasheed stumbled at its blistering ferocity, as terror raced through his unwavering mind to find a way out and take Fahimah with him. Sweat poured in buckets upon his bare chest seeping through Fahimah's galabiyah and dampening that of her mildly shivering skin. Nausea rushed to his throat at the crashing sound of the giant beast plowing through the underground cave and charging along behind him.

Incessantly, Seth blazed at Rasheed's heels with the fiery breath of the colossal sized beast blasting in caustic spurts upon the back of his hair, while the clanging of the heavy chain pealed within his aching panic-stricken head.

"Oh, sweet gods!" the words slipped through his panting lips as his weary legs raced against incredible odds at escaping Seth's unbridled fierceness. Thoughts of himself running through the palace grounds briefly entered his galloping mind and he frantically searched for somewhere to hide.

Suddenly, the mammoth-sized beast was atop him. Its breath was hot upon Rasheed's perspiring neck, as the stench of heated pelt was heavy upon his flaring nostrils. His body bolted forward as if slammed by a gigantic hammering fist and he was sent sailing through the blustery air. Abruptly, he crashed to the rough, rock strewn surface, then was snatched upward by that of the strong-fisted god. Kicking his feet wildly, Rasheed shielded Fahimah's unconscious body, while locking her within the tautness of his over-exerted arms. Crying out through the banded chords of his burning neck, Rasheed's eyes slammed shut. Tearing through layer upon layer of rock and granite, Seth's immense power plucked him and Fahimah from the earth and yanked them into the desert sky.

Rasheed's eyes fluttered open to view the sand covered terrain beneath his thrashing feet while ash and grit rained from his and Fahimah's emerging bodies. Blackness filled the vast void around him and he gasped at its obtrusiveness. The resonating of crashing earth and pouring sand upon howling man and beast below reverberated within his popping ears as his wide eyes frantically searched the darkness.

The LaHm rapidly enveloped the entirety of Nagid within their elasticized slimy sectors squealing in rhapsodic delight at the spastic thrumming of the giant's exploding heart and gravelly grunts. Hafiz watched in a fascinated enthrallment then shuddered. Shouldering his crossbow, he hurriedly retreated, slipping into the tunnels of the Haush Min Maut.

Nephthys hastily dove atop Cherinne's lifeless body rapidly melding her flesh and bone with that of the now deceased female while her decaying self disappeared completely.

The bracelet suddenly exploded to life sending Cherinne's corpse, now controlled by the wrathful goddess, hurriedly shooting skyward in the direction of her vile, evil intended husband. Nephthys irately snapped the protruding arrow ends from her front and back and angrily tossed them to the side.

"*SSSSEEEETTTTTTHHHHHH!!!*" She burst from the rumbling earth followed by the racing LaHm, who in suffocating and bringing to death the giant, pursued the path of their master. Transforming again to the qateefa they slipped beneath Nephthys's newly acquired body and transported her petite form upward toward that of the turbulent desert and her incensed husband.

Bringing forth immense light upon the shrouded land, she observed the terrain and the mass confusion that had been created by the development of war and the consuming darkness. Her gaze was set as she spied that of her loathsome brother blasting recklessly skyward. And utilizing Cherinne's body and the bracelet to the fullest of their ability, she, in resolute determination, prepared herself for battle.

CHAPTER 37

Astounded, the massive horde of men and beasts, scattered about the immense sandbox, blinked at the sudden burst of intense light; while the desert which had been enveloped in complete darkness, now burned with the heated light of day—hot, stagnant, choking air. Briefly pausing, they observed the rising of the celestial creatures and the fervent energy of the awakened bracelet as Seth and Nephthys crashed through the earth's crust. The armband's many jewels irately flashed with a lustrous sheen, as magnificence birthed from a mixture of ire and exhilaration—anger at the goddess's unsolicited tenure and excitement at attaining its potential supremacy. It pealed with the deadly cry of rage and destruction in multihued rays of flashing emeralds, magentas, yellows and indigo, as all the colors of the rainbow blasted forth from its band in a scintillating blaze of verve.

"Oh my God…it's Cherinne," Laddor shielding his stinging eyes breathed in a harsh whisper as he, unknowingly, observed her 'deity overcome being' racing through the lighted sky.

"Hey Red! Do ya' see what I see?" Deverall pointed a finger in Nephthys's direction. "Sweetheart's ridin' the beast that lunatic broad was on; and the bracelet's *kickin' ass!*"

Laddor watched as Cherinne spurred the magnificent creature onward, steering before the rays of the heated daytime sun. The tails of her black tunic whipped wildly in the passing wind and the locks of her golden hair, which had loosened from the black tie that secured them, waved behind her. Catching his breath, Laddor had nearly forgetting the profoundness of her beauty; while unreserved joy, at her being alive, momentarily appeared upon his haggard face. Swiping a sweaty arm across his harried brow, he silently mumbled a prayer of thanks.

In the far-off distance was the other mammoth-sized creature— Seth's. Laddor strained his eyes and peered into the searing white at two figures who were precariously suspended from beneath the large beast. Quickly rubbing his eyes, he prayed for his vision to be incorrect, then gasped with the accurate assumption it was Rasheed and Fahimah, who were dangling dangerously from Seth's inviolable grip, two hundred feet in the air.

"*Holy Shit!*" he crowed, kicking the dancing mare and frantically waving to Omar and the regime soldiers nearby. He charged through the collection of Jabali in the direction of the prince and princess while shouting in a panic, "*The amir! The amir!*"

Seething in uncontrollable savagery, Seth ripped through the blistering sky. Smoldering vapors of moldy green aura encased his tempestuous being, trailing like jet fuel behind his foaming beast. Blustering fury masked his normally fair features, with the awareness he could not toss the wretched human male intruder, without the loss of his female. For, if she is plunged into the grasping barbarous claws of the Jabali beast, she would be devoured instantly. "*Damn you! You human pest!*" He angrily jerked Rasheed's arm, nearly ripping the dangling appendage from its socket.

The tearing limb dislocated at the shoulder joint, sending Rasheed crying out in severe uninhibited pain; while, with all his god-given strength he endeavored to cling to Fahimah in the determination that, *no matter what,* he wouldn't let go. Excruciating pain rushed through the entirety of his side, bringing with it a cold sweat, which crawled upon his dampened skin and heated cheeks. He panted in rasping breaths.

He glanced at Fahimah who mildly groaned; while her milk white features, aiming to regain their color, drew upon the healing power of the small fiber encased within the inner fold of her garment. Her eyes fluttered lightly against the gentle wind and little by little she opened the weary lids that desperately struggled to remain closed.

"*Fahimah?*" Rasheed whispered, as she momentarily stared through sightless eyes into his which ached terribly to tear.

"*Rasheed?*" Her reply was barely a whisper upon her paled lips, while her face was drawn and gaunt; her lids gently fluttered closed.

Through immense pain, he attempted to focus on the low thrum of her steadily beating heart, while knowing he couldn't hold on much longer. His mind raced between the burning tattered arm, Fahimah, and the sword sheathed at his side which he was unable to wield.

The words, *I shall fix it* quietly formed on her parted lips. And, sliding a shaky hand within the fold of her galabiyah, she laboriously ran a small trembling finger over the tiny remnant of yarn which hummed against her flesh. Her arm then dropped to her side and one word slipped from her lips. *Rabba.*

The fragment of yarn hastily snaked its way around her aching body, ensnaring the astounded prince also within its shell. Crying out in unadulterated pain at the twisting armament which compressed and constricted the many aching parts of her body, Fahimah caught her breath. Arduously, she strived to focus on her undulated task, while her mind was still consumed in the darkness of Seth's quarters at the mercy of him and the vicious fiend, Hafiz. Within the darkness of the cocoon, she placed a quivering hand to her now empty womb and lowly began to weep.

Rasheed gently embraced her, while the cocoon raced to that of his dangling feet and into his burning fingertips, where he no longer felt the lord's fixed grip upon his panging arm. And, sensing the thrumming of Fahimah's beating heart and the wet of heated tears tracing his shoulder and down his back he lovingly squeezed her.

"Fahimah, my love…" he breathed into the nape of her neck while attempting to remain calm, "…we are going to fall…aren't we?"

Drawing him closer, she softly replied through a stream of grieving tears.

"…Yes."

Nephthys squalled in joyous delight while laughter danced within her flashing coffee colored eyes. "Brother, you are such a petty *fool!*" She observed from a distance as he sprung from the underground realm holding to that of the two humans—one undoubtedly the bedwench he had been keeping. She shook her head in mild amusement and a broad smile spread that of her now exquisite features.

A heated wind traced that of her lovely golden locks; and, running a hand through the rich, silken tresses she marveled at their touch. She had forgotten the sensuous feel of an elegantly alluring mane, with hers being stripped from her eons ago, when Seth had maliciously locked her in that underground pit from hell. The memory of it raced cold upon her warm skin and she shuddered at the recollection, while recalling the heated argument she had undergone with her husband over the heinous death of their joint brother, Osiris.

She had stormed from their empire with every intention to notify Ra, the supreme god of Egypt, of Seth's underhanded activities; and Seth, knowing of her intent, had laid in wait, calling to her deceitfully while simulating the voice of Osiris, ensnaring her in his deathly trap.

It was a pit, devised from the very bowels of the underworld which drew wickedness and demonic power from those who had lived sadistically upon the earth—the aspects of mankind's devious actions encased within its glutinous moltened slime. She had been swallowed within its bile, while being slowly absorbed like that of an insect, which has drawn too close to heated tar. Unable to free herself of its unrelenting grip, she remained trapped within the flesh absorbing gunk, weeping, as her flesh was slowly being devoured along with a portion of her bodily organs.

Nephthys briefly ran the small fingers of Cherinne's hand along the smoothness of her arm; the skin was velvety to the touch, while she pondered what may have befallen her if her sister, Isis, hadn't found her and released her from their brother's trap. Glancing at the hot noonday sun, and feeling the heat upon her newly acquired skin and face, she tore herself from the glum recollection and focused on the gratifying moments of entertainment before her eyes.

"Human!" Seth seethed through clenched teeth, endeavoring to shake his hand free of the large oddly shaped cocoon, which had suddenly formed around his inviolable grip on the prince. While any attack from a mere human would be ineffective; however, an attack from the Semus Bracelet or one of its sister jewels could be detrimental to the point of death. A slew of curses breezed his taut lips and he feverishly kicked at the immovable pupa with a sandaled foot. The layers of yarn, now interweaving within each other, formed an indestructible shell, which protected the administrator of that jewel's weapon. Irately, Seth, succumbing to its intense fortification, turned his attention to the unruly creature, which ardently strived to dismount him.

The brutish beast flailed its massive head about in irritation at the bulky fibrous form which had taken liberty of passage. And, angrily rearing, the rabid creature released a slimy secretion-filled snort along with frothy foam drippings which sprayed from his howling mouth, while sending a roar thundering across the searing sky.

Suddenly, the cocoon burst open, sending needles exploding in every direction. Seth, rapidly grasping onto the beast's over-sized neck, veered from their onslaught while striving to avoid the massive barrage of stinging quills.

"You miserable vermin!" He angrily bellowed through the bulging iron bands comprising that of his rigid neck as several had caught in his bare arm and leg. Rage quickened his storming black-heart, with fire blazing in his tempestuous stare. The right side of his divine being burned with immense searing pain as he recklessly kicked the violently thrashing beast, aiming to settle its storming savagery, while it had been unmercifully blasted full of razor-sharp needles.

Being suddenly released from Seth's grip, Rasheed gasped and his stomach rushed to meet with that of his dry throat. Gravity grabbed at him and Fahimah, and he thrashed his feet wildly, attempting to grab onto something with his dislocated arm. The wounded beast lurched forward and careened toward the sandy earth.

Rasheed reached for the dangling iron chain, which slipped within his burning damaged underarm. Gasping in heaving breaths, the pain soared throughout his body in flashes of heated white light and nausea rose to his chest. Fighting the urge to vomit, and blackness which attempted to overtake him, he shook his head while Fahimah's cry rang sharply within his popping ears, and the great beast plunged toward death. *"Raasshheeeedd!!!!"*

The gargantuan creature plunged toward the massive horde of eager Jabali Beasts below; and, spewing one vicious curse after another, Seth laboriously wrestled with the injured animal in the arduous attempt to steer it from a brutal crash-landing.

"I shall destroy you both!"

Suddenly, the creature made contact with the unyielding desert floor. Howling, it crashed headlong upon the terrain, slamming to the earth with an abrupt grunt. The sickening sound of snapping bone rose from the explosion of sand; and the creature, rushing like a freighted train, bouldered through the horde of mindless Jabali, crushing those within its path.

The chain, beneath Rasheed's arm abruptly ripped from his grip, sending him and Fahimah sailing into the wall of on-watching monsters who stared through greedy eyes and slobbering mouths.

Slowly, Rasheed, opened his burning lids, aware he was being ogled like that of lamb upon a spit; while the horde of massive Jabali foolishly shuffled about their crushed comrades, as if awaiting a signal to sup. A round moment passed, then, without delay, they dove headlong into that of their trodden cohorts. Rasheed painfully scurried to his feet; and drawing a sharp cutting breath, rapidly unsheathed his sword. The sickening sound of grinding marrow and ignorant grunts echoed within his throbbing ears along with the clanging of their sharpened weapons. Hastily, his eyes scanned the bedlam of tearing flesh and quarrelling beasts before him in search of Fahimah.

"No!" their vile master commanded through a snapped tone as they, finishing one meal, had quickly diverted their attention to Rasheed for another. Fear infested itself within the prince's bones as terror ran to that of his trembling hands and feet.

"Were you looking for this?" Arrogance reeked within Seth's silty tone, like the putrid stench upon his mindless beasts. He suddenly appeared through the stirring dust.

Rasheed slowly turned to face his adversary and the two sovereign's eyes met. Rasheed's gaze rapidly ran the full of the god's persona, briefly observing the icy azure eyes and unruly locks of red hair, then to the burgundy mantle and mist of aura that churned about his large being and Fahimah who lay within the god's arms.

"Put her down." Each one-syllable word was clipped, as panic hammered within Rasheed's pounding chest, threatening to reveal itself within his dark set eyes. Sweat rolled along his stern brow, with the knowledge he was completely outnumbered, and, with his injury, he didn't stand a chance.

"So—you are the amir of my lands." Seth glanced down at Fahimah's paled face, "...And, I assume this is your amiri—a ravishing creature." His icy stare then returned to briefly examine Rasheed, as his wicked steely gaze regarded him from head to heal. Disgust tinged his voice, "I would have expected more." He inhaled deep. "Well, Amir—you are no longer the ruler of my lands...or the female."

The tails of his wine-colored cloak and brimming ruby hair whipped about in the stirring of his demonic aura, as he abruptly spun on his heel to disappear into the immense horde of drooling beasts.

CHAPTER 38

Laddor anxiously spurred his horse, racing toward the location where Seth's beast had plunged headfirst into the legion of malformed swine. Glancing upward, he observed Cherinne flittering lazily about the sun-sweltering sky, like a butterfly that glides from here to there without any actual course of direction.

As she swooped in for a closer look, he noticed the blatant smirk riddled upon her face. His brows rose in mere surprise, at her jeering expression. And, while the battalion of men had been hot on his heels, with Omar, himself, and Deverall in the lead, he abruptly reined his horse. Laddor quickly waved the others on, while endeavoring to settle his dancing mare, whose wide eyes flashed in fear of the qateefa above.

Shielding his slatted vertical eyes from the searing light of day, he shouted up to Cherinne, unaware her body was now being possessed by Nephthys.

"*Cherinne.*" His voice carried along the arid desert breeze and disappeared within its billowing waves of heat. With no response, he shouted again. "*Cherinne—answer me! What's the matter with you?*"

Nephthys glowered down in annoyance at the commotion below her, as a human shouting out for someone named 'Cherinne', possibly the person whose carcass she had infested, had interrupted her few moments of enjoyment. Realizing it was the one who so closely resembled that of her egotistical husband, her ire peaked and she snarled, "*What is it you want, human?*"

"I…" Laddor stumbled upon his thoughts as he immediately knew he was not dealing with the Cherinne Havenstrit he had accompanied to this god-forsaken land. This person was now something different.

"Well—speak! You have disrupted my folly," Nephthys's irritation hummed to life. The qateefa tossed its head and brayed. "And, my beasts are anxious for a fight…now, *speak!*"

Laddor's mind raced for a rational reply. "Well, who are you to battle?"

Wrinkling her upper lip she snorted, "Surely, you jest. *I, Goddess Nephthys,* have come to defeat my brother and husband Lord Seth." The normally soft cocoa eyes of Cherinne suddenly blazed near black. "Now, leave me!"

She abruptly spun her fidgeting beast, while the diminutive amount of pleasure had been stolen by her distraction. Intending now, on returning to her original task at hand, she heeled the qateefa in the direction of the mayhem, in the not too far off distance.

"*Waaaiiitt!!* I'm not finished!" Laddor shouted spurring Nakia to keep pace with the departing goddess. "Where's Cherinne? I want to speak with Cherinne!"

Nephthys, quickly becoming impatient, glanced her shoulder and snapped, "She is gone—gone to the world beyond." Curiously, she observed his countenance, as all color drained from his already fair features turning him the color of milk.

"*No,*" he whispered shaking his head and burying his face in his quivering hands, "she can't be gone." His mind galloped in thought and he drew a shaken fist. "No! I don't believe it! She can't be dead!" The memory of the day they had notified him of his mother's death entered his mind. Teardrops formed in his flashing eyes—he fought their harsh coming.

"No! I won't accept that!" He shouted through the sudden onslaught of glaring tears. "She's not dead! She's inside of *you!*" He pointed an accusing finger at Nephthys. "Now—I want her back!"

"Impossible. And, besides…" she became slightly intrigued by his reaction, "…she no longer wishes to be your bedwench—to be used as you see fit."

"*What? No! It's not like that!*" He squalled in defense. "I have *never* touched her in that way—well, maybe *I tried*. But, that's all changed now...I love her...and want to take her as my wife!" Gazing up, through flaring eyes, he stood in determination. "Now—give her back!"

"I cannot give *anything* back. *She* has decided to complete her journey in this life; and..." Nephthys ran her fingers along a forearm, "...I think I am rather partial to this cadaver." Her eyes met Laddor's. "And, I can make ample use of it for...

"*Cheerriinnnneel!*" Laddor shouted ignoring Nephthys, whose conversation had fallen upon deaf ears. "*Cheerriinnnnee!! Come out! Please!* If not for *me*, then come out for the amir and his men! They need you...*pleeaassee!!*"

Perspiration streamed from his body, accompanied by the earnest words which poured from his pleading heart. He dismounted. "*Cherinne*," he dropped to his quavering knees in the hot dry sand, the granules clinging to his sweat pasted jeans. "I'm begging you."

Nephthys viewed him through narrowed, slightly amused eyes—the mere thought of a man groveling at a female's feet, enthralling, let alone one that so strongly resembled that of her contemptible husband, making this venture even more-so enjoyable. Suddenly, he toppled face first onto the sand as if he had been shot. With no shaft protruding from his body, Nephthys turned her mount and circled his silent being as it lay flat to the grainy surface

"*Hmmh?*" Cocking her head slightly, she, out of curiosity, swooped in for a closer look, while wondering what may have occurred. The coagulated cluster of LaHm irately snorted in objection to her wishes, as she guided the qateefa in nearer to the human's motionless body. The flapping of the great beast's wings mildly stirred the surrounding area of sand as she set down next to his unmoving form.

Briefly running her eyes the length of his body, she reached out with a dirt-encrusted foot and callously shoved him. With no response, she prodded him again; this time with more humph.

At lightning speed, he suddenly grabbed her ankle and rapidly yanked her from the braying qateefa to the sandy floor. "*Gottcha!*" He exhaled triumphantly throwing his weight atop her and attempting to pin her to the dusty ground.

"Get off me!!" Burning rage blazed black within her flaring eyes as she struggled in a heated fervor atop the stirring sand to break loose. *"Get off me…you meddlesome human!!"* Nephthys thrashed about as a wild animal baring teeth and nails endeavoring to tear herself free of his relentless grip.

"No! I won't let you go!" He grabbed her flailing wrists and pinned her petite form beneath him while his heart pounded and his harsh breathing matched that of hers. His dragonic pupils flashed in anxiety and frustration as he wrestled to keep her within his grasp. He shouted her name through a breath, as she whisked her head about wildly, her blonde tresses whipping to and fro before his wide eyes, making it near impossible to see her face. *"Cherinne!"*

"Let me go!!" She snarled again through clenched teeth.

"No." He firmly refused as the hair plummeted from her heated cheeks and their eyes met—a familiar warmth was hidden beyond the fuming layer.

"You've had your fun now, Human—so let me up," she glowered angrily through an icy stare. Her chest rose and fell abruptly in a raging disgust at the female's petite form, while she was unable to summon the LaHm from within her previously putrid skin *and* free herself of this pesky male.

Searching her scowling face, he pressed closer and closed his eyes. He and Cherinne's first kiss entered his mind, as he stood upon her balcony trying to explain his presence there, and also fearing the austere butler, who watched him like a hawk. As she had scolded him, he had taken a chance and nervously grabbed her within his quivering arms, and kissed her as passionately as humanly possible, while his nervousness and anxiety sent his heart racing just as it was doing now.

"I said 'no'," was a breath from his mouth into hers, as he covered her parted lips with his. "I love you, Cherinne…and I will *never* let you go."

His trembling lips lingered atop hers as his grip lessened and he drew her close, enveloping her within a warm embrace. *"Cherinne*—I've missed you—come back to me." He placed his face within her soft hair, relishing in the familiar scent of her wavy locks, determined to return this deity to the female he loves.

Squirming mildly beneath him, her small form shifted and her voice was no more than a breath of air, "Well, you wouldn't miss me so much if you weren't running off all the time."

Startled, he glanced through high arched brows, into her exhausted face. *"Cherinne?"*

"Yeah," she smiled meekly succumbing to a release of streaming tears that flowed from the corners of her warm eyes. "I thought you'd never come. I even thought you were dead, till I heard your flute." She buried her face within the swell of his neck as the tears dampened his skin through the cotton of his shirt. "Don't let me go, Laddor," she breathed through hiccoughing sobs. "…Don't ever let me go."

"Take him down!" Gulzar shouted angrily, as he charged headlong through the collection of beast toward the amir. His massive poleax cursed to and fro in a heated flash of arcing rage, like a swinging pendulum before his massive form. Hatred blazed from his beady eyes, as he blinked back the sting of tears from burning sockets, which had quickly dried from the sun's heated rays. And, glaring irately at the searing fireball, he then swiped a dowdy arm along the foam frothing from his slobbering mouth.

"Kill that human!"

The boundless numbers of Jabali eagerly converged upon the prince. Their mouths drooled with the taste of fresh blood, permeating upon their large snouts and pallets, as their unquenchable hunger drove them upon Rasheed in a hastened fury.

Rasheed laboriously swung his sword with his good arm, while he openly favored the dislocated one. The muscles of his chest and arms burned with each and every stroke; and beads of sweat sprayed from his soaked body. Utilizing every ounce of training and energy remaining, he fought for his survival.

"Come back here—Ssseeettthhh!" the cry lingered upon the stirring of dusty air, then disappeared within the grunts and groans of both man and beast.

Lateef fervently pressed forward, spurring his mare beyond her means. Her legs stretched along the sandy surface grabbing at the earth in a desperate race to reach the amir, while a bombardment of feathered bolts rained upon the terrain in a hailstorm.

"Move it! The amir is in danger!" the commander bellowed through the peal of his raging sword as he engaged two beasts, swung heatedly, then pressed on in the direction of his captain. *Hold on Sire; we are coming.*

An expansive shadow circled above the commander. Glancing up, he noticed it to be the great winged beast of the American female as she commandeered it en route toward the battling amir, the pilot and Sergeant Omar. Lateef frowned, as he noticed Laddor wrapped securely about his American companion, a terrified look affixed to his pale features. The situation seemed rather odd.

"No funny stuff, Nephthys," Laddor, shifting his weight, directed in Cherinne's ear, as they circled the vicinity.

While Cherinne had been revived, though fading in and out of consciousness, Nephthys had graciously stepped aside, allowing the human to reunite with her love. Her own feelings for Osiris flooded the remains of her fetid heart as she continued to mourn his death. And, though she had separated herself from Cherinne temporarily, and still required the use of the bracelet to defeat her malicious husband, Nephthys had grudgingly agreed to join forces with the humans.

They surveyed the situation below.

"There!" Laddor pointed a finger into the wind. "They're over there! And, Seth has Fahimah!" Rasheed suddenly plummeted to his knees. *"Hurry—help Rasheed! He's down!"*

Nephthys heeled the great winged beast. *"LaHm—make haste!* Now, hold your ears Human."

"I can't. I can't let go."

"You must."

A ruthless cry screeched forth from within her open orifice as she drew a breath and released its fury. The earsplitting shriek blasted through the air sending Laddor's hands rapidly slamming against the sides of his head while his eardrums screamed in unadulterated pain. *"Ggodd!"* he yowled as white heat rushed through his skull nearly sending him toppling from Nephthys's beast. His heart thrashed within his chest and he clinched his legs tighter around the swerving creature, as it dodged the mass of arrows suddenly blazing through the air.

The horde of Jabali below buckled to their knees in cursing pain, while attempting, unsuccessfully, to cover their small curved ears with bulky claws.

"Hop off and assist your friend," Nephthys shouted.

Laddor removed his hands from his thrumming ears. "What?"

"Get off and help your friend!"

He eyed her suspiciously. "No—you're liable to leave us."

She snapped the command. "I said, '*get off*'!" Abruptly spinning she shoved him from the qateefa sending him with a harsh thud to the sandy ground. "Now—Run!"

Glaring angrily, Laddor turned and high-tailed it through the heap of collapsed beasts, scaling with long legs the hunched backs of several to reach Rasheed. His blood raced within his pulsing veins as he glanced his shoulder to see Nephthys hovering just feet behind him and the amir's men colliding with the group of Jabali. Reaching the unconscious prince, he hoisted his battered body upon his shoulders and arduously made his way through the slowly rising beasts, just in time to hear the commands being shouted to the bracelet.

Laddor turned to see Nephthys, her façade strangely melding from Cherinne's features to that of her own, then gradually returning to that of Cherinne's. A hastened prayer quickly entered his mind in hopes that Cherinne would remain Cherinne, while the thought of embracing the putrid goddess was nauseating.

Inhaling deep, Laddor endeavored to quicken his step; and while he had always been commended for his speed, the weight of the prince had suddenly become a grueling task. Briefly, he caught a glimpse of the Jabali commander charging in his direction, with the multitude of beasts rapidly rising to their feet as they shook off the screeching that rang within their throbbing heads.

"*Red! Over here!*" Deverall shouted, waving him in his direction. The eager pilot twisted about and grabbed his pistol from the boy, who stared wide eyed at the scene before them. Slamming a loaded cartridge in, he sent off a few rounds that tore through the thick leathery hides of six beasts, which had been converging upon his friends. Grinning, he reached in his vest for another magazine and eagerly slipped it into its casing.

I gotta' get outta' here! Laddor whispered beneath a labored breath as he could hear Nephthys calling out to the shifting darkness above. Her voice reverberated in the language of the ancient gods, which brought life to the various gems derived from the Semus Jewels. Its call was one of majestic power from many millenniums past, whose strength was drawn from the galaxy of stars, which Nut had consumed within her wide spread orifice, as her weeping self had wallowed in the mourning for her beloved husband, Geb.

The bracelet exploded to life. Its vibrant prismatic rays, blasting through the horde of beasts below, cut through metal and armor, sending the dumbfounded creatures irately cursing and squalling in a rush to shoot the goddess from the sky. Multitudes of Jabali fell to their death.

"*Red—look out!*" Deverall hollered, taking aim and shooting at the Jabali commander who raged upon Laddor with determination to reach the amir. The bullet missed.

Instantly, the weight of the commander slammed as a giant swinging anvil into Laddor's back, sending him and Rasheed crashing to the sandy earth. The prince moaned lowly and Fahimah's name slipped from his wheezing chest to his parched lips. "Not quite," Laddor groaned; as he, unable to reach his sword, scrambled for Rasheed's.

Without a moment's hesitation, Gulzar plucked the prince's limp body from the ground. His glaring stare, which was aimed at Nephthys, became one of an unspoken challenge as he raised the amir high above his frothing head, aiming to tear the amir's body from limb to limb. A thunderous roar of triumph bellowed from his foaming mouth and cursed along the dry land; while the remaining Jabali, adhering to his voice, responded in a booming roar.

Laddor, scurrying to his shaking legs, hurriedly grabbed Rasheed's sword and held it before him. Terror burned through every fiber of his trembling being, as he, mustering the courage, rushed upon the huge swine-like beast.

Gulzar, slamming Rasheed's worn body to the unrelenting ground, sent a two-horned hoof thudding atop the prince's chest. And, speedily pulling his giant poleax from within its sheath, and spreading his bulbous lips to form that of a sadistic smirk, he swung.

"*Holy shit!*" Laddor squalled as the heated weapon blazed within inches of his head, sending him reeling backward.

Deverall reloaded and aimed. The bullet, ripping from its casing, raced through the buzzing air, plunging deep within the large beast's muscled thigh. Gulzar roared in a seething unbridled fury while rapidly sending the massive poleax crashing down upon Laddor who scrambled on all fours to escape. Another shot immediately discharged, ringing through the tumultuous air and tore along that of the commander's bulky chest. Abruptly, he dropped to a quavering knee.

The echoing sound of Nephthys's voice pealed throughout the wind gust sky; and, yet again, the bracelet released another barrage of burning rays that swiftly swept along the land, sending the remaining straggling beasts scattering in the direction of the amir's men. Their weapons drawn, Rasheed's men rushed upon the retreating Jabali with the intentions of battling to the death, till the last man or beast was spent.

Fuming, Gulzar assessed the situation; and irately succumbing to the pain tearing throughout his throbbing body, he was aware his incompetence would, most likely, bring him death. And, as blackness slowly settled upon his sweated dowdy head, he blared the word. *RETREAT!!*

The remaining beasts rapidly turned, heeding their commander's call. And, seizing their incapacitated leader, they suddenly dove beneath the hot surface, returning to the underworld, from which, they had come.

CHAPTER 39

An unnatural calm had settled upon the arid land as dusk crept along the horizon, welcoming that of the soon appearing moon. While the desert floor, slightly shifting in billowing waves of dissipating heat, aimed to compose itself, after the ravaging that had been committed upon its subdued sands.

Numerous palace soldiers lay strewn amongst the thousands of Jabali beasts scattered about the red terrain while Lateef hastily viewed the soiled land, desperately viewing his fallen men in search of the amir.

The ground before his mare's feet unexpectedly buckled, sending her hurriedly back-stepping in an awkward stumble; as the insatiable earth, readily drawing the slain Jabali creatures deep within its gluttonous self, left only those bore from a mother's womb. Through tired eyes, he observed his surroundings, endeavoring to absorb the magnitude of loss, while over half his men lay dead upon the blanket of sand—some merely bludgeoned through, while others would only receive prayer. He sighted the red-haired American wearily assisting the prince.

"Al-Jalab Al-doctoorra! Al-amir jaraH! Wa, sa'ad aHad akhar Had! Hal huwa al-eera alomeera?" the command bellowed along the quiescent air while he spurred his mare at an accelerated haste to reach the amir. The order also sent Omar speedily galloping in the direction of the tents to retrieve the physician.

The sergeant's eyes rapidly scanned the blood soaked sand for any sign of his younger brother, Mahir. Endeavoring to tear himself away from the battlefield, he willfully suppressed the sickening feeling which roiled within his tightened stomach. Pressing onward, away from the horrific scene, he cursed the overly-eager vultures overhead, which were gradually appearing in clusters, as they yearned for the pungent stench of death.

"*Fahimah*...? Where is Fahimah?" Rasheed, slipping in and out of consciousness, murmured the princess's name as Laddor gently laid him to the ground.

"We need the physician!" Laddor hollered while viewing the damaged shoulder, the dislocation worsened by use. Removing his shirt, Laddor gently brushed the collection of sand away from Rasheed's sweated face, visibly ashen and drawn; while the injury, which was dreadfully colored to shades of purples and blues, had swelled in enormity.

"Red..." Deverall shouted as he searched, along with the few remaining soldiers and the boy, for any survivors, "...the doc's on his way."

Hurriedly dismounting, Lateef dropped to his knees alongside the amir; his dark eyes quickly evaluated the prince's condition. "Hold on, Your Grace...Doctor Raghib will arrive very soon." He quickly shuffled to his feet and retrieved a rolled woolen blanket from his saddle and spread it over the amir's now shivering body.

Laddor observed anxiously, unable to understand the swarthy commander, only recognizing the word 'doctoora' which he recalled as doctor. A sour taste suddenly filled his mouth; he turned his head and spit.

"*Fahimah*," Rasheed again whispered her name.

As Laddor's gaze met with the commander's, an unspoken awareness passed between the two—an awareness, that *they* must recover the princess. And turning his attention to Cherinne and assuming she was still being possessed by Nephthys, Laddor watched as she bent to a knee and placed her ear near to the surface, appearing to be listening for something beneath the sand.

Nephthys frantically scanned the graying horizon. A marked sign of rage shaded her face as her narrowed eyes rested on the only mane of crimson shuffling about the upper surface; the realization her brother had escaped his inearth prison was infuriating.

"*Sssssssssssssseeeeeeeeeeeettttttttttthhhhhhhhhhhhhh!!!*" She screamed his name through a chorded throat while all those in close proximity rapidly cupped their hands to their paining ears.

"*Geez sweetheart*—I'd wish you'd give us just a little warnin' when you're gonna' do that!" Deverall howled in annoyance. "You've 'bout blasted my eardrums in two!"

"*Uuuggghhh!*" she snarled, rapidly spinning on her heels and racing in the direction of the awaiting qateefa. Sand spurted from beneath her running feet while, with precise agility, she leapfrogged onto the snorting creature, then urged it toward the darkening sky.

"Man—was it somethin' I said?" Deverall whistled low. "You'd best look out, Red," he shouted over to Laddor, "Sweetheart's mood swings sure have become atrocious—I'd sure hate to stumble in the midst of you two hot-heads. And, check out the way she mounted that beast!" His brow arched. "Where's she goin' anyway?"

Laddor silently shook his head and watched as Nephthys blazed skyward toward the jibing moon, hovered along the shroud of night, and keenly observed something beneath the heavy layers of sand. A chilled breeze drifted along the heated terrain bringing with it a much needed tuft of brisk air; he inhaled deep. With the reassurance that Cherinne was alive and safe, his mindset became one of searching for the princess, then possibly departing for home. He returned his attention to the amir who lay defenseless before him and the physician who was rushed by horseback to the prince's aide; the doctor's smug countenance bringing along with it a rash of irritation.

Doctor Raghib hurriedly slipped from Omar's mount while the sergeant briefly conferred with Commander Lateef. Worry shadowed the large sergeant's face as he then turned and began a search of his own— one which was for his brother. Hastily, he spurred his horse in the direction of the fallen men that lay about the dimming terrain. While dusk, creeping along the earth, shadowed the few remaining survivors, as

Omar, running his eyes along the desolate desert, recalled his brother's frightened stare.

Recognizing that demon, of fear and loss, and, though Laddor had visions of pummeling the younger sibling, he observed the worried sergeant momentarily and mumbled a 'good luck', hoping the sergeant would understand. He then scurried to his feet, as the irate physician grumbled in his native tongue and viciously glanced with black eyes and furrowed thick brows, those nearby. His eyes met Laddor's dragonized stare and his swarthy features darkened most severely with the knowledge the Americans were still alive.

Laddor cringed; and, with no desire to remain in the physician's narcissistic presence, Laddor shoved his hands in his jeans pockets and headed in the direction of Cherinne's departure.

The heart-rendering sound of Rasheed's low grief-stricken voice, calling out in desperation for Fahimah, resonated beneath the barking orders of the doctor which sent the remaining men scattering, like frightened children, in an attempt to assist the amir as rapidly as possible.

A broad hand landed atop Laddor's shoulder, shaking him to awareness. "Hey Red—the sergeant's found his brother. He doesn't look good, so I guess those freaks did the job for ya'." He received an irate glare from Laddor's peculiar-looking slits. "Just kiddin', man. Anyway, what's next? We've gathered all the survivors, which only amounts to twenty-three. The boy's prayin' over the others now—the poor bastards who didn't make it—may God rest their souls. And, there are only twenty-eight of us remaining; which makes thirty in all out here in this blasted desert, including the princess and sweetheart. Where's she at anyway?"

Laddor's mind was lost in the distance, as he observed the billowing grey clouds overhead which rode upon the mild breeze and churned in wispy swirls like ashen smoke. "I'm not sure, Deverall." Laddor, aiming to slip into his formerly white t-shirt, removed it from the back of his jeans and suddenly paused. Opening the garment, he found it to be repulsive— sweat stained and blood sprayed. Thinking better of it, he crumpled the garment within a large fist and tossed it irritably into the dark. "I'm not sure what to do. All I know is that I'm responsible for some of this mess and I need to help Rasheed get Fahimah back. And now, with that *detestable goddess* possessing Cherinne's body to access the bracelet, I assume Cherinne will have to be involved."

"*Whoa!* Now hold on just one doggone minute!" He searched Laddor's face for a smirk or hint of fabrication. "Did you just say what I think you said—that *that thing*, that *ugly putrid looking broad*, is possessing sweetheart's body? *Holy cheese and crackers—that bitch is nasty!* And, you were makin' out with that thing! Damn Red—you've just become more of a man than I'd ever even think to be!" He slapped Laddor on the back. "This is really gettin' interestin'! And, here I thought sweetheart had just taken control of the armband." Scratching his head, he chuckled. "A beastly red-head and a beast—Dude, sex between you two is gonna…"

Laddor rapidly placed a hand to the pilot's flapping lips. "Shut up, man. Besides, I don't know what's gonna' happen. I don't even know if Cherinne'll ever be able to leave Egypt now." Abruptly, he turned in the direction of the tents. "I need a shirt."

An unsettling quiet had eased its way upon the surviving men, bringing with it a false hope that the Jabali army has been beaten and the wily god had merely taken his prize and retreated. This would give the remaining faction of men, the opportunity to regroup and make one more attempt at rescuing the Princess Fahimah. And, while they strategized their final attempt at rescuing the princess, with the slightest knowledge of how to attempt this, their spirits dampened with each passing hour that turned into night.

The chilled air drew bumps upon Nephthy's cool flesh with the knowledge her husband was just beneath the surface stirring, awaiting the opportune moment to unleash his bridled revenge. Irritation was a brash taste upon her cursing lips as she scaled the open skies debating on plunging headlong into the beachy terrain and risking the possibility of again becoming trapped. Inhaling deep, she examined the darkened landscape while observing from above. And, noticing the shifting of earth, as if something large was tunneling its way beneath the desert's sandy façade, she cautiously swooped in lower.

"*Seth*…what are you up to?" Her wary gaze swept the entirety of the vicinity as shadows, cast from the shimmering moon, roved along the land like spilled oil along the sea.

Tiny lights flickered on just before the rising and falling dunes like fireflies flittering about on a warm summer's evening air; while Nephthys watched through large chestnut eyes, the men gathering within their tents, preparing for the coming events. Their minds shuffled through the exploits of the passing day and raced into the crucial hours ahead.

Loneliness slowly seeped within her commandeered being, bringing with it an unexplained aching upon her chest—a feeling she had long since forgotten. Attempting to locate the red-haired American, she guided the qateefa in for a landing, just outside the campsite. Silhouettes in various shapes and sizes shuffled in and out of the lanterns' glow which filled only a small portion of the now empty tents.

"*Humans*—they are such a weak species; why the Scarab Beetle could outlive this sort." Spying a busy shadow, adorned with a long flowing mane, she clicked the great beast forward. Irately, it pounded a hoofed leg upon the sand, as the creature bulked with the remembrance of the pit still heavy within its previously oily flesh.

The human for whom Nephthys searched, emerged from within one of the small canvas tents en route to another slightly larger canvas structure. Nephthys quietly observed from the shadows, with anxiety and apprehension pounding as a living entity within her chest. Strangely, she endeavored to recall this emotion or feeling, while at the present it was quite annoying. She watched as he made his way through the maze of mildly flapping structures with a set determination riddling his measured steps and glancing ever-so-often toward the night sky in search of his female. Cursing herself, she hastily called to him, "Is your king living?"

Laddor abruptly paused and cocked his head; warily, he stepped toward the shadows. "Cherinne?"

Nephthys heeled the beast into the low light, suddenly experiencing a feeling of nervousness. "Your king—is he living?"

"*Cherinne?*" Observing her momentarily and with the disappointing realization it was not her, he answered. "Oh, you mean the amir— Rasheed—he is a prince." Meeting her dark, near black gaze, with the desire to embrace her, a crushing burden, he inquired as to Cherinne's whereabouts.

Nephthys, for no apparent reason snorted—irritation at this human suddenly cursed like boiling water through her veins. Her reply was clipped. "She is sleeping, and will remain as such, till I have accomplished my task. And, why do you inquire of her so? Egypt is filled with an abundance of females who wish to have a male groveling at their feet."

"I do not come from this land; I am from the Americas."

"Ah, yes—the country of Want."

He eyed her skeptically. "And your country does not want?"

Her black eyes flashed with rising indignation while her chest banged loudly within her ears. "Yes indeed they do; but, what they *want* is what they *need*. And, right now I *need* to find my detestable husband." She hurriedly spun the qateefa, tiring of the conversation with this menacing human.

"Nephthys…we need to find them together; *your husband* has taken the amir's princess, and the amir desperately wants her back."

"*Humph!* Just another male who desires control—I will have nothing to do with such affairs."

Laddor spoke to her back which was stiffening from building ire. "No Nephthys…" his tone was set. "He has nearly died attempting to save her. So, don't ever put the amir in that class." A visible picture of his father appeared before his flashing eyes. "Rasheed is *nothing* like that. Now—this conversation is over." Turning, he irritably shoved his hands into his pockets; then, thinking better of it, he looked to the stirring dunes in the far off distance and continued, "…oh, and one more thing—you'd better take care of Cherinne." Then, nodding to the guard stationed just outside the tent, he proceeded to disappear inside.

Fuming, Nephthys turned to view his dark shadow, formed by the lights of the flickering lanterns' flames, which danced along the canvas wall within the tent. Wrinkling her upper lip, she cursed, "*Lashr!*"

Her thoughts turned to Osiris, her brother and true love, whom she had pleaded and begged to choose her over their sister, Isis, while he had ruefully rejected her and had chosen Isis. "Osiris, my love," she spoke to the darkness, "I would have loved and protected *you* with my life; and, while your body lay consumed beneath the earth, mine lay consumed in squalor—trapped within the putrid pits of hell by our wicked brother,

Seth. *Oh, Osiris*—I loathe and despise that of our sibling. He has made a mockery of your kingdom and brought famine and waste upon your lands."

Again, she glanced back to view the familiar shadow shuffling about, with him bending to a knee beside the injured amir. She listened intently to their conversation as the prince lowly murmured the name of 'Fahimah', while the person resembling her husband gently spoke words of encouragement, reassuring the amir they would retrieve the princess soon.

Unexpectedly, he turned in her direction and gazed through the fire's temperate glow. Startled at his awareness she was staring, she hastily back stepped with the dancing beast and caught her breath. "Curse you, human male!" she snapped, glaring angrily at his smug, self assured shadow.

Tiring of this place and the humans, she wearily turned the qateefa to leave. Suddenly, an icy hand wrapped its way around her knotting throat and covered that of the thrumming bracelet.

"*Hello—Nephthys.*"

"*Seth.*" She abruptly choked his name.

CHAPTER 40

Kneeling alongside Rasheed, Laddor quietly removed the tepid cloth lying upon the prince's forehead, dipped it into a nearby basin of fresh water, and then replaced it.

"Thank you, my friend," Rasheed whispered through a drawn cracked voice. "I have been informed that you were a great asset in that of my survival."

"Well, I wouldn't go as far as naming your first born after me. I certainly haven't done much to be praised for…" Laddor immediately winced. "Oh, I'm sorry, Rasheed. Cherinne had mentioned something about Fahimah being with child when she came to. I didn't mean to bring it up. I'm really sorry."

Rasheed inhaled deep, while his eyes slowly opened and closed with him wearily fighting consciousness and steadily losing the battle. While the medication administered by the heartless physician, eliminating the excruciating pain, would afford him a restful night of sleep. "It is okay," his tone was weak. "Is there any news?"

Laddor stared off into the direction where Nephthys had been hiding within the darkness; mindlessly, he observed the oil lantern's flickering light as it danced along the beige canvas wall. "No. But, don't worry— we'll find her."

An uncanny feeling pricked at the hairs upon his skin as Laddor

noticed a shadowed movement just outside the tent. "Hold on, Rasheed."
He slowly rose to his feet as his blood quickly chilled within his veins. He
summoned the soldier posted at the entrance. "Guard." And, realizing
the Egyptian did not speak English and may not understand, he
cautiously made his way toward the entry and listened carefully to the
sounds beyond the faintly snapping canvas flap. Hurriedly, recalling the
appropriate pronunciation of the word 'guard', in their native tongue,
which Rasheed had used quite often, he ventured a guess and called,
"'*Askari*." Receiving no reply, his eyes rapidly searched the amir's belongs
to find the prince's sword, while his had been left at his tent.

"What is it?" Rasheed opened his creased eyes slightly. Exhaling, he
attempted to rise to his good elbow.

Laddor peered just outside the flap, immediately breaking into a
clammy sweat with the realization the guard was, without authorization,
gone. "I'm not sure. Just rest and I'll check things out."

"Thank you, again." His voice was low, barely a whisper. "I haven't the
strength…"

Laddor turned to see he had lain back down and closed his eyes.
"That's right, Rasheed—go back to sleep; we'll find out what's goin' on."
He peeked his head back out.

"Hey!" Deverall suddenly appeared from within the shadows nearly
sending Laddor toppling backward in surprise.

Laddor lashed out in a clipped whisper, "Damn, Deverall! You scared
the shit outta' me! What the hell you doin' anyway?"

Grinning, he laid a hand to Laddor's shaken shoulder. His voice
remained low, as he glanced beyond his friend's shoulder to see Rasheed
resting. "Well, I just wanted to tell ya' your Egyptian buddy's doin' okay.
The doc is just finishin' up with him—had ta' set a few broken bones an'
all, but he's gonna' make it. Plus, they'll be holdin' some kinda' service for
the men who didn't make it—a prayer to Allah or somethin' before they
bury 'em. We've all taken shifts to ward off any hungry vermin; at least,
that's what I think I agreed to.

Anyways, I also wanted to ask ya' what that beast of sweetheart's is
doin' wanderin' round the camp. Wasn't she ridin' that thing? It sure is a
beautiful…"

"*What?*" Laddor burst from the tent and sprinted around the corner where Nephthys had just recently been. He called to her, "*Nephthys?*" Her name rode upon the brisk breeze to quickly wink out into darkness. "*Nephthys!*" panic produced itself within his voice while the scent of Seth's aura was a pungent odor upon the air, similar to that of smoldering wood.

"He's here."

"Who's here? Seth?"

Laddor's eyes flashed in multiple colors of blue, the vertical slits broadening, as he carefully inspected the area. "Yes, Seth. Now, alert the commander."

Deverall scratched his head, an uncertain grin spreading his broad stubbly cheeks. "And, do you have any idea as to *how* I do that—or, have you forgotten, I don't speak Arabic."

"I will inform him," Rasheed breathed as he, wavering upon his feet, grasped at the canvas tenting. "Summon him to me. And, where is the guard?"

"*Rasheed,*" Laddor hurriedly rushed to seize the collapsing prince in his grip. "I'm not sure where the guard is. And, you shouldn't be up."

A haze of tangled thoughts ran through the amir's woozy mind, "Now, what kind of leader would I be if I just laid around and let you do all the work?"

"A smart one, Princey," Deverall retorted, taking the other arm and helping to assist Rasheed back inside. "I'll retrieve the commander. Red, you help get the amir settled. And, don't go lettin' him up—hog tie em if ya' havta'. I'll be right back."

Nephthys raked her torn fingers along the craggy layers of earth as Seth arduously drug her frail body beneath the continent's coating of sand. His cloak slapped at the curvature of his booted ankles with the flaming locks of his tempestuous hair screaming in orgasmic ecstasy as he plowed deeper within the earth's core.

Callously dragging Nephthys by the banded wrist, he made it impossible for her to administer the bracelet's power and free herself of his merciless grip.

The screeching rock and soil warped and coiled as their bodies plunged deeper and tore through layer upon layer of sandstone and clay. The taste of ash was thick upon her protesting tongue, as she, shielding her head with a scraped bloodied arm, scrunched close to the unfettered god.

A round moment passed, seeming to have been the duration of hours. Abruptly, they landed with a harsh thud to the underground domain while the majority of the lord's realm now consisted of a pile of rubble.

Nephthys ran the back of Hafiz's sleeve along her stinging eyes while the cloud of fine particles and dust scratched her throat. Bending slightly, she retched.

"What's the matter, my love?" He briefly observed her wiping away a spray of spittle, then yanked her near to his massive figure. His icy stare, glared sardonically down into her paled face, while his roving locks snaked their way around her slightly trembling form. "Has your brief release from the Pits of Hades afforded you the loss of remembrance as to what it is like to be consumed within the darkness of the earth's bowels? Now that I have *you*, the females *and* the bracelet, I shall remove, from my lands, those pesky humans and anyone else who aims to deter me from my rightful throne. Do you understand this, my darling wife?" He ran a curved nail along her stiffened cheek, while his heated breath was heavy upon her blinking eyes. "*My*—you have become quite lovely—a delectable creature." Turning, he briefly studied Fahimah who lay unconscious upon his undamaged bed, while the majority of his underground kingdom lay in ruins. His brow furrowed while a perverse smile covered that of his jeering expression.

"My, oh my—and by the looks of things, these two are sisters—twins to be exact." Squeezing the metal of the armband firmly within his vice-like grip, he observed her through sparking cobalt eyes as if searching for an answer to a hidden riddle—the course of action which would best suit his wishes of ruling all of Egypt, in a cruel, malicious manner while holding captive these two ravishing females, without the interference of his atrocious wife.

Nephthys winced as a lengthy lock of his hair slipped beneath the cowl of the black tunic she wore, snaking along that of her banded throat.

The bracelet hummed and vibrated in a heated tempo, its power being restrained by Seth's almighty supremacy. He sniggered at the sight of her eyes widening in fear, as the crimson tresses tightened their grip and a gurgling sound rose from within her throat. Grabbing at his arm with her free hand and unable to budge his concrete grasp while in this petite form, she began to panic. Thoughts of returning to the pit brought her stomach to boiling and her mind raced in the attempts to escape. Her near bulging eyes darted about the destructed cavern to settle on the princess who lay less than twenty feet away. She watched as the female's chest lightly rose and fell and Fahimah's eyes fluttered beneath their elongated lashes.

A mild pulsating rhythm—soft as slightly fluttering wings—breezed upon the bare sections of Nephthys's flesh. Blocking out the cold biting words of her ruthless husband, she listened for its melodic tone, its call to the armband upon her wrist. And, while she had felt its presence earlier when Seth had brutally ripped the female and the royal monarch from the earth with the aide of his hideous beast, she had known there was another remnant of the jewels present—the fragment of yarn.

Nephthys suddenly saw an escape; a slightly mocking jeer escaped her gasping lips and the lids of her saucer eyes slammed shut. The cadaver, in whom she was abiding, immediately fell limp. And soaring rapidly through the dank air, she plunged rapidly into the princess's body.

Fahimah's eyes flew open and her kaleidoscopic pupils flashed in a heated ferocity. Suddenly she, being possessed by Nephthys, jumped to her feet which sank deep within the kingsized mattress and disappeared within the folding layers of down. Nephthys's heart banged within the rapidly beating chest of this newly acquired body, and blood flowed like lava through her pulsing veins as she, momentarily, adjusted to the rhythms and motions of her newly obtained flesh and bones. Wildly scanning the underground wreckage, she hastily searched for a way out as her roving eyes steadily came to settle on the disgruntled lord. Panicked alarm raced along her suddenly chilled flesh and rapidly she tore her gaze away from his mesmerizing stare.

"*Nephthys…*" her name was acid upon his tongue as he viewed the limp female within his arms. His icy glare then quickly returned to her, "…don't be coy." He tossed Cherinne's flaccid body to the nearby chaise lounge while his eyes never left Nephthys's recently attained form.

"When your little game is over, I shall wipe your existence from the face of this universe; and that meddlesome sister of ours, Isis, will *never* find the severed pieces of your mangy corpse." His silty voice scratched at the very fibers of her thrumming soul.

Speedily, she reached into the inner fold of Fahimah's garment, searching diligently for the woolen thread. Terror glazed that of her flashing eyes and her face drained of all color, while the yarn was no longer there. Panic-stricken, she watched as Seth retrieved the fragment of yarn from within his smoking cloak.

Smugness choked at the stirring air within the room. "I believe you are looking for this." A spark of triumph cursed through his silty tone as he held the thread up between two elongated nails. Impassively stepping toward a lantern stalk, he held the small beige string near to the flickering flame. His one-syllable words were clipped, "Now—*come here.*"

Nephthys anxiously watched as the tiny fibers upon the thread began to smoke and slowly curl to black. And, with the woolen strand her only possible weapon for escape, she was aware she must take immediate action.

"*Nnnnnooooo!!!*" She suddenly raced across the heavily padded bed and sailed through the air. Her petite form crashed headlong into the maniacal god sending them both toppling to the chamber's wooden floor and the thread airborne. Scrambling wildly, Nephthys rapidly ran her hands along the slatted boards, searching frantically for the lost piece of yarn while the sound of Seth's raging cry blasted within her muffled ears and the stench of burning cloth and flesh filled her clouded senses.

Thrashing about violently in an attempt to remove his fire doused cloak, Seth snarled a collection of curses which, in the process, had produced a violent squall of wind aimed at extinguishing the burning cloth. His fury was rapidly unleashed.

Feeling the strand of thread beneath her fingers, Nephthys grasped it tightly and immediately cart-wheeled backward, sending a foot deep within Seth's unsuspecting chest. The blow sent him stumbling into an awkward stagger giving her the opportunity she needed to grab the original cadaver, from which she had just come, and race from the room. Nephthys then shouted for the LaHm.

"N*nneeeppphhhttttthhhhhyyyyyssssss!!!!!*" her name roared along the underground structure, reverberating within every crack and crevice.

Frantically, she shouted yet again to the LaHm. "*LaHm!*"

Suddenly, the grand qateefa burst through the many layers of earth and crashed before her feet. Braying and snorting, it tossed its magnificent head while she rapidly heaved Cherinne's weakened body upon the creature's back and agilely climbed on behind her. "*Make haste, great beast!*"

Exploding through the plates of solid rock and clay, they swiftly plowed skyward to emerge upon the upper desert terrain. And while feeling as if her heart would tear from within her racing chest, her eyes darted about the quiet of the campsite. Diligently she searched for the human, endeavoring to warn him of the coming conflict.

"*Human!*" the echo of Fahimah's voice filled the silence of the night.

CHAPTER 41

The moment Fahimah had been waiting for had finally arrived. While she had greatly yearned to possess the power of the Semus Bracelet, one of the most powerful weapons in the entire universe, the supremacy of being inhabited by a goddess was completely stupendous. But, with the knowledge that two combatants are better than one, and having her own score to settle with Seth, she set her mind for battle. Her flaxen hair shimmered within the moonlight's dazzling glow, as she shook her head to free her mind of Nephthys thoughts, and resume control of her own body. And, while the goddess's strength still resided within her, flowing through her veins like heated molten lava she tucked the yarn within her tunic and prepared herself for combat. Spurring the great beast between her legs toward Rasheed's tent, she called out again; not for the American male this time, but for her Prince who she prayed survived the dreadful fall.

"*Rasheed!*" She glanced at her twin lying semi-unconscious before her and the bracelet which lightly thrummed upon her sister's wrist.

"*Fahimah?*" Rasheed whispered into the dimmed light of a nearby lantern as he strived to open his heavy lids which struggled to remain closed. The various sounds of running feet and clamoring of war preparation, seeped their way into the prince's jumbled mind, like water trickling through mud. And succumbing to the over-powering medication, he returned to his rest.

A handful of soldiers raced from their tents, armed and ready for battle while Deverall had summoned them to the amir, preparing them for what was to come.

"Princess Fahimah?" Lateef cautiously eyed her being, as he waved the men in the direction of Rasheed's tent, with the intentions of protecting the amir at all costs.

"Prepare the men, soldier—Seth is on his way. And, where is the amir?" She hurriedly shouted; her flashing prismatic pupils scanned the meager amount of men before her including the approaching Americans.

"This is all, Prin…" the commander's rueful words were abruptly cut short as the enraged god suddenly blasted through the sand.

Sitting atop another wicked beast, nearly identical to the last, he pointed an enraged finger at Fahimah. "*You.*" Venom seeped from each word, "*I shall kill you!*"

Fahimah quickly glanced at Cherinne and the awakening armband; and readying herself for what was about to come, she retorted with assuredness, "No Seth. You are now speaking with *Fahimah—Princess* Fahimah; and, *I* will kill *you!*" She kicked the qateefa, driving the braying beast toward the fuming god.

"*NOW!*" she shouted grabbing the radiating bracelet and willing, with all her strength, to rid her body of Nephthys and send her back into Cherinne.

Nephthys plunged deep within the resting cadaver as Cherinne's body instantly awakened and Fahimah jumped to the ground.

"*I like it,*" Nephthys exhaled from her smug lips as she rapidly adjusted to the familiar cavity's cadence. "Seth—" she shouted leeringly, as she guided the LaHm toward the nighttime sky; a slight, malicious laugh slipped from behind a triumphant countenance. "Vengence is ours!"

Fahimah scaled the sand in the direction of Seth, as if skimming across a carpeted floor; her bare feet scarcely contacted the surface as she headed toward the open dunes, away from the campsite and Rasheed's tent. Quickly retrieving the yarn from within her tunic and rubbing it hurriedly along her arm, she swiftly sailed through the air.

"*RABBA!*" the command raced throughout the darkness, bringing with it the power of the heavens, while the yarn rapidly snaked around her airborne body. The mesmerized soldiers below, observing her enrapturing transformation, were frozen upon their unmoving feet; and, while the fiber was near to covering her face, she hastily shouted the word—*RUN!*

Tearing their awestruck gaze from her newly formed cocoon, they gathered their wits and scattered within the darkness below.

Laddor's pulse buzzed erractically as he raced through the darkness in the direction of Cherinne and the snorting qateefa, an anxious sweat forming along his squinting brow.

He drew his sword from within its sheath.

"Red! Wait up!" Deverall shouted doubling his steps in the attempts to catch his friend, as he hurriedly slipped a magazine into his readied pistol.

"I have'ta help Nephthys!" he yelled through a drawn breath.

Deverall puffed out a response. "How'd ya' know its Nephthys and not Cherinne? Aren't they one-in-the-same now?"

Laddor mulled over his friend's reply. Well—No, he thought to himself. At least, hoping that wasn't the case. Abruptly, he stopped in his tracks. "I don't know."

The sound of Cherinne's laughter suddenly filled the the night sky, as Nephthys seeing Fahimah's cocoon, relished in its coming. "*Lovely,*" she whispered. "Now, blast him!"

The yarn structure rapidly exploded, sending its sharpened needles discharging in Seth's direction in a violent rushing storm.

Veering to avoid their contact and throwing her head back, Nephthys immediately shouted toward the moon and stars activating the armband. "Great Gods of the universe—send me all your glorious power!" The bracelet's jewels exploded upon her wrist, scintillating in a prismatic kaleidoscope of colors, sending a barrage of deathly rays raining upon the incensed god and his howling creature.

Seth heatedly spun and yanked his wine-colored cloak before the storm of raging artillery. "*Rrrraaaaahhhhhhhh!!!*" he bellowed. His stippled gray-green aura curled about him in an inferno of infuriated anger while he was only able to ward off a portion of the assailment.

Suddenly, the hideous beast, upon which he was mounted, stumbled forward and crashed with a disgruntled snort, landing snout-first in a cloud of sand. Seth lumbered to his feet; and shaking his head, ran to conceal himself behind the fallen creature.

Resting the Mauser on his forearm and sighting the scurrying god within the shadows, Deverall shouted, "*I* got 'im." Slowly pulling the trigger, he fired. Shots rang out, racing along the darkened terrain and tearing through that of the smoking cape, again sending Seth tumbling to his wavering knees.

"I'm out!" the pilot beamed as he watched the god struggling to keep afoot as a slew of arrows immediately screamed through the air sent by Lateef and his men.

Seth again shielded his injured self with the use of his cape.

"Nephthys! Hit him again!" Laddor shouted up to her, as she circled through the gray black sky.

Enraged, Seth turned to observe the human who had encouraged his appalling wife. His glaring cerulean blue eyes locked on the punitive person who so closely resembled himself.

"*How dare you!*" he sneered, jumping to his feet with anger blackening his angelic features. And, parting his lips to the width and length of his own skull, Seth exhaled a fierce gale, blasting them all with a torrent of cutting sand.

Laddor threw himself to the ground, covering his head, as the sharp granules shaved along his bare skin, like sandpaper smoothing wood. "*Ggoddddd!!!*" he hollered into the gritty earth, with every muscle in his body stiffening against the brutal scouring.

Seeing the American was in danger, Nephthys landed with a harsh thud beside him. "*Get on!*" she shouted into the violent wind, as the grains of sand tore at her normally lovely skin puckered and scraped to bleeding. Reaching for Laddor's outstretched hand, she unexpectedly heard the word, 'Rabba' as it reverberated throughout the howling wind and drifted upon her humming ears. Immediately, she threw herself upon the human while the blast of needles rapidly sailed through the air and sunk into the shrieking qateefa, sending it slamming on its side to the ground.

Nephthys, crying out in agony, cringed from the painful damage inflicted to such a large area of her body—the LaHm. And yet, while the great creature had protected her from receiving the brunt of the needles' fury, the LaHm had sustained severe injuries—possibly too many for them to recover.

"*Nephthys?*" Laddor gently took her shoulders and pushed her away, while attempting to see her face in the dark. The long locks of hair stayed to her sweated skin. "Nephthys—are you okay?"

Carefully rolling her to the ground, he tenderly brushed the hair aside. Perspiration streamed in rivulets along her heated cheeks and her chest rose and fell, in a laborious struggle to regulate itself. She gazed up at him through hazy eyes.

Laddor's flashing eyes frantically raced along the darkness in search of help, as he anxiously shouted out to the others. Then, feeling a drop of moisture run along his bare arm, he momentarily paused, thinking to be imagining things.

Suddenly, the sky burst open, and it began to rain.

"Dude!" Are you alright?" Deverall approaching at a steady trot shouted through a damp grin, as water snaked along the brim of his hat and dripped to the ground. "Man! It's raining! Can you believe this?" He threw his head and arms back and looked skyward to the volley of drops plummeting from the darkeness above.

"Deverall—its Nephthys…something's wrong; she must be havin' some kinda' reaction to Fahimah's needles which got her, but mostly injured her creature." Laddor laid a hand upon the qateefa, as its breathing had slowed to no more than a sporadic patch of breaths.

They watched in awe, as suddenly its large body, shuffling within the sand, slowly disappeared within the desert's layers of gritty earth—as if it had been swallowed.

Deverall's open mouth slammed shut, then abruptly reopened. "Holy Mother! Did you just see that?"

"*Nephthys?*" Laddor called to her while suddenly the ground beneath Cherinne began to shift, as if preparing to receive her also. "*Nnnoooo!!*" Laddor frantically grabbed Cherinne's arm, as the wet earth aspired to claim that of her water soaked body.

"*Holy Shit!*" Deverall clamored, as he rushed to grab the other arm. He and Laddor's eyes met through the downpour of chilly rain. Nodding in an unspoken agreement, Deverall shouted, "Ready, set—*heave!*" And, yanking Cherinne's wet, trembling body onto the rapidly flooding terrain, they tumbled backward with a splash.

Tears stung at the corners of Laddor's eyes, threatening to add to the wetness streaming his face and hair. Immediately, he embraced Cherinne, as he watched her lids and they lightly fluttered. And, as quickly as the rain had appeared, it vanished.

CHAPTER 42

Rasheed irritably tapped his pencil upon his notes with two fingers which extended beyond the discomforting cast that ran from his shoulder blade to the pivot joint of his wrist. His gaze narrowed, as he observed Fahimah seated on the edge of the large mahogany desk, with the silken garment she had purposely worn revealing more than deemed necessary for day attire. Shifting her smooth legs most alluringly before his dark watchful eyes, she performed diligently.

"Fahimah—I know what trickery you are up to, my love." He strived to remain firm while pleasure danced within his opposing stare.

"Do you now—my Prince?" Leaning across his desk, she intentionally brushed a taut breast along that of his mildly trembling fingers as they grasped tighter at his motionless pencil. Her honey breath quickened and hummed upon his neck then slipped between the locks of silken black curls to reach his ear. Rasheed shuddered as her lips brushed his skin and she sultrily whispered one word—*please.*

With his good arm, he achingly pushed her away as his dark eyes briefly scanned her lovely breasts and flowing hair, then quickly returned to her large pleading eyes, the colors flashing as she awaited an answer.

"*Hey Rasheed…*" Cherinne quickly pushed through the partially open office door followed by Laddor, who laboriously endeavored to keep step, while weighted down with several pieces of their luggage. "…I thought we had discussed this." Slipping her pack from her shoulder, Cherinne glanced irately at her sister. "*Fahimah*—why don't you put some clothes on?" She rapidly covered Laddor's gawking azure eyes while the vertical slits had slightly enlarged at the sight of Fahimah's skimpy attire and bare flesh.

"*Humph!*" She hopped from the desk, crossed her arms and threw her petite nose skyward. "No. I'm not doing anything until Rasheed says 'yes' and lets me go with you two."

The amir eyed Laddor and Cherinne skeptically; while the rememberance of their recent experience, running through his mind like a bad dream, was taking its toll on them all, especially him. For, while Seth had been bombared with hundreds of needles from Fahimah's cocoon and had disappeared within the earth's crust, Rasheed strongly believed that the god was still alive and would surely come for revenge. And, with Nephthys also being a *goddess* and perhaps being alive; it made it near impossible for his kingdom to rest.

Rasheed turned in his desk chair. The leather creaked slightly as he shifted, trying to remain comfortable while his injury had suddenly stiffened from stress—the thought of Laddor being the girls' guardian adding discomfort to his throbbing shoulder. Yet, he knew the importance of Fahimah traveling to the United States and finding herself within the few remnants of her family. And, also with his injury and him still dealing with those involved in the abduction of the children, especially the previous commander Rasool *and* Doctor Raghib, it made it impossible for him to accompany them back to the North American continent.

Laddor shrugged his shoulders and his brow arched into his hairline. "Don't ask me, Rasheed. Personally, if it were me, I wouldn't be able to let her go." Laddor suddenly flinched at the death stare he received from Cherinne. "But, that's entirely up to you." Observing Cherinne from the corner of an eye, he quickly added, "…three."

Rasheed's pencil tapping quickly resumed while he was unable to reach his lip with his good finger. Impatiently, he observed the trio before him. His dark stare came to rest on Cherinne. "I would like to speak with you privately, if that is okay with Mr. Zeandre." He looked to Laddor for approval.

"Sure Rasheed—Fahimah can wait in the hall with me."

"No—I don't think so." Cherinne took Fahimah's arm. "My sister will return to her quarters and dress while we speak."

Escorting her to the hall and watching as her twin lackadaisically sashayed through the palace corridor and out of sight, Cherinne then turned to Laddor who had followed and lovingly embraced him.

Laddor gently wrapped his arms around her and kissed the top of her head. "Hey—what's this all about?"

Her voice was muffled within the breast of his jacket. "I'm just so glad to be going home. I'd thought we'd never see this day." Smiling, she turned and quickly disappeared inside the amir's office.

Seating herself across from Rasheed and watching as he shifted uncomfortably within his chair, Cherinne's heart couldn't help but pain for the prince. Perhaps it would be best for Fahimah to stay at this time— at least until his injuries were healed—the thought crossed her mind as he began to speak.

"Cherinne." A mild insistence edged his voice as he suddenly felt tired. "*Please*—can you not dissuade Fahimah from leaving here *so soon?* These are dangerous times, and I truly fear for her safety; *and* we have only returned to the palace within the past *thirty days.* Isn't there *something* you can do to advise her against this? And, truthfully, *I* need *her*; my heart aches *miserably* at the thought of her leaving. Can't you make other arrangements?"

A soft knock sounded upon the office door and two of the amir's wives quietly peered inside—both were lovely Egyptian females slightly younger than Cherinne. Bronze in color and raven haired, one possessed a shorter, cropped style of hair, while the other adorning long wavy ringlets, slightly resembled that of the Princess Haneefah. Both emitted the alluring scents of cinnamon and ginger while their attire was lovely.

Noticing Cherinne, they quickly averted their gaze to the floor and waited permission to enter.

"Khash'sh." Rasheed waved them in, immediately realizing that the timing of their arrival was detrimental to his persuading Cherinne to side with him on the matters concerning Fahimah. His forehead creased along with his lips which attempted an apologetic smile, while, suddenly, he knew he had lost his argument.

Bringing him pillows and a tray of food, they worked diligently to make his highness comfortable, all the while keeping their eyes to the parquet floor, till each one's task was finished. Bowing to a knee before his desk, they awaited dismissal.

Inhaling deeply, Cherinne rolled her eyes toward Heaven. Then locking her large chestnut, disapproving gaze with the prince's, she began to shake her head shamefully.

Suddenly flustered, Rasheed hastily waved them away. "Rah! Rah!" His stare then returned to Cherinne. "Are you happy now?"

"*No,*" she snorted.

Moving toward his desk, she lightly touched his fingers. "Rasheed," her tone was soft and her eyes became warm, like a cozy fire during a winter's solstice, "Fahimah needs this—*I* need this. She is my sister, *my identical twin*; and, from what I gather, her life here has been...*less* than fair."

He endeavored to intercede. "But I..."

Advancing closer she placed a finger to his moving lips; and looking directly into his dark eyes, she stated, "but this isn't about *you*—this is about Fahimah."

Unaware he had been holding his breath, he exhaled; his body suddenly sagged in defeat.

"*Okay*—against my better wishes she may go. *But...*" he leaned toward her, his tone was set and uncompromising, like the stern look upon his face. "I will accompany you in the United States the very moment I have healed and my business has been completed. Also, she needs to remain fully covered at all times—from head to toe. I shall not have those American men eyeing the princess—she is royalty and shall be treated as such."

Pulling a key from within his snow white tunic, he proceeded to unlock his desk and remove a metal box slightly larger than a child's lunchbox. He handed it to Cherinne.

"What is this?" Her brows creased as she took it.

Rasheed leaned back and turned to glance out his window, not quite the size of his previous one, but adequate; for, while they had been in the desert, there had been major reconstruction going on to repair his palace. He observed the gardens below. A few potted flowers adorned its pathways while several of the granite statues were missing. His thoughts turned to Haneefah, sending an irrepressible ache to his heart.

Speaking to the distance, he replied, "It is currency for Fahimah's trip along with her passport and an identification card along with several documents for her arrival into the United States."

Opening the box, Cherinne's brows twisted in mild confusion. "Rasheed—there must be fifty thousand dollars in here," she remarked slightly amused as she leafed through the American currency. "Are you sure you wanna' send this much?"

He spun to face her. "You think it is too much for the princess?"

"*Well*—" she suddenly paused unsure as to how to answer his question, while Fahimah *was* royalty, and he had made it quite clear that she was to be treated as such, "...I guess not."

She closed the lid and set the box on the floor beside her chair.

He concluded, "Besides, I am sure that she will like shopping. She has never been outside of Egypt before and I am sure she will want to purchase many American things while she is on her trip. In fact, I would like it very much if she would bring me a *candy apple* when she returns—the one with nuts—I believe they would be quite delicious." He grinned mildly then remained quiet as his thoughts drifted into that of concern.

Smiling warmly, she stated, "of course. And, yes...they are delicious."

Worry, like an old wound, returned to his face and he shifted uncomfortably.

Cherinne leaned forward and took his good hand. "Rasheed—please don't worry. You need to concentrate on mending that shoulder. Fahimah will be okay and Reynolds is an old military man; he'll make sure Fahimah is looked after. In fact, he'll be so happy to meet her, with knowing she's my sister and all, he'll be estatic. Plus Laddor will be with us most of the time and he lives at the estate—in a separate section, of course."

She ran her fingers along the gold of the armband, aware that the amir had not only lost the majority of his military, trust to his previous commander, the physician's credibility, but also, a wife. *And*, not only those things, but the princess to a whole other life, *plus* the protection of the Semus Bracelet. Suddenly, her heart began to ache, as his burden steadily became hers. For while she had not intended on causing him grief, or *anyone* for that matter, the fact was, that if she had not been in possession of the bracelet, the chances were the majority of his troubles would not exist.

Inhaling deep, Cherinne rose from her seat, while the inflating of the leather cushion was the only sound filling the silence of the room.

Moving around the desk, she knelt before Rasheed, who observed her through dark solemn eyes as she gently took his hand free of the cast. Looking up into his austere face, which remained handsome through any façade, she gently began to speak.

"Rasheed—I am terribly sorry about all that has happened because of Laddor and me. I pray that someday you will find it in your heart to forgive us for invading your world and causing you so much grief." She lightly averted her gaze while shaking her head. "Laddor does things sometimes that just aren't the most…how shall I say it…commonsensical; but, he means well and never ceases to continue trying."

She began to fidget with a wavy strand of hair that had fallen along her face. And returning her wide cocoa colored eyes to meet with his, she asked, "Is there anything I can do to help fix this? I know you've lost a large amount of your military and you have other issues which have to be dealt with, *plus* concerns that have to do with Fahimah's abduction from my parents…Is there anything at all?"

Suddenly, the thought of her mother never getting to see Fahimah pained at her already stinging heart. Refusing to allow any tears to form in her glazing eyes, she then continued, while Rasheed, observing her pain, laid a hand sofly to her hair and gently stroked it. Both of their gazes settled on the armband; then he took her chin in his hand and quietly stated, "You could remain here as the administrator of the jewels. Just your presence would be a welcomed asset to the rebuilding of my military, while you and Fahimah could both remain here, and live as sister's within the palace, protecting me and its people."

Gently removing his hand from her chin, she replied, "Rasheed—you know I can't do that. I have a life of my own from here. And, though the palace is lovely beyond compare and you are a wonderful prince, I have school and Reynolds and Laddor, who is very anxious for the first time, to spend a few days at my father's cabin in Maine—I think we're both a little tired of the sand and heat."

Sighing deeply, he stated, "Well, in that case, then I have lost yet another jewel—you. I guess that I shall be forced to visit you all at your home, then possibly join you in Maine. I have heard they get great amounts of snow there and I have never seen snow before; and if my shoulder permits, perhaps I would like to try skiing." Turning toward his desk he began to jot some notes. "Then it is settled. After my affairs are completed here, I shall take a much needed vacation to the Americas."

"But…" Cherinne began, hating to put a damper on his enthusiasm, "…what about Seth? Do you think there's a chance he'll come for revenge?"

Without turning, he replied. "Yes, I am certain he will. That is why I had my people sent to your estate to retrieve the remaining jewels."

"*What?*" She rapidly rose to her feet. "And, what about Reynolds; I'm certain he'd fight to the death before letting anyone take anything from the estate." Anger began to boil beneath her skin, flushing her cheeks to pink, while she tried to remain calm. "He'd better not be hurt."

"No, he was not hurt, though he gave quite a struggle," he responded nonchalantly while he continued his note taking as if they were conferring over the weather.

Laying a hand atop his document, she irately retorted, "And, when were you going to inform me of all this, *Rasheed? What*—am I going to find Reynolds bound and gagged in the basement beaten to a pulp? If that's the case, then you won't be welcome…"

He raised a hand to silence her. "Do not get yourself in a tizzy. Remember—*you* stole from *me*. I am just retrieving what is mine."

"Does Fahimah know about this? And, *who* will use the jewels, if she's not here?" Anger flashed within Cherinne's eyes. "*One of your wives?* Fahimah won't be happy if someone else is overseeing…"

Rasheed immediately rose to his feet and slammed his hand upon his desk, his dark eyes sparked with irritation. "This kingdom does not revolve around Fahimah, I am sorry to say, Cherinne. Fahimah has matters that she aspires to pursue while I have a regime that I must manage and protect.

Now—I have a meeting I must attend to shortly and I wish to say good-bye to the princess before she leaves. So, if you will excuse me, Cherinne…" he made his way to the door and opened it to find Laddor, who had been listening, nearly stumbling to the floor, "…I must see to some business. And, oh," he stated observing Laddor as he embarrassedly collected himself, "this conversation is just between you and me. Fahimah need not be concerned with the affairs here; she will need to spend her time wisely, then return home as promptly as possible. Now, I bid you both farewell and I pray that you will journey safely." Turning, he proceeded to make his way in the direction of Fahimah's quarters.

"What in the world was that all about?" Laddor arched his brow in curiosity, as he handed Cherinne her pack and embarked on collecting their luggage.

"Nothing—absolutely nothing," she snorted. "Now—hand me that box. It's time for us to go home."

Rasheed stroked the hard coarse layer of cast in the attempts to relieve the tension tightening the muscles of his injured shoulder. "*Lashr!*" The curse slipped between his clenched teeth along with his grumblings which echoed lightly along the corridor walls. "Why does she have to be so difficult? Does she have *any idea* as to what she and Mr. Zeandre have done? And *now*, I am supposed to adhere to her every wish concerning Fahimah and my kingdom! American women—they are nothing but troublesome intrusive meddlers, wishing to rule those around them while they cannot even decide on which pair of shoes to wear, with many of their clothes closets containing dozens. A *foolish breed.*"

Without knocking, Rasheed entered Fahimah's room. Glancing up from where she was seated upon the bed, her prismatic eyes flashed in anxiety as she awaited the answer as to whether or not she may leave. A brief glimpse upon the amir's shadowed face and narrowed gaze assured her he was extremely displeased.

"Fahimah—come to me," he snapped the command as he closed the door.

Hastily, she rose from the bed and immediately embraced her prince.

CHAPTER 43

Shifting awkwardly within the confining space of the airplane seat, Laddor stretched his lengthy legs in an attempt to get comfortable for the long flight home. Gray, dark clouds drifted about the aircraft making it impossible to see into the nighttime sky. And while flying in itself was bad enough, flying at night was even worse.

"*Man*, Deverall's probably half way home by now," Laddor griped into his drink as he sipped at the golden liquor sloshing within his plastic cup. Deverall, making repairs to the Amphibian, had left Egypt earlier that day, while they had awaited Rasheed's answer as to whether or not Fahimah could accompany them back home. Also, the prince had wished for her to arrive in America in a proper manner—the Amphibian not quite meeting the standards.

Laddor glanced at Cherinne who sat quietly with her head back and her eyes closed, her V-8 juice untouched and her crackers unopened. "Hey, Cherry, you haven't said much since your chat with Rasheed—what's goin' on?"

As if she had not heard him, Cherinne glanced sidelong at the empty seat beside her. "*Where is Fahimah?*" Bolting forward, she then leaned over the vacant seat to peer down the long isle of seats in search of the princess. "*Laddor*—I specifically told you to keep an eye on *her!*"

"I didn't know you were sleeping," he retorted in his defense, "you were just mumbling something about Reynolds a minute ago. Plus, we're thirty-six thousand feet in the air; where could she go?"

"That's beside the point! She's never even been on a plane before; *and*, there are way too many shady-looking men on here, that may try and pick her up!"

Laddor stood and scanned the dozens of occupied seats, while over half of them were taken by someone in either a white or black tunic. Then, he looked to the nearest lavatory. "Maybe she's in the restroom."

Before he was reseated, Cherinne was already in the aisle heading in that direction, her eyes roving along the many passengers of the Boeing 747.

Suddenly she paused, as she noticed beneath a silken maroon beret of one of the many passengers, several locks of streaked golden hair which closely resembled that of her sister's. Engrossed in a detailed conversation with a rather handsome young gentleman, the female beneath the hat, hadn't even noticed Cherinne's presence.

"Excuse me," Cherinne gently tapped her on the shoulder, "have you seen…" Suddenly, Cherinne caught her breath, as the person turning toward her, *was* her sister.

"Hi." Fahimah smiled broadly at her twin, who was flabbergasted at the sight of the princess's attire and how she had become so quickly sidetracked by someone, especially of the opposite sex.

"May we help you?" The gentleman viewed Cherinne, barefacedly portraying the many thoughts which cursed through his full head of blonde—thoughts of there being, not only *one* but *two*, exceptionally attractive females on board—especially those who were twins.

"*No!*" Cherinne snapped; her eyes flashing like that of a provoked cobra whose nest had just been disturbed. "*Fahimah! What are you doing?*"

Irritably taking her sister's arm and aspiring not to cause a scene, Cherinne led her through the isle of onlookers. Then turning, she ran her disapproving gaze over the princess's attire, starting with the hat. "And, what are you wearing?"

Fahimah's garments were not that of the long white tunic and veil she had left Egypt with, but now the maroon beret, a low-cut white button blouse tied above the waist, frayed jean shorts which would barely cover a ten year old, and white heeled sandals. *"Oh my God! Rasheed's gonna' kill you! And me*—for that matter! Where did you get those clothes?"

Fahimah tilted her head and stated mildly confused, "Why, they are yours. Is this not American attire? And, am I not going to America? I need to dress like its people."

Reaching their seats, Laddor whistled low. *"Boy oh boy*, Rasheed is *not* gonna' be happy with this," he stated raising his brow. "Where'd she get those?"

"I purchased the shoes and hat in the market terminal, while we were waiting for the plane," she stated proudly, "and the shorts and top are Cherinne's."

"What? Those are *my* shorts?" Cherinne instantly recognized them. "You cut them off! Why?"

Fahimah pulled a magazine from within the netting behind the airplane seat and pointed to the girl on the cover. "Because this is how you are supposed to look." The three gazed upon a blonde model dressed in cut off jean shorts which barely covered her hind cheeks, while ample-sized breast popped from the button blouse she sported. Bent exaggeratedly, she was picking berries from a bush, somewhere in the Outback.

Cherinne rolled her eyes. "Where are your clothes, Fahimah? We have to get you changed." Throwing open the overhead compartment, she grabbed Fahimah's bag.

"No—I do not wish to dress as the Egyptian women; I am American—and shall remain in their attire."

Laddor chuckled beneath his breath, pulled his collar up around his neck and closed his eyes. "Boy, have you got your work cut out for you, Cherry. I surely wouldn't wanna' be in your shoes."

Allowing the warmth of the brandy to relax his tensed muscles, Laddor then closed his shade and attempted to shut out the many sounds drifting about him. The sound of Cherinne's voice scolding Fahimah, while endeavoring to convince her she was not properly attired, and the sound of the stewardesses, making their way up and down the isle, as they strived to meet the many needs of the passengers who had remained awake during the nighttime flight.

His thoughts sifted through the past weeks and the many dangers they had faced while trying to rescue the girls, and also Rasheed. Replaying the entire trip from home to Egypt through his tired mind, Laddor slowly began to relax; and setting his cup down, he drifted off to sleep.

Laddor's eyes flew open as the plane veered sharply right and a loud thounderous crack rang, like a clanging bell throughout the cabin, sending Cherinne and Fahimah awkwardly to their seats. Emergency lights flickered on and off in an irradic tempo with the sound of metal trays and people's belongings clamoring within Laddor's ears. While the low muddled voice of the stewardess, striving to maintain calm amongst the distraught passengers, filtered throughout the aircraft, instructing everyone to return to their seats and buckle in.

"What the hell was that?" Laddor screeched, throwing open the window shade and peering out. Bolts of lightening streaked along the darkness of the nighttime sky, illuminating everything, while flames rushed white hot from the right wing engine. "*Holy shit!* I think we were hit by lightening—the engine's on fire!" Laddor's heart banged like a big bass drum within his suddenly sinking chest, and nausea quickly rose to his throat, with the realization this metal contraption could end up being their tomb.

Grabbing Cherinne's shaking hand he looked to her for any possible comfort. And, unable to find any within the terrified look upon her face, he immediately found himself beginning to pray.

All of a sudden, the earsplitting sound of tearing metal raced through Laddor's petrified being as the roof of the aircraft rapidly began to peel back, like a fruit being skinned. Horrific terror echoed in the shrill screams of the many passengers who clung to someone or something in the frantic desperation to avoid being sucked out into the darkness of the nighttime sky.

"*Oh, my God!*" He barely heard the words slipping from between his terrified lips as his face, slamming forward, met with that of the leatherbacked seat before him. Suddenly, Seth reached a large hand inside the plane and grabbed Cherinne.

"*Holy shit!*" Laddor bolted forward. Sweat dampened his forehead and shirt; while his heart raced wildly within his panting chest.

Glancing frantically at the empty seats beside him, he could see Cherinne wearily leading Fahimah toward the lavatory. "*Holy shit! What a dream!*" he breathed. Loosening his grip on the leather armrest, he glimpsed at the closed shade of his window. And, endeavoring to regulate his breathing and settle himself again, he closed his eyes while the feelings of terror were still fresh upon his crawling skin.

"Shit."

Seth allowed the breeze to run through the long locks of his wine colored hair, while enjoying the feeling of freedom cursing through the blood of his vile being.

Pulling the gold and platinum anklets, he had aquired from the princess from within the fold of his cloak, he smiled, realizing this was only the beginning—a beginning to an end. And, shifting slightly, he adjusted to the aircrafts sudden jolt as lightening streaked along the sky and hit the nearby wing. "Oh, this is going to be fun," he sneered into the coming turbulence.

Manufactured By: RR Donnelley
                     Breinigsville, PA USA
                     July, 2010